KT-430-580

A SISTER'S SORROW

Kitty Neale was raised in South London and this working-class area became the inspiration for her novels. In the 1980s she moved to Surrey with her husband and two children, but in 1998 there was a catalyst in her life when her son died, aged just 27. After joining other bereaved parents in a support group, Kitty was inspired to take up writing and her books have been *Sunday Times* best-sellers. Kitty now lives in Spain with her husband.

To find out more about Kitty go to www.kittyneale.com

By the same author:

KITTY NEALE

A Sister's Sorrow

Published by Avon
A division of HarperCollins*Publishers*
1 London Bridge Street,
London SE1 9GF

www.harpercollins.co.uk

A Paperback Original 2019

1

A catalogue record for this book is
available from the British Library

ISBN-13: 978-0-00-827088-9

Typeset in Minion by Palimpsest Book Production Ltd, Falkirk, Stirlingshire

Printed and bound by CPI Group (UK) Ltd, Croydon CR0 4YY

MIX
Paper from
responsible sources
FSC™ C007454

This book is produced from independently certified FSC™ paper
to ensure responsible forest management.

For more information visit: www.harpercollins.co.uk/green

For my husband
Sweet love of mine and best friend too,
I'm blown away by all you do.
My life is enriched because of you.
One love, one life, a love so true.
Now we're here, we made it through,
Many would have faltered, but no, not you.
We're strong, we're great and we're together,
Eternally, I'll be yours forever.
Before this ends, there's just one more thing . . .
Because of who you are, I'm so proud to wear
your ring xxx

Chapter 1

Battersea, London, 1948

Sarah Jepson's legs jigged under her desk as she anxiously waited for the school bell to ring for home time. Her mother Annie had woken up with labour pains that morning, and Sarah was desperately worried about her.

Earlier, when Sarah had shown concern, her mum had told her to bugger off and go to school. She'd called her useless and said she'd be no bloody help. Comments like that weren't unusual and hadn't surprised Sarah. She was used to her mother's contemptuous remarks, and though they hurt, she tried her best to ignore them.

At last, the bell trilled, and Sarah hurriedly placed her books in her desk before dashing out of the classroom and then through the school gates. Dirty rainwater splashed the backs of her skinny legs as she ran through the narrow streets of run-down terraced houses. I wish I could fly, she thought, sprinting as fast as she could, as her thin coat billowed out behind her. It was at least two sizes too small, so she couldn't button it up. It did little to keep out the chill of the cold October wind, or protect her from the hammering rain. Sarah didn't care about the stormy weather, she just wanted to get back home and silently prayed that everything would be all right this time.

She finally arrived at the staircase of the tenement block, then paused as she caught her breath. Her heart was pounding in her chest and her long, dark hair hung like wet rat's tails. She rapidly tapped her forefinger and thumb together, something she unconsciously did when she was nervous. Apprehensively, she grabbed the hand-rail and stood still, her emerald-green eyes staring up the uninviting stairwell as she urged her legs to keep going. She'd come this far, but the reality of what she might find at home had stopped her in her tracks. Please don't let it be like last time, she thought, remembering the dead baby her mother had birthed three years earlier. Mrs Brown, a neighbour upstairs, had taken the baby away, but Sarah could still picture his wrinkled little face, and shivered at the memory of his limp, scrawny body.

Sarah recalled Mrs Brown having a go at her mum, telling her she'd brought it on herself and should have stayed away from the gin. She'd told her scornfully that she didn't deserve to be a mother and had murdered her own child. Sarah didn't understand how her mother could have killed the baby, as she'd witnessed his lifeless body being born. As she'd listened to Mrs Brown, Sarah had seen her mother glaring at the woman. She had seen that vicious look in her mum's eyes before, one that she'd now become accustomed to receiving. It was in sharp contrast to the look of pity in Mrs Brown's eyes as she had carried away the dead baby and said a solemn fare-well to Sarah. She wasn't sure what she disliked most:

the hateful stare from her mother or the look of pity from their neighbour.

A distant scream echoed through the tenement, piercing Sarah's thoughts. She knew immediately that it was her mother, and flew into action. She took the stairs two at a time, then she heard her cry out again, which drove Sarah even faster up the three flights. Please live, her mind raced, please let the baby be alive.

The front door was wide open. Sarah ran in then pushed it closed behind her. The room was dark, but she could see her mother lying on her filthy mattress on the floor, panting hard. As Sarah got closer, she noticed beads of sweat running down her mum's face even though the room was cold.

'Get this bloody thing out of me!' her mother screamed, and gripped the holey blanket that was covering her legs.

'I don't know what to do,' Sarah cried in a blind panic. Though she'd seen her mum give birth before, she'd only been ten years old at the time, and had been overwhelmed with horror through most of it. Now thirteen, she was still unsure.

She knew it would be useless to appeal to any of the neighbours for help. Mrs Brown had passed away and none of the other women in the block would have anything to do with her mum.

'Shall I get the doctor?' she said desperately.

'Don't be so stupid. I don't need a doctor, I just need some gin. Pass me that bottle,' her mother demanded, indicating to a bottle of alcohol in the tiny kitchenette.

'But . . . but that ain't no good for the baby,' Sarah pleaded, though she was loath to disobey her mother's orders.

'Don't you backchat me, just get it. I need it for the pain,' her mother ground out through gritted teeth.

Sarah reluctantly handed her the almost empty bottle, which she quickly drained.

'It's no good, I need more,' she cried, groaning again and writhing on the mattress.

'But we ain't got no more,' Sarah answered, recoiling at seeing her mum in such discomfort.

'You'll have to get yourself down the offie and get me a bottle on tick,' her mother said, then closed her eyes and moaned loudly again.

It was obvious to Sarah that another painful contraction was washing over her mother. She waited for it to pass before saying, 'They ain't open yet, it's too early,' grateful that she wouldn't have to go out begging again. She found it humiliating, and would much rather scavenge for food to eat or clothes to wear.

'Oh, for Gawd's sake, gal, use your bleedin' head for once, will ya! I can't bloody think straight. Go and have a word with Eddy in the next block, and tell him I'll see him straight next week. I don't care where you get it from, just get me some bloody gin!'

Fearing her mother's violent temper, Sarah rushed from the room and back out into the damp corridor. She didn't want to leave her mother in pain, but considering the mood she was in, Sarah knew it would be useless to try to reason with her. She ran down the stairs, but couldn't face going around to Eddy's flat. She'd tell her mum that he wasn't in. His place stank, and she wrinkled her nose at the memory of it. She found him a rather odd man, and the way he leered at her gave her the creeps and made her feel uncomfortable. He was one of her mother's long-term customers, and, for as long as Sarah could remember, Eddy had called in to see her mum once or twice a week.

Sarah began to aimlessly wander around the small estate while racking her brain for a solution. It was impossible. She couldn't think of anywhere to wangle any alcohol. As it was, she didn't like going into the side room of the pub to get her mother's booze, and liked it even less when she was made to go cap in hand.

After half an hour, the sun from behind the clouds was almost set and the temperature was rapidly dropping. Sarah's teeth began to chatter. She'd have to return home empty-handed and face her mother's fury, though it was of some consolation that her mum would be sober for once.

Outside her front door, Sarah reached through the letterbox and pulled out a piece of string with the key tied on the end. She opened the door and walked back into their one-roomed flat. All was quiet, so she assumed her mother must have fallen asleep. Then she heard a strange gurgling noise.

Curious, Sarah quietly tiptoed over to the mattress where her mother lay, and gasped in shock. She stared in disbelief at a naked new-born baby, lying on the linoleum and kicking his bony legs out. She reacted instinctively and quickly gathered the child in her arms. He felt cold, but she was thankful that he appeared to be well. She grabbed a towel and gently wrapped the small boy, hardly believing she was holding her new baby brother.

Sarah gazed at the bundle and smiled sweetly. He was so thin, his tiny ribcage was sticking out, which put her in mind of a lame sparrow she'd once found. 'Hello, little one, I'm your big sister,' she whispered, and kissed the boy on his bloodied forehead.

Her mother stirred and pushed herself up onto her haunches. 'Oh, you found him then. Where's me gin?'

'Sorry, Eddy was out so I couldn't get any. Look, Mum, you've had a little boy,' Sarah said, holding out the baby.

'Yeah, I know, you stupid cow. Who do you think cut the cord, eh, the bleedin' stork? Now get him out of my sight.'

Sarah frowned. 'But . . . but I think he might be hungry . . . you need to feed him.'

'I ain't having that little bastard hanging off my tit. Get rid of him. I don't want to see him again.'

Sarah blinked, hardly able to take in what her mother was saying. 'What do you mean? How can I get rid of him?'

'I don't know, sling him in the Thames or dump him in the park. Just get rid of it. I can't afford another mouth to feed, not with you bleeding me dry.'

With that, her mother turned her grubby body to the wall, leaving Sarah bereft. She gently rocked the baby in her arms, and Mrs Brown's words came into her head again. She'd said her mother had murdered her last child. Maybe it was true, as she now wanted Sarah to do the same to this one.

Chapter 2

Sarah huddled on her mattress in the opposite corner of the room from her mother, and gently cooed at her brother in her arms. She'd wrapped a blanket around him now, but it hadn't pacified his crying. Now she worried that his screams would wake her mother, who was snoring loudly, and she started tapping her finger and thumb together. 'You're hungry, little one. What are we going to do with you, eh?' she whispered.

Though it was early evening, Sarah hoped her mum would stay asleep, but knew that even if she did it would only be a short reprieve. All hell would break loose when she woke to find that Sarah hadn't got rid of the baby. Still trying to hush her little brother, she rose to her feet and quietly left their flat, to walk along the corridor to knock on her best friend's door. Jenny was thirteen, the same age as Sarah, in the same class at school, and Sarah inwardly prayed that as she was appealing for the baby, Jenny's mother wouldn't turn her away.

'Hello, Jenny, I couldn't ask a big favour, could I?' Sarah pleaded when her friend opened the door. Jenny was short for her age, and her blonde hair and blue eyes gave her a baby-faced appearance, making her look much younger than Sarah.

'What have you got there? Your mum had the baby then?' Jenny asked as she craned her neck to peer into the bundle Sarah was holding.

'Yeah, a little boy. Thing is, my mum's worn out and she's asleep, but I can't stop this little blighter from crying. Could I cadge a bit of your mum's formula and a bottle, only 'til the morning? I'll bring it back, I swear.'

'Come in, you can ask her yourself,' Jenny replied and opened the door wider. 'So what's he called?'

Sarah looked at her brother and it occurred to her he didn't have a name. 'Er . . . Tommy. His name's Tommy Jepson.'

'Ah, that's lovely,' Jenny said as they walked into the kitchen. 'Mum, Mrs Jepson's had her baby, a little boy called Tommy.'

Jenny's mum's expression was stern, and four small faces peered at Sarah from around the kitchen table. The flat had the luxury of four rooms, but as Jenny had five siblings it still felt cramped and overcrowded, yet warm and cosy. If Jenny's dad was home, Sarah wouldn't have been invited in, but now, as she stood in the kitchen, she wished her flat was like her friend's. It always smelled of freshly baked bread, unlike the damp smell that greeted Sarah in her flat.

Sarah's eyes quickly scanned the room, and she spied the tin bath under the kitchen workbench. She'd have loved to soak herself in hot water, but instead had to make do with a shivering strip wash at her small kitchen sink. Jenny was so lucky to have a dad, she thought, as her stomach grumbled at the sight of bowls of stew in front of the little faces sitting at the table.

'Stop standing there gawping, girl. I suppose your mother's sent you down here on the cadge for something?' Mrs Turner said. She was a plump woman, and short like her daughter, but Sarah knew she ruled over her household and kept her brood in order.

'Er . . . sorry, but Mum's a bit poorly, and the baby needs feeding . . .' Sarah nervously answered.

'Poorly my arse! More like passed out drunk,' Mrs Turner snapped.

Sarah felt ashamed and lowered her head. Everyone on the estate knew her mother had a drinking problem, and they also knew she'd sell herself for a jug of beer or a bottle of gin.

'I'm sorry, love, it ain't your fault,' Mrs Turner said, her tone softening. 'I can't see the poor mite go hungry, but you tell your mother this is the last time I'll help her out.'

Sarah had found it hard to bring herself to ask for food, without the added degrading comments about her mother, but felt a surge of relief.

'I don't suppose your mum's got anything in for the baby, has she?'

'Erm . . . er . . . no, Mrs Turner, she hasn't,' Sarah answered, and could feel her cheeks burning red with discomfiture.

'The woman's a disgrace. I don't know what she'd do without you. Jenny, get a bowl of stew for Sarah. I doubt you've had your tea, have you?'

'I . . . er—' Sarah said but was quickly interrupted.

'No, I thought not. Jenny, take the baby while I sort out a few things for him. Bloody good job I've not long had one of my own!'

Sarah took a seat at the large wooden table and ate hungrily, gratefully savouring every mouthful of the warm stew. She didn't care that Jenny's brothers and sisters were staring at her as she devoured the contents of the bowl, after all, she didn't know how long it would be until her next meal.

'He's going to be a proper little heartbreaker when he grows up, the handsome little thing. He ain't got your green eyes though, but you know babies' eyes change colour. Blimey, though, he's got a good pair of lungs on him!' Jenny said, holding Tommy as she swayed from side to side. 'I ain't being funny, but is your mum going to be all right looking after him?'

'Probably not,' Sarah answered, 'so I'm going to have to do it.'

'How are you going to manage that?'

'I'll have to leave school, I suppose,' Sarah said.

'But you can't do that. You're right clever, you are. You could have gone to grammar school if you'd taken your eleven plus.'

'Maybe, but we'll never know, will we, 'cos I didn't have any shoes at the time. Not that it would have done me any good now,' Sarah answered as she devoured the last of the stew.

Mrs Turner came back into the kitchen with a cloth bag bulging at the seams. ''Ere you go, love. This little lot will get you started, but I want the bag back.'

'Thanks, thank you so much,' Sarah said, taking the bag. 'Can you show me how to make up the formula, please?' She had a good idea of how it was done, but she wanted to quieten Tommy before returning home.

Mrs Turner prepared the bottle, while Jenny showed

Sarah how to put a nappy on the baby. 'We'd better put something warm on him too. Babies feel the cold, ain't that right, Mum?' Jenny said, and rummaged through the bag for something suitable.

'Yes, love, they do, so keep him wrapped up warm. And, Sarah, try to get some sleep when you can, 'cos if your Tommy is anything like mine he'll have you up most of the night.'

Once Tommy had been fed and drifted off to sleep, Sarah made her way back along the corridor. With her arms full, and Tommy content, she slowly pushed open the door to her flat, and was relieved to hear her mother still snoring. She placed Tommy on her mattress and emptied the contents of the bag. Mrs Turner had been very generous. She found towelling nappies and safety pins, and three little hand-knitted outfits, as well as some mittens and a hat. There was even a small stuffed toy.

She carefully moved Tommy over on the bare mattress, hoping it wouldn't disturb him. Then she lay down next to him and stared at him in awe before closing her eyes.

She gently pulled him close to her. 'I'll protect you,' she whispered, all the time worried her mother would wake up and snatch the child away.

Chapter 3

Annie had never felt so rough. She was sore down below and ached all over. This was one of the worst hangovers she'd ever had. She squinted against the daylight as she opened her eyes. A stiff drink would sort her out, she thought, then remembered with horror – she'd given birth.

Her head was thumping, but she managed to push herself up and saw Sarah sat at the table. To her disgust, her daughter was holding the baby and looked to be bottle-feeding him.

'I thought I told you to get rid of him,' she snapped.

Sarah didn't answer but, to Annie's surprise, she saw her daughter throw her a look of disdain.

'So what's he still doing here?' Annie demanded.

'Mum, I can't get rid of him. It ain't that easy.'

'Of course it bloody is! If you'd gone out last night when it was dark, like I told you to, you could have thrown him over Battersea Bridge and no one would have seen you.'

Annie saw her daughter's eyes widen in shock. The stupid little goody-two-shoes, she thought.

'I couldn't do that! It would be murder! I thought you

was kidding last night. Mum, how could you? Tommy's your child!'

'Tommy, eh. So you've given the bastard a name. Don't get too attached. I'm telling you, he ain't staying!' Annie said, and lay back down on the mattress.

'Please, Mum, I'll look after him. You won't have to do a thing. Look, I've got him some clothes and nappies ... Please ...'

Annie rolled her eyes and heaved a deep breath. She didn't want to be thinking about it. She could feel dried blood on her legs, so she'd have to get up and wash herself down. Bugger, she thought, as she realised she'd be out of action for at least a week. That would make it difficult to get her hands on any booze, and a bottle of gin took priority over a bastard baby.

'Do what you want, Sarah, just keep the bloody thing out of my sight, and don't expect me to feed it,' she answered dismissively. The sooner her milk dried up, the better, she thought, as she glanced down at her engorged breasts. She'd have to be extra careful in future and avoid any more unwanted pregnancies. After all, a swollen stomach wasn't good for business and was taking its toll on her body.

Worse still, as Sarah appeared reluctant to dump the child, it looked like she'd be burdened with this one too. She couldn't force the girl to do it, but that didn't mean she'd have to look after it. As far as she was concerned, if her daughter wanted the baby, then she'd be the one to take care of it, and woe betide her if she didn't keep the little bastard out of her way.

Chapter 4

Christmas came and went, and, as expected, Sarah's festive stocking had been empty. Her mother said she didn't believe in Christmas, and years before had told Sarah that Santa Claus didn't exist.

Now, another four months had passed and Sarah was pleased the bitterly cold winter was behind them. As the early afternoon spring sunshine broke through the April clouds, she pushed Tommy's pram through the housing estate. She'd found the pram broken and dumped at the bottom of the stairs, and though she didn't like Eddy, she'd been thankful that he'd managed to repair it.

Her stomach growled. It had been days since she'd eaten properly, just a few mouthfuls of vegetable broth here and there. Her mother had given Sarah some bread ration coupons, but she'd sold them to buy formula for Tommy.

Sarah stopped for a moment and pulled back the pram hood, allowing the sun to warm Tommy's face. As he happily gurgled, she smiled lovingly at him, satisfied that her sacrifice of food was worth it to see Tommy thriving. He was six months old now and she'd soon have to wean him off the formula, and then it wouldn't be long before he would be walking and talking. Though she was keen to see her brother develop, part of her wished he could stay forever a small bundle, safe in her arms. She feared once Tommy was a toddler, their mother's patience would wear thinner, and she wondered how she'd protect him against her vicious tongue and brutal ways.

'Hey, Sarah.'

Sarah heard her friend's voice calling her name and looked behind to see Jenny running towards her. Though they were both now fourteen years old, Sarah thought Jenny looked very young with her blonde hair in pigtails.

'I haven't seen you for ages,' Jenny said breathlessly when she caught up with her.

'I've been busy with Tommy. You know how it is.'

'Yeah, I suppose. A bunch of us are going over to the old bomb site. Stanley's dad made him a new cart and Molly and me are gonna have a leapfrog race with him. Do you want to come? It'll be a right laugh.'

Sarah thought for a moment. She would've loved to join her friends and play, carefree, but she had more pressing things on her mind. 'No, not today. I'm taking Tommy for a walk in the park.'

'Oh, Sarah, you're not off to see that old codger again, are you?' Jenny asked and rolled her eyes.

'Mr Sayers ain't an old codger . . . He's really nice.'

'If you say so. Well, suit yourself, I'm off. You're no fun any more.'

Sarah watched her friend skip away. Unlike her, Jenny didn't look as if she had a care in the world, and as much as Sarah loved Tommy, a part of her was jealous and yearned for her old life back. Dismissing her thoughts for now, and driven by the need for something substantial to fill her belly, she continued through the estate, heading for Battersea Park. A cool breeze caught her long dark hair and whipped it over her face. Tucking it firmly behind her ears, she marched on, hoping to find Mr Sayers working on his allotment.

Part of the park had been given over to the war effort and many allotments remained, though with the new sculptures they were erecting and the redevelopment of the park, Mr Sayers had told Sarah he wasn't confident he'd have his little piece of land for much longer. Still, it suited them both for the time being.

She had first met him in the park, when he'd seen her picking and scoffing wild blackberries which were growing in some brambles along one of the more discreet pathways. When he'd discovered she was eating the fruit because she was so hungry, he'd taken her to his allotment and offered her some cabbages to take home. That had been a year before Tommy had been born, and since then a firm friendship had developed. Mr Sayers' eyes weren't good, and he missed reading the daily papers. Sarah would sit and read aloud to him, and in exchange he would provide her with seasonal fruit and veg.

Once in the park and a little further on, she spotted her elderly friend, leaning into his shovel and digging the soil.

'Hello, Mr Sayers,' Sarah called, waving eagerly.

The man stood up and arched himself backwards as he squinted into the sun to see her. 'Hello, love. I thought you might come down today so I've just been digging up some lovely rhubarb for you. Come and have a look at this! I can't believe how big it's grown, especially after all that snow we had a couple of months back!'

Sarah had heard of rhubarb but she'd never eaten it.

She looked at the red and green stalks with a dubious expression on her face.

'Boil it up in a saucepan, that's all you have to do. With these blinking rations, I doubt you've got any sugar, but if you have, sprinkle a bit on, and there you have it, stewed rhubarb. You'll love it, and so will the boy,' Mr Sayers said, and handed Sarah the fresh fruit before looking into the pram at Tommy, who greeted the toothless old man with an equally gummy grin. 'Blimey, he's getting big.'

'Yes, he is, and I think it's time he came off the milk, so I'll give him a bit of this rhubarb later. Thank you.'

'Sarah, come and sit down, pet. There's something I need to tell you.'

She noticed a troubled expression on Mr Sayers' lined face, and instantly her heart began to pound in anticipation of bad news. She sat on a rickety bench and watched with concern as he slowly lowered himself down beside her. His back must be playing up again, she thought, wishing there was more she could do to help the dear old man. His wife had passed away many years ago, and now Mr Sayers rented a room in a house owned by an elderly couple. The rent was reasonably cheap and was supported by the fruit and vegetables he supplied, and though it was not ideal, he always said he was happy enough, although his landlady was a mean-spirited miser. He'd once told Sarah he was even charged extra for using the shed. On a few occasions, Sarah had helped Mr Sayers carry his tools back to the shed, but she'd never been invited into the house.

Mr Sayers took Sarah's hand, and sighed a long, deep breath. Though his palms were calloused, she noticed

17

the papery skin covering the back of his hands, and could feel him shaking.

'What is it, Mr Sayers?'

'Thing is, Sarah . . . well, I'm an old man and I've had a good innings. I've seen five kings and queens come and go, and I've lived through two World Wars. But my time's about up and it won't be long before I'll be seeing my Dulcie again.'

Sarah knew Mr Sayers' wife had been called Dulcie, but she was dead.

'I don't understand . . .' she muttered, praying it wasn't what she thought.

'I ain't going to mince my words, so I'll tell you straight . . . I'm dying, love. The doctor says I've got this blinking disease that's gonna finish me off within a few months.'

At the thought of losing her substitute granddad, Sarah instantly felt tears welling up in her eyes. Mr Sayers was such a caring, sweet man, and as most of her old schoolfriends now shunned her, he was pretty much the only friend she had. He couldn't be dying – it wasn't fair!

'Now, now, now . . . we can't have any of that sad stuff. Like I said, I've had a good and long life, but I've missed my Dulcie. It'll be good to be with her again.'

Sarah pulled her hand away from Mr Sayers' and wiped her snotty nose with the cuff of her sleeve. 'But . . . but . . . but I'll miss you!' she blurted out.

Mr Sayers shuffled further along the bench and placed his arm around Sarah's shoulders.

'I'm sorry, pet. There's nothing I can do about it. Death is a part of life and comes to us all eventually. I didn't want to tell you, but I had to 'cos I won't be coming up here no more. It's getting a bit much for me now. Come on, stop crying, you'll upset young Tommy . . .'

Sarah heaved in a juddering breath and looked into Mr Sayers' grey, watery eyes. 'So . . . is this the last time I'll see you? No, it can't be! Let me come and look after you . . . please . . .'

'You can't, love. My son and his wife are coming to pick me up tomorrow morning. They're taking me to live out my days with them in a town up north called Liverpool,' said Mr Sayers, then chuckled before adding, 'It ain't my cup of tea – they talk funny up there! Cor, you should hear the way my daughter-in-law sounds. Still, it's for the best, I suppose.'

Sarah threw her arms around the old man, sobbing hard. Mr Sayers was like the granddad she'd never had, and her heart was breaking at the thought of never seeing him again.

'You've got to be a brave girl. No more tears,' he said, and gently eased himself away from her.

'I'm sorry,' Sarah said as she tried to pull herself together. 'Can I walk back through the park with you?'

'Of course you can, though when we get to the gates, I don't want any of this mushy long goodbye stuff . . . just a quick wave and a "see you later". OK?'

'All right,' Sarah reluctantly agreed. She knew she was going to mourn Mr Sayers for a long time to come. As they walked through the park, she wondered what would happen to him. If he really was going to see his Dulcie again, would he be able to get a message to her dead brother?

Chapter 5

Annie drew a long breath on the roll-up she'd made from old dog-ends that Sarah had collected off the streets. She sat at the kitchen table, irritated at the thought that at any minute the front door would fly open and her children would be home.

Eddy had just left and given her a jug of beer. She poured some into a tin cup and drank quickly in the hope of getting rid of the disgusting taste he'd left. She hadn't wanted him to finish in her mouth but he'd forcefully held her head to his manhood and had almost choked her. She had thought of biting down, that would have taught the bugger a lesson, but then he'd have been annoyed with her and wouldn't have given her the beer. So, with little choice, she'd been compliant, but if he wanted that again, she'd demand gin next time.

'Hello, Mum,' Sarah said, sounding subdued as she came in, holding Tommy in one arm and a bunch of rhubarb in the other.

Annie managed a grunt, but she couldn't be bothered to get into a conversation with the girl. Tommy flashed her a wide smile. The brazen little brat, she thought as she glared at him, and was pleased to see him turn his head and bury it in Sarah's shoulder.

'I don't suppose you've had anything to eat, have you, Mum?' Sarah asked.

Annie didn't bother to answer.

'I'll take that as a no then. I'm making me and Tommy some stewed rhubarb. Do you want some?'

Annie rolled her eyes and shook her head. No, she bloody didn't want any rhubarb. Just the thought of it made her want to heave.

'Oh, Mum, you've got to eat. You're so thin, come on, it'll do you good.'

Here she goes again, Annie thought, her righteous daughter, nagging and mithering as usual. Annie didn't want to hear it. She scraped her chair back, then grabbed her coat and walked to the front door.

She heard Sarah say, 'Mum . . . where are you going?' but didn't bother to turn around.

'Out,' Annie snapped back. She had enough coins in her purse to visit the pub. She knew she wasn't welcome in there, but anything was better than sitting indoors and watching her bastard son stuff his face with Sarah fussing over him. If Sarah had dumped the brat when he'd been born she wouldn't have to keep looking at him. Every time she saw his face, she wanted to punch it in. The little bleeder looked just like his father, and that was a face she'd sooner forget.

Ten minutes later, Annie pushed open the door to the pub and was immediately hit by the smoky atmosphere. She made her way to the bar, ignoring the snide comments from men in flat caps supping on their ales.

'A large gin, straight, and half a beer,' Annie said to the landlord.

'Let me see your money first, Annie,' the man demanded.

'You know I'm good for it, Cyril, but . . .' She pulled some coins from her purse and slapped them down on the counter.

Cyril nodded and proceeded to pour her drinks, and as Annie waited, she caught sight of a woman in the mirrored wall behind the bar. The woman could have been very attractive with her long, dark hair and olive skin. Her black eyes gave her an exotic look, but she appeared old and haggard. With a jolt, Annie realised she was staring at her own reflection. She hadn't recognised herself.

Cyril placed the drinks in front of her, and she quickly knocked back the gin. How had it come to this, she thought, looking again at the aged image of herself. Men had used and abused her as far back as she could remember, but now she thought she had the upper hand. Surely it was her using them? She was in control, sleeping with them for what she could get. Granted, it wasn't much, but it was enough to keep a roof over her head and fill her belly with beer.

The trouble was, it had also filled her belly with three kids. Two had lived and she despised and resented them. They had different fathers, but she hated both men equally. Sarah's dad, Ron Lyons, had been her first love. When they'd got together, he was a married man, but had promised to leave his wife and marry her. She'd been fool enough to believe him, only to be dumped at sixteen as soon as she'd told him she was pregnant. Now every time she looked at her daughter, she saw Ron's emerald-green eyes looking back at her. As for Tommy's dad . . . a shudder went down her spine when she thought of him. The man was pure evil and she regretted the day she'd ever breathed the same air as him.

Annie took a large swig of the beer and belched loudly. A short, balding man who was standing next to her offered a smile. 'Bloody rotten, this ale. I think Cyril needs to give his pipes a good clean,' he said with a chuckle.

Annie eyed him up and down. He looked well fed, with a paunchy stomach, and he had a good pair of shoes on, not like the other men in the bar with their work boots and braces. She noted his hands and clean finger nails. He couldn't be a manual worker, and she guessed he probably had a few quid in his pocket.

'Yeah, you're right there. I should stick to the gin,' she replied. 'I'm Annie. I don't think I've seen you in here before?'

'Philip,' the man answered. 'I don't get out much these days, but many moons ago, Cyril and I used to be in the army together.'

'Philip, you say, like the Prince? Oh, I say, pleasure to meet you,' Annie said, trying her best to be charming as she gave a mock curtsey.

'Ha, yes, that's right, though I'm no prince.'

'Well, you look pretty dapper compared to the blokes in here,' Annie said with a seductive smile.

'Thank you. It's been a long time since anyone has flattered me so I think that deserves a drink. Cyril, I'll have another, and I think this young lady would like a large gin, if I'm not mistaken?'

'Lady, blimey! You ain't no prince and I ain't no lady, but I like the "young" bit!'

'Well, you're a lady tonight,' Philip said and clinked his glass against Annie's.

'So why don't you get out much?' she asked.

'It's the wife. She's ill, bedridden in fact, so I spend a lot of time looking after her.'

'Oh, I see. I bet it's been a while since you've had a bit of fun then?' Annie asked as pound signs flashed in front of her eyes.

Philip looked a bit taken aback and laughed before he answered. 'I suppose it has.'

'Don't be shy with me, Philip. I'm a broad-minded lady and for the right price, I could show you a good time.'

Cyril leaned over the bar and said quietly, 'Oi, I'll have none of that in here, Annie. I've warned you about it before. Either stop touting for business or sling your hook.'

Philip intervened, saying equally quietly, 'Don't be like that, Cyril. Annie seems like a lovely lady and was only offering to keep me company.'

'If you say so,' Cyril answered cynically, 'but if there's any funny business going on, I'd prefer it not to be under my roof.'

'Tell you what, Philip, how about we go back to my place,' Annie offered, loud enough for Cyril to hear. 'It ain't posh, far from it, but it'll stop that nosy bugger sticking his beak in.'

'I think that's a smashing idea. Lead the way,' Philip replied, and then gave Cyril a wink.

Once outside, Annie took Philip's hand and almost dragged him across the road towards the tenement blocks. They stopped at the bottom of the stairs, and in the dim light she said, 'This is gonna cost you, and I want the money up front.'

'How much?' Philip asked, his voice husky.

'Call it a quid and I'll make sure you have the time of your life.'

Philip took the note from a wad in his pocket and handed Annie the money. 'How about we do it here?' he urged as he pushed himself against her.

'No, someone might see us.'

Annie took Philip's hand again and led him up the stairs. As they got to the top, she noticed he was panting for breath. 'You all right?' she asked. ''Cos if you ain't up to a bit of how's your father, I'm warning you now that I don't do refunds.'

'Don't you worry about me, I'll be fine.'

Annie wasn't convinced as she could see Philip was perspiring profusely, but the man followed her into the flat. She took off her coat and scowled at her daughter, saying, 'Go on, bugger off for an hour and take the brat with you.'

Sarah was sitting cross-legged on her mattress with Tommy beside her, and instead of doing what she was told, she pulled her blanket closer. 'But, Mum, it's dark and cold outside, and Tommy's asleep. Where are we supposed to go?'

'That ain't my problem. Just clear off, will ya!' Annie snapped, her temper rising at her daughter's stupid question.

'Hang on a minute, Annie, you can't expect the girl to wander the streets in this weather. It's starting to rain,' Philip said as he eyed Sarah.

'Oh, yeah, so you want an audience, do you?' Annie asked.

'No . . . Look, I'm having second thoughts. I don't think this is such a good idea,' he said. 'Maybe we should call it a night?'

'That's up to you, but like I told you downstairs, I don't do refunds.'

'Fine, keep my money. It looks like you need it,' the man said as he made a hasty retreat for the door. 'You dirty cow!'

The door slammed shut behind Philip, and Annie laughed. 'That was the easiest quid I've ever made.'

'It's not funny, Mum. I wish you wouldn't bring all these men back here.'

Annie's face hardened as she glared at her daughter. 'Do you now? Well, let me tell you something – if it wasn't for me selling myself, you'd be on the streets, you and that brother of yours. So if I was you, I'd keep me mouth shut and stop bloody complaining!'

Annie slumped onto one of the kitchen chairs, angry with Sarah and thinking what a blinking cheek the girl had. She knew she wasn't a great mother but her daughter didn't know the half of it! She'd always provided a roof over her head and protected her from stinking, rotten men. In the past, she'd had some of her customers wanting Sarah too, but Annie had always denied them. She didn't care much for her children, but she wouldn't allow her daughter to have the same haunting memories she'd carried throughout her own life. The girl was lucky, thought Annie, and she shuddered at the recollection of her so-called father lying on top of her.

She walked over to the sink and grabbed the jug of beer before sitting at the table and downing a cupful. The smooth liquid calmed her, and after another cupful, the room became blurry. She looked at her daughter. The girl was pretty, like she'd once been before years of drinking had ravaged her. She thought Sarah could have a better life than she'd had, but first she'd need to impart some of her wisdom.

Sarah was horrified by her mother's attitude, but wasn't surprised. She was used to men coming and going at all times of the day and night. Mostly, her mother would give her the nod and she'd wait outside in the corridor. Sometimes, Annie would bring a man home when Sarah was in bed, so she'd pretend to be asleep and plug her ears with her fingers to block out the horrid grunts and noises.

'Sarah, get yourself over here, and cheer up. You've got a face like a smacked arse,' Annie said as she poured a cup of beer from the jug. ''Ere, get this down your neck, and don't say I never give you nothing.'

Sarah was astounded. Her mother's beer was so precious to her and she'd never shared it before. 'Thanks, Mum,' she said as she took a swig of the alcohol. It didn't taste anything like Sarah was expecting, and she grimaced, the bitterness almost making her gag. She couldn't understand why her mother enjoyed it so much.

'Give it back if you don't bloody like it,' her mum said, snatching the cup from her hand. She then heaved a sigh. 'I know you think I'm a bad mother, and, well, I admit I could have done more for you, but you don't know what it's been like for me. I don't want you having the same shitty life I've had, so I want you to promise me one thing . . .'

Sarah stared wide-eyed at her mother. She had never sat her down and spoken to her before, not like this, without yelling or criticising her. She quickly nodded her head, wondering what her mum would make her promise to do.

'Sarah, you're all grown up now, and you'll be having men after you soon. I'm telling you, don't trust any of them! They're all pigs, the bloody lot of them. Stay away from them, but, most of all, keep your legs shut.'

Sarah blinked hard. She knew what her mother meant about her legs, but if that's how her mum felt, why did she so readily have sex with all and sundry? She daren't ask. 'OK, I promise,' Sarah replied, and tried to smile at her mother.

'Good, now get out of my sight, and don't you ever show me up like that in front of a bloke again!'

Sarah scampered back to her mattress, almost relieved to hear her mum scolding her again as she'd found that little chat unnerving. She snuggled in close to Tommy and pulled the thin blanket up under her chin.

Thoughts of Mr Sayers floated through her mind, and a tear dropped from her eye. It was hard to accept that she'd never see him again. She'd miss him, and the fruit and vegetables he supplied. She'd have to get her thinking cap on, or she and Tommy would be going hungry.

Chapter 6

Four years later
February 1953

'Tommy, pick your feet up or you'll wear your shoes out,' Sarah said to her brother. She glanced behind to see Tommy reluctantly trudging along the pavement and dragging his shoes as he did so.

'But they're already worn out. I've got a hole in the bottom,' Tommy replied in a whiny voice.

'Well, there's no need to make them any worse. Anyhow, with that cardboard I patched them up with, they'll be good for months yet. Come on, get a move on, we'll be home soon.'

Sarah's basket had been full this morning, but now, as dusk drew in, she was pleased to see it was empty and all her kindling sold. It had been a good day's work, and she was looking forward to getting home and resting her aching legs.

'I'm hungry,' Tommy moaned, coughing chestily.

'I know you are, love, but we haven't got much further to go,' Sarah said, trying to placate the child. It wasn't much fun for him, in the cold February winds, wearing

29

short trousers and having to traipse the streets with her as she went door to door hoping to get a ha'penny for her bits of wood for the fire. She worried about his chest, as the boy suffered with coughs that rattled his small body.

'You said that ages ago . . .' Tommy moaned again and huffed.

Sarah fished in her coat pocket and pulled out a shiny coin.

'See this, Tommy?' she asked and held it out. 'If you're a good boy and stop complaining, I'll give it to you at the end of the week and you can buy whatever you like with it.'

Sarah smiled as she saw Tommy's blue eyes widen with delight. 'Really? Will you take me to the sweet shop? Can I buy some cough candy?'

'I haven't got any sweet coupons, but I'll take you to Woolworth's on Saturday and you can have ice-cream, but only if you behave yourself, mind.'

Tommy skipped up to walk alongside her. 'I'll carry your basket tomorrow, Sarah,' he said, then ran on a few feet ahead.

He's such a good boy, she thought, and was glad that he'd soon be going to school so she wouldn't have to drag him around with her. He'd also get a proper meal at school, something she wasn't able to ensure he got daily, though she tried her best. February was chilly so Sarah found her kindling was still in good demand. Soon, though, the weather would turn, and during the warmer summer months she'd pick wild flowers and make little posies to sell in the High Street. She'd got the idea from a gypsy lady she'd once seen selling tiny bouquets of lavender. It didn't make her a fortune, but it paid enough for her to provide basic nourishment for Tommy. The wind was beginning to whip up, so Sarah quickened her pace. 'I'll race you home,' she said to Tommy as she passed him on the pavement.

'It's not fair, wait for me,' Tommy called, 'you've got taller legs than me.'

Sarah panted, waiting for Tommy to catch her up. She couldn't help giggling at the silly faces he began to pull at her. He was such a joy, and she loved him as if he were her own son.

Annie was cold and fed up with hanging about outside the pub. She'd been standing on the corner for nearly two hours, yet hadn't received even so much as an enquiry. She loathed touting herself on the streets, but had been forced to as business had been slow lately. It had been a while since she'd seen three of her usual punters and she was really feeling the effect of the pinch in her purse.

'All right, Annie,' a voice said.

Annie spun round to see Eddy hopping from foot to foot with his hands stuffed deeply into his donkey jacket. Though he was about the same age as Annie, his face was deeply lined, and his salt-and-pepper hair had receded.

'Hello, stranger. Where have you been lately? You ain't been round to see me for ages,' Annie said. She kept her voice sweet in the hope of winning back one of her long-time regulars.

'Yeah, sorry 'bout that, you know how it is.'

'No, actually, I don't, Eddy, so why don't you enlighten me?'

Eddy hunched his shoulders, and Annie decided he looked shifty. He was hiding something, and she intended to find out what.

'I've been . . . busy,' Eddy answered, but Annie thought he still looked very uncomfortable with the conversation.

'Too busy to come and see me for half an hour?'

'I've been meaning to . . . I will come and see you.'

'When?'

'I . . . I dunno. Soon.'

'This ain't good enough, Eddy Sterling. We've been friends for years and I know when you're up to something . . . Come on, spill the beans,' Annie said sternly, placing her hands on her hips.

'It's . . . I don't want you getting annoyed or nothing . . . but . . . I've been seeing someone else.'

'What do you mean, seeing someone else? Who?'

'Her name's Cathy . . . she lives down Bullen Street. I saw Jerry coming out of there the other day too, seems she's onto a good little earner there.'

Annie bit her lip as her mind turned. That explained a lot. Jerry was one of her regulars whom she hadn't seen lately. 'Well, thanks for the loyalty, Eddy. I've been sorting you out for bloody years and expected a bit better from you! She must be some looker – I mean, you've had your head turned quick enough! So what's this Cathy got that I ain't, eh? What does she do for you that I don't?'

'See, this is why I didn't want to tell you. I knew you'd act like this.'

'What do you expect? . . . I'm bloody fuming! This Cathy tart has pinched some of my best blokes, you included. Why do you think I'm stood out here freezing my tits off! I've a good mind to go round there and rip her blinking head off!'

'I wouldn't do that, Annie. She's got someone looking after her, and I don't think he'd be too pleased with you interfering in their business.'

'So I'm just supposed to stand back and let them nick all my customers? It ain't on, Eddy. I've got mouths to feed and I need to put a roof over my kids' heads. I can't afford to lose the business. What's so bloody special about her anyway?'

Annie glared at Eddy as his mouth opened and closed, but no words came out.

'Well, tell me! You obviously prefer her to me, so . . .'

'She's a lot younger than you, Annie . . . and, well, pretty. Her gaff is nice too . . . she's got a proper double bed, and it's . . . clean.'

Annie gritted her teeth. Her blood was boiling. She quickly pulled her arm back, swung it at Eddy and slapped him hard across his face. 'You've never bloody well complained before! How dare you insult me! You want to take a look at yourself, you ain't no oil painting . . . You're welcome to her. Don't you ever come near my place again!'

Annie saw Eddy rub his red cheek before she spun on her heel and marched towards home. She was too wound up to do any business now, but at least she had a bit of gin waiting for her indoors.

Sarah closed the front door behind her and Tommy, then flopped down on the newly acquired but stained second-hand sofa, courtesy of one of her mother's customers who was a bin man. 'I'm bushed!' she said to Tommy.

'Me too,' Tommy replied as he sat next to Sarah. 'Where's Mum?'

'I don't know, love, but best you get yourself quickly washed and ready for bed before she gets home.'

Tommy tilted his head to one side and screwed his pale face up before asking, 'Why is Mummy always so horrible? I try really hard to be a good boy, but she always shouts and says bad things to me and you.'

Sarah gulped hard. She'd been dreading this day. She'd hoped Tommy hadn't noticed their mother's spiteful tongue, but he was more than four years old; it was apparent he had, and she'd have to find the answers to some very difficult questions. 'I don't know, Tommy, it's just the way she is. Some people are made of sugar and spice and all things nice, others are made of sharp bits of glass.'

'I don't like her. She's all right sometimes when she's quiet, but when she drinks that stuff that smells funny, she's loud and nasty. Do you like her, Sarah?'

'She's our mum, Tommy. You shouldn't say things like that about her. If it wasn't for her, you and me would be in a children's home or on the streets. She can't help being the way she is. She's ill, and the gin, the stuff that smells funny, she has to have it to make her better.'

'But if the gin makes her better, why does she get horribler when she drinks it?'

Sarah could see Tommy's bottom lip beginning to quiver. It broke her heart to see the child so upset. 'She doesn't mean most of the stuff she says. You've got to learn to do what I do . . . ignore it. Just let all her words go in one ear and come out the other. Don't keep them in your head and then they can't hurt you.'

34

Tommy nodded, and Sarah was thankful that the boy seemed satisfied with her answer for now. 'Right, now hurry up, get yourself ready for bed,' she urged.

Tommy scampered off to wash at the kitchen sink while Sarah rested her head back. I'll just have five minutes before I get his tea ready, she thought, closing her eyes.

'You wicked little brat! How dare you!'

Sarah's eyes shot open at the sound of her mother's angry voice. She didn't know how long she'd been asleep, but it must have been for a while. She saw her mother standing at the kitchen sink with an empty gin bottle in her hand, and Tommy shaking as he cowered behind a kitchen chair. 'What's going on?' Sarah asked, confused.

'You're supposed to be looking after him, but while you've been snoring your head off, the little bastard has tipped me gin down the sink! I'll kill him, I swear I'll skin the bleeder alive!'

Sarah jumped from the sofa and ran to scoop Tommy into her arms. 'Sorry, Mum. He don't know any better. Please, don't take it out on him ... I'll get you some more gin.'

'Too right you will, but I'm telling you that little sod is still gonna get a good hiding from me, and if you try and stop me, you'll get the same!'

Sarah knew only too well what her mother was like and that she wouldn't back down. Though Annie was small-framed, she could still pack a punch, and Sarah feared for Tommy more than she did for herself.

'Please, Mum, I'll go now and get the gin. Don't hit

the boy, he won't do it again,' Sarah said as tears began to roll down her cheeks.

'For Christ's sake, girl, you're too soft with that precious brother of yours. I don't care how much you turn on the waterworks, he ain't getting away with it!'

Sarah could feel Tommy quivering in her arms and watched in horror as her mother went for the cane she kept next to her mattress. Annie didn't use it often, preferring to deliver a slap or a punch, but when she did produce the cane, Sarah knew it meant business. She still had the scars across her buttocks to prove it.

Tommy seemed to sense Sarah's fears and began crying hysterically. She'd do anything for the boy, whatever it would take to protect him from the intense pain she'd experienced from one of her mother's lashings. 'I won't allow you to whip Tommy!' she said firmly.

'You won't *allow* me? Who the hell do you think you are? You'll do as you're bloody well told, so either hand over the boy or get out for good, the pair of you!'

Sarah's heart raced. She could tell her mother was on the brink of complete rage. If they were to avoid a beating, she'd have to act fast. In a panic and without stopping to collect any of their belongings, she drew in a deep breath, bracing herself before heading for the front door. If she left now, she knew there would be no turning back, but what other choice did she have? She threw her mother one final look, then turned quickly and walked through the door.

Tommy could see over her shoulder and suddenly screamed, 'Run, Sarah! Run!'

As she picked up her pace and ran along the corridor, Sarah looked behind her and caught a glimpse of her mother hard on their heels, hand raised in the air, ready to lash out with the cane. It was the last thing she saw before she turned and fled down the stairs, gasping with relief when her mum didn't follow, but her foul language echoed down the stairwell as she threatened to shred the skin off their backs if they dared to come back.

Tears streamed down Sarah's face as she vowed never to return to her mother's flat again.

Chapter 7

Annie paced the floor. Her daughter had really messed things up for her this time. She had no gin, no money and no customers. She knew it would be pointless to go begging to Cyril as he'd recently thrown her out of his pub, and on more than one occasion too. She could go cap in hand to Eddy, but after the slap she'd given him earlier, she doubted she'd get a welcome reception there either.

Feeling exhausted and exasperated, she slumped on the edge of the sofa and sat with her legs splayed, chewing her fingernails. The agitation caused by the need for a drink was driving her crazy. In a bid to calm herself and think clearly, she drew in a few long deep breaths and leaned back to rest. Sarah's coat was over the back of the sofa, and as Annie laid her head on it, she felt something hard in the pocket.

She grabbed the coat and frantically began rifling through the pockets. Then, to her relief and delight, she found several coins. This is the least you owe me, Annie thought as licked her lips at the thought of buying some gin. She gathered the money and glanced around the flat. It felt strangely empty and lonely, but Annie was resolute.

If her kids had the audacity to show their faces here again, she'd give them what for. Good riddance to 'em, she thought, and untied the key on the back of the door so they couldn't get in. After all, Sarah was eighteen now, and hardly a child. Annie had done her bit to bring her up, and now she reasoned it was time the girl made her own way in the world and found out what life is really like.

It was getting dark and Sarah could see Tommy was tired and cold, especially as all he had on his legs was a pair of thin shorts. She wished she'd taken the time to at least grab their coats, but with the fear of their mother's wrath, she hadn't been thinking clearly.

'Sarah, I'm so worn out. Can't we go back home now?'

'No, love, sorry. That's not our home any more,' she told him as she reached for his hand to gently pull him along.

'So, where's our home then?'

That's a very good question, thought Sarah. She knew she had to find somewhere for them to sleep but with no family, friends or money she felt at a complete loss.

'Please, Sarah, my feet hurt, let's go home,' Tommy whined, and began coughing.

It sounded chesty again, and Sarah knew she had to find them somewhere to rest. 'Here, sit on this wall a minute while I get me thinking cap on,' she said, trying to sound cheery, though really she felt in utter despair. She lifted the boy and placed him on a garden wall.

'I'm cold . . .' Tommy moaned again.

'I know you are, love,' Sarah said, then wrapped her arms around her brother.

Then it came to her. Mr Sayers' shed! It had been four years since she had been there, and she hoped the old couple still owned the house. If they did, the back gate might still be unlocked and so would the shed. It wasn't ideal, but it would do for tonight. At least they would have some shelter. 'Come on, little man, we're going on an adventure!' she said with a renewed vigour.

'What adventure?' Tommy asked, not showing quite the same enthusiasm as his sister.

'We're going to find a secret hut, and maybe, if we're as quiet as mice, we may find some treasure in there!'

Tommy's eyes lit up and he jumped from the wall. 'What treasure, Sarah? Where's the secret hut? Have pirates been in the hut? Is it Captain Hook's treasure?'

Sarah chuckled. *Peter Pan* was Tommy's favourite story. 'I don't know, we'll have to find out for ourselves, but remember what I said – we have to be very, very quiet.'

Tommy nodded, and they set off for Mr Sayers' old shed.

Half an hour later, Sarah was pleased to find the back gate unlocked and, as she looked up the garden path, she was relieved to see the house in darkness. She turned to Tommy and placed a finger over her lips. 'Shush,' she whispered.

Tommy clung on to Sarah's skirt, almost hiding behind her. With trepidation, they crept through the gate and up to the shed. Sarah pulled on the door. Thank goodness, she thought as the door creakily opened. She shot a look over her shoulder. There wasn't any sign of movement from the house, so she quickly pulled Tommy inside with her, then gritted her teeth at the sound of the door creaking again as she closed it. She just had to hope the noise hadn't disturbed anyone.

'I don't like it in here . . . it's dark, Sarah,' Tommy said.

'It's all right, look,' she replied, and then pulled back a piece of gingham material that was stretched on a curtain wire over a small window.

Once the curtain was open, half of the shed was illuminated with moonlight.

'There you go, now we can see a bit better. I wonder where the treasure could be? Don't touch anything yet, but can you see it?'

Sarah watched Tommy, who looked animated as he scanned the shelves for treasure. Then her eyes fixed on Mr Sayers' shovel. It was in the corner, leaning against the wall. She instantly recognised it, together with his old flat cap, resting on top of the handle. She felt a lump in her throat and fought to hold back tears. She hadn't expected to react like this, but it upset her to see his things, forgotten and covered in spiders' webs and dust.

'Where's the treasure, Sarah?' Tommy whispered.

'I'm not sure. It's a bit too dark to look tonight, so let's get some sleep and we can have a look in the morning when the sun comes up.'

'Sleep in here? But, Sarah, it's cold and I don't like spiders.'

Sarah looked around and saw a pile of old newspapers. She picked one up and could just about make out the date. 1948. The last time she'd seen Mr Sayers. These must be his papers, the ones she used to read to him, she thought. Then she spotted a ball of string on one of the shelves.

'Sit yourself down in this chair,' she told Tommy,

pulling an old deckchair forward and opening it. The stripy cloth looked worn, but she thought it would be a comfortable place for Tommy to rest. 'Now don't you worry about any spiders. You're a lot bigger than they are so they're more frightened of you than you are of them. Anyhow, spiders can't hurt you.'

Tommy looked apprehensive but did as he was told, while she took sheets of the newspapers and scrunched them around his feet. Then using the scissors that had been with the string, she cut it into lengths and tied it around the paper. She rubbed his legs briskly.

'There you go, your feet will be as warm as toast now,' she told him.

'What if Captain Hook comes back for his treasure and finds us here? He'll make us walk the plank!'

'Don't be daft, have you seen any pirate ships round here? If there is any treasure, it's been here for years and long forgotten by the likes of Captain Hook. I'm going to put some newspaper over you then I want you to close your eyes and get some sleep. We'll have to be up really early in the morning.'

'But what about you, where are you going to sleep?' Tommy asked.

'Right here, on the floor next to you.'

Once Tommy was covered with the paper, it didn't take long for him to drift off. Sarah tried to make herself as comfortable as she could, but there was a terrible draught coming under the shed door. She felt something crawling on her face, and grimaced as she brushed off a bug. At least they were safe for tonight, but she couldn't sleep as her mind churned with thoughts of the challenges she knew the daylight would bring. Tommy would wake up hungry, they were homeless and without a penny to their name. She wondered if Tommy would be better off in a children's home. He'd get fed and watered, which was more than she could offer the child.

Her eyes focused again on Mr Sayers's flat cap. Thinking about him seemed to give her comfort. He had cared for her, more than her own mother ever had. She'd loved him dearly and missed him. It had broken her heart when he'd died.

She eventually closed her eyes, and though it was cold in the shed, she found that she felt warm, and as if she was lying on soft feathers. 'Goodnight, Mr Sayers,' she whispered, feeling a strange sense that he was watching over her. It gave her courage and, before she gave in to sleep, Sarah decided her mind was set. She wouldn't be separated from Tommy. Come what may, she'd make sure he wasn't taken from her. She might not be able to give him a home and proper food, but she could give him all the love he needed, and that was something she knew he'd never get in an orphanage.

Chapter 8

Sarah was already wide awake when the sun came up. By the time Tommy awoke, she'd had a rummage through the shed but had only found a few things that she thought may come in handy: the scissors and string, an old dark-grey utility blanket and, of course, Mr Sayers's flat cap. It didn't appear that anyone had been in the shed since Mr Sayers had died, so she didn't think taking the small items was stealing. The garden tools might be worth a few bob, but then that really would be theft so Sarah decided to leave them. Best of all, she'd found an old tobacco tin filled with small lead soldiers. She'd left the tin hidden, but in a place where she knew Tommy would easily find it.

Tommy brushed off the newspapers and pushed himself up in the deckchair. 'Can we look for the treasure now?' he asked as he untied the string on his feet.

'Good morning to you too!' Sarah said with a small laugh. 'Go on then,' she added, 'but make sure you keep the noise down.'

Tommy scrambled out of the chair and began mooching around. Dust filled the air and spiders ran for cover as he carefully moved things. Then, just as

Sarah had anticipated, he found the tobacco tin, and gently shook it. The metal soldiers rattled inside, and Sarah smiled as Tommy gasped.

'What do you think is in here?' he asked excitedly.

'I don't know, it could be the treasure. Open it and find out.'

Tommy pulled the lid open and raised his eyebrows at what he saw. 'Look, Sarah. These are so 'mazing,' Tommy said as he studied the painted soldiers in their red coats and black hats.

'Yes, they are. Well done for finding the treasure but now we have to sneak out of here. Put the tin in your pocket, there's a good boy,' Sarah said as she placed Mr Sayers's flat cap on his head.

She peeked through the small shed window. There didn't seem to be any movement from the house and all the curtains were still drawn. 'Come on, Tommy,' Sarah said and took him by the hand. She pushed open the creaky door to make a dash for the back gate and when they emerged from the back alley, they began wandering the streets of terraced houses.

'Where are we going? I'm hungry,' Tommy said as he dragged his feet.

'How about a trip to Battersea Park?'

'Can we have something to eat?'

'Yes, later,' Sarah replied, not knowing where their next meal would come from.

'I'm cold, I want to go home.'

'I told you, we don't live with Mum any more. Here, this'll keep you warm,' she said, and wrapped the utility blanket like a cape around Tommy, securing it with a knot under his chin.

Tommy was beginning to lag, but as they turned the corner onto Battersea Bridge Road, Sarah noticed his mood suddenly perk up.

'Sarah, Sarah . . . the bridge. Please can we go on the bridge and look down at the boats . . . please?'

She hadn't planned on walking over the bridge, but it seemed it would be a welcome distraction for Tommy. 'OK, but no throwing things over the side like you did last time.'

'All right, I promise,' Tommy said, and skipped ahead.

Sarah quickened her pace to keep up with him. Though he could see the boats through the Moorish-style latticing balustrades, he was almost tall enough to see over the top. She was nervous about him reaching too far and toppling into the Thames. 'Hey, wait for me,' she called.

Tommy stopped and began to jump up and down. 'Pick me up, please, Sarah . . .' he asked excitedly.

She wrapped her arms around her brother's waist and held him up to look out along the river.

'I wish we could go on a boat,' Tommy said.

'Maybe you will one day. You could sign up with the Navy and live on one of them big battleships.'

'Nah,' said Tommy, 'I'd miss you too much 'cos you couldn't come on the boat 'cos no girls would be allowed.'

Sarah affectionately squeezed Tommy and he giggled in response.

Just as her arms were beginning to ache and she was about to put him down, he squealed, 'Look – Sarah – I can see treasure!'

'Can you? What treasure can you see?' Sarah asked, playing along with him.

'Down there, in the mud . . . LOOK.'

Tommy seemed very insistent, so Sarah put him down and leaned into the balustrade for a closer look. The mud and shingle appeared almost black, but Sarah spotted something gold glistening in the sun's rays. 'You're right, Tommy, there's definitely something down there.'

'Come on, let's go and get it. I bet it's real treasure that's fallen off a pirate ship,' Tommy said, and began running towards some concrete steps that led down to the banks.

As he made a dash down the steps, Sarah gave chase. 'Wait,' she shouted, 'it's too dangerous. You stay here, I'll go.'

'But . . . but . . .'

'No, Tommy, there's no buts about it. I want you to sit on this bottom step and don't move, OK?'

Tommy put on a sulky face but nodded his head.

'Good boy. Sit tight and I'll be back in a minute with the treasure.'

Satisfied that Tommy would follow her instructions, she cautiously stepped down onto the foreshore, half expecting her feet to sink in the stinking mud. Thankfully, it wasn't as mushy or as deep as she had expected. She looked again for the shiny object and mapped a path in her head which would take her mainly across the shingle.

She slowly made her way through the mud, wrinkling her nose at the foul smell. Her black lace-up shoes were soon covered in thick gloop, and she nearly lost her balance a couple of times, slipping on green algae-covered rocks. As she got closer to the object, her heart began to race. She was sure it was a piece of jewellery. Finders, keepers, she thought, desperate for the money it could be worth.

Finally, she reached down and pulled the gold from the mud. It was filthy, but she could see it was a very thick and heavy gold bracelet adorned with several jewelled charms. It must be worth a fortune, she thought, quickly heading back towards the steps.

'Is it treasure, Sarah?' Tommy asked, as he jumped up excitedly.

'Oh, yes, it most certainly is,' Sarah replied, holding out the bracelet for Tommy to see. 'Look.'

'Wow, I've never seen nothing like that. Is it ours now? Can we keep it?'

'Well, really, we should try and find the owner or take it to the police station, but given that it was in the mud down here, I doubt we'd ever know who lost it. So, yes, I suppose it is ours, but we can't keep it 'cos I'll have to sell it or we'll be going hungry.'

'But I saw it first, so it's mine, and I don't want to sell it,' Tommy complained.

'What good is a gold bracelet to you? Would you rather you kept this and we starved to death? Stop being so selfish, it isn't like you.'

Tommy hung his head. Sarah could see he was about to start crying, and she hated to see him upset. 'Come here, give me a cuddle. You're a clever boy, spotting that in the mud like you did. Well done,' she said, and wrapped her arms around him.

'Geroff me – you smell,' Tommy said and chuckled.

Sarah realised she did. In fact, they both needed a wash and so did the bracelet. With no money for a tram, she knew it would be a bit of a trek, but decided on heading to Clapham Junction. They could use the public toilets, then make their way to the market at Northcote Road.

Once there she hoped to sell the gold and finally fill their empty bellies.

The streets and shops at Clapham Junction were bustling with people, and as they passed Sarah she felt a little fearful, wondering if the bracelet in her pocket belonged to any of them. She had no way of knowing, but she knew she had to risk trying to sell it.

To her relief, Tommy had been quiet for most of the journey, but she could see the child was tired, and knew he was hungry. When she looked down at him and he greeted her back with a warm smile and twinkling blue eyes, the guilt she felt was like a stab to her heart. He was such a sweet child and she wished she could do more for him.

As they passed Hastings' furniture store, Sarah caught a glimpse of her reflection in the shop window. Her shoes were caked in mud, and her thin blouse and holey cardigan were grubby from lying on the shed floor. Her skirt was wrinkled, and her hair was tangled. With Tommy in his oversized flat cap and blanket wrapped around him, she realised they must look like a couple of vagrants. She crossed the road to a central reservation which was locally known as Bog Island. There were toilets in Arding and Hobbs' department store, but, looking as they did, she thought it best to avoid them.

'Sarah, I'm a big boy now. Can I use the men's toilet by myself?'

'No, Tommy, you're still not old enough. Sorry, I know you don't like it but you have to use the ladies' with me,' Sarah answered as she led Tommy down the curved steps to the public toilets located under the street, noticing how clean and white the tiled walls were.

Once downstairs, she saw how the brass pipes and door knobs gleamed in the light coming through the opaque glass tiles in the pavement above. She quickly scanned the room, and, pleased to find the char lady wasn't around, took off her shoes and rinsed them under the tap in one of the sinks. She filled another sink with water and instructed Tommy to wash himself.

'What with?' Tommy asked.

Sarah took a corner of the blanket and dampened it before wiping it over her brother's grubby face. 'There you go. Now wash your hands too.'

'I need the loo, Sarah.'

'Me too, but I haven't got a penny. We'll have to wait for someone to come down, then when they come out of the cubicle, we'll grab the door before it closes.'

'But what if the door won't open again and we get locked in 'cos we didn't pay?' Tommy asked, looking concerned.

'Don't worry, that won't happen,' Sarah reassured him.

She had just about finished doing her best to tidy herself up, then gingerly took the bracelet from her skirt pocket and rinsed it under the tap. 'Keep an eye out and tell me if you see anyone coming down the stairs,' she said to Tommy.

A moment later, 'Someone's coming!' Tommy said quickly.

Sarah stuffed the bracelet back into her cardigan pocket and began to finger-comb her hair while looking in the mirror. She covertly watched as a middle-aged woman with a scarf covering her hair rollers fished a penny from her purse and placed it in the big brass lock on the toilet door. The woman turned the knob, entered, then closed the door behind her.

A few minutes later, Sarah heard the chain pull in the cubicle. She winked and whispered to Tommy, 'Now's our chance.'

As the woman came out, Tommy grabbed the door.

'Thanks, missus,' he said, and flashed her a cheeky grin.

That boy could charm the birds from the trees, thought Sarah. He deserved so much more than she could offer. She put her hand in her pocket and fingered the gold bracelet. She thought she'd had a lucky run, first with Mr Sayers' old shed and then finding the jewellery. Now she hoped her luck wasn't about to run out.

Chapter 9

'Come on, ladies, I've got a smashing suit and tie 'ere. It'd smarten up your old man a treat,' George Neerly called out to the passing shoppers milling around in the market. He'd been working on the second-hand clothes stall for as far back as he could remember, at first with his father, but after his dad was killed when a doodlebug had dropped on their house, George had taken over the business.

'How about this lovely little number for you bootiful ladies, guaranteed to make him indoors sit up and take notice of you,' George shouted as he held up a green and yellow flower-patterned dress. When there were no takers George looked over to Roger, who ran the fruit and vegetable stall next to his, and said, 'Slow today, mate, ain't it?'

'Yeah, if it carries on like this, I might pack up early,' Roger replied.

Unlike him, Roger was tall and slim, with a chiselled jaw, black hair and striking ice-blue eyes. His good looks always seemed to attract the housewives, which George thought was a blessing as it would inevitably bring business to his stall as well. After all, it wasn't as if he could rely on his own looks, not with a heavily scarred face. However, it seemed Roger's appeal was letting them both down today, and George sighed heavily as he thought back to the bomb that had killed his father and left himself almost unrecognisable. He still had flashbacks, mostly when he was sleeping, and would often wake in a cold sweat, remembering the smell of his own flesh burning and the searing pain as flames licked his once handsome face.

This won't do, George thought to himself, and shook his head. The bomb had dropped eight years ago when he'd been thirteen years old, and though the memory was vivid, he tried not to dwell on the past. He walked around to the front of his stall and began tidying some of the clothes that had been left strewn around when a woman had been rummaging earlier. As he folded a pair of striped pyjamas, he caught sight of a young woman sitting on the kerb at the edge of the market. He thought she looked very pretty with her long, dark hair and slim legs which she had pulled up in front of her. He could see she was holding something out to the few passers-by. It looked like gold, maybe jewellery, and he wondered what she was playing at. He knew PC Plod would be passing on his beat any time now, and if the young woman was trying to sell knock-off bits of gold, she'd soon find herself having her collar felt. By the looks of it, she had a young lad with her. George felt compelled to go and warn her.

''Ere, Roger, keep an eye on my stall, I'll be back in a tick,' he said.

Roger gave him a nod, and George walked off. He passed a flower stall, then a book stall, and then approached the young woman. 'What you got there then?' George asked.

She looked up at him and George immediately noticed

her shocked expression. He was used to that sort of reaction from strangers when they saw his face.

'It's . . . I . . . erm . . .' she replied.

'Look, I'm only here to warn you. The Old Bill come down here and if they see you trying to flog that bracelet, you'll find yourself down the nick. They don't take kindly to stolen goods being sold on the market.'

'But it ain't stolen!' the young woman protested, 'I found it!'

'Yeah, all right, if you say so. It's up to you, I'm just giving you the heads up,' George replied.

He saw her unusually green eyes begin to well up and realised she was about to start crying. Judging by the state of her and the lad, he thought they looked like a pair of ragamuffins and had obviously fallen on hard times. He suddenly felt very sorry for her. 'Please, don't cry. I didn't want to upset you. Tell you what, come with me to my stall. I've got a nice wool coat that would look smashing on you. You look half frozen,' he offered.

'Thanks, but I ain't got no money,' she answered, and sniffed.

'Don't worry about that. I've had the bloody thing for weeks now, can't seem to shift it. It's nice, mind, and a gift to you.'

George held out his hand to help her up and was glad when she accepted. He led her back to his stall, with the little lad in tow who was clutching a blanket around himself. Poor mite, he thought, hoping to find something suitable for the boy too.

Sarah felt so uncomfortable. She hated accepting charity, especially from strangers, but she was cold down to the bone and her teeth were chattering. She welcomed the thought of a warm coat to wear.

'I'm Sarah, and this is my brother Tommy,' she said.

'Pleased to meet you both. Me name's George and this 'ere is that coat I was telling you about.'

George held up a dark-blue coat, and then helped Sarah into it. She thought he was very gallant, and was pleased when the coat fitted well. She instantly felt warmer, but also embarrassed. 'Thank you, George. I'm so grateful but I wish I could pay you for it. If I can sell this bracelet, I'll come back and give you some money. How much do I owe you?'

'I won't hear of it. I told you, it's a gift. Now, let me see what I can find for the young man,' George said and turned to smile at Tommy.

Tommy had been very quiet, but suddenly said loudly, 'Sarah, why has that man's face melted?'

Sarah felt her cheeks burn and wished the floor would open up and swallow her. You couldn't help but notice George's scars, but she hadn't expected Tommy to ask such a direct question.

As if sensing her awkwardness, George quickly responded. 'I like a man who says it as it is. That's right, lad, my face has melted, but it was a long time ago. I got injured in a fire, so you watch yourself and stay away from fires. You don't want to end up looking like me now, do you?'

Tommy shook his head and asked, 'What fire? Was it the Great Fire of London?'

'Tommy, that's enough. It's rude to ask questions. Now say you're sorry,' Sarah chastised.

'Sorry,' Tommy said and pouted.

'No need. Now, I'm sure I've got something in that box that'll be good for you,' George said and pointed to a crate under his stall. 'Have a look through there and see if you can find yourself something to wear instead of that old blanket.'

Tommy got down on his bare, dirty knees and began delving.

'Right, let's have a look at this bracelet you're selling. My old mum loves a bit of gold and her birthday's coming up soon,' George said, clapping his hands together.

Sarah took the bracelet from her pocket and handed it to George. 'Honest, I did find it. Tommy spotted it down on the river banks off the bridge. I didn't steal it, I wouldn't.'

'It's all right, I believe you, thousands wouldn't,' George said. 'Tell you what though, I've never seen anything quite as fancy as this. It must be worth a fortune. How much do you want for it?'

Sarah knew it was worth much more than she could ask, but she didn't care. She'd take whatever she could get. She pulled a figure from the air and answered, 'Ten pounds.'

George coughed and for a moment, Sarah thought his eyes were going to pop out of his head.

'Well, I wouldn't normally spend that much money on a pressie for my mum, but—'

Sarah quickly interrupted, worried she was about to lose her sale. 'Five pounds,' she said.

'Whoa, slow down, girl. I was going to say—'

Once again Sarah cut in. 'OK, three pounds but that's my final offer.'

George laughed. 'You drive a hard bargain. Tell you

what, I'll give you a fiver for it. That way, you've got it sold and I've got me mother a bit of tom that she's going to love. You'd be hard pushed to get rid of it round here. People ain't got that sort of money going spare. You'd be better off going up town to flog something like this.'

'No, a fiver is fine. Deal,' Sarah said, relieved she would at last be able to feed herself and Tommy.

George handed Sarah a five-pound note. She'd never had so much money in her hand and studied the white piece of paper with its writing in black ink. It said, '*Bank of England*' in fancy swirly letters and underneath was written, '*promise to pay the bearer the sum of five pounds*'. Sarah wasn't sure if the money was real, and couldn't afford to be ripped off.

'What's this you're trying to fob me off with? Do you think I'm stupid, George?'

'What do you mean? Of course I ain't trying to fob you off. That there's good money,' George replied.

His tone of voice made Sarah think she'd hurt his feelings with her accusation, but she had to be sure she had real money. 'I'm sorry. I don't mean to sound ungrateful. Truth is, I've never seen a fiver before and didn't know they looked like this. If I'm honest, I'd much rather you paid me in coins.'

'Give it here,' George said, tutting. 'I don't know, you women, there's no pleasing you sometimes.' He chuckled.

As George was sorting out some coins from his money belt, Tommy jumped up from the crate he'd been looking through. 'Can I have this please? It's really brilliant.'

George and Sarah looked at the man-sized khaki army jacket that Tommy was holding up, and both laughed. It almost reached to his feet.

'If that's what you want, but better check with your sister first.'

'Can I, Sarah . . . please?'

Sarah saw the delight on her brother's face. It wasn't as if the child had much to be happy about, and she supposed it would at least keep him warm. 'Yes, all right. Just make sure you thank George.'

Tommy dropped the blanket to the floor and put on the jacket, then spontaneously ran and threw his arms around George's legs. 'Thanks. This is the best coat I've ever had!'

'You're welcome,' the man said, ruffling Tommy's brown hair.

Sarah picked up the blanket, roughly folding it while thinking that George looked quite moved by Tommy's display of affection. She saw him smile when Tommy began marching back and forth.

'He's a proper nice lad. A real credit to your mum and dad,' George said.

'Yeah, he is. But it's just us two, no mum and dad.'

'Oh, I'm sorry, I didn't mean to say anything out of turn. Well, you're doing a fine job of looking after him.'

Sarah didn't think she was and the guilt jabbed at her again. She thought she might burst into tears, but before she could, George handed her the coins and she croaked, 'Well, it was nice meeting you, but now I've got this money I can pay you for the coats.'

'Nah, I've got a good deal with the bracelet, so we'll call them a bonus. It's been a pleasure doing business with you,' George replied.

She managed a watery smile then called, 'Tommy, come on, time to go.'

Tommy swung round and marched towards her, stomping his feet, pretending to be a soldier. 'Yes, sir,' he said in a deep voice.

Sarah gave George a small wave and, tummy rumbling, turned to head for the nearest fish and chip shop.

She didn't look back, but she heard George call out, 'Don't be a stranger. Come and say hello next time you're up the market.'

Tommy had wolfed down his fish and chips and had even licked the newspaper they were wrapped in. Then the rest of the day had been spent ambling around the park, but now as the sun was beginning to set, Sarah thought about heading back to the shed.

She had enough cash in her pocket to get a room for a few nights, but thought it best to save the money instead. After all, she didn't yet have a plan for how to make any more. 'Come on, Tommy,' she called to her brother, who was halfway up a small oak tree. 'Time to go.'

Tommy whined, 'Ow, I don't want to go yet. Can we go to the funfair?'

'No, it's going to be dark soon, come on and stop answering me back.'

Tommy jumped down from the tree then minced towards her with a sullen expression. 'Have we got to go back to that shed again?'

'Yes, we have, but I don't know why you're looking so miserable about it. You slept OK *and* found some treasure in there!'

'I know, but I don't like it. Please, can we go home? Mummy might not smack me now.'

Sarah had twelve years' more experience than Tommy,

so she knew only too well that their mother would not have calmed down, and if they walked back through her front door they'd both receive the hidings of their lives. 'Sorry, Tommy, I'm not risking you getting beaten black and blue. I love you too much to see you get hurt, so like it or lump it, we're going back to the shed.'

Tommy didn't protest, but hung his head as he walked alongside her. They were soon in the alley which led to the back gate. 'Remember, just like last time, quiet as a mouse,' Sarah said, and pushed open the gate.

Once inside, Tommy made himself comfortable on the deckchair. 'My soldiers, I can play with them now,' he said as if just remembering them, and pulled the tobacco tin from his pocket.

As he played quietly and happily, Sarah found an old broom and swept the floor. She pushed the big pile of dust to a corner, and then arranged some of the newspapers to fashion a bed. The moon was veiled by clouds, so the shed wasn't as illuminated as it had been the previous night. It's not too bad, she thought, at least no worse than her mother's flat.

Half an hour passed, and Sarah strained her eyes in the darkness to see that Tommy had fallen asleep. She carefully took the toy soldiers from his hands and placed them back in the tin, then covered him with the grey blanket. He'd be as snug as a bug in a rug, she thought, grateful for the oversized army jacket George had given them.

She took her own coat off and lay down on the newspaper, then pulled her coat over her like a blanket. She'd sleep better tonight knowing she had money in her pocket to feed Tommy tomorrow.

Chapter 10

'Wake up, Sarah. Time to go.'

Sarah awoke with a start. She rubbed her eyes and tried to focus. The morning sun was beginning to stream through the small window. She looked at Tommy and was surprised to see him still soundly asleep. Who had spoken to her?

'Who's there?' she whispered.

She stood up and tiptoed to the window, but couldn't see anyone, though she was sure she'd heard someone speak to her. Tommy began to stir and yawned as he stretched.

'Tommy, have you been playing tricks on me? Did you tell me to wake up and then pretend to be asleep?' she asked, keeping her voice light.

She could tell from the confused expression on her brother's face that he didn't have an inkling of what she was talking about. Time to go, she thought, recalling the words she'd heard. It was a warning, it had to be. They had to get out of the shed, quick! 'Come on, Tommy, get up, hurry! We've got to go.'

'All right,' Tommy said slowly, rubbing the sleep from his eyes.

Sarah was irritated to see he wasn't rushing himself. 'Now,' she said firmly.

Tommy stood up, and Sarah grabbed his hand before opening the door. To her horror she saw an old woman coming towards them. The woman's back was bent and she was walking with a cane, but Sarah was amazed at the speed of the woman's pace. Her hair was long and grey, which put Sarah in mind of a witch. She knew she should run but fear froze her to the spot. She stood stunned and watched as the old woman stopped just yards in front of her and began to angrily wave her cane, shaking it at Sarah. She had no doubt that the woman was more than capable of hitting her with it.

'Go on, clear orf. I've called the police, you thieving bloody gypsies,' the woman screeched.

'I – I'm sorry . . . we – we just needed somewhere to sleep,' Sarah said fretfully.

'Well, you ain't kipping in my shed. Go on, bugger off.'

Sarah glanced at Tommy. The child looked terrified. She yanked on his hand, and within seconds they were through the gate, but she could still hear the old woman shouting obscenities.

Once they were back on the streets, Tommy seemed to relax. 'We was really, really, really quiet so how did she know we was in her shed?' he asked.

'I have no idea,' Sarah answered, shaking her head, but as she remembered the voice, she knew that Mr Sayers had saved them. The woman had called the police and if they hadn't been woken, the rozzers would have been on them before they could have made their escape.

George was busy setting up his stall, but he couldn't shake the thought of Sarah from his mind.

'Penny for them,' Roger called. 'You look like you've been away with the fairies for the last half hour.'

First thing in the morning, George would normally be full of banter and larking around with the other coster-mongers, but today he felt subdued. If he'd been blessed with Roger's fine face, he might have had the courage to ask Sarah on a date, but, as was usual for him, he'd let the opportunity slip him by and now deeply regretted it. He could have kicked himself. He just hoped she'd pass his way again soon. 'Sorry, mate, just got stuff on my mind,' George answered, and forced a smile.

'Oh, yeah. That wouldn't be the pretty little thing I saw you chatting up yesterday, would it?'

'Cor blimey, mate! You don't miss a thing, do you?' George replied, his mood lightening.

'You know me. You've gotta keep your eyes and ears open here. Seriously though, who was she?'

'I ain't got a clue. I saw her sitting on the kerb. She looked down on her luck, but all I know is her name's Sarah and her little brother is Tommy and they ain't got no parents.'

'You silly sod, fancy not asking her out! She was a looker, that's for sure,' Roger said, then tossed a potato over to George as he added, 'That's you that is, a proper spud head.'

George caught the potato and laughed. Yes, when it came to women, Roger was right, he was a spud head, though he'd never heard anyone being called it before.

Sarah held Tommy's hand as she marched determinedly to the local shop. She knew they had a notice board where people would pay a small weekly amount to advertise on a card, and she was hoping to find a cheap room to rent.

'Are we going to see George today?' Tommy asked.

'Not today.'

'Ow, why not?' he said, sounding disappointed.

'Because it's more important to find somewhere to live,' Sarah answered, though she was reluctant to spend her money before she knew when more would be coming in.

'Are we going to live in a proper house then?'

'I hope so, let's see,' Sarah answered as they arrived at the shop. 'Wait here, I won't be long.' She knew there would be an array of sweets displayed in jars behind the counter, so, to avoid temptation, she thought it best to go in alone.

'Good morning, Miss,' the shopkeeper chirped, but Sarah noticed he hardly lifted his eyes from the magazine he was reading.

'Good morning. Is it OK if I have a quick look at your notices?'

'Yes, of course, just don't go unpinning any off the board. You'd be amazed at the number of people who see something they fancy and take the card with them.'

'I won't, but do you have a pen and paper I could use?'

The shopkeeper looked up from his magazine and eyed her up and down. She knew she looked a mess, but she hoped her blue coat covered her scruffy clothes.

'Here you go,' he said, and took a pencil from behind his ear, handing it to her with a scrap of paper. 'I shall want my pencil back when you're done.'

Sarah thanked the man and scanned the notice board. There were plenty of adverts for rooms and flats, but most were too expensive. Then she spotted one that looked affordable. A ground-floor room in a shared house. It was unfurnished but at least it would be shelter from the cold, wet nights. She quickly scribbled down the telephone number before thanking the shopkeeper and returning his pencil.

The bell above the shop door rang as Sarah opened it to leave, but once outside, her stomach flipped as she realised her brother was nowhere to be seen. 'Tommy,' she frantically called, 'Tommy . . .' Her eyes darted up and down the deserted street, and she began to panic. It wasn't like him to wander off alone, and she wondered what could have happened to him.

A middle-aged woman appeared on her doorstep. 'Are you looking for the young lad in the army coat?'

'Yes, my brother. Have you seen him?'

'He ran off up the street with a couple of other boys. You'll probably find them round the back. There's an old warehouse there that the kids like to play in.'

'Thank you,' Sarah replied, feeling some relief. She ran along the street and around to the back of the houses, and soon found the disused warehouse, just as the woman had described. She noticed the windows were smashed, and, from what she could see, half the roof was missing. She didn't think it looked like a safe building for children to be playing in, and could feel her heart hammering hard in her chest.

Sarah pulled open a metal door that was hanging only by its upper hinges. The concrete floor was littered with dead leaves, and she was startled by a pigeon taking off from its roost. 'Tommy,' she called again, and listened as her voice echoed through the derelict building. 'Tommy, I know you're in here, so stop playing silly beggars.'

She heard some giggling from around a wall, and young voices saying, 'Shush'. As she turned the corner, she found herself locking eyes with Tommy, who was obviously oblivious to the fear he'd just caused her.

'You little bugger,' she said through gritted teeth, then stomped towards him, grabbed his arm, and laid three hefty whacks on his backside.

The other boys ran off, leaving Tommy sobbing.

'I was only playing hide and seek with my friends,' he cried.

Sarah suddenly felt awful for hitting the child. She'd never laid a hand on him before, and memories of her mother snapped into her mind. 'I know, I'm sorry for smacking you, but you scared the living daylights out of me. You mustn't ever run off like that again, do you understand me?'

Tommy nodded his head and wiped his snotty nose on the cuff of his coat.

'And who are those boys? You don't even know them. They're not your friends.'

'They is Jerry and John and they said I could play with them.'

'Well, next time, you ask me first,' Sarah said in a softer voice.

Both calmer, Sarah led Tommy back to the street and they walked in silence to the post office. She'd seen a red telephone box outside, and was keen to ring the number for the room rental, hoping it was still available.

Once they found the telephone box, Tommy squeezed inside with Sarah. 'I've never been in a telephone box before,' he said, and breathed on one of the small glass windows. The window misted up and Sarah watched as he amused himself by drawing pictures with his fingers in the condensation.

She was relieved when she got through to Mrs Preston, who had placed the advert, and found the room was still available. The woman agreed to meet Sarah immediately at the house, though she didn't sound over-enthusiastic at letting out one of her properties to an unemployed woman caring for a young child. She told Sarah she'd require a significant payment of rent in advance, and, with little choice, Sarah agreed.

When they arrived at the terraced house, Mrs Preston was waiting outside. Sarah could tell by the woman's attire that she was wealthy. Her gloves were pristine white, and on her grey hair she wore a smart hat with a diamond pin. Her car was parked outside, and Sarah noticed a man in an official-looking cap sat at the steering wheel.

'Mrs Preston, pleased to meet you. I'm Sarah Jepson and this is my brother Tommy.'

'Yes, well, I don't have time for chitter chatter.' She opened the front door, and led them to a good-sized room with a window above a sink that overlooked the street.

Sarah instantly smelled the damp, but the room was cheap and it would have to do.

'As we discussed, I will require six weeks' rent in cash,' Mrs Preston said, holding a white handkerchief to her nose.

'Yes, that's fine. We'll take it,' Sarah replied, and counted out the money.

Mrs Preston took the cash and wrote a receipt which she handed to Sarah, saying, 'In future, Mr Terence will collect your rent, due fortnightly. I don't normally visit the properties myself, but Mr Terence is unavailable today. If you cannot pay, you will be evicted. I am not a charity, and I will not tolerate any sob stories.'

'I understand,' said Sarah, noting that the woman was looking down her nose.

With that, Mrs Preston handed Sarah the keys and walked off in a haughty manner. Sarah closed the room door, then turned happily to Tommy. 'This is ours. This is our new home.'

'But where are the beds?'

'All in good time, we'll make do for now. Anyway, who cares about beds and stuff? No more sheds for us, we've got our own home.'

Sarah was pleased to see Tommy smile, and felt proud of herself for providing a home for him, though she was worried that the rent she'd paid had left her with very little money.

'Can we have something to eat now? I'm so hungry that my belly thinks my head has been chopped off.'

Sarah laughed. 'I'll tell you what, how about we put this old blanket on the floor, go and get some food, then come back and have a picnic?'

'Yes,' Tommy said with delight, 'can we have cake?'

She fumbled the remaining coins in her coat pocket. They'd eat like kings tonight, but tomorrow would be a different story.

Chapter 11

The next day, Sarah sat on a bench in a churchyard close to the Thames. She liked it there. It was quiet and tranquil, which gave her time to think clearly.

'I'm bored, can we go now?' Tommy asked.

He'd been wandering around looking at the head-stones, but now sat next to Sarah on the bench.

'In a minute,' she answered.

'Can we go back to the bridge and look for more treasure?'

'That was a bit of a fluke the other day. I doubt there would be anything else there now.'

'Please, Sarah. It's much more fun than sitting here with all the dead people in their forever boxes under the ground.'

He had a point, she thought, and reluctantly stood up to leave. She didn't expect there would be anything in the mud again, but she'd humour her brother, if only to stop him moaning.

Battersea Bridge was just around the corner, and soon Tommy was racing off again to look over onto the banks. 'Pick me up,' he asked as he held onto the balustrades and jumped up and down.

Sarah lifted him up, and Tommy squealed in delight.

'I don't believe it, Sarah . . . there's more treasure!'

'Don't be daft,' she said, and placed him on the ground to look over the edge for herself. To her utter amazement she saw something glistening in the mud again, but she couldn't believe it could be anything like what she'd found before. It was more likely to be an old tin can, she thought.

'Told ya . . . I told you there'd be more treasure, didn't I?'

'Yes, Tommy, you did.'

They both ran to the steps and raced down to the foreshore. When Sarah got to the bottom, she noticed the water's edge was closer than it had been last time. It was later in the morning, so she assumed the tide must be coming in.

'Stay here, like before. I'll go and get it,' Sarah instructed, and set off across the mud. She'd never taken much notice of the river before now, and wasn't sure how quickly the water would rise. She'd heard stories of people drowning in the Thames, so with her heart pounding she hurried to retrieve the item before it could get lost under the water.

'Got it,' she called over her shoulder to Tommy. She looked towards the water to see it approaching faster than she had anticipated. With no time to hang about, she made a hasty retreat to Tommy on the steps.

'What is it, Sarah?'

'I'm not sure,' she said, looking curiously at the item in her hand, but she thought it might be valuable.

'Can I see?' Tommy asked.

Sarah handed it to him. It was round and silver with a chain attached. He wiped the round part on his shorts, then pushed in a tiny catch on the side which flipped a lid open.

'Wow, Sarah, look. It's a clock.'

Sarah took the watch from Tommy and noticed the time read half past eleven. She guessed it must have been the time it had fallen into the water, but she didn't know if that had been in the night or morning. Then she looked closer at the silver lid and saw it was engraved with the initials A. S. and dated 1903.

A wave of guilt washed over her. It was easily identifiable so she should take it to the police station, but she already knew she had no intention of doing so. She reasoned Tommy's well-being was more important than a watch. Whoever had lost it was obviously wealthy. If she could sell it, it would be a small loss for the owner but a life-saver for them.

George was pleased to have sold several garments from his stall, and the continual flow of customers had kept him from thinking about Sarah. Now, as lunchtime loomed, and with a lull in custom, his stomach groaned.

'George, fancy a pie?' Roger called.

'Cor, do I, yes, great idea,' George answered, thinking Roger must have read his mind.

'Do you want to nip to the pub and get them? I'll keep an eye on yours, only I've got my hands full here,' Roger said as he weighed out some carrots for a middle-aged woman.

George clapped his hands together and headed off towards the pub on the corner of the market. He thought the landlady, Violet, baked the best pies in Battersea, even better than his mum's, and he was looking forward to biting into one. Several people said hello to him as he passed them. He was well known in the market and his old wounds had left him easily recognisable. The pub was busy, so George found himself having to wait a while to be served, but it'll be worth it, he thought to himself, as he discussed the weather with a couple of acquaintances at the bar.

Eventually, with two pies in hand, he headed back to the stalls. He could see Roger had his fingerless gloved hands cupped to his face and was blowing on them to keep them warm. 'There you go, mate, this'll help keep the chill out,' he said and handed Roger one of the hot meat pies.

'Cheers, George. You've been gone a while, and you'll never guess what?' Roger said.

'You've sold all my stock and made me a small fortune?' George joked.

'No, you only bloody well missed that girl . . . what's her name . . . Sarah.'

'You're kidding me.'

'No, straight up. I saw her and that little lad walk past the end of the road. In fact, I'm surprised you didn't bump into her, you must have only just missed her.'

George shoved his pie into Roger's hand. 'Which way did she go?' he asked.

Before Roger had a chance to answer, George spun around and ran to chase after Sarah, but he heard Roger shout, 'Right, turn right.'

Sarah had been into the public toilets again, and now, with the silver watch cleaned up, she was hoping to find somewhere suitable to sell it. She didn't want to go up town like George had suggested when she had the bracelet. She'd never been over the bridge before, but had heard the people on the other side of the Thames were right toffs. That's probably where the watch came from, she thought.

George had told her the police walked along the market, so she decided it was probably better to stay away from there too. With Tommy alongside her, she searched the streets in the hope of finding a pawnshop. She'd never been in one before but remembered, when she was about Tommy's age, she'd had to wait outside while her mother went in to sell a ring a man had given her. Sarah had been fascinated by the three brass balls hanging over the shop sign. When her mother had come out, she'd been delighted and had dragged Sarah to the pub, where, once again, she had been left to wait outside.

She didn't miss those days, she thought, as she scanned the shops looking for the three brass balls. Then she unexpectedly heard George's voice.

'Hey, Sarah.'

As she stopped and turned, to her surprise, Tommy yanked his hand from hers and ran towards the man, clearly very pleased to see him.

'Hello, little man,' George said to Tommy.

'We found more treasure!' he squeaked.

'Did you indeed? What did you find this time?'

'We found a silver clock, didn't we, Sarah? Show George our clock.'

Sarah suddenly felt very embarrassed. George would never believe she wasn't a thief and had found the watch in the Thames. She could hardly believe it herself.

'Let's have a look at it then, Sarah,' George said.

She fumbled in her pocket, then held out the watch on the flat of her palm.

'Wow, this is a nice piece,' George said, as he took the watch from her hand. 'You say you found it? The same place where you found the bracelet?'

She knew George would question her and she looked for suspicion in his hazel eyes. As he stared back at her, she couldn't see any doubt, but suddenly felt awkward and looked at the ground.

'I reckon you've hit lucky twice. The watch ain't working, but I bet this is solid silver. Where are you taking it?'

'I was looking for a pawnshop.'

'I don't think you'll be able to sell it in there. Guaranteed they'll think you've nicked it. Tell you what, save you getting into trouble, how about I sell it on my stall for you?'

'Really? You'd do that for me?'

'Of course I would, but it'll cost you,' George said and winked at Tommy.

'I knew there'd be a catch. How much?' Sarah asked.

'A date . . . with me.'

Tommy giggled, but Sarah was taken aback. How could she possibly go on a date with anyone? She had Tommy to look after, and she had no clothes or anything, not even so much as a hairbrush. 'I'm sorry, George, but I can't.'

'Go on, Sarah, yes, you can,' Tommy urged.

'Shush, Tommy. Who'd look after you, eh?'

'Tommy can come too, it'll be fun,' George said.

Sarah still didn't think it was possible. George knew nothing about her and had no idea they were destitute.

Even if she could accept his offer, she didn't really want to. He was a kind man, but she found it difficult to see past the dreadful scars on his face. 'No, George, I can't. Thanks for the offer, but can you tell me where the pawnshop is? I'll offer it to them and the worst they can say is no.'

Tommy looked disappointed, and George must have noticed too, because he patted the boy's head and said, 'Don't worry, Tommy. Your sister doesn't want to date me, and who could blame her, but we're still mates and I can still sell that watch for you.'

Sarah had upset George; she could see it in his eyes and his tone of voice didn't sound quite as cheery, yet he was still willing to help her out, and she was grateful. 'I really appreciate you doing this for us, but I think it would be fair if you take a cut from the profits of the sale,' Sarah said, and held her head high. They might be penniless, but she still had her pride.

'What, you mean like a commission?' George asked.

'Yeah, I think that's what it's called. That way, we both benefit from it.'

George rubbed his chin, as if deep in thought. 'OK, I can see that would work. What sort of percentages are we talking here?'

Sarah's eyes widened. She'd never understood percentages and didn't know how they worked, but she didn't want George to think she was stupid. 'What would you suggest?' she asked.

'How about I take ten per cent, so, say I sell this for ten pounds, I'd take a pound and give you nine.'

Sarah was pleased that George had explained the numbers to her, and she thought it seemed more than reasonable. 'That sounds fair to me. Thing is though, George, I really need the money, so how quickly do you think you can sell it?'

'I can't make any promises, but I'll give it my best shot and hopefully I'll soon make a sale. Come on, let's get back to my stall and you can help me work out the best way to display it.'

Sarah walked through the market with renewed vigour and self-esteem. She wasn't a beggar or homeless, she was a businesswoman. Once she had the money from the sale, she'd find some half-decent furniture for their new home, and then set her mind on a plan to keep the cash coming in.

Then a light-bulb seemed to switch on in her head. If the watch sold for good money, maybe she could use some of it to buy stock for George to sell on commission. Yes, that could work, she thought, and remembered her mother's warnings about keeping her legs shut. Whatever the future held, she knew she'd never sell her body like her mother did.

Chapter 12

The next morning, George was washed, dressed and ready to leave for work. As he ran down the stairs in the house he shared with his mother, he had a definite spring in his step. He knew Sarah would be coming by his stall today to see if the watch had been sold.

'Morning, love,' Lena said as George came into the modern kitchen. 'There's tea in the pot.'

'Morning, Mum. Thanks, I'd love one,' George replied as he sat opposite his mother at the kitchen table. He thought she looked very trendy in her close-fitting cream-coloured dress with her brown hair styled in mid-length waves. She'd always looked younger than her years, and didn't have a grey strand on her head. Her smooth skin veiled her real age, and though she was over fifty, she could quite easily be mistaken for a woman in her early forties.

Lena poured a cup from the teapot. 'What are you so happy about? You look like the cat that's got the cream,' she asked, as she eyed her son suspiciously.

'Nothing. It's just a nice sunny morning and I've got a feeling today is going to be a good day,' George answered, taking a swig of his tea.

'So how come you're wearing your best shirt?'

George would have liked to have said to his mother that he'd met a beautiful girl and had fallen in love, but as Sarah had turned him down, there was nothing to tell. However, as his mother always said, he was the eternal optimist and he hadn't given up hope yet. 'Leave it out, will you? Can't a fellow look good without getting interrogated?'

'I know you, George Neerly, and it's more than a bit of sunshine that's put that twinkle in your eye! I hope she's a nice girl,' Lena said, and smiled warmly at her son.

'She is, and her name is Sarah, but she ain't interested in me . . . yet.'

'Give her time, George. I know it's difficult for you with women, but once she gets to know you and your shining personality, I'm sure she won't be able to help but fall head over heels in love with you.'

'I hope you're right,' George said wistfully.

'I am, son. Trust your old mum,' Lena said, then scraped back the kitchen chair and smoothed down the front of her dress. 'I'm off now. I'm going to pop in and see Mrs Harris before I go to work. I'll see you later . . . oh, and good luck with your lady friend.'

George waved as his mother left the kitchen to go to her job in the local grocery corner shop. It'd been three years since she'd started working there, and George thought it was the best thing to have happened to her. After the death of his father, she had sunk into a depression, hardly bothering to even get out of bed, but since working at Bosco's she'd come out of her shell. It seemed his mother loved the local chit-chat and gossip, and would often relay tales to George about her at number seventeen or him from the candle factory.

George heard the front door close, and sat back in his chair. He took Sarah's silver watch from his pocket and stared at it, knowing there was little chance of him selling it down the market. He didn't want to disappoint her though, and she looked as if she needed the money.

If his mother knew, she would call him a fool in love, but undeterred he made his way back to his bedroom and from the bottom of his wardrobe he pulled out a carved wooden box. He picked up the bracelet he'd bought from Sarah, and then took two five-pound notes from his small savings, which he stuffed into his trouser pocket. Then he placed the bracelet back in the box and the silver watch alongside it.

She's worth it, he thought, hoping he'd see her breathtaking smile again.

Sarah awoke to the musty smell of mould, which made her nostrils twitch. She threw her coat off, pushed herself up from the bare concrete floor, and walked across the room to open the curtainless window. Though the sun was shining, it was cold outside, but a blast of freezing fresh air would be better than the awful smell of damp.

The room she'd rented for her and Tommy wasn't much. In fact, it reminded her of the room she'd grown up in with her mum, only this one had more black mould growing up the walls than she would have liked. Unlike her mum's flat, which was in a purpose-built block, this was a ground-floor room in a small house, and she could hear footsteps walking back and forth above her. The shared bathroom was at the back of the house, but Sarah had found the taps over the bath had ceased to work, and the sink was cracked. At least the toilet flushed and was clean.

They didn't yet have any furniture, but the floor with a roof over their heads was better than the streets, and, having been found in the shed, she didn't have any other options. The small sink under the window had a cold tap, so at least they could have a bit of a wash. When she'd first turned the tap, the water had been a murky brown colour, but after leaving it to run it had cleared. The water was icy cold, but at least she didn't have to resort to going to the public toilets on Bog Island to clean them both up now.

Thankful for this small mercy, Sarah gently woke Tommy. 'We've got work to do today, so come on, lazy bones, time to get up.'

Tommy opened his eyes, and Sarah was delighted to see him smile widely. 'Are we going to see George today?'

'Yes, and fingers crossed he's sold our watch,' Sarah said, and after a chilly wash, she did her best to tidy their hair with an old comb she'd found.

'I'm hungry,' Tommy moaned.

'All right, we'll something to eat before we go to see George.'

By the time they arrived, the market was a hive of activity, and Sarah spotted George shoving a jumper into a woman's shopping trolley. He hadn't seen Sarah as he had his back to her.

'See you next week, Ethel,' George called as the woman walked off looking happy with her purchase.

'Hello, George,' Sarah said.

George spun round to look at her, and once again Sarah was reminded of his terrible disfigurement. Though she'd seen him a couple of times now, she was still shocked by the scars on his face, though she tried her best to hide it.

Tommy didn't appear to be the least bit bothered by George's appearance, and gleefully greeted the man.

'Hello, you two,' George replied, 'how are you both?'

'Do you want to see my soldiers?' Tommy asked.

'Yes, mate, I'd love to,' George answered, and scooped Tommy up in his muscular arms.

'Have you managed to sell the watch yet?' Sarah asked.

'Blimey, give us a chance,' George replied. 'Your sister, eh, what's she like?'

'She's like an ice-cream,' Tommy answered.

'How's that?' George asked, looking bemused.

'Well, she's a bit cold sometimes but she's all soft and creamy really, and I really like ice-cream.'

Sarah felt her heart melt. If only her mother could have opened her eyes to see what a wonderful son she'd had.

'I like ice-cream too,' George said, and Sarah noticed him looking at her in a way that made her blush.

George put Tommy down and fished in his pocket for some coins. Then he handed them to Tommy and pointed down the road. 'See that ice-cream shop over there, De Marco's? – best ice-creams in Battersea. I know it's cold today, and a bit early, but go and get you and me a nice cornet, any flavour you like. Would you like one, Sarah?' George asked.

'No, thanks, George. We've not long had something to eat, but I won't stop Tommy having a cornet. Mind you, straight there and back, Tommy, no mucking about.'

Tommy skipped off, and George turned to Sarah. 'I've sold your watch, but not for as much as I would have liked. We got six pounds for it, so I hope you're not too disappointed with this?' George said as he handed Sarah her money.

Sarah took the cash, and was more than delighted with the amount.

'That's great, thanks, George. I was thinking—'

'Oh, no,' George cut in, 'this could be dangerous.'

Sarah smiled and continued, 'I wondered how you'd feel about selling more of my stuff? On commission, not for free.'

'Have you got more stuff then?'

'Well, no, not at the moment. But I was thinking, I could use some of this money to buy some.'

'I'd be happy to. After all, it's easy money for me and no skin off my nose, but what sort of stuff are you thinking of buying?'

Sarah was pensive. She hadn't really thought it all through, and even if she had a plan of what to buy, she'd no idea where to buy it. 'I'm not sure yet. More jewellery, I suppose. It seems to sit nicely with your clothes. What do you think?'

'I reckon that's a smashing idea, but make sure you don't buy nothing too fancy,' George answered. 'My customers aren't flush with money, but they might be tempted by some beads or brooches, stuff like that to dress up an outfit.'

'Yes, good idea,' Sarah said, but as they shook hands to seal the deal, a large clap of thunder exploded overhead. I hope that's not a bad omen, Sarah thought worriedly.

As the skies opened and rain began to pour, George suddenly sprang into action and began pulling tarpaulin over his stall. Sarah ran around to the other side to help. In her haste, she bumped into Roger who was hurriedly trying to cover his stock.

'Sorry,' she said, and caught her breath as she found herself looking into the most striking blue eyes she'd ever seen. Tommy had blue eyes, but this man's were ice-coloured and rimmed with black eyelashes.

'That's all right, love. You must be Sarah?'

'Er . . . erm . . . yes . . .' she managed to stutter, feeling like an absolute idiot. She thought the man was gorgeous, and could feel her heart rate quicken as butterflies flitted in her stomach.

'I'm Roger. George has told me all about you. Nice to meet you.'

Sarah found herself unable to speak, and instead just gazed at him. She heard Tommy call her, and was pleased to realise that hearing her little brother had brought her back down to earth. She spun around and saw her brother with water dripping off his oversized coat and flat cap, holding a cone in each hand. The rain had washed away the ice-cream. He must have been disappointed, yet still had a huge smile on his face.

Sarah, George and Roger all chortled at the lad, which in turn gave Tommy the giggles. This is nice, thought Sarah. It had been a long time since she'd laughed so hard and she wasn't going to let a thunderstorm dampen her spirits. George had agreed to her business proposition, and at last her future looked brighter.

Chapter 13

Two weeks passed, and George hadn't seen Sarah. He was beginning to worry about her. She'd appeared very keen to purchase stock and have him sell it, so he wondered why she'd not been back.

'Why are you sitting there looking like you're chewing a bee?' his mother asked as she dished up a plate of sausages and mashed potatoes.

George folded his arms across the kitchen table. 'I'm all right, Mum, just thinking.'

'What you thinking about?'

'That girl, Sarah. I said I'd sell some gear for her on my stall, but that was a few days ago and I ain't seen her since.'

'Oh, well, son, it's her loss. Now stop being so blinkin' maudlin and eat your tea before it goes cold. I haven't stood over that hot stove for you to waste good food.'

'Yep, sorry, Mum,' George said, then scooped up a large forkful of mash. 'This is lovely, got any more gravy?'

'In the pan,' she answered. 'So this Sarah, is it purely business between you two, or do I need to be buying meself a new hat?'

'Pack it in, Mum. It's business, that's all. I'm just helping her out, though I would like it to be more. Thing is, I think I'm barking up the wrong tree. I saw the way she looked at Roger and she ain't never gonna look at me like that.'

'There's no getting away from it, that Roger is a good-looking man, but he ain't a patch on you. Once you get past his pretty face, there isn't much left. Shallow, that's what he is, and from what I've heard, he's a right woman-iser too. Any girl worth her salt would be well advised to stay clear of that man. I knew his father, he was a friend of your dad's, and I'm telling you, Roger is a chip off the old block. His father was terrible to his mother. He'd knock about with all the local tarts and made no secret of it! Poor Viv, I'm sure him carrying on like that sent her to an early grave.'

'Cor blimey, Mum, you don't 'alf go on sometimes,' George said with a smile.

'I'm just saying she'd be an idiot to pass you over for that Roger.'

He knew his mother was right. Roger often bragged about his latest conquest. 'Love them and leave them,' he would say, and freely offered tips to George on how to bed a woman.

George wasn't interested in playing the field. He under-stood it would take a special woman to see him for himself, and not just his burned face. He thought any woman who could love him would be a keeper, and he hoped it would be Sarah.

Tommy jumped up and down on his bed while Sarah was busy cooking Spam fritters.

'If you break that, you won't be getting another one,' she called over her shoulder.

'I love my new bed. I've never had my own one before,' Tommy said.

It wasn't new, but it was to Tommy. It had been delivered earlier, along with a bed for Sarah, two armchairs, a small stove and a coffee table.

Sarah turned with two plates in hand, and scanned the room. She decided it now looked quite homely. She'd scrubbed the walls and managed to remove most of the mould, though she knew it would soon return. The yellowing wallpaper which had been hanging off the walls was now temporarily fixed back with a paste Sarah had made from flour and water. The second-hand furniture was neatly arranged, and they even had a pretty bit of green material at the window that matched the green rug.

'Come and eat your supper,' Sarah said, and sat on one of the armchairs with her plate on her lap.

'When are we going to see George again?' Tommy asked as he ate his fritter.

'Don't talk with food in your mouth,' Sarah replied, then added, 'I don't know. I haven't managed to find anything for him to sell for us.'

'Let's go back to the river then. There might be more treasure.'

Sarah rolled her eyes as if it was a ridiculous suggestion, but she had already contemplated the idea herself. After all, she hadn't managed to find any suitable stock, and their money was rapidly diminishing. With her funds running low, she was getting worried and regretted spending so much on furniture. She should have waited until she'd found stock for George to sell, but hadn't been able to resist furnishing the room.

Sarah was eating the last mouthful of her fritter when she heard a knock on the door. 'Just a minute,' she called, guessing it was Mo from upstairs.

She'd bumped into Mo a week earlier when they'd both gone to use the shared bathroom. Mo had relayed her life story in a matter of minutes, and from what Sarah could understand, Mo was living in sin with Samuel, her West Indian boyfriend, and her family had ostracised her.

Sarah had instantly liked Mo's bubbly personality. With her red hair which framed her blue eyes, Sarah thought she was one of the prettiest women she'd ever met, and hoped Mo would become a good friend.

She opened the door, but gasped in shock. Mo's face was swollen and bruised almost beyond recognition. 'Oh, no, what's happened?' she asked, and gestured Mo in.

Mo walked in and instantly began to cry.

'Tommy, go outside and play. Make sure you don't leave the street. I'll be watching you from the window,' Sarah said.

'But . . . I haven't got any friends,' Tommy answered slowly, looking stunned at the sight of Mo.

'Well, go and flippin' make some,' Sarah said firmly.

Tommy skulked out of the room, and Sarah turned her attention to Mo. 'Sit down, I'll put the kettle on.'

'It looks nice in here,' Mo said and sniffed.

'Thanks. Please tell me Samuel hasn't done that to you.'

'Of course not!' Mo said, sounding indignant. 'He'd never hurt me. It was my dad. He came round this morning and 'cos I wouldn't come home with him, well, you can see for yourself.'

'Oh, Mo, that's awful. Where's Samuel? Does he know?' Sarah asked.

'No, and by the time he gets back I'm hoping I'll be all better. He's over the East End for a few days, visiting his brother. I reckon my dad knew he was away and that's why he turned up. He wouldn't have shown his face if Samuel was home, I'm bloody sure of it.'

'That's a nasty shiner, Mo, and your lip is split. I wouldn't count on that healing before Samuel comes home.'

'Oh, blimey, what am I going to do? I don't want my Sam getting into trouble, but if he knows my dad did this to me, he'll kill him, I know he will.'

Mo began to sob harder, so Sarah rushed over and tried to offer some comfort by placing her arm around the woman's shoulders. 'Don't worry, Mo, we'll think of something. Maybe we can make up a story about you getting mugged in the street or something.'

'Yeah, I suppose that could work,' she agreed, drawing in a juddering breath. 'Oh, Sarah, I hate my dad. He's always been heavy-fisted with me and my mum but he's never laid a hand on my brothers. He's a bloody coward, that's what he is. A coward and a bully. My Samuel's worth ten of him.'

Sarah had never known what it was like to have a father, and though she'd envied Jenny having a dad, she realised they weren't all good. 'He's done this to you before then?' she asked, trying not to sound too surprised.

'Oh, yeah, this ain't unusual. When I told Sam about how my dad would hit me, he wanted to go round to give him a good hiding. Oh, Sarah, Samuel must never know the truth about this. Promise me you won't say anything?'

'Of course I won't,' Sarah reassured her new friend.

'Thanks,' Mo said, and winced as she sipped her tea.

'Can I do anything to help?' Sarah asked.

'No, I've patched myself up as best I could, but I just needed to get out of that room and speak to someone. It felt like the walls were closing in on me, and then I got scared that my dad might come back.'

'Tell you what, why don't you stay down here with me 'til Samuel gets home? Tommy can get in with me so you can have his bed.'

'Oh, I don't know. That's ever so kind of you, but I don't want to be a burden or nothing.'

'Don't be daft. It'll be nice to have someone my own age to talk to for a change. Don't get me wrong, I love Tommy to death, but his conversation can be a bit limited.'

'If you're sure, I'd love to. I'll nip back upstairs and get a few bits and bobs . . . will you come up with me?'

'Yes, but let me just look out on Tommy first.'

Sarah walked over to the sink and glanced out the window. She could see Tommy leaning against a wall watching a small group of boys playing marbles. She hoped he would join in with their game, but for now she was satisfied he was safe, and proceeded upstairs to Mo's room.

When Mo opened the door and Sarah followed her in, she stood in awe as she gazed around the room. The walls were adorned with paintings of brightly coloured, exotic flowers. They were so vivid, Sarah almost felt as if she could inhale their fragrant scent.

'Lovely, ain't they?' Mo said.

'I've never seen nothing like them,' Sarah replied. 'They're beautiful.'

'Samuel painted them. He's an artist, and was getting quite a name for himself in Jamaica. Trouble was, his younger brother saw one of them ads about the better life in Britain and got sucked in by it. Samuel didn't want to let him come across alone, so they both got a cheap ticket on the *Windrush* ship, and now the best he can hope for is a stinking job on the railway.'

'Couldn't he sell his paintings?' Sarah asked.

'He tried, but people round here ain't into this sort of art. It's a bit too "foreign" for them. He tried over Chelsea way, but none of the galleries were interested in him. It ain't easy being a black man in a white man's country.'

Sarah had never thought about it before. She'd seen signs outside some boarding houses saying, 'No blacks or Irish', but she'd never understood why. She stared at one of the paintings as Mo rushed around throwing some clothes into a bag.

'I'll just scribble him a quick note to let him know where I am,' Mo said.

Sarah nodded, hardly noticing what Mo had said. She found the paintings fascinating and wondered if Samuel was as striking as his artwork. Then, to her surprise, she felt her belly flip as the thought of Roger popped into her head. She'd found him striking too, and cringed at the memory of their first meeting and her dumbstruck behaviour. She didn't have anything to give to George to sell, but nonetheless she'd visit the market tomorrow and hope to bump into Roger again.

Chapter 14

It was unseasonably warm for March, and as always, Fridays were good days for George. He'd found that women loved to have something different to wear for a weekend night out, whether it be a dance or the cinema. So, every Friday morning, he'd set his stall up to display his fanciest goods. Today was no exception, and the pleasant weather promised to bring him plenty of custom. His star item this week was a fur stole he'd acquired from a house clearance of an elderly lady who had passed away. As he placed it in a prime position, he thought it oozed class and elegance, then thought how lovely it would look across Sarah's shoulders. He could imagine her wearing it, but wished he hadn't, as now he knew he'd be stuck with her image in his head for the rest of the day.

'That's right nice, that is . . .' Roger said.

'Yes, it is,' George replied and turned to look at his friend.

Roger was leaning against his stall with his arms folded, eyeing up a young lady walking along the other side of the road. That's when he realised Roger wasn't referring to the fur stole but to the woman.

The woman seemed to sense she was being stared at,

and turned to look at Roger before flashing him a sultry smile. It was no surprise to George. He was used to seeing girls almost drop at Roger's feet. He just hoped the man would keep his hands off Sarah.

The morning whizzed by, and George patted his money belt, pleased with his takings. He'd been busy so hadn't had a lot of time to think about Sarah, but as he stretched his back and looked around the market, he felt his pulse quicken when he saw her walking towards him. He thought she looked different, smarter maybe, or did she have a new hairstyle?

As she got closer, he couldn't help but smile broadly. There was no hiding how pleased he was to see her. He wanted to open his arms and for her to fall into them, and to feel the soft caress of her lips on his. Instead, Tommy came gleefully running up to him and gave him a warm hug. Sarah said hello, but George's heart sank when he noticed she was looking over his shoulder, probably searching for Roger.

'I was getting worried about you. I thought you was going to bring me some gear to sell?' George said, hoping to grab her full attention.

'Erm ... yes ... I was ... I am,' Sarah replied. 'I've been looking for stuff, but I just don't know where to start. Truth is, I'm seriously giving some thought to going back to look on the Thames banks.'

'Can't say I blame you considering what you've found there before. I bet there's all sorts down in that mud. 'Ere, I've got a new nickname for you – the mudlark,' George said with a snicker.

'The mudlark, what sort of name is that?' Sarah asked.

'It was given to kids who used to scavenge on the banks

when Queen Vic was on the throne. You want to be careful though, 'cos I'm pretty sure it's against the law now.'

'Well, I don't suppose the police are going to be bothered about me picking up a few bits and pieces. It's unlikely that I'll find any more jewellery, but when I was down there before, I did see a few clay pipes and some funny-looking shells. I had a nose in the fishmonger's yesterday and saw them in there – oysters. The shells are proper ugly outside but they're ever so pretty on the inside. I was thinking maybe I could fashion some jewellery from them.'

Those shells are just like me, thought George. If only she could look at me in the same way as the oyster shells, and see past my ugliness. He doubted it would happen though. He had to push his gloomy thoughts to one side.

'I'll be interested to see what you manage to make with clay pipes and oyster shells, but I'll have a go at selling whatever you bring me,' George said, and winked at Tommy.

'Thanks, I'll see what I can do.'

'So if you haven't found anything for me to sell yet, what brings you down here today?' George asked, but he'd already guessed it was something to do with his mate on the next stall.

'Nothing really. I just thought I'd have a mooch around,' Sarah said, her eyes immediately going to Roger's stall.

He must have sensed her eyes on him, because he turned to her with a smile.

'Hello, Sarah.'

George thought he looked as if he was undressing her

with his eyes, and wanted to tell him to bugger off, but instead bit his tongue.

'Hi, Roger,' she answered coyly.

'Would you like an apple, Tommy? I've got some nice juicy ones.'

Tommy nodded enthusiastically, and Roger walked to his stall and returned with two large Coxes.

'One for you,' Roger said and handed Tommy an apple, 'and one for the pretty lady.'

As he gave Sarah the apple, George noticed Roger's fingers momentarily stroke her hand. He clenched his fists as his anger rose. Roger knew how he felt about Sarah. What sort of mate would step on his toes like this? He'd have words with him, but it would have to wait until later, when Sarah and Tommy were out of earshot.

On her way home, Sarah felt as though she was floating on air as she recalled the way Roger had looked at her. She'd found it difficult to meet his gaze, and had averted her eyes to the ground, sure he'd see her feelings in them. She bit into the apple he'd given her, and remembered the tingle of his touch on her skin. At the time, she'd quickly pulled her hand away, but now she imagined how it would feel to kiss him.

'Fancy a cuppa?' Mo called from over the upstairs banister as soon as they stepped into the hall. She had moved back up to her own room when Samuel was away longer than expected, and so far, thankfully, there hadn't been any further trouble from her family.

'Can I go out to play?' Tommy asked, tugging on her arm.

Sarah had been happy to see Tommy had made some

new friends, but they had work to do on the Thames banks. 'Yes, but only for ten minutes. We've got to go treasure hunting again.'

'Oh, but I want to play with Micky and Larry . . .'

'You can leave him here with me, Sarah. I ain't going nowhere,' Mo offered. She worked in the evenings as an usherette at the Grand Picture House, and had offered Sarah free tickets.

'If you're sure, that would be great, thanks. I'll have this cuppa and get going. Tommy, you can go out, but behave yourself and do what Mo tells you.'

Tommy ran out of the front door, and Sarah smiled at her friend.

'Who is he then?' Mo asked.

'I don't know what you mean,' Sarah replied. She could feel her cheeks flushing, as she hadn't realised her feelings for Roger were so transparent.

'I know that look. You've got a boyfriend, haven't you?'

'No . . . but I have met this gorgeous bloke . . .'

'I knew it! Has he asked you out on a date?'

'Not yet, but even if he did, I'm not sure I could go.'

'Why not?' Mo asked.

'Well, there's Tommy to think about . . .'

'Don't let that stop you. When I'm home I can always have him, and on my evening off. From what you've told me, you deserve a bloody good night out!'

Minutes later, Sarah had finished her tea and set off for Battersea Bridge with Mo's words still buzzing in her head. If Roger asked her out, there was no reason why she couldn't accept. She wasn't homeless any more, she had new clothes, soap and a comb. If she found anything good on the banks today, she might even treat herself to a hairbrush and a new lipstick, a pink one, just like the one Mo wore.

Before long, she was on the bridge and looking out along the Thames, but to her dismay the tide was in, and murky water covered the banks. She wouldn't be searching for anything she could sell today. Her heart sank and she also began to feel a bit panicky. She'd been too quick to spend money on things, and now she didn't have much left to put into purchasing stock. Until Tommy started school she couldn't find a job, and even then, with school hours, it would have to be part-time. She'd been depending on finding things in the mud and slumped with disappointment.

'Sarah, is that you?'

Sarah turned to see Jenny, her old friend from the tenement blocks, walking towards her from the other side of the bridge. 'Jenny! I haven't seen you in ages. How are you?' Sarah asked, genuinely surprised and pleased to see her.

'I'm all right, just on my way home from work. What about you?'

'Yes, not bad, thanks. Me and Tommy are living just off Shuttleworth Street now. We've got a room there. Where are you working?'

'In a big house in Chelsea for Mrs Alderton-Steele. I do the cleaning. It's all right, but the lady is a bit weird sometimes. She's got this son called Godfrey who blinking hates me 'cos he tried it on with me once and I told him where to get off! How's Tommy?'

'He's fine. In fact, I'll be getting him into school soon.'

'I'm sorry to hear about your mum . . .'

'What about my mum?' Sarah asked.

'Oh, I assumed you'd heard . . . she's not well.'

'She's not been well for years, Jenny, we both know that.'

'No, this is serious, Sarah. I think . . . she's dying,' Jenny said awkwardly.

Sarah caught her breath. She hadn't been expecting to hear that. It hadn't been that long since she'd left home. How could her mother have suddenly gone so far downhill? She'd never thought of her mother's demise, and somehow just imagined she would live forever.

'I can see I've shocked you. Tell you what, why don't you walk back with me and call in to see her?'

'I . . . I don't know, Jenny. We didn't exactly part on good terms.'

'Come on, you'll regret it if you don't.'

'Yes, probably. All right then,' Sarah reluctantly agreed.

As they walked, she asked, 'Do you know what's wrong with her?'

'Yes, it's some medical word called sir . . . eye . . . orsus, or something like that. My mum said it's her liver that's packed up 'cos of all the booze. She's refusing to go into hospital though, so my mum is doing what she can and that bloke Eddy has been to see her a few times. Maybe she'd listen to you and go to the hospital if you told her to?'

'I doubt it, my mother has never listened to me before.'

'But it's different now, you know, with her being so poorly.'

The rest of the journey was filled with small talk until Sarah found herself at the bottom of the concrete stairs that led to her mother's flat. She'd vowed she'd never come back here, and recalled the night her mother had chased them out with a cane in her hand.

They arrived at the third floor. Sarah thought her heart might pound out of her chest. Not because of the hike up the stairs, but for fear of how her mother would react to seeing her.

'Do you want me to come in with you?' Jenny asked.

'No, I'll be fine, thanks. I'll see ya,' Sarah said and nervously approached her mother's home.

She stood for a moment and looked at the front door, which was slightly ajar. Her mother never closed the door, and it used to irritate Sarah. Taking a deep breath, she pushed it open. As she slowly entered the room, her nose picked up the familiar musty odour. She could see her mum lying on her mattress with a blanket up to her chest, but her stomach looked swollen and her skin was yellow. Sarah quietly knelt on the floor and studied her mother as she slept. Her long black hair looked greasy and unwashed, and her eyes appeared to have sunk into her head. She was wondering if she should disturb her, when her mum slowly opened her eyes. Sarah was shocked to see that even the whites of them were now very yellow.

'Hello, Mum, it's me, Sarah,' she whispered.

'I can see who you are, you stupid bitch,' her mother said, though Sarah noticed her voice was weak and without its usual venom.

'I hear you're not feeling too well?'

'Yeah, that's right. Come to gloat, have you?'

'No, of course not. I've come to see if you need looking after . . .'

'You needn't have bothered. I don't need you looking

after me, or anyone else. I know I'm going to meet my Maker, and the sooner the better. Did you bring me any gin?'

'No, Mum, that's what got you in this state, so of course I didn't. Please, Mum, let me help you . . .'

'Why would you want to help me? It ain't as if I ever did much for you,' she asked, then began to cough heavily.

Sarah waited for her mother's chest to clear, and gazed at her with pity. It was a shock to see her so desperately ill, and now she was glad she'd plucked up the courage to come. 'You're still my mum. If you won't let me look after you, will you at least go into hospital?'

'No,' Annie replied firmly, 'I'll die in my own bed, not in one of them places with them taking blood out of me and doing Gawd knows what to me. I'll go out of this filthy world the same way I came in . . . alone.'

'Please, Mum, you don't have to be alone. I want to help.'

Sarah saw a tear slip from her mother's eye and streak down the side of her face before disappearing into her dirty hair.

'You've always been a good girl, better than me, and you've been a good mum to your brother. I ain't got long left . . . hours, maybe a couple of days. There's something I should have told you . . .'

Sarah took her mother's clammy hand. She'd never seen her mum cry before, or heard her speak so gently. She noticed her mother's arms were scabby and covered in scratches.

'Your father . . . Ron Lyons . . . he lives on Lavender Hill. It's up to you what you do, but you have a right to know.'

Sarah took in a sharp breath as her mother's words sunk in.

'But I thought my dad was dead?'

'No, he's alive and well, but he didn't want nothing to do with us.'

'What do you mean?'

'I told you he was dead 'cos I met him when I was just a kid. Sweet sixteen – yes, I was sweet once. He was a big man, full of charm, and he knocked my socks off. I fell in love with him, absolutely besotted I was. Life at home was pretty crap with my dad treating me like his wife, and, well, Ron said he would marry me and take me away from it all.'

'So what happened?'

'He never left his wife and kids. Yeah, that's right, he was a married man, but I was so blinded by love and desperate to get away from home, I stupidly believed all his lies. When I told him I was carrying you, I thought he'd be over the moon, but no, he dropped me like a ton of bricks and broke my heart.'

'Oh, Mum, why didn't you ever tell me any of this?'

'What was the point, eh? See, once my dad got wind of my pregnancy, he gave me a good hiding and threw me out. Ron didn't want me, I had nowhere to go and no money. That's why I had to start selling myself. It wasn't for the booze – well, not at first. It was for us. But as the years went by, I hated myself and what I was doing more and more. I started drinking to blot out the pain, and look where that's got me.'

'Oh, Mum, you've had a terrible life, but it's not too late to change. You can stop drinking and get better.'

'No, Sarah, it's gone beyond that. I've poisoned my

body and I'm at death's door. I'm glad I've been able to make amends with you though. It's been a long time coming and I wish I'd spoken up sooner.'

'Me too, but what about Tommy's dad?'

Sarah saw a black look come into her mother's eyes, and Annie turned her face away.

'Just go now, will you?' her mother said coldly.

'No, Mum, I won't. Tommy deserves to know about his dad too.'

Annie tried to sit up, but fell back into her mattress. 'You really want to know?'

'Yes, Mum, I do.'

'OK, I'll tell you. I just hope for your sake that I haven't spawned the child of the devil, 'cos I'm telling you, his father was evil.'

Sarah saw her mother shiver. She wasn't sure if she had a fever or if the memory of Tommy's dad had made her react that way.

'He was a customer, nothing more, and a bit of a brief encounter really. I didn't know his surname, I only ever called him Bert. He used to come round three times a week, but he never liked to talk. He'd pay me a fair bit over the odds so that he'd be my exclusive client. He always paid up, but I had this strange feeling about him. Nothing I could put my finger on, but he . . . well . . . he scared me. Anyhow, after a few months, I realised I was pregnant with Tommy and told him he'd have to stop visiting. I lied to him, and told him I was still seeing other blokes, Eddy and a couple more. I said I didn't know who the father was, but I knew it was him. It was just an excuse to get rid of him, he gave me the creeps.'

'So what was so evil about him?'

101

'Water,' Annie said, and pointed to a cup by her side.

Sarah held her mother's head up as she struggled to drink from the cup. Then she laid her head back down and sighed heavily.

'Does it hurt, Mum?' Sarah asked.

Her mother nodded, and Sarah could see her face was twisted in pain.

'A few days later, I was in the pub and someone had left a paper on the bar. I couldn't believe it, I saw Bert's face on the front page, staring out at me, and the headlines said "Bert – The Blood Bath Murderer". Honestly, I was shaking when I read what he'd done. Turns out, after he'd left me, he'd gone home and murdered his pregnant wife and young child. He'd chopped them up into pieces in their bath. That could have been us, Sarah. He could have killed us all.'

Sarah gasped in utter shock. She'd heard of the murders. The kids in the playground had talked about it. Everyone had been disgusted, and to think that man was Tommy's father! 'What happened to him?'

'He was found guilty and swung for it. But now can you see why I wanted to get rid of Tommy? What if he turns out like his father?'

No, thought Sarah, Tommy was such a sweet child, he was nothing like his dad, she was sure of that. 'He won't, Mum. He's such a good boy, and so loving. He ain't got a bad bone in his body. I can never tell him about this though.'

'Like I said, I hope for your sake that you're right. Look, I've said my piece, you know everything now, and I'm tired Sarah, really tired. Let me be now, eh? Leave me in peace to die.'

'I'm sorry, Mum, but I can't just leave you like this. I can see you're uncomfortable, and it's only going to get worse. I'm going down the road to call an ambulance. They'll give you something for the pain in hospital. At least you'll feel more comfortable.'

Sarah saw her mother grip the blanket and nod.

At last, she thought, and ran from the flat to the telephone box before her mother could change her mind.

Annie heard the front door close, and tried to suck in a deep breath, but it was almost impossible now as her swollen stomach inhibited her breathing. Her itchy legs were driving her crazy, but she didn't feel she had the energy to scratch them. She was glad she'd given in and allowed Sarah to call for an ambulance. She knew she'd be dead soon, but welcomed the thought of some pain relief.

So, her daughter knew everything now, the whole sordid truth about her father and Tommy's. She was pleased she'd finally told her, but regretted not being honest earlier. The girl deserved better, and Annie wished she could have lived her life over again and treated her daughter with more kindness.

Her head throbbed, and her body ached. The years of alcohol abuse had finally caught up with her. She'd killed herself, slowly drinking herself to death, and she knew it was too late to do anything other than accept her sorry fate.

She scratched her arms. They began to bleed again as she took off several scabs. In the distance, she could hear children playing, and footsteps overhead from the upstairs occupants. All around her, life was carrying on, but hers was coming to a self-inflicted, premature end.

Fear gripped her, and her shallow breaths quickened. I don't want to die, she thought, terrified of what it was going to feel like. Would she just close her eyes and that would be it? Did she have a soul, and if so, where would her soul go? She knew she didn't deserve a place in heaven and hoped she wouldn't meet up with her wicked father again. She'd heard that people close to death experience their life flashing before their eyes. She hoped that wouldn't happen to her. She'd rather not be reminded of most of hers. Whatever happened, she prayed it would be quick and soon. There was no fight left in her, and she felt she had no reason to live.

She thought of her daughter again. She loved the girl, though she'd never shown her and couldn't recall ever telling her. If anything, she'd done the complete opposite and behaved despicably towards her, probably making her feel unwanted. She remembered when Sarah had been a babe in arms, so sweet and innocent. She'd vowed to love her and always look after her, but somewhere along the line, it had gone all very wrong. The biggest mistake she'd made was taking out her own frustrations on Sarah, yet still the girl was now showing her pity. It was too late, she knew her time was limited, but she dearly wished she could make up for all the wrongs she'd bestowed on her child.

The front door opened again, and Annie felt the waft of a cool breeze come in with her daughter.

'The ambulance won't be long, Mum,' Sarah said as she knelt by her side.

Annie suddenly felt very confused. 'What ambulance?' she asked.

'The one I've just called to take you to the hospital,' her daughter answered.

Hospital? She managed to slowly lift her head and saw her engorged stomach. Was she in labour? She didn't remember being pregnant.

She felt Sarah hold her hand. 'It'll be all right, Mum.' Her daughter's voice was soft, it felt soothing, but what would be all right?

'No hospital, I ain't got time to be mucking about, and I don't want another child.'

'What are you talking about, Mum?'

Annie moved her head from side to side. She didn't know. Her mind was fuddled. 'What's going on?' she asked, beginning to panic. She wanted to sit up, but her body wouldn't respond.

'Mum . . . calm down . . . please.'

'I need to get up. I've got to go to work,' Annie said, again scratching at her arms.

'I think you're a bit confused, Mum. Shush, lay still . . . relax.'

Annie listened to the sound of her daughter's voice, then it seemed like a fog was clearing and she could think straight again. 'I think I'm going mad,' she said, unsure of what had just happened.

'It's all right, Mum. You'll be in the hospital soon and they'll know what to do.'

Oh, yes, the hospital. That was right, she was dying. Her liver wasn't working. She remembered, but she wasn't sure how long the clarity would remain. She had to tell Sarah something, something important, but what was it? Then it came back to her. 'Sarah, my girl, I'm sorry I never told you . . . I love you. I always have. You've always been so precious to me and I'm so sorry I let you down. Be good to Tommy. Tell him every day how much you love him.'

Annie could just about see the shocked expression on her daughter's face, and she was sure her eyes were welling up. She didn't want to see Sarah cry. She'd caused the girl enough tears, and didn't want to hurt her any more. 'Don't cry, love. Find a man who really loves you. I'm sorry I wasn't better.'

Annie closed her eyes. She could hear her breath making a strange noise. It was the death rattle, and she knew her time was nearly up. She could go now, leave the world she held in so much contempt, and know she'd made her peace with her daughter. She opened her eyes again, and focused on Sarah. The girl she'd created was so beautiful, almost like an angel. At last, it was time to let go.

Sarah felt her mother's hand go limp. She looked into her eyes, but there was nothing there. It was as if the life had just gently slipped away from them, and she knew her mum had died.

Her mother had told her she loved her. Sarah had been so taken aback that she hadn't answered. She'd wanted to tell her she loved her too, but now it was too late.

'Ambulance service,' a gruff voice said.

Sarah looked over her shoulder to see two uniformed men, and heard their heavy footsteps as they walked across the room.

She looked back at her dead mother, and gently reached across and closed her eyelids. 'Oh, Mum, I wish things had been different,' she whispered.

Then she felt one of the men pull her to her feet.

'I'm sorry, we have to see to her,' he said.

Sarah allowed herself to be led to the side of the room, and watched as the other man leaned over her mother's body. She wasn't surprised when he turned to his colleague and shook his head. She'd already known her mother was dead, and thought it was strange that she didn't seem to feel any real emotion.

It was over. There was nothing more that could be said, or ever would be. One final thought passed through Sarah's mind, and she quietly said, 'Rest in peace, Mother. I hope you've finally found it.'

Chapter 15

The moment Mo opened her door to Sarah, she could see that something was troubling her new friend. 'What's wrong?' she asked, urging her inside.

'Where's Tommy? I didn't see him playing outside.'

'He's fine. He's got a new best friend, Larry, and he's gone to have tea with him. Don't worry, it's only three doors down.'

'Thanks, Mo, and I'm sorry I've been gone so long.'

Mo watched as Sarah sat on the armchair, then rested her head back and closed her eyes. 'You still haven't told me what's happened. I can tell you're upset about something.'

Sarah lifted her head and drew in a long breath. 'It's my mum . . . she's dead.'

'Oh, Sarah, I'm so sorry, that's awful. How do you know? I thought you was going down the Thames?'

'I did, but I bumped into an old mate who told me my mum was ill. I went to see her, but it was horrible. She looked so ill and weak, I ain't ever seen her looking like that. She seemed fine when I left, but now . . . Anyhow, she eventually let me call for an ambulance, but by the time I got back from the telephone box, she was almost dead. She said a few last words, then she was gone.'

Mo dashed across the room and knelt on the floor beside her friend. She took Sarah's hand, and though she wanted to offer some words of comfort, she felt at a loss what to say.

'It was so awful. It's the first time I've seen a dead person. Her eyes were open, but they looked vacant, just staring into space. I couldn't believe it at first, it didn't seem real. The ambulance arrived, and that's when they confirmed it. Funny really, she said she wanted to die alone . . . well, she almost got her wish, but I think she was glad I was there at the last moment.' Sarah began to sob while Mo held her.

'She's in a better place now, love,' Mo said.

'I don't know what I'm so upset about. I mean, she wasn't the best of mums, but just before she died, she told me some stuff. Now I sort of understand the reason for the way she was. I wish I'd known earlier, maybe we could have been closer.'

'Let me pour you a cuppa. You've had a nasty shock, it's bound to be upsetting,' Mo offered. As she poured the tea, she glanced at Sarah and felt relieved to see she'd finally stopped crying.

'I ain't got much money left and my mum didn't have any, so she'll be in a pauper's grave. I feel terrible about it, but there's nothing I can do.'

'I'd help you out if I could, but me and Sam are skint too. If we had any money, we wouldn't be living in this dump,' Mo lied. They had a few quid put aside, but she wasn't prepared to share it with a woman she'd only recently met.

'Thanks, Mo, but even if you did have anything, I wouldn't expect you to lend it to me. I don't suppose it really matters. After all, she's dead, and I should think I'll be the only person at her funeral.'

'I could come with you if you like?'

'That's good of you, but to be honest I think I'd rather you looked after Tommy for me. I don't want him seeing his mum put in the ground.'

'Of course, I understand. Now, splash some water on your face before the boy gets home. You don't want him seeing you upset.'

Mo sat on the other armchair feeling awkward. She wasn't very good at dealing with things like this, and didn't have much empathy. She thought the years of getting bashed by her father had knocked all the softness out of her and left her hardened. 'Sam will be home tomorrow. I can't wait for you to meet him,' she said in a bid to change the subject.

'Yes, me too. I'm looking forward to seeing the mystery man who paints the wonderful pictures,' Sarah answered.

Mo noticed Sarah's face was pink from the cold water, and though she smiled, Mo could see it didn't reach her eyes. Still, she was pleased that Sarah was no longer crying. She liked her, though she thought her a bit naïve. She'd enjoyed getting to know the young woman, but she'd missed Samuel terribly and couldn't wait to see him.

Sarah lay in bed that night finding it difficult to drift off. Tommy was fidgeting, and coughing again. Her thoughts wandered back to her mother. She didn't think she'd ever get the image of her dead face from her mind, and tried to think of happier times. It was difficult as there weren't many good memories to draw on.

Then she thought of Mr Sayers. She wouldn't miss her mother but she still missed the old man. She rolled over and heard Tommy cough again in the next bed. It really was just the two of them now, and for the first time she felt truly alone. The burden of being solely responsible for her brother weighed heavy on her shoulders. Her mum hadn't provided either of them with much of a life, but she was determined Tommy's would be better.

Sarah thought about the last conversation she'd had with her mother. Annie had revealed that she had a dad who could well be alive and kicking. Ron Lyons, a local man. She wondered what he might look like, and what sort of a person he was. Her mother had said he hadn't wanted Sarah, but maybe her mum had lied. After all, Annie wasn't known for being straight with the truth. Anyway, a lot of time had passed since Ron had first heard of her mother's pregnancy, and maybe he now regretted turning his back on them.

So many questions, thought Sarah, and tried to conjure up the image of her father as she wondered if he ever thought about her. There was only one way to find out and to have her questions answered – she'd have to find her dad.

Chapter 16

George thought the atmosphere between him and Roger had been a bit frosty since he'd warned him off Sarah. He'd called her 'his girl', but as Roger had quite rightly pointed out, Sarah was not his girl or anyone else's. He decided it was time to break the ice, and called over, 'Fancy a pint later?'

Roger turned to look at him, and George was sure the man had a smug expression.

'Yeah, why not. As long as you don't start accusing me of pinching your drink.'

'Leave it out, will you? Enough is enough. I'm holding out the olive branch here,' George answered, now almost regretting the effort to make amends with Roger.

'Sorry, mate. Yes, a pint after work would be nice,' Roger said, then turned to serve a customer.

George was pleased to have things back on an even keel with his friend, but if the situation was to arise, he still wasn't convinced that Roger wouldn't make a move on Sarah. Just as he was thinking about her, he was pleased to see her walking towards his stall. His excitement rose, but was soon replaced with concern when he noticed her solemn face.

'Hi, Sarah, you don't look very happy this morning. Is everything OK?' he asked, his voice caring.

'Hi, George. No, not really.'

'What's up? Is Tommy all right?' George asked, seeing that she was alone.

'Yes, he's fine, he's with my friend Mo who lives upstairs from me. It's my mum . . . she died a week ago so I'm looking for something cheap and black to wear to her funeral.'

George was confused. He'd thought her mother was already dead, but decided not to ask any questions. 'I'm so sorry to hear that, love. I've got a black dress here that should be about the right size for you, and look –' he reached across his stall and picked up a hat '– this is black too and would look proper smart on you.'

'Sounds perfect, thanks, George. How much does it all come to?'

'No, this one's on me,' George offered.

'Thanks, but I'd rather pay,' Sarah said.

George could tell from the tone of her voice that she was going to be stubborn, so instead offered the clothing for a few pence. He knew she was struggling for money, and she had little Tommy to care for. Then he had an idea that might help her out. He bagged her newly purchased items and said, 'I hope you don't mind me asking, but is Tommy going to school soon?'

'Yes, as soon as my mother's funeral is over, I'll sort it out.'

'Well, once you do, I know of a little job going, and the hours would work perfectly with Tommy at school,' George said, remembering a conversation he'd had with his mother the night before.

'Oh . . . what sort of job? I don't have much experience in things, and I didn't do no exams at school.'

'That won't matter. It's my mum, Lena. She works in a grocery shop and she happened to mention that Cissy, her part-time girl, is leaving soon 'cos she's up the duff. That means there'll be an opening 'cos my mum ain't going to want to work extra hours. I could put the word in for you if you like?'

'Sounds great, George, but I've never worked in a shop before.'

'Don't worry about that. My mum would show you the ropes.'

Sarah looked apprehensive for a moment, then answered, 'If you're sure, I'd really appreciate you asking for me.'

'Tell you what, you get Tommy into school for the start of the new term, and then you can come round mine for your tea one night. You can meet my mum, as she pretty much runs the shop, doing all the hiring and firing. The owner shows his face now and again, but it'll be up to my mum, and I know she's going to love you,' George said enthusiastically.

Sarah nodded, and though George could tell she was happy with the offer, considering the circumstances he didn't expect her to show too much eagerness.

'Thanks, George. I need something as I've not had much luck with finding any stock. I might have another go down at the Thames. If I can find just one more thing of value, that should tide me over 'til I can start work.'

'Are you off down there now then?' George asked. He wished he could do more to help her, but had already come to realise that she was fiercely independent and would only refuse any handouts.

'It's a bit late now, the tide will be in, but I'll have a look tomorrow morning. Let's face it, I'm unlikely to find my riches down there, but you know the saying, third time lucky.'

'Well, I'll keep me fingers and me toes crossed for you, even if it means I'll be walking funny,' George said, and was pleased when he saw a faint smile on her lips.

Sarah said goodbye, and before she left promised to come back soon either with some treasures from the river or for a job with his mum. He'd been pleased to see that she hadn't been looking for Roger. He watched her walk away, her shoulders slumped. He yearned to chase after her to offer comfort. Instead he turned to look suspiciously at Roger, but was surprised when he saw his friend had deliberately stayed well hidden behind some sacks of potatoes.

Roger popped his head up, and asked, 'All clear?'

George couldn't help but chuckle. 'Yes, mate, she's gone, but you didn't have to go to those extremes, or are you just taking the mickey?'

'I'm just doing as I've been warned. I wouldn't want a girl to come between us, and let's face it, there's plenty more fish in the sea, and I've got a bloody big net.'

By the time Sarah arrived home, it was late afternoon and the street was lively with children playing, though she couldn't see her brother. As she put her key in the lock of her front door, Tommy and Larry appeared and came running up to her.

'Guess what?' Tommy asked.

'I don't know. What?' Sarah answered.

'We met Samuel and he gave us a tanner to share.

We're rich, ain't we, Larry? We've never had so much money! Larry's mum said she'll take us to the shops later . . . can I go, Sarah, please?'

'If Larry's mum says it's OK, then yes, you can, but make sure you're a good boy.'

'I will, thanks, Sarah. Come on, Larry, let's go and tell your mum that I can come.'

Sarah watched as the boys ran off together, and then plastered a smile on her face in anticipation of meeting Samuel. After hearing so much about him from Mo, she'd been looking forward to seeing him, but with her mother's death and little money, her mood was dark. She was opening the door to her room when she heard Mo's cheery voice, and turned to see her friend skipping down the stairs with a tall dark man following closely behind.

'Sarah, this is Samuel,' Mo said, grinning widely as she placed her arm around her lover's waist.

'It's a real pleasure to meet you, ma'am,' Samuel said, and offered his hand to Sarah.

'Likewise,' Sarah said, trying to hide her surprise at being addressed as 'ma'am'. As she shook his large hand, she covertly eyed him up and down, and thought how funnily he was dressed. His smart brown trousers were very high-waisted and baggy. Though Samuel was a big man, she reckoned two of him could have fitted in his slacks. He wore a matching long, double-breasted jacket, and a smart shirt and tie. He didn't dress anything like the men in Battersea.

'I wanted to thank you for looking after my gal while I've been away.'

For a moment, Sarah was mesmerised by his Jamaican accent, but eventually, she answered, 'I think we've been looking after each other. Would you like to come in for a cup of tea?'

'Thank you, that would be nice, but I've not seen my Mo for a while, so if you don't mind I'll have that cup of tea with you another day.'

Sarah nodded and saw Samuel wink at Mo. She felt her cheeks burn as she watched the couple run hand in hand back up the stairs to their own room.

Mo called, 'See ya later, Sarah.'

She heard her friend giggle as their door closed behind them, and felt a pang of jealousy. She'd have liked her own boyfriend, someone to snuggle up with and share her worries and joys. Not just any boyfriend, though – he'd have to be special. She'd seen too many bad men in her mother's bed, and wouldn't settle for anyone less than perfect.

Roger was perfect, she thought, and wondered again what it would feel like to have him kiss her. She hoped one day to find out.

Chapter 17

Nearly another week had passed and Mo was looking after Tommy at home while Sarah sat on the steps that overlooked the Thames foreshore. She was tired after spending another restless night wondering about her father. Now, she was deep in thought. It would be her mother's funeral the day after tomorrow, a chance to say a final goodbye and put the past well and truly behind her. She felt she had many demons to lay to rest, and though she'd forgiven her mother, she still found it difficult to forget the beatings and her cruel tongue.

Her thoughts were broken when she saw something fall from the sky and heard it crack on a rock. Then a large seagull swooped down and picked it up with its beak before flying off again. Curious, Sarah carefully walked across the mud and shingle to the rock where it had landed. She looked around and found an empty mussel shell. 'Well, I never,' she said out loud as she realised the gull must have dropped the mussel onto the rock to crack open the shell to eat the creature inside. She'd never given it much thought before, but she'd seen stalls outside some of the pubs selling cockles and mussels, and wondered if they were fished from the

Thames. She wasn't having much luck finding anything else of value, but now she wondered if she was looking for the wrong sort of treasure.

She picked up the shell, and began to amble back towards the steps while her mind drifted into daydreams of the feasibility of becoming a fisherwoman, if only for a while until she secured a proper job. Then, out of the corner of her eye, she saw something glimmering that instantly caught her attention. She looked down and saw a red object poking out of the mud. She bent down and pulled it from the dark gloop, then wiped it on the underside of her skirt. As the mud came away, her heart soared when she saw she was holding a gold ring set with a large ruby. This couldn't be happening again, she thought in disbelief, and quickly shoved the ring into her coat pocket.

Feeling happier, she dashed back towards the steps, intent on getting to the market as soon as possible. She felt sure that George would have no problem selling the ring, and the money she would earn from the sale would keep them going until she could start work in the shop with his mum.

Once she reached the top step, Sarah stopped for a moment to catch her breath. Still in shock, she shook her head and looked to the skies. Thank you, Mr Sayers, she said in her head. Someone must be looking out for her, and she doubted it was her mother.

'Sarah, fancy seeing you here again!'

Sarah almost jumped out of her skin at the sound of Jenny's voice. She'd been so busy thinking that she hadn't seen her friend on the bridge. 'Oh, hi, Jenny. Are you on your way to work?'

'Yes, but I think it might be my last day.'

'Why is that?' Sarah asked. She could see the disappointment in her friend's eyes so was curious to know the reason Jenny would be leaving her job.

'I think Mrs Alderton-Steele is going to sack me. You know I told you about her son being narked 'cos he tried it on with me and I told him where to go . . . well, some of her stuff has been going missing and I reckon she thinks I've nicked it. I bet it's him, though, that flippin' Godfrey. I wouldn't put it past him to have nicked it, just for me to get the blame!'

'Oh, Jenny, that's horrible. I know you, you'd never pinch anything from anyone. Have you told her that?'

'Yeah, but the old cow is never going to believe me over her precious son. It's a shame, though, because I like the job. The hours suit so I can get home and help out Mum. Not only that, Mrs Alderton-Steele pays me well, more than most would for a bit of cleaning. Still, if the battleaxe gives me my marching orders, there's nothing I can do about it.'

'You'll soon find another job,' Sarah consoled.

'Probably, but I won't get a good reference, and I doubt I'd find one which pays as well.'

'Have you confronted that Godfrey and told him you know what he's been up to?'

'Yes, but he just laughed. He's a nasty piece of work who lives off his "allowance" from Mummy and couldn't give two hoots about anyone else. I don't know what he's done with the bits he's nicked, 'cos I've searched high and low and can't find them anywhere. I suppose he's sold them, but he don't need the money, and one of the things was a pocket watch that belonged to his father. When that disappeared it really upset Mrs Alderton-Steele, but it didn't bother Godfrey, the horrible git.'

Sarah gulped hard as all at once she realised she'd been in possession of the watch. She remembered it had been etched with the initials A. S., which she now knew had represented Alderton-Steele. She felt consumed with guilt – the watch had been sold so she couldn't return it, and now her friend could lose her job. The other items too, the gold bracelet and the ring in her pocket. It all made sense. She'd thought it had been too good to be true and now realised that Godfrey must have been throwing the jewellery over the bridge.

She placed her hand in her pocket and held the ring. It wasn't hers to keep, not now she knew who it belonged to, and it was stolen. If she gave it to Jenny her friend might be able to convince Mrs Alderton-Steele that she wasn't the thief, and Jenny could keep her job.

Though reluctant, she went to hand Jenny the ring, but an image of Tommy popped into her head and she quickly stopped herself. It was wrong to keep it, but if she didn't, Tommy would go hungry. Mrs Alderton-Steele didn't need the money, and Jenny would easily find a replacement job. Without the ring, Tommy wouldn't eat and she reasoned that he had to be her priority.

'I'm sorry, Jenny, but I've got to dash. Good luck today, I hope it works out,' Sarah said and fled over the bridge in the opposite direction from her friend. She'd felt so bad that she hadn't been able to meet Jenny's eyes, and inwardly recoiled at what she'd done.

For the first time, Sarah could see what her mother

had meant when she'd spoken about hating herself and turning to drink. Sarah realised that no matter what it took, a mother would do whatever was needed to put food in the bellies of her children. She never thought she'd think the words, but as Sarah made her way to the market, she inwardly thanked her mother. She was finally grateful that her mum had sold herself, and understood the sacrifices and choices that a lone mother is forced to make.

At this moment, just as her mother had hated herself, Sarah didn't like herself very much either, but her feelings of self-loathing were irrelevant compared to the drive to provide for her brother.

Mo was happy to look after Tommy as it helped relieve her boredom. Samuel was busy working long hours, and though she had tried working days too, it never went well for her. Either one of her brothers or her father would always turn up and cause trouble, so she'd end up getting her cards. It wasn't ideal working evenings in the cinema, but it was dark most of the time, and so far her family hadn't discovered she worked there.

She wasn't content with the situation though. It meant she hardly saw Samuel. She'd suggested to him that maybe she shouldn't work at all, but he wouldn't hear of it, reminding her how important it was to save to buy their own house.

Tommy was sat quietly on the floor with the paper and paints he'd bought with the tanner Samuel had given him and his friend. He'd said he was painting a picture for Sarah to put on the wall next to her bed. Mo sneaked a peek and smiled. He was doing his best to copy one of

Samuel's paintings, and she thought how nice it was that her man had inspired the lad.

She stood up and began to pace the floor of her cramped room. The radio had broken, and the silence was driving her crazy. At least when Sarah came back she could enjoy some girlie gossip.

Meeting Sarah had been a lifeline for her. If it hadn't been for her new friend, she wasn't sure how long she could have stuck out the boredom. It was beginning to cause a rift between her and Samuel, and though they had made love when he'd returned from the visit to his brother, there hadn't been any desire in the bedroom since, at least not on Samuel's part. By the time Mo got home from work, Samuel would be fast asleep, and no amount of coaxing had worked. She'd tried on many occasions, but he always brushed her off, saying he was tired and needed to sleep.

She wondered if he had gone off her, especially as there had been such a passionate attraction when they'd first met. She'd asked him but he'd told her she was being silly and reassured her how much he still fancied her.

Now, as she paced the floor, she caught sight of her reflection in the mirror. Her wounds had healed well, and she felt back to her old self. She leaned in closer to the mirror and pouted. I could have been a pin-up girl, she thought to herself as she admired her full lips and high cheekbones. Her red hair made her stand out, just like Rita Hayworth. She placed her hands on her hips and wriggled from side to side. Yes, she was just as attractive as all the film stars she saw on the silver screen night after night, and had a curvaceous figure that caught the attention of men. The difference was, unlike the women who lived the glamorous Hollywood lives that she so badly wanted, she was stuck in an almost frigid relationship, in a filthy bedsit, with no family and just one friend. She swung her hips some more then tutted.

Tommy giggled. 'What are you doing?' he asked.

He'd been so quiet, she'd forgotten he was there. 'Just being silly. Don't you ever imagine you're someone else?'

'Sometimes I think I'm one of Peter Pan's lost boys, or sometimes me and Larry play cowboys and Indians. Who was you pretending to be?'

'A beautiful film star. A girl can dream.'

'I think you're bootiful, Mo. Not as bootiful as my sister – well, maybe nearly.'

Mo laughed, Tommy was such a sweet child and it was obvious he adored Sarah. Despite the pleasure she took in looking after him for her friend, that was as much as she wanted. Samuel had talked about having a large family, five kids or more, but Mo hadn't told him she'd decided a long time ago that she wasn't the mothering sort, and babies were off her agenda. After all, she didn't want an expanding waistline to ruin her hourglass figure.

'Look, Mo, I've finished. Do you think Sarah will like it?' Tommy held up his painting.

Mo thought it looked like a load of coloured blobs, but said, 'It's really good, Tommy, and I'm sure your sister will love it.'

'Yeah, I bet she will,' Tommy agreed happily.

Mo took out her compact and studied her face in the mirror. She knew that she was better-looking than Sarah and patted her wavy hair. She took great pride in her appearance and always liked to look her best. She loved Samuel, or at least she believed she did, but a girl's gotta keep up her standards, she thought, because you never know who you might meet.

George saw Sarah walking towards him. He was pleasantly surprised as he hadn't expected to see her again until after her mother's funeral. As she approached he studied her face to gauge her mood. He thought she looked worried, and as he saw her eyes flitting around the market he wondered why she seemed so nervous.

'Hello, Sarah. You all right?' he asked, noting how she kept looking over her shoulder.

'Hello, George. Yes, I'm fine thanks. I . . . I . . . erm . . . I've got this ring . . . Can you sell it for me?' Sarah pulled the ring from her coat pocket and held it out, but she kept her hand close to her body and was still flicking her eyes all over the place.

George got the impression she was trying to hide something. 'Blimey, that looks a bit special. Did you find it down on the banks again?'

'Yes . . . yes, of course I did,' Sarah snapped.

'I tell you what, girl, you ain't half bleedin' lucky with all that gear you find. Some poor bugger's loss, but your gain. Are you still interested in working with my mum, or are you going to stick to treasure hunting? You're bloody good at it!'

'What's with all the questions? Can you sell the ring or not?'

George stepped back, shocked at how sharply she'd spoken to him. 'Sorry, I was only being friendly. Pardon me for breathing. Yes, of course I can try to sell it for you.'

Sarah stuffed the ring back into her pocket. 'On second

thoughts, forget it,' she said, then spun around and marched off.

George blinked as he tried to understand what had just happened. If he'd offended her, he certainly hadn't meant to. He gave chase, and called to Sarah, but she continued to storm on ahead.

Once he finally caught up with her, he pulled on her arm. 'Hey, Sarah, wait up. Sorry, love, if I said something to upset you. Look, come back to my stall and we'll see about getting this ring sold for you.'

Sarah stared wide-eyed at George, then lowered her head, and her shoulders beginning to shake.

'Hey, come on, what's wrong?' George asked as he saw big tears rolling down her cheeks.

'Oh, George . . . I'm such a horrible person,' she cried.

'Don't be daft, you're lovely. Look, there's a little café over there. Let me buy you a cuppa and you can tell me all about what's troubling you.'

Sarah nodded and allowed George to gently lead her towards the café. Once she was seated, he dashed to the toilet and came back with some paper for her to dry her eyes and blow her nose. Then he ordered two cups of tea and a couple of Eccles cakes, and sat himself opposite her, asking, 'Are you going to tell me what's wrong? I don't like to see you upset like this.' He thought she was probably distressed about her mother's recent death.

'I've done something terrible . . .' Sarah answered quietly as she gazed into her cup of tea.

'I bet it ain't as bad as you think,' George offered with a warm smile, though she didn't look up to see it. He wanted to reach out across the table and hold her hand, but he guessed she'd probably yank it away.

'It is, George. I've let a friend down. Because of my own selfishness, I've let her go off like a lamb to the slaughter . . . I could have helped, but I turned my back 'cos I thought . . . well, I don't know what I thought . . . but I've done it, and now I regret it.'

'This all sounds like a bit of a riddle to me. Start at the beginning and tell me exactly what happened.'

'The ring . . . it's stolen,' Sarah said, and lifted her eyes to meet his.

George tried his best not to look astonished, but blurted out, 'What, you stole it?'

'No, no, I found it, but I know it's been stolen and I know who it belongs to.'

'Sarah, I'm normally a good judge of character, and you seem like an honest person to me. Don't upset yourself, love, you didn't 'alf-inch it, you found it. That makes it yours.'

'But I should return it to its rightful owner, otherwise I'm just as bad as the person who did steal it.'

'Depends how you look at it. In my book you've just been fortunate. Did you go looking for the ring knowing it was stolen and who it belonged to?'

Sarah shook her head. 'No, I was just down on the banks again and came across it. It wasn't until after I found it that I bumped into my friend and she told me about the lady she cleans for who has this son who's been nicking her stuff. He wants my mate blamed for stealing it and for her to get the sack 'cos she turned him down. It was the watch. She told me about the watch. You know it was marked A. S. The lady's name is Alderton-Steele. Now do you see? This ring must belong to her too.'

George rubbed his forehead and sighed deeply as he

tried get a grasp on Sarah's story. 'So, what you're telling me is you know who the watch belongs to, and that this woman's son must have lobbed it into the Thames?'

Sarah nodded, her eyes still wet with tears as George continued, 'Yeah, well, it's too late to do anything about it 'cos you've sold it. Your friend never mentioned the ring, though, did she, so how do you know it belongs to this Steele woman?'

'Well . . . I don't. I'm just assuming it does, and the bracelet, 'cos according to my friend, this bloke Godfrey has pinched a few items from his mother. It's got to be hers, hasn't it?'

George thought quickly. He was in possession of the bracelet and the watch. If the items had been reported to the police as stolen and they found he had them, he'd likely get charged with receiving. He thought it was a good job he hadn't tried to sell them on and they were safely tucked away in his wardrobe. He'd have to convince Sarah to give him the ring too. At least then he could protect her from the long arm of the law. He knew she was innocent but he doubted the courts would believe her. 'I suppose it could belong to her, but you don't know that for definite. It could just as likely have belonged to some woman who lost it years ago in Windsor or some-where, and it got washed up where you found it. I think you're beating yourself up needlessly. You found the ring, it's yours, job done.'

'Oh, George, I wish I could see it in black and white like you. I know what you're saying is a possibility, but in my heart I know who this ring belongs to, and 'cos I'm desperate for the money, I chose to lower myself. I ain't done the right thing, and now it's probably too late.'

'Give me the ring, Sarah. What's done is done, and you're worrying about it too much. I'll buy it off you now for. . .' George rummaged in his money belt and slapped several coins on the table. 'There's about three quid there. It ain't much compared to what the ring is worth, but it'll see you over 'til you get the job with my mum. And before you say another word, this ain't me doing you no favours. I can sell that ring on for a lot more than three quid, so there'll be a tidy profit in it for me.'

'You really think this is OK? You don't think I should take it back to Mrs Alderton-Steele?'

'No, you definitely shouldn't take it back! Think about it, Sarah. Do you really reckon she'll believe you weren't somehow involved in the robbery? It ain't worth risking it, not for a few quid and a poxy ring.' George sounded more forceful than he wanted to, but he had to convince her.

He was pleased when, without saying a word, Sarah slid the ring across the table towards him, then scooped up the cash.

'Good girl. Now, we won't ever mention this again, and you stay away from that blinkin' river, OK?'

Sarah nodded, but George wouldn't be satisfied until he'd seen a smile on her beautiful face. 'What do you reckon to these Eccles cakes? They taste good but I have to close my eyes when I eat them.'

'Why?' Sarah asked.

'It's these currants . . . they look like dead flies.'

At last, Sarah's lips turned up and her eyes creased in the corners.

'Thanks for telling me that, George. Now I'll have to

close my eyes too,' she said, but smiled as she picked up her cake.

George was pleased to see that Sarah looked happier. She'd been beating herself up, feeling guilty, and that endeared her to him even more. It proved she had a conscience, and he had no worries about recommending her to his mum for a job in the corner shop. She'd be safe there, with no more foraging on the banks of the Thames. Her days of being a mudlark would be well and truly over.

Chapter 18

On the day of her mother's funeral, Sarah wore the black outfit she'd bought from George. She wasn't surprised when nobody turned up to bury her mother. Annie had made more enemies than friends, but Sarah had thought that at least Eddy might have put in an appearance. As it turned out, she stood alone at the side of the shared grave to see her mum off.

She laid a bunch of wild flowers on the ground. It was a poignant reminder of her struggle to provide for Tommy when she'd sold hand-picked flowers in the High Street. She shouldn't have been put in the position of having to leave school and look after Tommy. It was something her mother should have done. However, she no longer resented her, and in some ways she felt sorry for her. Sarah understood how difficult life could be with no money and the responsibility of a child. She could see why her mother had prostituted herself.

Yet despite that, there was no need for the abuse, and instead of feeling loved, Sarah had only ever felt unwanted. Her mother had declared her love for her on her deathbed, but it had been too late, and Sarah wondered if her mother had really ever loved her or was just easing her conscience as a dying woman. With one last look at the pauper's grave, Sarah whispered, 'Bye, Mum,' and without shedding a tear she walked away.

Samuel was forever bringing home old newspapers, magazines and books that commuters had left behind on the trains. As Mo sat on her sofa and turned the page of yesterday's broadsheet, she huffed in frustration, then threw the paper to her side. She struggled to read and she found the pictures all very boring.

Tommy was outside playing with Larry, but Sarah would be home soon and offer some respite from the tedium. She just hoped her friend wouldn't return full of pity and woe, though she'd appeared to be fine when she'd left.

Mo crossed her legs and drummed her fingers. She could bake a cake, that would pass some time, but she'd painted her nails earlier and didn't want to chip the varnish. She stood up and walked around the pristine room. Samuel had left the rent money in an empty fruit bowl that sat on a small table which had two chairs tucked neatly underneath. It was due today so she was expecting Mr Terence to call any time soon. She considered putting the kettle on and offering the man a cup of tea, but he didn't seem the friendly sort and she didn't want him getting the wrong idea. Still, anything was better than going out of her head with the monotony.

She heard the front door close, then footsteps coming up the stairs. The steps were too light and quick to belong to Mr Terence, so Sarah must have come home earlier than she'd expected.

Mo eagerly rushed to the door to greet her friend and was pleased to see a smile on Sarah's face. 'How did it go?' she asked, though in truth she didn't really care and hoped Sarah wouldn't relay all the depressing details.

'Just as I thought it would. There wasn't anyone else there except me, and in a way it was good,' Sarah replied as she took off her coat and moved the newspaper before sitting on the sofa.

'How do you mean, good?' Mo asked.

'Well, it gave me time to think. My mum's gone now, and I'm ready to build a new future for me and Tommy, but there's just one thing I have to do first, and I don't think I'll be able to get on properly with my life until I've done it . . . I'm going to find my dad.'

Mo handed Sarah a cup of tea, then pulled out one of the chairs from under the table before sitting down. 'You've just lost your mum, so I can understand that you probably feel very alone, but are you sure that's a good idea? I mean, you said your mum sounded pretty adamant that he hadn't wanted you.'

'Yes, I know, but it was such a long time ago. I can't shake him from my head. Every night I lie in bed and try to imagine what he's like. I won't rest until I know the truth for myself.'

'You've got to do what feels right for you, but just watch your step. For all you know, he could be a right bastard like my old man.'

'Yeah, I know he could, but on the other hand he might not be,' Sarah replied positively.

Mo sipped her hot tea. 'That Mr Terence will be here any minute now. What did you think of him?'

'I've never met him. He wasn't around when I came to look at my room. Mrs Preston showed it to me and she was a right snooty cow!'

'Oooh, I say, you are honoured. Mrs P don't show her face often, not round here. You're right though, she is proper stuck up but it's all fur coat and no knickers with her.'

Sarah spluttered on her tea. 'What do you mean, fur coat and no knickers?'

'She thinks she's a cut above the rest of us, but she's nothing special. My gran knew her from years back when they were neighbours. Mrs Preston, or Connie Spittal as she was known then, grew up in a two-up two-down with an outside lavvy just like the rest of us. Connie had a sister called Edna and together they were known as phlegm and gob, the Spittal sisters.'

Sarah spluttered with laughter.

'Yeah, funny, ain't it?' Mo said, grinning. 'Anyway, from what my gran said, God rest her soul, Edna went on to marry a milkman and had loads of kids, but Connie had ideas above herself. She'd tell my gran, if you're going to fall in love, it may as well be with a rich man rather than a poor one. So, that's what she did. My gran said you could hear everything through those walls, and Connie was always getting in bother with her dad for pinching the rent money and buying herself fancy clothes to wear up town. Eventually, the rent arrears mounted up and the family got thrown out. My gran lost touch with Connie then, but she said a few years later she bumped into her again and hardly recognised her. She was talking all posh and boasting about some property tycoon she'd married who was forty-five years older than her and would pop his clogs soon. That's how she did it, you know, got rich. He died and she was left with everything, which included a couple of dozen houses, a few of which are here in Battersea. She's what you would call a gold digger.'

'I never would have guessed, and to think she looked down her nose at me!' Sarah said. 'At least I'm going to be working for what's mine.'

'And that's not all,' Mo continued. 'With all that money, she never once helped her family out. I heard Edna died a terrible death in pain 'cos they couldn't afford the doctor. She was good enough to house her parents, but charged them rent.'

'But that's awful,' Sarah exclaimed.

'I know, and now she lives in a bloody huge house near Victoria, but the only visitors she ever gets are a load of stray cats. Mr Terence worked for her husband, and she's got a driver and a cleaner, but they say she wanders around the house at night counting her money then hiding it again. She's obsessed with it. Rumour has it that she's got money sewn in the curtain hems, the mattress, stuffed in saucepans and even in the toilet cisterns.'

'See, money can't buy you happiness,' Sarah said.

'No, it can't,' Mo replied, 'but it can help make being sad a whole lot easier.'

'Yeah, I suppose, but I'd rather be poor and happy than rich and lonely.'

Mo nodded her head in agreement, but thought that if she was a film star, she'd be rich – and she knew that would make her happy, very happy indeed.

Chapter 19

On the Monday that Tommy was to start school, Sarah awoke to him jumping on her. 'Wake up, Sarah, I want to go to school now.'

Sarah rubbed her eyes and could see it was still dark outside. 'Tommy, it's far too early, the school won't be open yet. Go back to bed and get some sleep or you'll be shattered later.' She turned over in her bed, but Tommy wasn't having any of it.

'Please, Sarah, get up. We've got to get ready.'

'Oh, for goodness' sake, Tommy. Move then, let me get out of the bed. I can see I'll be wasting my time trying to sleep with you this excited.' She swung her legs over the bed and stretched her arms, as she noticed Tommy's bed was neat and tidy for a change. 'You've made your bed?' she asked Tommy, surprised.

'Yes, and I've got my bag packed with my paints and marbles, and an apple. You don't have to come with me today 'cos I'm going with Larry and his mum. Larry said I'll sit at the desk next to him. He said my teacher is really nice and hardly ever throws the blackboard wiper.'

'Tommy, do you even know what a blackboard is?'

'Yeah, the thing the teacher draws on.'

Sarah could tell that Tommy and his friend had obviously been having lengthy discussions about school, and she was pleased that he was so keen to go. She had feared that he'd be scared and put up some resistance, but it looked as though the opposite was true.

A couple of hours later, Tommy skipped out the door, and Sarah realised she was going to miss her little brother. She stood at the front door and watched as he and Larry went running up the street together. It didn't appear that he was going to miss her quite as much as she would him, although he did give her a brief wave as he ran off.

Sarah went back to their room and sat on the edge of her bed as she drained the last of her tea. Tommy starting school was the beginning of something new for them both. She was nervous and excited at the same time, but before she went to see George about the job with his mum, there was one more thing pressing on her mind. Ron Lyons.

George was really pleased when he spotted Sarah walking towards him with a big grin on her face. It was nice to see her looking happy.

'Good morning,' he said. 'I take it little Tommy got off to school all right then?'

'Hello, George. Yes, he couldn't wait to go and had me up at the crack of dawn. Still, it's nice to see him so contented, albeit a tad excited.'

'Right, then you'll be wanting that job with my mum now. I've already spoken to her about it and she's looking forward to meeting you. Do you want to come round tomorrow evening?' George hoped she'd say yes. His mum had taken a bit of persuasion, but eventually she had agreed to give Sarah a chance.

'Yes, thanks, that would be great. There's just one more thing I was hoping you could help me with?'

'Always a pleasure to lend a hand to a beautiful young lady . . . What can I do for you?'

'Well, it's a bit of a long story . . .'

George laughed and interrupted, 'It usually is with you.'

'Thing is, I want to get in touch with someone. I know his name and I know he lives on Lavender Hill, but that's about it. It's a bit of a delicate situation, so I can't just go and knock on every door until I find him. Any suggestions?'

George rubbed his chin as he thought. He wanted to know more about the man she was looking for. If it was a love interest, then he wasn't sure that he really wanted to help. 'I know it's none of my business, but why is it "delicate"?'

'Like I said, it's a long story, but . . . I think the man I'm looking for is my dad.'

'Oh, I see,' George said, feeling chuffed that she wasn't chasing after another bloke. 'I take it that he doesn't know about you then?'

'No. He knew my mum was pregnant, but that's about it. From what I know he's got a family of his own, so he ain't going to want me banging on his door.'

'This bloke, your dad, what's his name? Chances are, if he's a local, I might know him.'

'Ron Lyons,' Sarah answered.

'Ron Lyons,' George parroted as he thought hard. 'The name sounds familiar . . . In fact, there was a girl in my school called Theresa Lyons. She was a few years below me, but she could be related. Hang on a tick.'

George walked over to Roger who he noticed was staying out of the way, but still eyeing Sarah from a distance with a lustful look. 'Mate, do you remember Theresa Lyons from school?'

'Yes, and I tell you what, that ugly duckling has grown into a right looker. I saw her at the Town Hall dance with Freddie the Fish. Don't know what she was doing with him though, she's well out of his league.'

'I don't suppose you know where she lives?'

'On Lavender Hill. Why do you want to know? I thought you was well into Sarah?'

'It's not me who wants to know, it's Sarah, she's looking for Theresa's dad, Ron.'

'Ha, I see. You want to be her knight in shining armour. Buy me a pint later and I'll tell you exactly where she lives. In fact, I can do even better than that. Ron Lyons works at Battersea Bridge nick, he's a desk sergeant,' Roger said and playfully punched George on the arm.

'Great. I'll buy you two, cheers.'

George walked back to Sarah with the information he had gleaned from Roger, hoping it would earn him some extra brownie points.

'Well . . . do you know where I can find him?' Sarah asked eagerly.

'Yep, and even more than that, I can tell you where he works,' George said, feeling rather smug.

'Oh, that's great, George, thank you. I wouldn't want to cause him any embarrassment with his family, so if I can find him at work that'll be so much better.'

'You ain't got far to go from where you live. Turns out he works at the police station.'

'What, Battersea Bridge station?'

'That's the one.'

'My dad's a copper?'

'I think so. By all accounts he's a desk sergeant, so you shouldn't have any problems finding him.'

'George, I can't believe it! All this time, when I've been scavenging down on them banks, I've been right under my dad's nose and didn't know it.'

'It's a small world, love,' George said. 'So, what are you going to do now?'

'I'm going to go and see him.'

'What, just like that? You're going to march in off the street and announce that you're his daughter?'

'Pretty much, unless you've got any better ideas?' Sarah said.

'No, not really. Do you want me to come with you?'

Sarah was quick to reply, 'No, but thanks, George, and that's really good of you to offer. I'll be off now, but I'll see you tomorrow evening.'

'Not so fast, missy,' George said, then took a pencil from his money bag and scribbled down his address on a brown paper bag. 'You'll be needing this. Mum's expecting you about half six.'

Sarah took the bag and smiled at George before walking off. 'Wish me luck,' she called over her shoulder.

George wished her all the luck in the world and thought she was going to need it. Ron Lyons was in for the shock of his life, and George hoped the man would be welcoming. Even before Sarah had been born, her father had abandoned both her and her mother, and now she could be facing the hurt of being rejected again.

Chapter 20

Sarah stood outside the large redbrick building and held onto the black railings as she tried to muster up the courage to walk through the main door. Two bobbies came out and walked past her. They were young, too young to be her dad. She had no idea what her father looked like, but she hoped that as soon as she saw him, she'd somehow recognise him.

She drew in a long breath before apprehensively climbing the few steps that led to the entrance, then slowly pushed open the door. As she stepped inside, she looked around. The stark walls were painted pale green, and there were several doors leading from the reception area.

'Can I help you, miss?' she heard a policeman ask from behind a long wooden counter.

She looked at the man, but felt nothing, and wondered if he could be her father. She approached the desk, all the time studying the policeman's face, trying to see something that reminded her of herself.

'I . . . I . . . I'm looking for Ron Lyons . . .' she managed to say nervously. She could feel her heart beating fast, and her hands were clammy. She tapped her left finger and thumb together.

'And who shall I tell him wants to see him?' the policeman asked.

Sarah had to think quickly. She couldn't say her own name. 'Sarah Neerly,' she lied, thinking George wouldn't mind her using his.

'And can I ask what it's about?'

'I . . . er . . .' Her mind went blank.

'Just a minute, I'll find him for you,' the policeman said impatiently, then exited through a door behind the counter.

Sarah sighed with relief. She saw a long wooden bench and walked across to sit down. Her legs felt strangely shaky and her head was swimming. She'd been full of bravado at George's stall, but now she wasn't feeling quite so brave and regretted declining George's offer to accompany her.

Sarah jigged her leg and began to bite her nails. This wasn't going to be as easy as she'd originally thought, and now she wondered what she was going to say. It felt as if she'd been sitting waiting for hours, but really it was only a few minutes before she heard the door open and the policeman walked back through, closely followed by another uniformed man.

That's him, she thought to herself. That's my dad! He was a large man, with brown hair thinning on top, and his complexion was rugged, but when she saw his eyes they were deep green, and it was like a reflection of her own.

'I understand you're looking for me. I'm Sergeant Lyons,' he said in a deep voice.

Sarah felt rooted to the wooden bench. She wanted to get up and move closer to him but her legs wouldn't work, and it felt as if her voice had become stuck in her throat. She gulped hard, but it wasn't easy as her mouth was so dry.

'Miss . . . Are you all right?'

Sarah nodded, but she felt light-headed, and for a moment, she thought she might faint. She heard her father tell the other policeman to fetch her a glass of water, and suddenly she realised she was causing a scene and needed to pull herself together. She didn't want to draw too much attention to herself. 'Thanks, but I'm fine.'

'What did you want to see me about?' her father asked.

Sarah finally moved from the bench and stood in front of the counter. Both policemen were staring at her, and as she looked into her father's eyes, she hoped he'd realise who she was. 'Can we speak somewhere in private?' she asked in almost a whisper.

She saw the men exchange glances.

'Come through this way,' her father said, lifting the flip-up counter. Sarah followed him into a long corridor. He led her through to a room with a table and chairs in the middle, and pale-grey painted walls. It didn't feel very friendly. Then her father spoke.

'Sorry, this is normally an interrogating room, but please, take a seat.'

Sarah pulled out a chair and sat down, gripping her shaking hands in her lap.

'Now then,' her father said as he took a seat opposite her, 'do you want to tell me what this is all about? I hope you're not wasting police time, young lady.'

Sarah had thought about what she was going to say, but all the words evaded her now, and instead she blurted,

'I lied. My name isn't really Sarah Neerly. It's Sarah Jepson and I believe you knew my mother, Annie?'

Ron Lyons leaned back in his seat, and Sarah watched as the colour drained from his face.

'Annie Jepson . . . Yes, I remember her well. How is she?'

'Dead,' Sarah said bluntly.

'Oh, I'm very sorry to hear that.'

Sarah couldn't detect any sincerity in his voice and his face was deadpan.

'She told me something on her deathbed . . .' Sarah paused, hoping her father would work out what she was about to say so that she wouldn't have to spell out the details.

There was silence between them for a moment, but then it was broken as he said, 'Are you going to enlighten me?'

'Well, it's a bit delicate. My mum, Annie, she told me that you're . . . you . . . Oh, blimey, I'm just going to come straight out with it. She said you're my dad.'

Ron Lyons shifted uncomfortably in his chair. He looked very awkward and Sarah wondered if she should have broken the news a little more gently.

He cleared his throat, before saying, 'I think Annie, your mother, is very much mistaken. I'm sorry you've had a wasted journey to see me. Now, if there's nothing else, I'll see you out.'

She hadn't expected her dad to welcome her with open arms, but she hadn't been prepared for such a quick and cold denial. 'Wait, I'm sorry, but I think you are my father. Look at my eyes, they're the same as yours. My mum told me all about you, and how you left her when you knew she was pregnant. It was a long time ago, I don't bear grudges as you were both much younger then, but you are my dad.'

Ron quickly scraped his chair back, and began pacing up and down the small room. He looked worried, panicked almost, but Sarah couldn't understand why. Yes, she'd just dropped a bombshell on him, but according to her mother he must have known he had a love child and surely he'd thought about her turning up one day?

'I'm not sure what you want from me, Sarah. You can't prove anything, and you can't go around accusing people of being your father just on your mother's word.'

'I'm not accusing anyone! I know you're my dad and I'm not here because I want something from you,' Sarah answered, feeling hurt.

'Then what *do* you want?'

Her father's voice was harsh, and Sarah could feel tears beginning to pool in her eyes. She hadn't wanted to cry in front of him – at least not tears of upset. 'I don't know really. I suppose I just wanted to know you,' she said, and looked imploringly at him.

'I'm sorry, Sarah, but you're wasting your time. I never believed your mother was pregnant. I thought she was just trying to trap me into being with her. For all I know you could be the result of whatever Tom, Dick or Harry she took to her bed after me. I don't mean to sound unpleasant, but I know all about your mother and what she did for a living. She's been nicked for it a few times. Look, whatever silly notion you've got in your head, just forget about it.'

Sarah couldn't hold back any longer and the tears began to fall, splashing on the table as they landed. 'How dare you talk about my mum like that! She was forced to be a prostitute 'cos you left us high and dry. How else was she supposed to look after me when you abandoned us?'

'Stop it. Shut up and stop what you're saying right now. I won't have you talking like that. Your mother was a tart and I'm not your dad! Now get that through your skull.'

It wasn't easy to hear him talk about her mother in that way, yet Sarah still felt she should try and convince him, make him see the truth, accept her as his own. It was clear he was her father, his eyes were so distinct, and exactly the same as hers. 'Please, Ron. I don't want anything more than your acknowledgement and maybe to find out a bit more about you. I'm your daughter . . . surely you want to know about me and my life?'

'To be honest, Sarah, I couldn't give two hoots about your mother, you or your life. I didn't know you existed until ten minutes ago, and that's the way I'd prefer to keep things.'

'But you can't deny it, you do know now. You know I exist!' Sarah said, almost pleading with the man for his acceptance.

'You can go on as much as you like, but as far as I'm concerned, you're a fantasist and your mother was a whore, so that's an end to all this nonsense.'

Sarah's tears were falling harder now, and she drew in a juddery breath. After several more snivels, she looked up at Ron, who had sat down opposite her again. She stared into his eyes, hoping to find some glimmer of recognition, even a sign of empathy towards her. But they were cold, devoid of any emotion, and she doubted she'd be able to change his mind.

'Ron, I'm not expecting you to welcome me into your family or anything like that. In fact, I'm not even expecting to meet them or for them to know anything about me,' she said, hoping the promise of staying away from his family would soften him.

'Why would you mention my family? What do you know about me and mine?' Ron asked suspiciously.

'I . . . erm . . . I just know you have a family of your own, and I wouldn't want to cause you any embarrassment with them.'

'Yes, well, as it happens, I'm happily married with six kids and if you start blurting out stuff about me being your father, I could lose them all. My wife, my career, everything.'

'Is that what you're worried about, your wife finding out?' Sarah asked disappointedly.

'Yes, of course it is! But you already knew that, didn't you?'

Sarah didn't know what he meant and shook her head. She'd guessed he'd want to keep her a secret, but he seemed to be implying something else.

'Ah, that's it! I should have known. I know your game, missy . . . you think you can come in here with your wild stories and I'll pay you money to shut you up so that my wife doesn't find out. I'm right, aren't I? You want to blackmail me.'

'No,' Sarah answered emphatically, 'that's not true!'

'Of course it is! I bet you thought you'd butter me up first, get me to admit to being your father, then you'd stick the knife in and see what you could get out of me. How much did you think your silence would be worth?'

'It's not like that! I'm not after your money,' Sarah protested, but she could see Ron wasn't listening.

'Yes, you're bound to say that, aren't you? You're hardly likely to admit that you're in this for what you can get out of me. I've been in this job for thirty-odd years and I've met plenty of people like you before. You're a nasty piece of work, just like your slag of a mother,' he said angrily as he brought his fist down hard on the table.

Sarah gasped. The sudden thud had made her jump. Her father's face was twisted in fury, though he couldn't have been further from the truth. She could see he was never going to accept her as his daughter, and now she was becoming frightened of the man. 'No, you're very wrong. I would never do that and I wish I hadn't come here now,' she said as her tears dried, only to be replaced with anger and fear. Yes, her mother had been a tart, but at least she'd tried, which was more than could be said for her father. She stood up and pushed her shoulders back defiantly. 'You've got it all wrong.'

'No, I think you'll find it's you who's got it wrong,' Ron answered quietly as he looked at her through slitted eyes.

'I'm sorry you feel this way,' Sarah said. 'If you want nothing to do with me, fine. I'd like to leave now.'

Without saying a word, she followed Ron back through to reception. He held the main entrance door open, and as Sarah walked through, he covertly grabbed her arm and squeezed tightly. She felt his breath on her cheek as she heard him whisper, 'Keep your mouth shut about what you think you know, or else you'll regret it.'

Sarah put on a show of bravado and threw him a look of disdain as she yanked her arm from his grip. She hurried down the steps and dashed around the corner from the police station, but once out of sight she stopped and leaned forward with her hands on her thighs as she gasped in lungfuls of fresh air.

She could hardly believe what had just transpired. He'd threatened her, and now she thought it was a good job that he'd left her mum. She dreaded to think what sort of life her mother would have had with such a vile man, and thoughts of Mo's violent father came into her mind.

Ron Lyons was a wolf in sheep's clothing, and she had no doubt in her head that his policeman's uniform was the perfect disguise for hiding an explosive temper.

Mo had finished cleaning her room and was looking around for something else to fill her time when she glanced out of the window to see Sarah walking home. She went down to the front door to greet her friend, and as Sarah drew closer, she could see the woman looked pale.

'Hello, love, what's happened?' she asked. 'You look as white as a ghost.'

'I can't tell you.'

'All right, but come on, I'll make you a cup of tea. You look like you could do with one.'

Sarah followed Mo upstairs, and once inside she flopped onto a chair. 'Oh, Mo, I wish I could tell you what happened, but for your sake it's better if you don't know.'

'Look, if you can't tell me, that's fine, but I ain't one to gossip and anything you say won't pass these walls.'

As though her words had released a dam in Sarah, it all spilled out, until at last she slumped, seemingly exhausted.

'I hate to say I told you so,' Mo said as she gave her

friend a cup of tea, 'but I did warn you. I'm sorry for you 'cos I'm sure you had this romantic vision in your head, and now that illusion has just been shattered, but trust me, there's some men you're better off without.'

'Yes, that's exactly what I think now. I know my mum's life was pretty dismal, but at least she wasn't knocked about too much by her punters. I reckon it would have been a different story if Ron had stayed with her.'

'What about your dad's other kids? They'd be your half-brothers and -sisters. Are you gonna try to get in contact with them?'

'No, good riddance to the lot of them. I don't need anyone else in my life, I'm fine with just me and Tommy. And by the way, my dad is no longer called my dad . . . we'll call him Ron from now on.'

Mo was pleased to see that Sarah didn't seem to be upset, though she had obviously been shaken by the experience.

'I'm off to have tea with George and his mum, Lena, tomorrow. Hopefully, by this time next week, I'll be working. Onwards and upwards.'

Mo felt a twinge of envy, and selfishly hoped that Lena didn't like Sarah. She enjoyed having her friend around during the day and found her a welcome distraction from her usual boredom. 'Yeah, onwards and upwards,' she repeated through a forced smile. 'What about that other bloke you like, Roger? You ain't mentioned him lately.'

'I ain't seen him. To be honest, with my mum's funeral and everything else, I haven't really had time to think about him. Oh, Mo, I wish you hadn't mentioned him because now I've got butterflies.'

Mo suddenly burst into song, and began waltzing

around the room as she sang Doris Day's 'Secret Love'. Then she giggled along with Sarah, noticing her once pale face was now blushing pink.

'Thanks for the cuppa and the entertainment,' Sarah said, 'but I'd better get downstairs and tidy up before I pick Tommy up from school. Honestly, he was so excited this morning, he was like a little whirlwind.'

Mo nodded her head and tried to hide her disappointment. She'd hoped Sarah would stay longer. 'I could give you a hand if you like,' she offered. She didn't particularly like housework, but at least she'd still have the company of her friend.

'No, it's all right, thanks, Mo. It's only one room, it won't take me long. I'll see ya soon.'

Sarah walked out, leaving Mo feeling lonely. She missed Samuel and wished he would take more time off work. Trouble was, it appeared he was becoming more and more obsessed with saving to buy their own place, but the extra hours of overtime weren't helping to fulfil Mo's idea of a happy relationship.

Mo slumped in her chair, finding the silence of the room almost deafening. Well, whether Samuel liked it or not, she decided she'd dip into their savings and treat herself to a new radio. After all, if he was going to leave her alone so much, she needed some sort of entertainment.

A while later, Sarah stood at the school gates waiting for Tommy to emerge. A light drizzle was beginning to fall, but she doubted it would dampen her brother's spirits.

She heard a bell ring, then all at once there was a mass exodus from the school building as young boys and girls filed out into the playground. She immediately spotted Tommy, who was running alongside Larry, both chuckling mischievously.

'Sarah, I had the best day ever!' Tommy said as he ran towards her. 'Larry and me are going to be in the class play, and guess what? I'm going to be a talking tree!'

'Sounds like fun. What else did you do today?' Sarah asked as she went to hold Tommy's hand, but missed as he ran ahead.

'I'll see you at home, Mum. I'm going to run after Larry.'

Shocked at what she'd heard, Sarah stopped walking and ran Tommy's words over again in her head. He'd called her Mum, there was no mistaking it. She had always felt like his mother and loved him as if he were her own son, but to hear him call her Mum melted her heart.

What did it matter if she didn't have a dad, especially one like Ron Lyons! She and Tommy had each other, and for Sarah that was enough. She began walking again, only now she was prouder than ever, and soon she'd be working and would be able to give Tommy all the things she'd missed out on.

Especially love, Sarah thought. Yes, especially love.

Chapter 21

'George, stop fussing about like an old mother hen and relax, will you. It's only Sarah coming for tea, not the Queen Mother,' Lena said as she stood over the gas stove, poking a knife into some potatoes on the boil.

'Yeah, I know, Mum. I was just having a bit of a tidy up,' George replied as he scanned the kitchen.

'You cheeky bugger! Are you trying to imply that my house ain't clean enough?'

George laughed. 'No, of course not,' he said, and walked across the room to kiss his mother on the cheek. He checked the clock on the kitchen wall. Sarah would be here any moment.

'George, do me a favour, love, and plump the cushions on the sofa. Anything to get you out from under my feet.'

George walked into the front room but instead of plumping the cushions, he stood in front of the green-tiled mantel and stared at his reflection in the mirror hanging above the hearth. Who was he trying to kid, he thought to himself. His scars covered most of his face. His bottom lip was swollen, and part of his ear had burned away. He only had patches of brown hair on his damaged scalp, and his nose was almost flat to his face because of the scar tissue. His skin felt tight, and though he rubbed in creams every day, it still caused him discomfort. Sarah would never want to be with him. If she did, it would be like Beauty and the Beast – and that, though the story was fantasy, gave him hope.

George heard a knock at the door, and his mother call out, 'Can you get that, George?'

He opened the door, and Tommy immediately threw his arms around his legs. 'I've done you a painting, George. Mum's got it. I'm at school now.'

So, he was calling Sarah his mum now, George mused as he ruffled the boy's soft hair. It was sweet, and as Sarah had raised him, he could understand why, but he hoped it wouldn't cause any tongues to wag. People could be spiteful if they thought a girl was an unmarried mother, and he wouldn't want that for Sarah. 'Come inside. You can show me your painting and tell me all about school.' As he spoke, his eyes were fixed on Sarah. He thought she looked stunning with her long hair tied in a neat bun on top of her head. It emphasised her eyes and long dark lashes, and gave her an air of elegance. 'You look nice,' he said, trying to sound more nonchalant than he felt.

'Thanks. I thought I'd put my hair up to make myself look a bit more professional. I hope your mum likes me,' Sarah said in almost a whisper.

'Don't worry, she'll love you,' said George, and, whispering too, he asked, 'How did you get on when you went to see Ron Lyons?'

'I got it wrong. He isn't my dad,' Sarah said, and looked at the floor.

'Oh, right. Well, come on into the front room.'

Lena appeared in the doorway and whipped off her apron. 'Hello, Sarah, and you must be Tommy,' she said. 'Sit down, my dear. George, have you offered our guests some drinks?'

'Give me a chance, Mum, they've only just walked through the door,' George said and hid a smile. His mum was putting on airs, but he knew she wouldn't be able to keep it up.

'Thank you,' Sarah said equally formally as she sat down prettily on the sofa.

'What can I get you?' George asked.

'I'd love a cup of tea,' Sarah answered.

'Would you like a glass of lemonade, Tommy?'

'Yes, please,' Tommy answered with gusto.

'Tea won't be long. I hope you like meat pie?' Lena asked.

Sarah nodded and Tommy said, 'That's my favourite.'

Lena went back to the kitchen. George wanted to sit next to Sarah on the sofa but Tommy had already positioned himself there, so instead he took an armchair next to the fire mantel.

'Is it OK if I go through to the kitchen to see if your mum wants a hand with anything?' Sarah quietly asked.

'Yes, I'm sure she'll appreciate that, though be warned, she's always slinging me out of her kitchen. Tommy can tell me all about school.'

George watched as Sarah left the room, then listened as Tommy told him about his new ventures.

Twenty minutes later, Sarah came back into the room. 'Dinner's ready!'

George and Tommy followed her through to the kitchen, and George was pleased when he saw his mother give Sarah a warm smile. He didn't know what had been said in the kitchen, but the ice had been broken and conversation flowed freely around the kitchen table as they ate.

'That was delicious, Mrs Neerly,' Sarah said as she finished her meal.

'I'm glad you enjoyed it. Now, if you're going to be starting work with me tomorrow morning, I think you should call me Lena.'

Sarah's eyes widened with delight, and she clapped her palms together. 'Really? You're offering me the position in the shop?'

'Yes, I'll be expecting you there at ten sharp and then you'll finish at three. The hours should fit in nicely with Tommy's school. Once you've learned the ropes, I'll be able to leave you to it and just open up in the mornings and cover the late afternoons. Suits me a treat.'

'Thank you, thank you so much, Mrs Neerly ... I mean Lena.'

'You're welcome, love. We all deserve a chance, ain't that right, George?' Lena said, and looked at her son wryly.

He knew his mother was referring to Sarah giving him a chance, but he hoped Sarah didn't cotton on. 'Yes, Mum. Now, who fancies a game of cards in the front room?'

'You three go through, I'll wash up in here,' Lena said.

'I'll help,' Sarah offered, but Lena wouldn't hear of it and ushered them all away.

'I'm really looking forward to working with your mum tomorrow, George.'

'Good. It's nice to see a smile on that pretty face of yours.'

The rest of the evening passed with lots of laughter, and George soon found himself having to say goodbye to Sarah. He offered to drive her home in his van, but she insisted on making her own way. Though he found her stubborn independence frustrating sometimes, he also admired her for it.

Later that night, as he lay in bed, images of Sarah's face floated through George's mind. He began to feel aroused, and tried to dismiss his thoughts of her. They'd had a very enjoyable evening together, and the least he could hope for was more of the same.

It was dark by the time Sarah arrived home, and Tommy was yawning. She felt bad for keeping him up later than usual, especially now that he had school in the morning.

As she turned into her street, she gasped when she saw two policemen walking towards her. They were some way away, but as they passed under a street lamp, it illuminated their faces. 'Oh, thank Gawd,' Sarah said with relief.

'What?' Tommy asked.

'Nothing, I'm just glad we're nearly home.'

The policemen greeted her a 'good evening' as they passed, but their friendly manner did nothing to abate her qualms. Neither of them had been her father, but she still had concerns that he would one day turn up and ensure she was never able to tell the truth about him. She pushed her fears to one side. She had enough to be worrying about with starting her first ever real job in the morning.

Once indoors, Tommy didn't take long to settle and fall asleep, and Sarah decided it would be wise for her to do the same. However, as soon as her head hit the pillow, she realised she was full of nervous energy, her mind turning as she wondered what it would be like to work in a shop. George had reassured her there was nothing to worry about, but his words hadn't calmed her fears. She wanted to be good at her new job, but years of her mother telling her she was useless had left her doubting her own self-worth. If it turned out that her mother was right, Sarah felt she'd be letting Tommy down, as well as Lena and George.

Stop it, she chided herself. This was her chance to prove that she wasn't useless, and, feeling more determined than ever, Sarah eventually drifted off to sleep.

Chapter 22

The next morning, Lena checked her watch. It was ten to ten so she expected Sarah to walk through the door at any minute. She hoped the girl wouldn't be late on her first day. George had talked her into taking her on, but Lena still had her doubts. She thought Sarah seemed nice enough, but she had no experience and little education. Her regular customers were looking forward to meeting her, though one had mentioned she'd heard a rumour about Sarah's mother being a drunk and a prostitute. Since meeting the girl, Lena had put the rumour down to nasty gossip, and had decided that if it was true, then Sarah was nothing like her mother. At least, she hoped not.

The door opened and Sarah breezed in. Lena thought she looked petrified and could see straight through her cheery manner. 'Good morning, pet, right on time. That's a good start.'

'Hello, Lena,' Sarah chirped, but Lena could hear the crack in her voice.

'First things first . . . Get yourself out the back through there and take your coat off. You'll find a spare pinny on the peg. The toilet is on the left and the stove is on the right. Put the kettle on and make us both a cup of tea, then we'll get down to business.'

It wasn't long before Sarah reappeared holding two steaming cups. Lena could hear them rattling on the saucers as the girl's hands shook, and noticed much of the tea had sloshed over the side and into the saucer. 'I don't bite so you don't have to be so scared,' she said, trying to put the girl at ease.

'I know, I'm sorry. My nerves are all jangled. This job means so much to me and I don't want to mess it up.'

Lena's heart went out to her. She was such a young woman with the huge responsibility of raising her little brother, and from what she'd seen, she thought Sarah was doing a great job with Tommy. 'You'll be fine. Don't get me wrong, I'm going to make sure you work hard, but as I've always told my George, hard work is good for the soul. Now, your first job this morning will be restocking the shelves. The goods are all boxed up out the back. Just bring through one box at a time and make sure you put the new stuff at the back of the shelf. That way, the old stuff gets sold first. Do you think you can manage that?'

'Yes, no problem,' Sarah answered.

Lena kept a close eye on Sarah as she very efficiently stacked the shelves. Customers came and went, and Sarah's affable ways impressed Lena and charmed the customers. She thought the girl was a natural at shop work, but she still had the till and money to cope with yet. The till didn't do any adding or subtracting, and was only used to store the takings. She hoped Sarah wouldn't find it too difficult. 'You've done really well, love. Now come and join me behind the counter and we'll have a go at you serving the customers.'

Lena had thought that Sarah was beginning to relax, but then she saw the panicked look in her eyes that had been there earlier. 'It's easy, honest,' she said, hoping to reassure her.

It didn't take long for Sarah to grasp how the monetary system worked. Lena had a pad and pencil on the counter for writing down the prices to add them up, and was astonished when, nine times out of ten, Sarah would add the numbers in her head. At first she felt compelled to check the girl's figures, but soon found out they were always correct. In fact, Sarah could do it faster than she could. 'I told you there was nothing to worry about. You're really good at this, and I know I'm not going to have any problems with leaving you here alone soon.'

'Do you really think so? Thanks, Lena. I love working here and I can't believe how quickly the time passes. I've only got one hour to go, but I can't wait to come back tomorrow.'

Lena chuckled. 'Huh, I doubt you'll be feeling that enthusiastic after a few weeks.' She then told Sarah to fetch another stool from the storeroom, and they sat together behind the counter. 'We normally have a quiet spot about now and it won't get busy again until the schools finish for the day. This is when I normally do my stocktaking. I'll go through that with you another day, and in the meantime, it gives you and me a chance to have a natter.'

The obvious topic of conversation was George, and Lena explained to Sarah how he'd come to have such horrific scarring. When she told Sarah about George screaming in agony as his flesh had blackened and melted from his face, she saw tears in the girl's eyes and regretted being so graphic. But her son was a brave young man, and rarely talked about what had happened to him. He was better at putting on a cheery face that betrayed nothing of the excruciating suffering he'd been through. No one but she really understood how much George had endured, and seeing her son in unbearable pain had deeply affected her too. It was good to talk and get it off her chest, and though the bomb had dropped years earlier, Lena realised she'd been left traumatised. George had physical scars, but she had mental ones.

Nevertheless, once Lena realised she was upsetting Sarah, she changed the subject. An hour passed, and in that time, Lena gently probed. She found out that the rumours she'd heard were true. She didn't think Sarah was anything like her mother, but she'd keep an eye on the takings for now, just in case.

Her day's work over, Sarah dashed from the shop and collected Tommy. When they arrived home, Mo called over the banister, 'Congratulations on your first day at work. How was it?'

'Fine. I enjoyed it.'

'Come up and tell me all about it.'

'I want to get these shoes off, so why don't you come down here?'

'Yeah, all right,' Mo agreed.

'Can I go out to play with Larry?' Tommy appealed.

'Yeah, all right,' Sarah agreed, and once inside their room she flopped on the sofa, kicking off her shoes.

Mo came in to sit next to her and wrinkled her nose, 'Phew, those feet of yours smell a bit cheesy.'

'You cheeky mare. Yours would too if you'd been on

them for hours, and my shoes ain't exactly new,' Sarah protested, but smiled, unoffended.

'Well, come on then, tell me what it was like in the shop.'

'I love it. Lena is so nice. She's a bit nosy, and I found myself telling her all about my mum, but I've seen her with the customers. She loves a gossip, but it's all one-sided. She's got this knack of getting information out of people, but she don't gossip back. I like her.'

'Good,' said Mo, though Sarah thought her friend didn't sound very sincere. 'Was she shocked when you told her about your mum?'

'Not really. You know what it's like around here and she'd already heard stuff. I found out today that I'll be getting a bit of a discount, so next time you want a bit of shopping, I can get it for you.'

'Samuel will love that, you know how he is about saving money. You know I bought that radio the other day? Well, he only made me take it back to the shop, the tight bugger. I swear his bum squeaks when he walks!'

Sarah laughed. She always found Mo funny and wished she had her wit. 'Lena's invited me over for Sunday lunch. You'd think she'd be sick of my company after working with me all week.'

Mo gave her a knowing look. 'Haven't you worked it out yet?'

'Worked what out?'

'George. From what you've told me it's so obvious he fancies you, and now Mummy is going to play Cupid and get you two married off.'

Sarah sipped her tea. George had asked her out when they'd first met, but he hadn't pushed it since. 'No, you're way off the mark. George knows we're just friends.'

'He may know that, but does Lena?' Mo asked teasingly.

'Oh, stop it, Mo. Whatever Lena has got in her head, I hope she soon realises it's never going to happen with me and George.'

They continued chatting for another hour, then Mo left and Sarah began to get Tommy's tea ready. As she stirred a saucepan of mutton stew, her mind began to wander and she found herself thinking about Roger again. It wouldn't be so easy to see him now, not with her working during the week. She wouldn't be getting a full week's pay packet on Friday, but she'd have enough to treat herself and Tommy to some new clothes. She'd visit George's stall on Saturday, and would hopefully see Roger. She'd make a special effort and make sure she looked her best. Maybe she could get Mo to help her with some make-up. Her stomach flipped at the thought of him and, with her new-found confidence, she dared to dream that one day he would ask her out on a date.

Chapter 23

Sarah was happy in her work, and the weeks passed quickly. One Saturday morning in April she woke in the early hours to hear the front door close. She knew it would be Samuel leaving for work and closed her eyes, hoping to fall asleep again. She didn't work on Saturdays and wanted to look her best for when she went to the market, hoping to see Roger. She was disappointed that he still hadn't asked her out, but didn't want to give up hope that one day he would.

She was still wide awake when the sun rose and light spilled through the thin material at the window, illuminating the room. Sarah climbed out of bed and trudged over to the stove. She might as well put the kettle on, as it was unlikely she'd get any more sleep now.

As she stood with an absent mind and waited for the kettle to boil, Tommy jumped up from his bed and ran from the room, calling, 'I need a wee.'

She could hear muffled voices in the hallway, and guessed Tommy must be talking with Mo.

A few minutes later he returned, Mo close behind him. 'Morning, love. Tommy said you're making a brew.'

'Yes, sit yourself down,' Sarah said and yawned.

'Looks like that job is wearing you out,' Mo commented.

'No, it's not my job. I just didn't sleep very well. I've been awake for hours.'

'Something on your mind? Or someone?' Mo asked with a knowing smile.

'Well, funny you should mention that. I was thinking of popping up the market later and now that I've managed to buy some, I wondered if you'd do my make-up for me?'

'Sure, no problem. Tell you what, Samuel won't be home until late, so how about I come with you? It'd be nice to put names to the faces of the people you talk about.'

'Are we going to see George today?' Tommy asked. He'd obviously been listening to the conversation, and was now jumping on his bed excitedly.

'Yes, we are,' Sarah told him, 'and what have I told you about breaking that bed?'

'Sorry,' Tommy answered and sat down.

'We can make a day of it,' Sarah said to Mo, 'it'll be fun.'

'Just as long as I don't spend too much money. You know how Sam is.'

'You're doing my make-up so we'll have fish and chips for lunch and it'll be my treat.'

'Yummy,' two voices said in unison, both Mo and Tommy grinning happily.

A few hours later, Mo strode into the market with Sarah, Tommy running a little ahead. She was looking forward to meeting George and checking out Roger. Sarah had told her about George's face, not that it would have shocked her. Things like that didn't bother her. She'd seen the broken bodies and aftermath of many accidents when her oldest brother had been an ambulance driver. It wasn't allowed, but she'd often sneaked a ride with him.

As they walked into the market, it wasn't difficult for Mo to recognise George and she spotted him immediately. It didn't go unnoticed that his eyes lit up as soon as he saw Sarah approaching. 'I see he still fancies you,' she said, and nudged her friend in the ribs.

'Behave yourself, Mo,' Sarah said quietly out of the side of her mouth, 'or there'll be no fish and chips for you later.'

'Hello, George. This is my friend Mo, she lives upstairs from me,' Sarah said.

'Nice to meet you,' George said, though Mo wasn't taking much notice as she was too busy looking past him to see Roger. He was just as good-looking as Sarah had described and she could see why her friend was so besotted with the man. She was admiring his profile as he turned his head and looked straight at her, catching her staring. He eyed her up and down, then flashed her a flirty smile. Mo glanced sideways at Sarah and saw she was occupied with looking at some of George's stock, so returned his smile with equal flirtatiousness. She could tell by the way he was looking at her that he found her attractive, but Mo was used to this. Most men did.

'What do you think of this dress?' Sarah asked.

Mo pulled her eyes away from Roger and looked at the outfit Sarah was holding up. She thought it was hideous and very old-fashioned. 'It's nice. I'm sure it'll really suit you,' she lied.

As Sarah paid for the dress, Mo turned her attention back to Roger and was pleased to see him grab a few apples before making a beeline towards them.

'Hi, Sarah. Are you going to introduce me to your friend?' Roger asked.

Mo noticed George was frowning, and Sarah seemed to get herself in a bit of a tizzy.

'This is Mo,' Tommy answered for her. 'Can I have an apple, please, Roger?'

'Yes, there's one here for you, and one for each of the beautiful ladies.'

Mo thought Roger's voice sounded like smooth, dark velvet, and as she took the apple from him, she offered him a wicked but sly grin. His eyes met hers, but Mo looked away quickly, chastising herself for flirting with him. After all, she was virtually a married woman, and Sarah had first dibs on him.

'I heard that you're working with Lena now?' Roger said, turning to Sarah.

'Er . . . yes,' Sarah replied, her cheeks flushing.

George was looking at Sarah too and though she couldn't fancy him, it annoyed Mo that she wasn't the one getting all the attention. Butting in, she said, 'We're out and about because it's Sarah's day off.'

'What have you got planned then, something nice?' asked Roger.

'Well, I was thinking of suggesting a matinee film, but I've changed my mind. I work at the Grand, see, and it'd be a bit boring for me. Apart from a bit of fish and chips later, we're at a bit of a loose end. Got any good ideas?'

'Saturday is normally our busiest day, but how about

we all go to the funfair later on this evening?' Roger suggested.

'Please, Mum, I've never been to the fair. Please can we go?' Tommy asked, emphasising the 'please'.

Mo would have quite enjoyed squeezing up to Roger on the Jets. The fellas would always sit their girls on the inside of the flying airplane, so when the merry-go-round picked up speed, the men would lean in and squash up against the ladies. She couldn't go out this evening, though, as Samuel would be home. 'I'm sorry, I can't go tonight.'

'That's a shame,' Roger said, 'I quite fancied a ride on the Big Dipper.'

'Me too,' Tommy whined. 'I really wanted to go.'

'There's nothing to stop you taking Sarah and Tommy, eh, George?' Roger said.

'Yes, good idea,' he agreed.

Mo thought it sounded a little like a set-up. It was obvious to her that Roger knew how much George was enamoured with Sarah. Trouble was, Sarah's feelings weren't reciprocated – well, not towards George.

'Oh, Mum, say yes, please say yes!' Tommy begged.

Sarah looked at the boy's eager face and sighed. 'Oh, all right, I suppose so, but I won't be going on that Big Dipper thing, or the Jets. I'll wait down the bottom while you two go on the rides.'

Roger winked at George and then returned to his stall as a queue was beginning to form. Sarah made arrangements to meet George later, and then they left the market to head for Clapham Junction. They walked in silence for a while, but then Mo asked, 'Are you all right, Sarah?'

'Yes, but I was hoping to be going out with Roger tonight, not George.'

'Maybe Roger hasn't asked you for a date 'cos they're friends and he knows that George likes you,' Mo offered in consolation.

'Maybe, I hadn't thought of that. To be honest, I don't really want to go to the fair with George tonight, but I couldn't think of an excuse to get out of it and I didn't want to let Tommy down. I just hope I haven't given him, or Roger, the impression that it's a date.'

'No, I wouldn't have thought so, especially as you'll have Tommy with you.'

They walked to the Junction with a few stops now and then to admire goods displayed in shop windows. It had been a long time since Mo had felt so carefree, and wasn't preoccupied with looking over her shoulder for one of her brothers or her dad.

They bumped into Tommy's friend Larry and his mum, and after several pleas from the boys, Sarah allowed Tommy to go off with them. She watched them leave and then said to Mo, 'Fancy a tea and bun in Arding and Hobbs?'

Mo hesitated, but then said, 'I'm not ready for fish and chips, so yeah, that sounds like a good idea.'

The large department store stood grandly on the corner of the Junction, and apart from the bargain basement, it wasn't a shop Mo would normally frequent. Her only concern was that she knew her brother often visited the store on a Saturday to buy a record from the music department and as they walked towards the entrance, she looked around her nervously.

'Now it's my turn to ask you if you're all right?' Sarah asked.

Mo thought she'd hidden her worry well, but Sarah

must have seen through her act. 'You can read me like a book,' she answered and tutted. 'Yes, I'm OK, just a bit nervous in case I see one of my family. I'm sick of hiding away and being cooped up in that room, especially with Sam working. It's great to be out and about, and I shouldn't let them get to me and spoil my fun.'

'Surely they wouldn't make a scene in front of me and in such a public place?'

'Oh, you don't know my family! It's never bothered them before when they've come into where I've worked. One time, Danny, my middle brother, he turned up at Gilson's factory and literally dragged me out by my hair. I screamed and kicked and punched him, but he wouldn't let me go. Needless to say, I wasn't welcome back after that. Then this other time, I had a job at the fair on the candy floss stall opposite the Big Dipper. I loved that job but it didn't last either, not once my dad got wind of it. He showed up, effing and blinding, and scared all the kids. I couldn't promise he wouldn't do it again, so they let me go. Believe me, I could go on, they're relentless, that's why I get nervous when I'm out.'

'Oh, Mo, I knew you'd had a rotten time of it, but I didn't realise it was that bad. Well, like you say, let's not let them spoil our fun. Fingers crossed we won't see any of them today. If we do, you won't be alone.'

'Thanks, Sarah,' Mo said, though she didn't know how her friend would be able to help against her dad and brothers. She thought it was nice of Sarah to stand by her, but her friend hadn't seen the size of the muscles on her family. Nor had she heard their foul mouths.

'Come on, let's go to the beauty department and you

can help me pick out a new lipstick,' Sarah urged. 'I doubt we'd bump into your dad or brothers in there.'

'OK, but I bloody hate them snooty make-up women. They're probably all posh Chelsea girls who think they're so much better than us.'

'I've never been in there before, but I bet none of them are as pretty as you, Mo.'

'I wouldn't bet on it,' Mo answered, 'you wait 'til you see them. They always look immaculate and have a right air about them.'

Mo and Sarah climbed the red carpet of the impressive sweeping polished wooden staircase, and looked in awe at the fine dresses displayed in the centre.

'Cor, I wish I could have something like that red dress instead of second-hand gear from George's stall,' Sarah whispered.

'I know what you mean, but where would we wear an evening gown like that?'

'Good point. Oh, well, it's nice to look,' Sarah said.

Mo nodded in agreement, but she imagined herself in the designer dresses, riding in a flash sports car with an attractive film star by her side. That was the life she believed she should have been born into. Not this tedious one of poverty and beatings. It's not fair, she thought, trying not to sulk.

As they walked past the cosmetics counters and admired the expensive perfumes, Mo thought Sarah seemed rather animated, like a child at Christmas. She could see her friend was enjoying herself, and couldn't understand why. It wasn't fun to look at things they could never afford, and the women behind the counters made Mo feel inferior. She felt like everything in the store was teasing her, mocking her life and reminding her of all the things she would never have.

'Let's get out of here,' she snapped to Sarah.

She saw the look of surprise on her friend's face, but nonetheless hooked her arm through Sarah's and dragged her quickly back towards the grand carpeted staircase. She had to get out of there and back onto the dirty streets.

'Hey, slow down, Mo. What's wrong?' Sarah asked.

'Nothing. Nothing's wrong. I just don't like it in here,' she answered through gritted teeth.

Just as they began to descend the stairs, Mo stopped in horror as she saw her brother Danny walking up towards them. There was no mistaking him, he had the same red hair as her. 'Quick, run,' Mo said, and pulled Sarah back through the beauty department.

'What's happening? Where are we going?' Sarah asked as she trotted alongside Mo.

'It's my brother! He's on the stairs. Oh, God, I hope he hasn't seen me.'

'What are we going to do? Hide?'

'Yes . . . yes . . . in the ladies' toilets. No – we won't know when he's gone. Bloody hell, let's just get out. This way – quick. We'll use the lift.'

Mo pressed the button to summon the elevator, and was glad to see no one else was waiting. She looked over her shoulder, grateful to see no sign of Danny. He was unlikely to be on this floor, amongst the cosmetics. No, as she'd suspected, he'd be heading for the record department.

The lift stopped and a short, thin man in a smart purple uniform and cap opened the doors. 'Which floor?' he asked politely.

'Ground,' Mo answered quickly.

The lift operator closed the gated door first, then the inner door, and moved the lift down. It wasn't going fast enough for Mo, and she could feel her panic increasing. 'Come on . . . come on . . .' she muttered.

'It's all right, Mo, we'll soon be out and clear of him,' Sarah whispered.

Soon enough, they were on the ground floor, and Mo fled for the exit with Sarah closely following. As she came out onto the street, she turned right and began to run up Lavender Hill.

'Mo, wait . . . you're safe now.'

She heard Sarah speak, but her own heartbeat was pounding so hard it was ringing in her ears. 'Are you sure?' she asked breathlessly.

'Yes, it's fine. There's no one following us. He couldn't have seen you.'

'I'm so sorry, Sarah. I had a feeling I was going to bump into him today. My mum always said I had the gift of foresight, but I never understood what she meant. She told me to always listen to my gut. Now I know what she was on about. I knew it, I bloody knew he'd be in there.' Mo cursed herself for daring to be bold and ignoring her instinct. She wouldn't make that mistake again, but now, though she hated feeling like a prisoner in her own home, there was nothing she wanted more than to get back to her room and wait for Samuel to return from work.

Chapter 24

Sarah could see the lights of the fair ahead. George had picked her and Tommy up in his van, even though she'd insisted they could walk to the park and meet him there. He'd found a convenient place to park, then turned to Sarah. 'Wait there,' he said, and got out of the van.

Sarah sat bemused as George walked around to the passenger side, then opened the door, and with a sweeping gesture of his arm, said, 'Milady . . . If you'd care to join me.'

Sarah climbed out of the van and smiled. She hadn't wanted to come tonight, but already she was enjoying herself and they weren't even at the fair yet.

George opened the back doors and Tommy clambered out happily and exclaimed, 'That was so much fun . . . I've never been in the back of a van before.'

'If you thought that was fun, just wait 'til we get on them rides!' George said.

Tommy squealed and grabbed Sarah's hand as he yanked her towards the bright lights. 'Hurry up, come on, Mum,' he urged.

Sarah was walking as fast as she could and was looking forward to seeing Tommy's face when he would have his first ever ride. She'd never been to the fairground herself, but she wasn't as keen as Tommy. From what she'd seen, most of the attractions looked ever so big and fast. The fair had been built two years before for the Festival of Britain, but it cost sixpence to get in, and Sarah had never had the money. The Pleasure Gardens were free though, and she and Tommy had spent many hours being amazed and amused by the Guinness Clock. It was at least four times as tall as her, and decorated in wide black and white stripes. When it chimed, the clock's performance would take at least four minutes to run through, with funny characters popping up and out of little doorways, and windmills spinning around. It would fascinate Tommy and he would try to guess what was going to happen next, but it always surprised him.

As they approached the fair, Sarah could see the words 'Funfair' in lights over the entrance, and yellow-painted booths. George walked ahead, but Sarah caught him up. 'I hope you don't think you're paying for me and Tommy to get in,' she said.

'Of course I am. What sort of bloke would take a woman and kid out and expect them to fork out for themselves?' George asked, his expression one of hurt, so Sarah grudgingly allowed him to pay.

Once through the booths, she watched as Tommy's eyes widened and could see he wasn't sure where to run to first. 'He's going to have the time of his life. Thanks, George,' she said, though she still would have preferred to pay their own way.

'Follow me,' George said, 'I've been here more times than I've had hot dinners. If we go on the Ferris wheel first, once we're up the top it's so high you can look around and see what you want to go on next. When we've done all the good stuff, I'll take you through the tree walk.'

'Yes!' Tommy agreed eagerly.

Sarah wasn't so keen. Her hands were already feeling clammy at the thought of sitting so high above the ground, and walking through the tree canopies.

'No sweets before the rides though, Tommy. We don't want you chucking up halfway round,' George said with a laugh. 'My mate ate a packet of Spangles before going on the Rotor and threw 'em all back up afterwards.'

'What's the Rotor, George?' Tommy asked.

'It's a big circle thing that you stand in and it spins round so fast that you stick to the wall. It don't 'alf leave you feeling giddy and ill though.'

Sarah pulled a face, and George added, 'But I don't think we'll be going on that ride today.'

A few minutes later, Sarah found herself on top of the Ferris wheel, clinging on to one of the safety bars and barely able to open her eyes.

'Look, Mum, can we go on that?'

Sarah opened one eye to see Tommy pointing towards something on the ground. She felt too afraid to speak. She feared if she opened her mouth, all that would come out would be an ear-piercing scream. Thankfully George intervened.

'Ah, the Jets. You'll love 'em, Tommy. There's a stick you can hold that controls the plane going up or down.'

Once they had disembarked the Ferris wheel, Tommy led the way to the next ride. As they stood in the queue, Sarah felt weak at the knees. 'I can't do it,' she said to George.

'Can't do what?'

'I can't get on that ride. I'm going to sit this one out. I think the horses on the merry-go-round are going to be my limit.'

George chortled. 'You big chicken,' he said. 'Not to worry, Tommy and me will wave at you.'

Feeling relieved at being let off the hook, Sarah stepped out of the queue to look for a good vantage point. If she couldn't enjoy the rides, she could at least watch Tommy appreciating them. She found a place that offered a good view and waited for the ride to start. As it began to spin, she could hear squeals of laughter and a few anxious screams. As the ride began to speed up she felt queasy just looking at it and was glad she'd opted out. Tommy looked delighted when she spotted him and seemed to wave at her as a second thought. She waved back eagerly, but the airplanes were whizzing past so fast that she had trouble keeping her eyes on him. She saw a couple walking towards her, and suddenly, her stomach flipped, only this time it had nothing to do with the rides. Ron Lyons was approaching, presumably with his wife.

Sarah wanted to run and hide, but it was too late, he'd seen her and she noticed his face pale and his smile vanish. She stared at him, transfixed and terrified at what he might do. She felt intimidated, and as he walked past her, he grimaced threateningly. She kept her eyes on him, too afraid to look away, and eventually he walked around a ride and out of sight.

Tommy appeared in front of her. 'Did you see me, Mum? Did you see how high we went?'

'Yes, love,' Sarah answered, but she was looking out for Ron.

'You feeling all right, Sarah? You look a bit peaky,' George asked.

'Er . . . yes, I'm fine, George. Can we go in the Happy House next?' she asked, thinking it would be the ideal place to hide for a while.

'Ow, but that's boring,' Tommy moaned.

'How do you know? You've never been in there,' George said, 'and I think it's only fair that Sarah picks a ride too.'

The Happy House was dark, but had many long mirrors that reflected a distorted image, each mirror giving a different reflection. Tommy ran from one to the other, laughing at himself with an extra-long face and tiny legs, and giggling at another that made him look three feet wide.

'Something happened when me and Tommy was on the Jets, didn't it?' George asked while Tommy was out of earshot.

Sarah sighed. 'Yes, I saw Ron Lyons and he didn't look very happy to see me.'

'Why not? I thought you said he isn't your dad.'

'He denied it, and though I shouldn't tell you this, he . . . he sort of threatened me . . . told me to keep my mouth shut. Oh, George, you should have seen the way he looked at me just now. I grew up with my mother throwing evil eyes at me all the time, but honestly, she never made me feel as scared as Ron just did. There's something about him that frightens the life out of me.'

Sarah stiffened as George put his arm over her shoulder and gave her a quick squeeze. 'Don't worry about him. If he comes near you, I'll look after you, I promise. Now come on, put a smile on your face. We don't want to spoil Tommy's fun.'

She glimpsed herself in one of the mirrors, and thought about her mother. There were many things she hadn't liked about her, the list was endless, but her mother was brave. She'd never let men intimidate her, and for once Sarah wished she had more of her courage. Twice today she'd found herself running and hiding from bullying men, so it was comforting to know George would be there for her.

However, as much as she appreciated his promise, Sarah now wished she had kept her mouth shut. She didn't want George hurt and wasn't sure that, if it came to it, he'd be a match for Ron Lyons.

Chapter 25

It had been over a month since George had seen Sarah at the funfair in Battersea Park. He'd dropped her off that night and had arranged to pick them up the following Saturday to take Tommy on the boating lake, but Sarah had cancelled, owing to Tommy coming down with a nasty cough. She hadn't been to the market since either, and he was worried he'd done or said something to upset her.

His mother came into the kitchen, and George noticed she was still in her dressing gown. 'Ain't you going to work today?' he asked as he looked her up and down. She looked well enough, so he didn't think she was feeling poorly.

'No, George. I'm having meself a bit of a holiday. I've taken the week off so today I'm going to clean out the larder, then get my hair done. Tomorrow, I'm going with Kath to Brighton, and then to the cinema on Wednesday with Joan. Thursday I thought I'd get the train over to Croydon and see your Aunty Min. I'll be stopping over with her but I'll be back in time on Friday to do your tea.'

'Well, well, well, you have got a busy week, but who's looking after the shop?'

'Sarah, of course. She said she could do with the extra hours and she's more than capable.'

George felt his pulse quicken. She'd only be up the road and he could call in to see her under the pretence of checking how she was getting on alone. It was perfect! 'But what about Tommy?' he asked.

'I'm picking him up from school tonight and popping into the hairdresser's on the way home. Mo is going to help out the rest of the week. I think Sarah is going to get her in a bit of shopping to say thank you. She gets a good discount so it'll be worth more than bunging her a few quid.'

'So, is Sarah coming here tonight to pick up Tommy?'

'Yes, love, and I said I'll have some dinner ready for her. I should think she'll be bushed after doing a full day by herself.'

George jumped up from the kitchen chair and planted a big kiss on the top of his mother's head. 'Mum, you're a diamond,' he said, and walked towards the kitchen door.

'Hang on, son, not so fast. Come here and sit down. I want a little chat with you.'

George could see his mother's face was serious, and did as he had been instructed. 'What do you want to talk to me about? You're not ill or nothing, are you?' he asked, concerned.

'No, I'm perfectly well. It's about Sarah . . .'

'What about her? Have I upset her? I ain't seen her in ages. Has she said something to you?'

'Not in so many words, but I think she's keeping her distance 'cos she's worried she might have given you the wrong impression.'

'So, she has said something then?' George asked, beginning to feel irritated with his mother.

'Like I said, not really. I just mentioned that you was fond of her, and well, she said she was fond of you too . . . as a friend.'

George was annoyed with his mum for revealing things like that to Sarah, but pasted a smile on his face. It hurt to hear that she wanted no more than his friendship, but deep down he already knew. 'That's all right with me. Anyway, I reckon she likes Roger.'

'Yeah, I think you're right. When his name came up in conversation her eyes lit up. I didn't say anything to her, but you know my thoughts on that man.'

George did, and again his mother's words felt like a hefty blow. He thought it was probably time to stop lusting after Sarah and chasing a dream that was never going to come true, yet he knew it wouldn't be easy, not when he couldn't stop thinking about her.

Lena was pleased with her cut and set and even happier that she'd got home from the hairdresser's with Tommy before the rain had started. The weather was always a bit iffy in May and she hoped it would brighten up for her trip to Brighton the next day. She ruffled Tommy's hair. The lad had been as good as gold, even though he must have been bored stiff while she'd been sitting under the hairdryer. 'Tommy, go up to George's room and have a look under his bed. He's got an old train set under there, and I'm sure he wouldn't mind you playing with it.'

'Cor, thanks,' Tommy said, then ran from the kitchen and up the stairs.

That'll be the last I see of him 'til teatime, Lena thought, remembering how George would spend hours in his room playing with his trains. She made herself a hot drink, then sat in the front room with her legs up on the sofa. She must have dozed off, but was woken by the sound of the front door closing and George calling out hello. She checked the wooden clock on the mantel. He was early, and she could guess why. It appeared her little chat with him this morning had fallen on deaf ears.

She got up and walked to the hallway as Tommy came flying down the stairs to greet George. The boy was unmistakably taken with him, and Lena thought it was such a shame that Sarah didn't feel the same. She thought he'd be a smashing stepdad and a doting husband too, but if Sarah couldn't see past his scars to see that, then the girl was stupid.

'You're home early, love.'

'Yeah, I thought you might want a hand with this little monster,' George said and scooped Tommy up from the stairs.

'Oh, he's no trouble,' Lena said, pinching the end of Tommy's nose. She pretended to accept George's reason for his early arrival, but she could see straight through him and knew he'd come home to spruce himself up for Sarah. She'd have loved to see her son happy with a woman, and thought it such a shame that he was wasting his time on a girl who had no interest in him. She was blinded by Roger and his looks, which was a crying shame.

Later that evening, as Sarah walked through her front door, Mo appeared at the top of the stairs. 'The kettle's on if you fancy a cuppa?'

'Thanks, Mo, but I'm done in. I just want to get indoors and lie on my bed with a good book.' Sarah knew Mo was lonely as Samuel was working long hours, but she was so tired, she doubted she'd be good company.

'Oh, OK. Have you both eaten? I could do you some sandwiches and pop them down?'

'We've just had our tea at Lena's, but thanks again. I'll see you bright and early in the morning with Tommy. I warn you, he's very energetic and excitable before school.'

'He'll behave himself for his Aunty Mo, ain't that right, Tommy?'

Tommy nodded but was unusually subdued. Sarah wondered if he was just tired and hoped he wasn't coming down with a bad chest again. 'Night, Mo,' Sarah called as she walked through to her room.

When Sarah changed into her night clothes, she saw that Tommy was sitting very quietly on the edge of his bed. In fact, when she thought about it, she realised he'd been behaving out of character all evening. She sat on the bed next to him, then lowered her head to look at his face. 'You all right, Tommy?'

Tommy nodded but Sarah wasn't convinced. 'You know you can talk to me about anything that's bothering you?'

Tommy nodded again and glanced sideways at her. 'It's . . . I don't understand. George said he sold all the treasure we found, but he lied and you told me lying is naughty.'

'What on earth makes you think George has lied?'

'I saw the stuff in a box in his wardrobe.'

'Are you sure?'

'Yes, Mum, honest, it was all there. The bracelet, clock and ring.'

'What was you doing in George's wardrobe?'

'I was just playing. Lena said I could play with his train set. Am I in trouble?'

185

'No, you're not in trouble, but I know a man who is.'

Sarah settled Tommy down and got him ready for bed, and as she tucked him in, said, 'What you saw in George's wardrobe . . . it'll be our secret, OK?'

'OK,' Tommy replied, then rolled over to sleep.

Sarah climbed into bed, and though she felt exhausted, her mind raced. It made no sense. Why would George say he'd sold the jewellery if he hadn't? There was only one way to find out. She'd confront him tomorrow after work.

Chapter 26

The next morning, George was whistling a happy tune and found himself once again thinking about Sarah. She had looked beautiful last night and they'd had a right laugh. Sarah told him about Mrs Coombs coming into the shop and asking if she had any sponge fingers. They had all roared when Sarah told them she'd squeezed each of her fingers and said to Mrs Coombs, 'No, they're all real.'

He smiled again at the memory. As much as he tried to dismiss thoughts of Sarah, he couldn't. He thought she was fabulous – beautiful, clever and funny. Everything a man would want in a woman.

'You've seen Sarah,' called Roger from his stall, 'that's the reason you're whistling that bloody tune like one of the seven dwarfs – "Whistle While You Work".'

'Yep! She came round last night,' George answered, then carried on whistling, and ignored Roger pulling faces at him.

Hours passed, and George was becoming restless. Tuesdays were always a bit quiet in the market, so he decided to pack up early, eager to call into the shop to see Sarah.

'You off, mate?' Roger asked.

'Yeah, things to do, places to be and people to see,' George said.

'You mean you're off to see Sarah. Good luck, mate.'

'Cheers,' George called, but he knew it would take more than luck for Sarah to fall for him.

A while later, George pulled up outside the corner shop and took a few deep breaths to calm himself. Then he walked in with his stomach churning. Sarah was stacking some shelves, but when she heard the bell above the door ring, she spun around and looked at George. He saw her smile turn into a frown then watched her stomp across the shop and stand behind the counter with her hands placed on top. 'What a coincidence,' she said with a sarcastic tone, 'I was going to come to see you later, but you've saved me the bother.'

'Oh, what was you coming to see me about?' George asked, perplexed.

'Turn that sign round to "closed". I don't want anyone hearing this.'

George did as he was told, but couldn't work out why she sounded so angry with him.

'Would you like to explain to me how Tommy found the bracelet, watch and ring that you told me you'd sold?'

George could feel himself instantly deflate, and struggled to find an answer.

'Well?' Sarah pushed.

He chewed on the side of his mouth, reluctant to tell her the truth, but the mood she was in, he felt he had no other options. 'I couldn't sell them, Sarah, not round here. They're too fancy, so I bought them and kept them.'

'Why would you do that? And why lie to me about it?'

'I don't know . . . you seemed to be struggling, and I wanted to help you out. I thought I was doing you a favour.'

'So, you thought I was a charity case.'

'Yes . . . no . . . I . . .' George spluttered.

'You gave me a lot of money for those pieces, and seeing the state I was in, more than you needed to.'

George was beginning to feel exasperated. He wasn't very good at being put on the spot, and blurted out, 'Isn't it obvious why, Sarah? I'm in love with you. I have been since I first set eyes on you, sat on the kerb like a little lost stray.'

Sarah bit her lower lip for a moment, but then said, 'I'm sorry, George, but I can't return your feelings and though I'm grateful that you helped me out, you shouldn't have lied to me. When I told you about the jewellery being stolen and that I wanted to give it back, you said I couldn't because other than the ring it had been sold. I've not been able to see Jenny since – I'd never be able to look her in the eye – and all this time you had the jewellery stashed away.'

'I thought I was doing the right thing. I was trying to protect you.'

'Protect me! How?' Sarah asked, her voice high.

'I was worried that you'd be implicated in the robberies, so I thought if I hid the stuff away, the Old Bill could never connect you to it.'

'I need a minute to think,' Sarah said and sat on a stool behind the counter, her shoulders drooping. 'Go and put the kettle on.'

George did as instructed. He stood in silence, waiting

for the kettle to boil, but his mind was in turmoil. He'd really upset her. Tentatively, he took two cups of tea through to the shop, and placed one on the counter close to Sarah. 'I'm sorry. I've really messed up, haven't I?'

'Yes, you have, but I realise you had good intentions. I'm just disappointed that you let me so feel awful about my friend, when really you could have helped. Still, at the end of the day you've paid for the stuff, so I suppose it's yours to do as you please with, but if it was me . . .'

'What are you getting at, Sarah? Are you implying that I should give all the jewellery back?'

'Yes, of course you should. You know it's stolen and you know who from. I do realise it would leave you significantly out of pocket, but it would be the right thing to do.'

George rolled his eyes. He knew she was right, and it wasn't as if he would ever do anything with the items. They'd probably be sitting in the bottom of his wardrobe for years. If it got Sarah back on side, it was worth the loss of a few bob.

Sarah watched as George left the shop without saying another word. She was still reeling, still unable to believe that he'd kept the jewellery. She turned the sign to 'open' again and managed to carry on working, but between customers her mind kept going back to the jewellery.

At closing time, George came into the shop again. 'Here, have it back,' he said, handing her the jewellery wrapped in one of his large handkerchiefs.

'Oh, George, thank you,' Sarah said, 'I'll give—'

George turned abruptly and walked out, leaving her unfinished sentence hanging in the air. Sarah quickly locked up then hurried home, where she tucked the still wrapped jewellery in a drawer under her underwear. She didn't feel relaxed about having the items in her home, but it would only be until Saturday when she had a day off and could go to see Jenny. She was grateful to George for returning them, and was determined that one day, somehow, she would pay him back the money he had paid her for them.

Tommy was coughing again. The thick pea-soupers that plagued London didn't help his chest, and though she was constantly scrubbing the walls, she thought the mould added to the problem. Now that she was earning money regularly, Sarah had thought about moving into something nicer, but she enjoyed sharing the house with Mo and Samuel. Tommy's best friend lived three doors down and she didn't think he'd want to leave either, so though the room wasn't ideal, she'd stay put, knowing that at least with the cheap rent she'd be able to save a bit each week to pay George back.

Later that evening, with Tommy tucked up in bed, Sarah picked up her book from the coffee table. She was going to read for half an hour before going to bed herself, but her eyes were tired and she was having difficulty focusing on the small print in the dim light of her table lamp. The street outside was quiet, and she couldn't hear any noise from her upstairs neighbours. Then her peace was suddenly disturbed when the window shattered, and something landed on the floor with a loud thump.

Sarah stifled a scream and jumped from her chair. She looked at the shattered window, then her eyes followed the broken glass to a large brick.

'You fucking slag,' she heard a man's voice shout from outside. She wanted to run to the window to see who had thrown the brick, but fear stopped her, and instead she checked on Tommy. He had stirred, but she was relieved to see him still asleep. Her heart was in her mouth when she heard a bang on her door and froze on the spot, unable to move.

'Sarah, it's me,' she heard Mo say, and felt instant relief when she realised it wasn't the man from outside. She dashed to the door, grateful to see her friend.

Mo walked in and looked stunned at the scene. 'I'm so sorry, Sarah, it was my brother. I heard his voice. This was obviously meant for me. Are you both all right?'

Sarah was shaking and on the verge of tears. It had all happened so quickly and had been a shock. 'Yes . . . Tommy slept through it. Bloody hell, it made me jump though. I can still feel my heart pounding.'

Samuel came into the room panting for breath and said, 'I gave chase but I lost him down one of the alleys. Are you all right, Sarah?'

'Yes, I'm fine, just a bit shaken up, but nothing to worry about.'

'I'll get that window boarded up for tonight, then I'll make sure it's fixed before Mr Terence comes knocking. Mo, get a brush and sweep up the broken glass,' Samuel instructed.

'It's all right, I'll clean it up,' Sarah said.

'We've got to get out of here,' Mo said pleadingly to Samuel. 'They're never going to leave us in peace, can't you see?'

Samuel walked across the room and took Mo into his arms. 'It's OK, darling,' he soothed.

'But it isn't! What if it had been worse and they'd put petrol through the letterbox or something? It's not fair on Sarah and Tommy. My family are putting them at risk too. Please, Sam, we've got to move away,' Mo said, beginning to cry.

'Sarah, I think you should call the local police,' Samuel said over Mo's shoulder.

Sarah stared wide-eyed at Samuel. She had seen the threatening look Ron Lyons had given her, and the last thing she wanted was for him to find out where she lived. 'No, it's fine. I doubt they'd do much anyway. You know what they're like, they shy away from getting involved in family stuff.'

Mo sniffed and pulled away from Samuel. Black blobs of mascara were smudged on her face. 'She's right, the police have never bothered to help me before. I was black and blue from a beating my dad gave me, but once I told them who did it, they turned a blind eye.'

'They can't get away with this. I won't allow it. I'll go and sort them out myself,' Samuel ground out, his nostrils flaring and his eyes wild with anger.

'Please don't go round there, Sam, it'll only make matters worse and there's more of them than there are of you. I couldn't stand the thought of you getting hurt,' Mo pleaded. 'Tell him, Sarah. I'm right, ain't I?'

'I'm afraid to say I think she is, Sam. I wouldn't be surprised if this was done to goad you. They'll probably be waiting for you, so don't play into their hands. I'd stay well clear if I was you.'

Samuel heaved his shoulders. 'I refuse to be chased out of my own home by those thugs. We're not budging, Mo, and that's an end to any more discussions about it.'

Tommy stirred again, and began to slowly wake up. 'What's going on?' he asked in a drawl.

'Nothing love, go back to sleep,' Sarah said, then turned to Samuel and, speaking softly, said, 'Don't worry about the window tonight. It isn't cold and I was going to open it anyway to get a bit of fresh air, so let's all try and get some rest now, eh?'

Mo gave Sarah a small hug, then followed Samuel back upstairs. Sarah swept up the glass, and moved the brick so it was on the floor next to her bed before climbing in. She could feel the cool breeze coming through the broken window. It wasn't so bad, but what Mo had said about petrol had scared her. A brick through the window was bad enough, but the thought of them setting fire to the building was terrifying.

Sarah turned over and pulled the blankets up to her chin. Maybe she should think about moving after all.

Chapter 27

Sarah hadn't had a chance to thank George for returning the jewellery, so the next day she went to see him. She couldn't love him, but she was fond of him and didn't want to lose their friendship. It had mended bridges and three days later, on a Saturday, Tommy was at Larry's little brother's birthday party. Mo was spending some time with Samuel after she'd managed to persuade him to take a weekend off. That suited Sarah well as she didn't have to fib to anyone about what she was doing. She had thought about telling Mo her plans, but it was none of her business, and she was sure her friend would try and talk her out of it. As much as she liked the woman, she knew Mo would try to convince her that she was mad to return the jewels, and she had a niggling feeling that Mo wasn't entirely an honest person.

She stood staring up the concrete stairs that were so familiar to her. It felt strange to be back at her old block of flats, but with her mother not there. A couple of young boys came running down, and their laughter echoed through the stairwell. She remembered how she'd heard her mother's scream echoing the day Tommy had been born.

She began the arduous climb to the third floor, and hoped Jenny would be home. The ring, watch and bracelet, still wrapped, were tucked in the bottom of her handbag. She hadn't got used to carrying a handbag around with her, but Lena had encouraged her, saying she was a working woman now and should look like one.

Sarah fretfully knocked on Jenny's door, and smiled warmly at her old friend when she answered it.

'Sarah! What a lovely surprise. Come in,' Jenny offered and pulled the door open wider.

'Actually, I need to speak to you in private.'

'That's all right, no one's home.'

Sarah entered the flat and noticed it was much quieter than normal.

'Mum's taken all the kids over to my cousins for the day and Dad's at work. Do you want something to drink? Tea, orange squash?'

'Squash, thanks.'

'So what brings you here?' Jenny asked.

'It's a long story and I'm not sure where to begin.'

'Tell you what, let's take the drinks through to the front room then we can get comfy on the sofa and you can tell me all about it.'

Sarah arranged herself in the cosy front room and kept her handbag close by her side. 'You're looking really well,' she said, admiring Jenny's long blonde waves.

'That's 'cos I ain't getting up at the crack of dawn any more to go and clean up for Mrs Alderton-Steele. I've got a job round the corner as a trainee seamstress. The pay is crap, the hours are long and it's boring, but my mum said it's good to learn a skill so you don't have to rely on your husband for every penny.'

'Husband? Surely you're not getting married.'

'No, of course not,' Jenny said, and giggled. 'She's just talking about my future. Mind you, 'cos I work such long hours I think she misses me helping out here with the little 'uns, especially now she's got another bun in the oven. What about you? You're looking very grown up.'

'I'm working in a grocery shop up near the High Street. I'm really enjoying it. It's good your learning a trade, but what happened with Mrs Alderton-Steele?'

'She sacked me, just as I thought she would. She wouldn't believe it wasn't me who nicked her precious jewellery and, the worst of it, she called the cops on me. You should have seen the smug look on Godfrey's face when they marched me off. The bastard. I wanted to swipe the smile off his face. I didn't need to though. The police came here and searched the place but of course they didn't find anything so no charges were brought.'

'Blimey, Jenny, I'm so sorry you had to go through that!'

'It's not so bad, and I feel sorry for the poor girl who's got my job now. I heard through another mate of mine that Godfrey is getting his leg over whenever it suits him, and there's nothing the girl can do about it 'cos he's blackmailing her. He reckons he can prove she's nicked stuff and threatened her with prison. I'm in half a mind to go round there and tell the poor mite the truth, but, well, it ain't really any of my business any more.'

'Blinking 'eck, he sounds like a right horrible git.'

'He is, and I'd love to get my own back on him, but what chance have the likes of us got against the toffs?'

'Well, Jenny, as long as you don't ask me any questions, I might be able to help you to get your revenge.'

'Oh, yeah? How?' Jenny asked, looking intrigued.

Sarah reached into her handbag and pulled out the wrapped package. She placed it on her lap, and gently unfolded the handkerchief to reveal the missing jewellery.

'Oh, for the love of God, where on earth did you get that lot from?'

'I found them down on the river banks, nearly buried in mud, so I reckon that Godfrey was pinching the stuff then throwing it over the bridge.'

'Sarah, you're a genius. I always said you was clever. Are you thinking of giving it to me to take back?'

'Yes, well, sort of,' Sarah answered.

'But how can I get them back to Mrs Alderton-Steele without her thinking I nicked them in the first place?'

'Don't worry, I've got a plan. I just need you to give me a good description of Godfrey and, if this works, I promise you he's going to get his comeuppance,' Sarah said, going on to tell Jenny what she had in mind.

An hour later, Sarah was knocking on the door of a terraced house not far from her own. A timid-looking young woman poked her head around. 'Yeah?' she said.

'Hello, I'm Sarah. Are you Doreen?'

'Yes.'

'Doreen, do you mind if we have a little chat? I believe you work for Mrs Alderton-Steele and you're having a bit of bother with her son Godfrey?'

'I don't want to talk about it,' Doreen said, and looked scared as she went to close the door in Sarah's face.

'Wait,' Sarah said, and pushed against the door, 'I'm here to help you.'

'You can't help me, nobody can,' Doreen said.

'Trust me, I really can,' Sarah insisted, 'but you've got to let me in and talk to you first.'

Doreen slowly opened the door, and Sarah followed her up the hallway and into the kitchen. A baby was sleeping in what looked like a drawer placed on top of the kitchen table, and the sink was overflowing with dirty dishes. Wet washing was hanging on the back of the door and on a line which stretched across the room. Sarah's eyes settled on several empty beer bottles, and she thought of her mum.

'They ain't mine, it's my husband who likes a drink. Keep your voice down, he's passed out in the front room,' Doreen said, pulling her cardigan closer around herself.

'The reason I'm here is to get Godfrey back for all the wrongs he's done. My friend used to do your job at Mrs Alderton-Steele's, but she lost it after Godfrey pinched some jewellery and made sure she got the blame. They even had the police on her, but as she hadn't stolen it they obviously couldn't prove anything. Anyhow, I know Godfrey is giving you a bit of a hard time, and if you help me, we can stop him.'

'I can't afford to lose my job. Look around you. My husband drinks more than he earns, and my milk's dried up so I can barely afford to feed this little 'un. I know there's lots more jobs out there, but it ain't easy to find one when you've got a baby. The cook at Mrs Alderton-Steele's is my cousin and she lets me leave Joseph with her in the kitchen.'

'You won't lose your job. I just need you to tell a little white lie for me. I promise you, your job will be fine, and it'll put a stop to Godfrey.'

'I can't risk it. I hate him . . . hate what he's doing to me, but what choice do I have? He said if I don't do what he says, he'll have me arrested. I can't go to prison. Who'd look after Joseph?'

'It won't come to that,' Sarah said and as she had with Jenny, she laid out her plan.

'Yeah, yeah, that'd work,' Doreen said when Sarah had finished speaking, and at last she smiled. 'All right. I'll do it.'

Sarah was glad to be back outside in the fresh air. Doreen's house had been stuffy, and felt so depressing. It'd reminded her of where she grew up, and though she could see Doreen was unhappy but doing her best, she couldn't help feeling sorry for Joseph as she knew what it was like to grow up with a drunk.

She was pleased that Doreen had agreed to go along with her plan. She had felt so guilty for not speaking up sooner, but now she could help both Jenny and Doreen to get their revenge.

Mo rested the back of her hand on Tommy's forehead again. He didn't feel any hotter than the last time she'd checked him, but he looked deathly pale. 'So much for spending a nice weekend with you,' Mo said to Samuel.

'The boy can't help being unwell, and Sarah wasn't to know he was going to be taken ill at that birthday party. Are you sure we shouldn't call the doctor?'

'No, I think we should wait for Sarah to come home,' Mo replied as she walked across from her bed to look out of the window impatiently. Bloody kids and their diseases, she thought, another reason for not wanting any. 'If we're stuck indoors with a sick child, we may as well make the most of it. Do you want to pop out to the offie and pick us up a bottle of something?'

'I don't think we should be drinking with Tommy poorly in our bed. Once Sarah gets home, then I'll take you out somewhere nice.'

'Please, Sam, it's not often we get any time together or have a drink, and she could be hours yet. Come on, let's have some fun for a change,' Mo urged, and flattered her eyelashes at her man.

'OK, OK, you know I can't resist those eyes,' Samuel said, kissing Mo on the cheek. 'I'll be back soon.'

Samuel had been gone for about half an hour when Mo saw Sarah walking down the road. She went out to the landing and when Sarah came in she called out to her over the banisters. 'Sarah, come up here. Tommy's not well and I've got him in my bed.'

Sarah looked panicked as she ran up the stairs, so Mo said reassuringly, 'Don't worry, he's not too bad. It's just his chest playing up again. I reckon all the coughing has worn him out.'

'I'm so sorry to have ruined your day,' Sarah said after checking on Tommy. 'Where's Sam?'

'I sent him to pick up a bottle. In fact, he should be back by now,' Mo replied, and began to worry what was taking him so long.

'Maybe he stopped to have a drink. After all, I doubt he was too happy about minding a poorly child.'

'Maybe, but he doesn't normally like to drink in our local. He said he feels a bad atmosphere in there. Anyhow, he wasn't bothered about looking after Tommy.'

'He's a nice bloke.'

'Yeah, I know,' Mo agreed, but suddenly tensed. 'Sarah,

I know this sounds silly, but I've got one of those strange feelings again.' Mo could feel her stomach churning, and her instincts were telling her that something was wrong.

'What, like you had when we bumped into your brother?'

'Yes, exactly like that,' Mo said, and looked out of the window, tapping her foot. 'Panic over, here he comes,' she added with relief.

'I'll take Tommy downstairs. Thanks ever so much for looking after him,' Sarah said.

'Wrap him in the blanket. You can give it back to me later.'

Sarah smiled her thanks and as she was scooping the child from the bed, Samuel walked into the room.

Mo gasped. 'What on earth happened to you?'

'I . . . er . . . tripped on the kerb and fell over.'

'I'm not bloody stupid, Sam. I've seen enough fights in my life to know when someone's been in one, so what really happened?' Mo asked as she rushed over to Samuel and reached up to touch a cut above his eyebrow. She then took his hands and examined his swollen knuckles.

'I got jumped, nothing to worry about, just a couple of bumps and bruises,' Samuel said, but Mo could tell he was trying to fob her off.

'I know when you're lying to me, Sam. It was my dad or one of my brothers that did this to you, wasn't it?'

Samuel hung his head.

'I knew it! I said to Sarah I had a bad feeling. For Christ's sake, can't we even leave this dump for half an hour without you getting attacked?'

Samuel placed his arms around her. 'It's all right,' he said in a soft voice, 'It's not what you think.'

'Yes, it is. I hate them, all of them, and I wish they were dead! Who was it? Danny?'

'Yes, but he looks a lot worse than I do,' Samuel answered.

'What do you mean? You beat him up?' Mo asked. Her brother was one of the hardest blokes she knew, and she didn't believe that Samuel would be a match for him. She thought her man was more of a lover than a fighter.

'I'm sorry, Mo. I know you didn't want me causing trouble, but I saw him coming out of the pub and I just saw red.'

'Are you telling me that you attacked him?'

'Yes, I got the first punch in.'

Mo turned to look at Sarah to see she had placed Tommy back on the bed and was now sitting beside him, her mouth agape. She looked as surprised as Mo felt.

'Blimey, Sam, you must be mad! From what Mo has told me, Danny is a nutter and he could have battered you.'

'He's not so tough,' Samuel said with a shrug and a smile.

'What happened then?' Mo asked, intrigued.

'He saw me walking towards him and had an ugly sneer on his face. I think he thought I'd turn away, but I've had enough of your lot intimidating us, so I carried on towards him. He started telling me I should go back to my own country, and the next thing I knew, I had punched him. He looked so shocked, especially when he noticed his nose was bleeding. Before he had a chance to react, I punched him again . . . and again. I'm not sure how many blows I landed, but two men grabbed me and pulled me off him. There was a bit of a scuffle and that's how my face got hurt. It wasn't your brother that caused it because by then he was lying on the pub doorstep in a bit of a mess. He was still lying there when I left.'

'Oh, Sam, I love you,' Mo said, and threw her arms around his waist, thrilled that her man had overpowered her brother.

Sarah brought her down to earth when she said, 'If Danny is in a bad way, there might be repercussions from this, Sam. What if the police come looking for you?'

'Mo's family won't go to the police. They prefer to keep things in house, but I doubt we'll see Danny again. Men like him are nothing more than bullies, and now I've shown him we can't be terrorised any more.'

Mo pulled away from Samuel and went to the window. She scanned the street, suddenly panicking, but was momentarily calmed to see only children playing outside. 'I wouldn't bet on that. Danny won't let you get away with this. He'll be back, and he won't be alone. I know my family, they'll all be round here soon, mob-handed, vying for your blood, and mine too. This isn't going to stop a thing. It's just going to make it get a lot worse.'

'Let them come,' Samuel said boldly. 'I've told you, I won't be chased from my own home.'

'Don't be so stupid and bloody stubborn, Sam. I'm telling you, they'll be coming, and soon! We've got to get out of here, and you too, Sarah.'

Thankfully, Sarah hurriedly picked Tommy up and left, saying she'd pack a few things. Mo hoped Samuel would listen to her too. Though she admired his courage, she feared for their lives.

Chapter 28

It would always brighten George's day when he saw Sarah walking through the market, and today was no exception, though he could see she wasn't looking her usual bubbly self and was lugging a large, heavy bag. She'd forgiven his lies about selling the jewellery and they were once again firm friends, though he still cringed when he thought about his announcement of his love for her.

'Hello, Sarah, Tommy,' George said, then noticed how pale Tommy looked. 'Are you all right, little man?'

'Hi, George. He's got a nasty cough again and should be in bed, but we've got a bit of a problem,' Sarah said.

'I'm sorry to hear that. Anything I can help with?'

'As it happens, I hate to ask, but I really need a big favour.'

'You know me, Sarah. If I can help, I will,' George answered and then listened intently as she explained the situation with Mo's family.

'So,' she continued, 'we need somewhere to stay for a while until it's safe to go back or I find somewhere else to live. I would have gone straight round to your mum's and asked her, but I know she was going out.'

'Yeah, she told me about the shop being closed for a

205

bit of a refit. She's gone up town with Joan, but I know I can speak for her when I say she'd be happy to have you and Tommy come and stay. We can't have you two put at risk like that. Mo's lot sound like a right lovely bunch,' George said with a note of sarcasm.

'Thanks, George, you're a life-saver,' Sarah said, and seemed to cheer up.

George fished in his pocket for his front-door key, and handed it to Sarah. 'Here, take this and let yourself in. Put Tommy in my bed. You both can share it and I'll kip on the sofa. There's some cough syrup in one of the kitchen cupboards. Get some down the boy's neck – he won't like it but it'll make him feel better. My mum swears by the stuff. Have a root around for a bottle that says Pulmo Bailly.'

'Thanks, George, but I don't want to put you out. You can't sleep on the sofa,' Sarah protested as she took the key.

'You're not putting me out. I don't mind where I get my head down, and I ain't arguing with you about it. Anyhow, when my mum gets home, she'll throw me out of my room and put you in there, and I bet you won't argue with her,' George said with a laugh.

'You're probably right,' Sarah agreed. 'I'll go to yours now and get Tommy into bed before he drops where he's standing. I'll see you later when you get home.'

George noticed his van was boxed in and didn't recognise the vehicle in the way. 'Tommy looks really rough, so if you hold on a minute I can run you both back. Some blinkin' idiot has gone and parked where they shouldn't.'

'Thanks, but your house isn't far from here and it'll

probably be quicker if I walk. Don't worry, Tommy will be fine.'

George watched in admiration as Sarah walked away with Tommy. Her coat was open and he could see that the dress she was wearing came from his stall. Her hair was pulled into a ponytail that swung from side to side as she walked. As always, he thought she looked stunning. As she disappeared, though he wasn't happy about her not feeling safe in her own home, he couldn't help but be overjoyed at the thought of her staying in his house. He'd also noticed that she hadn't once looked towards Roger's stall, which added to his joy.

Tommy was tucked in George's bed, and was sleeping soundly after she'd given him a couple of spoonfuls of the cough syrup. He'd protested and baulked at the taste, but it had seemed to ease his coughing. She sat at the kitchen table and sipped a cup of hot tea. What a day, she thought to herself, feeling worn out.

Sarah rested her elbow on the table and with her chin in her hand, she wondered when it would be safe to return home, if only to collect the rest of their belongings. Samuel had yielded to Mo's pleas about going into hiding for a while, and they had left to go and stay in a hotel. Samuel hadn't been keen on breaking into their savings to pay for it, and had insisted they would return home in a few days. He'd refused to change his mind about moving to a new house, and though Sarah could see his point, thinking his stance was both brave and admirable, she had Tommy to think about. His well-being had to come first. She wasn't sure she'd still feel safe living in the house; after all, she'd already had a brick thrown through the window.

It wouldn't be easy to find new accommodation. With buying things for their room, along with food and clothes, she hadn't had the chance to save any money yet. She'd need enough to pay more than a week or two's rent in advance, and many landlords were reluctant to accept a single mother, though she was working now and felt sure Lena would provide her with a good reference.

She leaned back in the chair, deep in her thoughts. She would never have expected to find herself being labelled an unmarried or single mother, but with Tommy now calling her Mum, no one would believe he was her brother. She was becoming accustomed to receiving disapproving looks from strangers, but didn't mind. Stuff what other people think, she thought to herself, and hoped Tommy would soon be on the mend.

Lena arrived home to hear George laughing heartily and when she walked into the kitchen, she was surprised to see him and Sarah sitting at the kitchen table tucking into the pie and mashed potatoes she'd prepared earlier.

'Hello, Mum. Hope you don't mind us starting dinner before you, but I was starving.'

'You get stuck in. I've already had something to eat with Joan.'

'Mum, I hope you don't mind, but I've told Sarah that she and Tommy can stay with us for a while. She's had a bit of bother at home and it's too dangerous for her to be there. I've said they can have my bed and I'll take the sofa.'

Surprised, Lena pulled out a kitchen chair and sat next to George, facing Sarah. Her feet were aching after a long day window-shopping. She took the knitted cosy off the teapot and looked inside, glad to find it half full and hot. 'I don't mind at all, but what's so dangerous at home?' she asked, concerned about what Sarah might have got herself involved in.

Sarah reiterated the story she'd told George earlier, and Lena was satisfied that the girl was innocently caught up in something that she hadn't brought on herself. From what she'd heard, Lena didn't think Mo's family would come around looking for Sarah, and she was happy to allow them to stay for as long as they needed, especially as Tommy was under the weather again.

Lena poured herself a cup of tea, and quietly watched her son and Sarah. They seemed so relaxed together, and she could see that George looked happy. He was a hard worker and caring too, but Sarah only saw him as a friend. It was a shame, as she quite liked the idea of having Sarah as a daughter-in-law. It was all very well them playing happily families, but she knew, with Sarah living under her roof, her son's hopes would be raised again, and now she began to regret agreeing to let her stay. She had a dreadful feeling it would all end in tears.

Chapter 29

Sarah had been at George's for a few weeks, and had enjoyed every minute. It felt comforting to be in a family environment, and Tommy loved having George as a father figure to look up to. She was reluctant to leave, but knew that if she stayed any longer, she'd outstay her welcome. Lena refused to take any keep from her, so she'd managed to save a bit of money, and had viewed a couple of rooms, none she'd thought suitable. With nothing else on offer locally, she decided to bite the bullet and see if it was safe to return home.

It was Monday, 2 June, and a glorious Spring Bank Holiday morning. Sarah was sat in the front room with George and Lena as Tommy played upstairs with George's trains. Both the shop and the market were closed, and Tommy was on school half-term break. He had recovered well from his chest infection after Lena had shown Sarah how to put his head over a bowl of steaming hot water. She'd said it would open up his tubes, and it had appeared to work. In fact, Lena had offered lots of motherly tips, and taught her many useful things that she'd never learned from her own mother, including how to sew and knit. She didn't feel very accomplished with the knitting and kept dropping stitches, but Lena had encouraged her and told her she'd improve with practice.

'It's such a lovely day, how about I take us all out? We could go to the ponds on Wandsworth Common and feed the ducks. It'd make a nice change from Battersea Park,' George suggested.

'I've already told Joan that I'd go round to hers for lunch today. She gets lonely since her Pete passed away and welcomes the company. You three go, though, I'm sure you'll have a smashing time in this sunshine,' Lena said.

Sarah liked the idea, but thought now was a good time to mention leaving. 'Actually, George, I was thinking of going home today.'

'But you don't know if it's safe yet,' George protested.

'I never will know if I don't go and find out. I would have thought if Mo's family were out to get Samuel, they would have been and gone by now.'

'I'm not sure I like the idea of you waltzing back in there just yet. I think you'd be better off staying a while longer. You know you're more than welcome, ain't that right, Mum?'

'Yes, but if Sarah feels she needs to go home, then why don't you run her over there and check out the place first? I can take Tommy to Joan's with me and at least that way he'll be out of harm's way,' Lena suggested.

Sarah smiled thankfully. 'If you wouldn't mind, that would be great.'

'All right,' George said firmly, 'but if we get there and there's any doubt, you're coming straight back here with me.'

Sarah agreed and went upstairs to kiss Tommy goodbye,

warning him to behave himself with Lena. She quickly grabbed a comb from her handbag and ran it through her hair. As she placed it back inside her bag, she saw the handkerchief full of jewellery, and was reminded of her promise to Jenny and Doreen to get payback on Godfrey. Her plan to visit Mrs Alderton-Steele had been put on hold while she'd been staying at George's, but she'd make it a priority once she was back at home.

George pulled up outside Sarah's house, and immediately noticed the front door had been repaired in a makeshift fashion. He assumed it had been kicked in. 'Are you sure about this, Sarah?'

'I'm as sure as I'll ever be,' she replied, drawing in a long breath.

George climbed out of the van first and walked in front of Sarah. 'Looks like this door's had a bit of a bash,' he commented. 'Give me your keys.'

Sarah handed them to him and he slowly opened the door to step inside, saying over his shoulder, 'Wait there a minute.'

He walked across to Sarah's room and saw black scuff marks on her door, probably from heavy boots, but when he went to unlock it, the key wouldn't fit. 'Are you sure this is the right key?' he called.

Sarah walked into the hallway and answered, 'Definitely.'

George fiddled some more with the lock, but it wouldn't open.

'Sarah, you're back!' Mo called from the top of the stairs. 'Hang on a tick. Sam changed the lock so I'll get the new key,' she said before running back into her room.

'That explains it,' George said.

Mo quickly returned and came running down the stairs. 'Hello, George,' she said cheerily and handed him the new key.

'I take it your brother's been here then?' George asked as he opened the door.

'Go inside and I'll tell you all about it,' Mo said, 'but first, if you put the kettle on the gas to boil, I'll pop upstairs and bring you some sugar and milk for a cup of tea. I won't be two ticks.'

Sarah looked around her room and was pleasantly surprised to see everything looked intact, in fact, tidier than she'd left it. Even the window pane had been replaced, which she hadn't noticed when outside. She walked over to the stove, picked up the kettle and filled it with water from the single tap over the sink.

'Are you OK?' George asked.

'Yes, I'm pleased to see my place hasn't been damaged.'

Mo came back into the room carrying a small tray. 'Well, as you could probably see from the front door, they came, but I'm hoping that'll be the last we see of them.'

Once the tea was made and they'd all sat down, Mo continued with her account of what had occurred. 'We stayed in a hotel for a couple of nights, but you know what my Sam is like about spending money, so we came home. It was obvious they'd already been 'cos the front door was smashed in. Your door had been forced open as well, but it seems they didn't do any damage in here. Shame I can't say the same for upstairs.'

'How bad was it?' George asked.

'It was awful, they'd completely trashed the place. All of Sam's paintings were ripped up, my mattress, the sofa

. . . everything. They slashed the lot, but as Samuel said, it's just things and better they knifed all the furniture than us. It was a scary thought though, 'cos it showed they'd come armed and meaning to get us.'

George felt his blood run cold. Sarah could have been in the house and come to serious harm.

'Sam worried about them coming back and he didn't want to leave me alone here. He took the week off work on the sick and got his brother to come and stay too. His brother brought a mate with him, Tony. He's a bare-knuckle fighter. Turns out he's a bit of a legend in the East End, and as hard as bleedin' nails. It was a bit of a tight squeeze, but we managed and I felt quite safe with three big blokes in my room.'

'You should have put them down here,' Sarah said.

'To be honest, I did think about it but I didn't want to take liberties. Anyhow, later that night, just as Samuel had predicted, Danny and my dad came back, but we were ready for them. When they saw they were outnumbered, they ran off. Sam said to give it a couple of hours, and then they'd be back again. He wasn't wrong. Only this time there was seven of them. Honestly, Sarah, when I saw them marching towards the house, I've never been so scared. I could see they had weapons too, bats, hammers, all sorts.'

'Oh, Mo, no wonder you were scared.'

'I begged Sam not to go outside, but he wouldn't listen. I thought there was going to be a murder, and prayed it wouldn't be my Sam who copped it. Tony, the bare-knuckle fighter, was out the door first and managed to take three of them out before Sam was even at the bottom of the stairs. Then I saw Sam lay into Danny, and Sam's brother got into a scuffle with my dad. The next thing I know, there was only one of them left standing and he was begging Tony not to hurt him. Tony grabbed him round the neck, and warned the others that if they didn't leave me and Sam alone he'd find them all, one by one, and kill them.'

'Blimey, Mo, sounds like it was terrifying! Did Sam or the others get hurt?' Sarah asked.

'A couple of shiners and small cuts between them, but not a mark on Tony. I've never seen anyone fight like that before. No wonder he's a legend. He stood over the rest of them, fists clenched, and then one by one they staggered to their feet to leg it.'

'I take it they haven't been back? George said.

'No, it's been quiet since and with Tony's threat hanging over them, I don't think we'll see them again.'

'Are you sure that's an end to it, Mo?' George asked, feeling protective. 'I don't want Sarah to risk bringing Tommy back here if it's going to kick off again.'

'I'm sure it's all right. I managed to get one of my mum's neighbours to have a quiet word in her ear. I got a message back from her to say that as far as my dad's concerned I'm dead to him and my brothers. They never want see me again. So, that's it, all over and good bloody riddance to them.'

'At last. Now you can relax and get on with your life,' Sarah said.

'Yes, though I must admit to still feeling nervous when I'm out. Time will tell, but I'm pretty sure they won't bother me any more.'

'Well, Mo, it looks like I'm moving back home.'

George was pleased to hear there'd be no more trouble,

though his heart sank at the thought of Sarah leaving. He wanted her to remain at his house, but with no threat from Mo's family, there was no reason for her to stay. 'I'll run you back later with Tommy,' he offered and tried to hide the disappointment in his voice. At least he'd be getting his bed back instead of having to sleep on the lumpy sofa, though it was little compensation.

He had a few hours left alone with her, and his stomach knotted at the thought. If he could bring himself to be bold enough, he'd make his move later. He'd been thinking about it for a while, and now seemed like the right time to ask her the big question, before it was too late and the opportunity passed.

Sarah had been chatting all the way back to George's house, but she'd noticed he seemed very quiet. As they pulled up outside, she went to get out of the van, but George stopped her, telling her to wait.

She turned to look at him and saw he was staring straight ahead with his hands gripping the steering wheel. 'What is it, George?'

'I . . . er . . . I don't want you and Tommy to go back home,' he answered.

'It's been lovely staying with you and your mum, and I'm not sure I want to go home either. I know Tommy will miss you, but there's no reason for us to stay now.'

'There is . . .' George said, and slowly twisted himself around to take her hand in his.

'What are you doing, George?' Sarah asked as she laughed uncomfortably. From the look in George's eyes, she had the impression that he was about to become romantic.

'Would you really prefer to be here, you and Tommy?'

'Well . . . yes, I suppose. It's great for Tommy to have a loving family around him, and your mum is so nice to us both, but it's not our home, George.'

'It could be, Sarah, if you want it to be.'

'It can't, George. It's not fair on you to be turfed out of your room, and I'm sure your mum would like her peace and quiet back.'

'Sarah, can't you see what I'm getting at? Gawd . . .' George took a long breath, then blurted, 'Marry me?'

Sarah sat stunned and speechless. She knew George liked her, he'd told her before that he loved her, but she hadn't been expecting a marriage proposal.

'I know that wasn't very romantic, but if you say you'll be my wife, I'll do it again and properly, down on one knee with a ring.'

Sarah's mind was racing. She hadn't misheard him the first time, he'd just confirmed it. She thought maybe he was larking around, but one look into his eyes told her he was serious. She liked George as a person, but he didn't give her butterflies like Roger did. All the same, she didn't want to hurt him and searched for the right words to let him down gently.

'I know it's a bit of a bolt out of the blue, Sarah, so perhaps you want some time to think about it?'

She slowly pulled her hand away from his. As far as she was concerned there was nothing to think about, and if she didn't respond to him now it would only prolong his agony. 'I'm sorry, George, but my answer is no. You're like my best friend, and I love you, but not in that way.'

George turned away, his shoulders slumped and Sarah could see that she had cut him deeply. She wanted to take him in her arms to offer him comfort, but that might give him false hope. Instead, she climbed out of the van, hating that there would now be an awkward atmosphere between them.

'Don't feel bad about turning me down,' George said as he too got out of the van, 'but you've missed your chance now, woman. You'll be sorry when you see some other bird snap me up.'

She turned to see him grinning and kissed him on the cheek, relieved that he wasn't sulking. 'Just as long as she's good enough for you and makes you happy.'

They went indoors, and Sarah went upstairs to George's room to pack the clothes she'd brought with her. She took a moment to sit on the edge of the bed, and thought again about George's proposal. He was such a sweet, kind man, and though he'd put on a good front when she'd turned him down, she could see straight through him and knew he was upset. Sarah sighed heavily and decided that once she was back in her own home she'd put some distance between them for a while. It would give George a chance to get over her and maybe, just maybe, he might meet someone who could give him all the love he deserved.

Chapter 30

Lena was stacking tins of Spam, but her mind was on her son. It had been a week since Sarah and Tommy had returned to their own home, which seemed to have left George feeling down in the dumps. She missed his cheery smile in the mornings, and having been through a spell of depression herself, she hoped her son wasn't going down the same path.

The shop door opened, and Lena was surprised to see Albert Bosco walk in. He rarely came to his store, but was always amiable and polite when he did.

'Good morning, Mrs Neerly, how are you today?' he asked as he doffed his hat to reveal his thick white hair.

'Mr Bosco, hello. I'm very well, thank you, but you're lucky to have caught me here at this time. Sarah would normally be working now, but she's at a school play so I'm covering for her for the rest of the afternoon.' She thought he was such a nice gentleman and always dressed smartly. He had a Mediterranean look about him with light-brown skin in striking contrast with his hair. He wasn't much taller than her, and, unlike her, hadn't kept his youthful figure, so now had a paunchy stomach. Yet he had the deepest dark-brown eyes, which Lena thought were his best feature.

'I'm glad I've caught you then, as it's you I was hoping to see.'

Lena carried the box of remaining tins towards the counter.

'Here, let me help you with that,' Mr Bosco said as he rushed across the shop and took the box from her.

'Thank you. What did you want to see me about? I hope you're happy with the way I'm running the shop?'

Mr Bosco placed the box on the counter, then turned to look at Lena, but she noticed he looked somewhat uncomfortable.

'Yes, yes, I'm more than happy with all your hard work, and Sarah seems an asset to the business too.'

'Yes, she is.'

There was a long, silent pause, then Mr Bosco said, 'I have tickets to a dinner and dance being held at Battersea Town Hall. It's one of those events to promote small businesses in the area, and, well, can be a bit stuffy as it's a black-tie do.'

'It sounds like a good excuse to get dressed up and I'm sure you'll enjoy it,' Lena said.

'I'm not very good at this . . . It's been a long time since I've asked a lady for a date, so please excuse my fumbling, but would you like to come with me?'

'Oh,' Lena answered, taken aback, and stuttered, 'I . . . I—'

Mr Bosco interrupted, 'It's all right, I understand and I do hope I haven't embarrassed you. Sorry, it was a silly idea. Anyway, I'll be off now then.'

He turned to leave, but Lena called, 'Yes.'

Mr Bosco spun back around.

'Yes, I'd love to come with you, Mr Bosco.'

He looked delighted as a huge smile spread across his face. 'Wonderful, I'll pick you up at seven on Saturday, and please call me Albert.'

'Albert, seven is fine, and I think you should call me Lena.'

Albert doffed his hat again, then left, while Lena flopped down on the chair behind the counter. She couldn't believe she'd agreed to go out on a date. It would be the first since her husband had died, and suddenly she worried about what she would wear. Not only that, what on earth would George have to say about it?

Sarah had watched Tommy in his school play production of *The Three Little Pigs*. The short stage act had brought her so much enjoyment, and she'd swelled with pride at his performance as a talking tree. Now he was back in his classroom, but Sarah wasn't ready to go to work yet. Lena had opened up the shop and stayed on for a few hours, so now it was time to put her plan into action. It had been put on hold when she'd had to move in with George and his mum, but now that she was home again, she was ready.

Sarah stood at the bottom of the stairs leading up to Mrs Alderton-Steele's house, gazing with admiration at the three-storey building, with stairs leading down to a basement. The large front door was adorned with brass fixtures, and through the front sash windows she could see luxury drapes. Everything she'd heard about this side of the water was true. The people looked smart, and the houses were opulent.

It was a bold plan and Sarah had expected to feel nervous, but instead she was filled with determination to correct a wrong. She had no idea how Mrs Alderton-Steele would receive her, or if the woman would even allow her in the house, but walked up the wide stairs to ring the doorbell, her body stiff.

'Yes, can I help you?' an elderly gentleman asked when he opened the door. He was dressed in a black suit with a crisp grey shirt matching his grey hair, which was immaculately swept back. Sarah knew from what Jenny had told her that he must be Henry, the butler.

'Good afternoon,' Sarah said, trying to speak properly without her cockney twang, 'Miss Jepson to see Mrs Alderton-Steele.'

'She isn't expecting you,' Henry said, and eyed her suspiciously.

'No, but she will want to see me.'

'There are no service positions currently available,' Henry said, and began to close the door.

'Wait,' Sarah said, 'I'm not here for a job. I have some information that I believe she will want to hear.'

'You will have to be more precise.'

Although the man initially came across as being snobbish, Jenny had said he was a nice bloke, and Sarah could see he had a kind face. 'It's about a watch, and some other things that I believe belong to her.'

Henry's eyes widened. 'You'd better come in,' he said, and showed Sarah into a large hallway. 'Wait here,' he instructed before going through a door to the left of a large staircase.

Sarah gazed around her surroundings. The walls were panelled with rich dark wood, and statues stood on marble plinths. A sparkling chandelier hung from the ceiling, and scattered rainbow reflections of sunlight over the walls. Blimey, thought Sarah, the hallway was bigger than her entire house.

'This way, Miss Jepson,' Henry said from the doorway.

Sarah had been feeling brave, but suddenly felt out of her depth in the lavish house and began tapping her finger and thumb. She walked past Henry and into a large room where Mrs Alderton-Steele was sitting on the largest sofa Sarah had ever seen. She quickly scanned the room, taking in a grand piano, the oil paintings framed in gilt, and the foreign-looking vases. She thought the place looked how she imagined Buckingham Palace to be, and Mrs Alderton-Steele was like royalty. It even crossed her mind that perhaps she should curtsey.

'Henry tells me you know something of my late husband's missing watch,' Mrs Alderton-Steele said.

'Yes, that's right.'

'You had better sit down then, girl. Henry, bring us tea . . . oh, and a slice of Dundee cake. I'm sure Miss . . . Miss. . .' Mrs Alderton-Steele looked at Sarah with a furrowed brow.

'Jepson. Sarah Jepson.'

'I'm sure Miss Jepson would enjoy a slice of cook's cake with her tea.'

Sarah's eyes followed Henry as he left the room, then came back to Mrs Alderton-Steele. Jenny had warned her the woman was a bit eccentric, but she hadn't expected her to be dressed like a mourning Queen Victoria. She was even wearing a black hat with netting. The woman looked frail, and through the netting, Sarah could see she had deep wrinkles and thin lips.

'I rarely see visitors, so I do hope you have information of importance for me?'

'I do, Mrs Alderton-Steele. I have more than merely information,' Sarah said, and smiled at the old woman.

'Do tell. That watch is very precious to me.'

Henry entered carrying a silver tea service on a tray, and fine china cups. He placed the tray on a low table between the sofa and Sarah.

'Leave it, Henry. I believe Miss Jepson is about to tell me something very interesting,' Mrs Alderton-Steele said, and began to daintily pour the tea while Henry retreated and stood against the wall with his hands behind his back.

'As you can probably tell, I'm not from round these parts. I'm from across the river in Battersea, and where I grew up it was . . . well . . . rough. There were lots of shady people around and it's given me a nose for sniffing out when something ain't quite right,' Sarah said, forgetting her attempt to speak nicely. 'I was walking across the bridge and I saw this bloke throw something over. I waited 'til he was out of sight, then I went down to the banks and found this bracelet.' Sarah took the bracelet from her handbag and placed it on the table.

Mrs Alderton-Steele's bony hand picked it up. 'My bracelet! But how did you know it belonged to me?'

'I didn't at first. I used to spend quite a bit of time at the river, and then one day, a little while after I found your bracelet, I saw the same man on the bridge. He threw something over again, only this time I followed him and he came back to this house. When I went back to the river to look for what he'd thrown, I found this watch.'

'My goodness,' said the elderly lady as Sarah then handed the watch to her. 'I had almost given up any hope of ever seeing this again.'

'I'm assuming this belongs to you too?' Sarah asked and held out the ring.

'Yes, it does,' Mrs Alderton-Steele said. 'What did this man look like?'

'He was well dressed, very tall and slim, with black hair. I'd say he was in his late thirties. I reckon he must live or work in this house 'cos he used a key to get in the door.' She could see the old woman's face slowly changing as Mrs Alderton-Steele realised Sarah was describing her son. A look of shock replaced her uppity expression. Then Sarah continued, 'I racked my brains and couldn't think why a bloke would just throw away such expensive-looking stuff, and to be honest I did think about flogging it. After all, as they say, finders keepers.'

'I see. So why didn't you?'

'The likes of me could never afford jewellery like that, and I was frightened I'd get nicked for stealing it. I kept it hidden in my room, but eventually my conscience got the better of me, so here I am . . .'

'You are a very decent young lady, very decent indeed. I doubt there would be many who would be so honest, but tell me, have you found anything else?'

'No, I haven't been to the river for a while now, but there could well be more stuff down there.'

'Yes, I would imagine there probably is as I have several other items missing. Henry, where is Godfrey?'

'He went out earlier. He didn't say where he was going or when he would be returning, but I would assume he's at his club.'

'Henry, there's a photograph on the piano. Show it to Miss Jepson.'

Sarah took the framed photograph and as she looked

at it, Mrs Alderton-Steele asked, 'Is that the man you saw?'

Though she had never actually seen him, the description Jenny had given her matched, so she said without hesitation, 'Yes.'

Mrs Alderton-Steele held her hand to her head and closed her eyes. 'Henry, my smelling salts. This is all too much.'

Henry passed the woman a small bottle which she held in her handkerchief and lightly sniffed. 'Why would my son steal from me? It makes no sense.'

'The thing is, and I hope you don't think I'm talking out of turn here, but something odd happened when I arrived. I saw a young woman coming up from the basement and as she looked very upset, I asked her if she was all right. She was crying, but before she hurried off she warned me that if I was after a job, I should stay well away from this house, or I'd end up in trouble with the Mrs's son like she was. I'm not sure what she meant by that or if it's got anything to do with your stolen things.'

Sarah knew the old woman had no idea what was going on in her home right under her nose, but Jenny had said that Henry was aware of Godfrey's wicked behaviour, though he'd turned a blind eye to it. Sarah flashed the butler a look, and saw him shift uncomfortably, then discreetly clear his throat.

'I can only suggest you saw my cleaner, but I have no idea why she would say that. Do you know, Henry?'

'Actually, yes, ma'am. I think I do,' Henry answered.

'Spit it out then, man,' the old woman barked.

'Ma'am, I think this would be better discussed in private.'

'Well, it's becoming apparent that my son is a thief, so I think it's a little late to concern ourselves with privacy. Now, Henry, I demand to know what exactly has been occurring in my house!'

Sarah thought that Mrs Alderton-Steele was quite a formidable character when riled, and hoped Henry would have the bottle to tell her what he knew. It had to come from him, as Sarah didn't think the old woman would believe her.

'I'm afraid to say that Miss Jepson's story has confirmed exactly what I think Godfrey has been doing, but until now I've had no proof. I believe he has been taking your jewellery in order to have the staff blamed,' Henry said, and looked at Sarah with a look of relief as if he was glad to get it off his chest.

'Why would he do such a thing? What could he possibly gain?'

'Er . . . favours, ma'am, of the . . . er . . . feminine kind,' Henry said and lowered his head.

'I still don't understand, Henry. How is the theft of my jewellery involved?'

'I'm afraid Godfrey had his eye on our previous cleaner, Miss Turner, but she refused to be forthcoming with her favours. To punish her, I think Godfrey took your jewellery and Miss Turner was blamed for the theft. I think he's been doing something similar with this new girl, maybe blackmailing her to be freer with her favours as I caught them in somewhat of a clinch the other day.'

Sarah was pleased Henry had so readily provided the information, but hadn't expected him to give it up so easily. Now that he had, he looked very pleased with himself, though the same couldn't be said for Mrs Alderton-Steele.

'I see,' she said, her voice no longer forthright but tremulous. 'Henry, please reward Miss Jepson with the sum of fifty pounds, and Miss Jepson, thank you for returning my jewellery. I do hope a reward will secure your silence about everything you have just heard?'

'Yes, thank you, Mrs Alderton-Steele, and I can promise you that nothing I've heard today will be spoken about outside of these walls,' Sarah answered.

'Good, and I hope you keep your promise. I am deeply ashamed of my son, and he will be punished, but if any of my friends and acquaintances hear of his disgraceful behaviour, I will instruct my solicitor to pursue the perpetrator of the rumours for defamation of character.'

'It won't come from me,' Sarah said. She hadn't expected a reward, and was reeling at how generous it was, but the mention of solicitors frightened her. She hadn't liked telling lies, but it was the only way she could think of to make Mrs Alderton-Steele see the truth, and it had worked. Henry had blabbed, the jewellery was returned, and now Sarah hoped Mrs Alderton-Steele would see to it that Godfrey never laid a hand on Doreen again. She doubted Jenny would get her job back, but at least her friend would have the pleasure of knowing that Godfrey's sickening behaviour had been uncovered.

'Good, and now Henry will see you out.'

Sarah dashed back over Battersea Bridge feeling slightly dizzy and thankful the wind was behind her to speed her along. She'd stuffed the reward money into her bag, but hadn't dared to take a close look at it yet. Fifty pounds

– she could hardly believe it! It was more money than she'd ever seen in her life!

Once on the other side of the bridge, Sarah began to relax a little in the surroundings she found familiar, though kept her head down as she dashed past the police station where her father worked.

When she got home she'd have to find somewhere safe to keep the money. She couldn't risk losing it, not this amount of cash. If she was clever and kept a clear head, it would be enough to set her and Tommy up for life.

Chapter 31

It had been over two weeks since Sarah had visited Mrs Alderton-Steele's house. She knew she had to go to see Jenny to tell her what had happened, but so far guilt had held her back. She had decided not to mention the reward money. Jenny had a good home and a job so she was hardly in a desperate situation, while she had Tommy to think about. He was frequently poorly with his chest and living in a damp room didn't help. Some of the substantial amount Mrs Alderton-Steele had given her would go into finding them a decent place to live, and more of it would be used to repay George. She also had what she thought would be a profitable plan, and was hoping to get George on board too.

It was a Saturday morning and her day off when she at last plucked up the courage to see Jenny, and now she was walking up the three flights of stairs to her flat. Tommy began to ask questions. She hadn't wanted to bring him back here, but Mo was busy spending precious time with Samuel.

'Are we going to see our mum?' Tommy asked. His little face was screwed up in consternation, and his voice was barely a whisper.

'No love, she doesn't live here any more. I told you earlier, we're going to see my friend Jenny.'

'Where does Mum live now then?'

'She lives in heaven with the angels and my good friend Mr Sayers.'

'If she lives in heaven, does that mean she went to her forever box?' Tommy quizzed.

'Yes, Tommy, she went to her forever box and now she's in the sky.'

Tommy seemed satisfied with her answers and happily skipped on ahead. She was pleased to see that the discovery of their mother's death hadn't upset him. In fact, it hadn't seemed to bother him at all.

Tommy knocked on Jenny's door and was greeted warmly by Mrs Turner.

'Hello, young man, look at you, you've grown. Is your sister standing you in horse manure?'

'Hello, Mrs Turner,' Sarah said. 'Yes, he's shooting up quicker than I can keep trousers on him. Is Jenny home?'

'Yes, pet, come through. I can see you're doing a fine job with that child, so well done, 'cos I know it can't have been easy for you. Jenny tells me you're working in Bosco's grocers. I've not been in there for years, but you've landed on your feet there. Mr Bosco is a lovely man, and so was his late wife. There's some squash made in a jug, go through and pour some for yourself and Tommy while I give Jenny a shout.'

Mrs Turner's pregnancy was showing, though Sarah thought she had a while to go yet. As Sarah helped herself to a glass of orange juice, Jenny appeared in the kitchen, pleased to see her friend.

'I didn't hear you knock. I had the radio to my ear.

Tommy, do you remember where my bedroom is?'

Tommy nodded.

'My little sisters Pat and Carol are playing with my old dolls' house. You can go and see what they're doing if you like.'

Tommy went off to play and Mrs Turner came back into the kitchen. 'I'm sure you girls would like to have a chat, but we've got a bit of a houseful today. Tell you what, leave Tommy here with me for an hour and go for a walk. It's a lovely day, and the girls will look after him.'

'Thanks, Mum. Come on, Sarah, let's go down to the old bomb site, you won't believe how much it's changed and what they're building there now.'

As the two of them strolled through the estate, Jenny linked her arm through Sarah's, which reminded her of the old days when they would walk to school together.

'Come on then, spill the beans. I've been dying to know what happened at the big house,' Jenny said.

'It was just like you said it would be. She's a right old character, that Mrs Alderton-Steele, but I liked her. I did as you said, waited for Godfrey to go out, then rang the bell and met Henry. Anyway, I got invited in, gave her back her stuff and managed to drop Godfrey in it. You was right, the butler knew everything and it didn't take much persuading for him to admit to it. He seems like a nice old boy, and I got the impression that he ain't too keen on Godfrey.'

'Sarah, you're brilliant! I knew Henry would back up your story. He wasn't happy when I was forced out, but it was my word against Godfrey's so there wasn't much he could do to help. What did the old girl say?'

'She was pleased to get the watch back, but really upset that her son was the one who'd stolen it.'

'She believed you then?'

'Yes, and she knows he's been bribing Doreen for – how was it Henry worded it? Feminine favours.'

'Yeah, that sounds like Henry, sort of pompous, but he's a nice man.'

'Mrs Alderton-Steele will sort Godfrey out, so Doreen won't have to worry about him in future. She's safe now and not only that, your name has been cleared.'

'That's bloody marvellous, Sarah. I've never been in trouble with the law before, none of my family have. I wasn't charged with nothing, but that's not the point. Knowing people think that about me is horrible, but now the old girl realises I'm innocent and it's her own flesh and blood what stole from her . . . ha, it's sweet revenge.'

'I'm sorry, Jenny. Mrs Alderton-Steele doesn't want any of this getting out. She said if it does she'd instruct her solicitor to go after the person responsible for defamation of character.'

'Bloody hell. What's that?'

'I dunno, but it don't sound good. We wouldn't want to go up against someone with her sort of money. We wouldn't stand a chance against her fancy lawyers.'

'Well, in that case, I ain't going to open me mouth, and you should have a word with Doreen too.'

'Don't worry, I will,' Sarah said.

With nothing else to say on that subject, they spent another half an hour wandering the estate reminiscing about the fun times they'd shared as children, until Sarah suggested they went back. She wanted to collect Tommy and then head for the market.

She had business to discuss with George, and hoped to see Roger too.

The morning had flown by, but it always did on busy Saturdays. George hadn't seen Sarah for a while, not since he'd dropped the bombshell question and been rebuffed. It hadn't been easy, but he'd picked himself up, dusted himself down and was smiling again at customers on his stall. He thought he'd got over her rejection, until he spotted her in the crowd heading his way. Nothing had changed. As always, his stomach flipped and his pulse quickened. For Gawd's sake man, pull yourself together, he told himself, and stretched out his arms to scoop up Tommy, who had run towards him.

'George,' Tommy squealed, 'can I come and live with you again?'

'I reckon Sarah would miss you too much. Ain't that right, love?'

'Yes, I would, and hello, George,' she said with a warm smile.

As Tommy's arms tightly squeezed his neck, he looked over the boy's shoulder and noticed Sarah was wearing new clothes that she hadn't bought from his stall. Her fashionable straight skirt with a high-necked red blouse tucked in emphasised her small waist. He thought she looked stunning in her high heels, which showed off her shapely legs, and he saw a few heads turn to admire her.

'Mum said I can have an ice-cream. Do you want one too?' Tommy asked him as George placed him back down. The lad was growing, and George could feel how much heavier he'd become.

'Yes, mate, it's a scorcher of a day so that that would

be nice, though it'll be my treat,' George said, fishing in his money bag for some coins.

Tommy skipped off, and George turned his attention back to Sarah, but was saddened to see her gawking at Roger. She looked as if she was daydreaming as she stared wantonly at him. George couldn't help but feel jealous and said quietly, 'He'd break your heart.'

'Eh? Oh . . . I was . . . I was . . .' Sarah stuttered.

'It's all right, Sarah, I know you like him, and I can't say I blame you. He's a good-looking chap, but I'm warning you as one friend to another – you're best off staying well clear of him.'

'I don't know what you mean, George Neerly,' Sarah said in a haughty manner.

'By the way,' George continued, 'I've heard some posh bloke has been looking for you, asking around. I'm betting it's the bloke from the house where the jewellery come from. I take it you've returned it?'

'Yes, I have. You'll be pleased to hear that my friend Jenny was as pleased as punch when I told her what happened. Godfrey has fallen out of favour with his mother and now you think it's him snooping around. What's he been asking?' Sarah said, finally taking her eyes off Roger.

'I heard from a few of my mates on the market that he was asking if they knew you. You're all right though. You know this lot – they wouldn't say anything to someone like him. Just watch your back.'

Sarah's eyes darted around nervously as she said, 'I wonder what he wants?'

'Don't worry about the likes of him. If he causes you any trouble he'll have me to deal with. Now, what did you want to talk to me about?'

'I told you, not here,' Sarah said. 'If you aren't doing anything tonight, come round to my place and we can talk in private.'

Tommy returned with two ice-cream cones. It was clear he'd been licking them both. 'It was dripping,' he said to George as he handed him one.

'I'll see you later then,' Sarah said, and grabbed Tommy's hand to lead him away.

'See ya, George,' Tommy called.

'Ta ta,' George shouted, but they were soon lost from sight in the throng of shoppers. Oh well, he thought, he'd see her again soon and as far as he was concerned the rest of the day couldn't pass quickly enough.

'That was the bestest. Thanks, Mum,' Tommy said as he licked melted ice-cream from between his fingers.

They had walked a good way from the market, and the streets were quieter here. Sarah looked down at Tommy, took a handkerchief from her bag and lightly spat on it before crouching down to wipe his face. 'Don't thank me. George paid for it. Now look at the state of you! I reckon you must have more ice-cream on your face than in your belly.'

'Ew, get off,' Tommy moaned, as he tried to push away Sarah's hand with the moistened handkerchief.

Sarah stood up then gasped as she found a tall man blocking her path. She'd never seen Godfrey, but judging by the way he was dressed and the photograph, she instantly knew it was him.

'You must be Sarah Jepson. I've been looking for you,' Godfrey said with a sneer.

'No, I think you're mistaken. Excuse me, please,' Sarah

answered. Her heart pounded as she looked into his threatening eyes. She went to walk around him, but he stepped sideways, again blocking her.

'I'm not mistaken. You weren't that hard to find. You told my mother you live in Battersea, and I've been asking around. It didn't take me long or cost much to find out that you often use that market. It seems people around here will quite happily open their rotten mouths for a cheap price.'

Sarah looked around her. She didn't recognise anyone, but that didn't mean people wouldn't know who she was. Gossip was rife in the area, but George had said no one would say anything. He'd obviously been mistaken.

Tommy was standing by her side looking suspiciously at Godfrey. She hoped the man wouldn't make a scene and scare her brother. 'Yes, I'm Sarah Jepson. What of it?' she said, trying to make herself sound more brazen than she felt.

Godfrey didn't answer, but she suddenly felt his tight grip on her arm, then he began to pull her off the street and down a narrow deserted alley. She tried to yank herself free, but his clutch was too strong. She couldn't allow him to drag her into the alley. He could do anything to her and no one would see.

Her mind raced. Tommy was standing as though transfixed, looking terrified so she daren't scream or it would frighten him even more. 'Get George,' she called before Godfrey managed to overpower her.

Sarah didn't see if Tommy had run off, but then she was aware of a pain shooting across her shoulders as Godfrey slammed her against a brick wall. She gasped for breath, feeling winded, then felt the weight of Godfrey's body as he pushed against her.

'There's no one to help you, and nobody will see us in here,' he ground out, dragging her deeper into the gloom and behind a pile of rubbish.

'Get off me,' Sarah gasped.

Godfrey's fingers wrapped round her throat, forcing her head back and his face just inches from hers. His eyes looked hard and cold, like flints, as he tightened his grip. She couldn't breathe, couldn't make another sound, her body trapped between the wall and the man who was trying to squeeze the life out of her.

'You bitch!' Godfrey hissed. 'You've ruined my life. I've lost everything because of you. Did you think you would get away with it?'

Sarah could feel his saliva on her face as he spat his words with such venom. She struggled for breath, knew she had to somehow placate him and managed to croak, 'Sorry.'

'Sorry! You're sorry! I've been disinherited, thrown out of my home, and all you can say is you're sorry! You fucking whore! I'm going to make sure you pay for this.'

Sarah's skirt was tight but she could feel his other hand roughly grabbing at the bare flesh on her thigh. She couldn't scream for help and feared he was going to rape her. The more she fought against him, the tighter he gripped her throat, and she began to panic. She felt her windpipe being crushed, and as she desperately tried to suck in air, she became aware that the world around her was spinning until it slowly faded.

George was surprised to see Tommy running towards him again, but soon became alarmed when he saw the child's frightened face and no sign of Sarah.

'George . . . George . . . a man's got Mummy in an alley and he's hurting her,' Tommy shouted as he approached.

He knew instantly that it must be that Godfrey bloke, and quickly yelled, 'Roger, come with me. Sarah's being attacked.' He looked down at Tommy and grabbed the boy's shoulders, 'Wait here, don't move and don't worry,' he said, before running off with Roger closely on his heels.

'Move . . . move . . .' George shouted as he charged through the crowd and waved his arms like a man possessed. Once away from the market, he ran the route that Sarah would have taken to go home. Tommy had said she was in an alley and he stopped to look up the first one he came to. There was nothing in it except empty boxes and a dustbin. His legs pumping like pistons, he ran to the next street, then the next, until he came to another alley. He paused, panting, sure he could see something at the back in the corner. He ran in, and behind some rubbish saw a man standing over something. His stomach lurched. It was Sarah.

'Get your fucking hands off her,' George yelled.

Godfrey looked startled when he saw him, but as George pulled his arm back to punch Godfrey, he felt a blow to his stomach which knocked him off his feet. He landed with a thud on the floor. Had Godfrey punched him first? He was unsure of what had happened, but he was aware of pain. He sat up and looked down. Blood was beginning to spread across his white shirt. His hand was shaking as he tentatively touched the wound. It felt wet and strangely warm. Then he realised, he'd been stabbed. 'Look out. He's got a knife,' George screeched as he saw Roger running towards Godfrey.

Godfrey turned to look at George, and in that moment Roger swung his fist, landing it heavily on Godfrey's jaw. The force of the blow sent him flying and as he landed close to George, the knife fell from his hand. George quickly grabbed it, and managed to get himself onto his knees. 'Don't move,' George warned as he held the knife aggressively towards Godfrey.

It had all happened in seconds, but it had felt like an eternity and had played out in slow motion in front of George's eyes. He looked over at Sarah and was relieved to see she was pushing herself up from the floor with Roger gently helping. He could hear her coughing and her voice sounded raspy.

'I thought he was going to kill me . . .' she cried.

'It's all right, I've got you,' Roger reassured her.

'Roger, what am I going to do with him?' George called.

Roger turned to look and his face went pale. 'You're bleeding, George.'

'I know, but what about him?' George repeated and indicated with his head at Godfrey, who was sitting passively on the floor 'What about you, Sarah, are you all right?'

'Yes . . . I think so . . .' Sarah said huskily, rubbing her neck. 'Where's Tommy?'

'He's safe, he's at my stall. Roger, I think you'd better go and find a copper . . . and call me an ambulance.' George could feel himself becoming weaker as blood began to pool on the floor next to him. He wasn't sure how much longer he could hold the knife at Godfrey.

Roger had one arm under Sarah's, and the other across her shoulder. She looked a bit unsteady on her feet and was leaning heavily on him. It was stupid, thought

George, but even in this crazy situation he felt jealous and wished it was him helping Sarah.

He'd taken his eye off his prisoner, and, with Roger concentrating on Sarah, Godfrey unexpectedly jumped to his feet and swiftly ran from the alley. 'After him,' George shouted, but it was too late. Godfrey vanished out of the alley into the busy street.

With that, George finally slumped. He closed his eyes and felt someone lift his head. With a force of will he managed to open his eyes again and saw Sarah's face looking down on him.

'It's all right. George . . . hold on . . . you're going to be all right . . .'

Her voice sounded like the soft tones of an angel, but then, as everything around him seemed to darken, the last thing George heard was the sound of a siren.

Chapter 32

Lena held her son's hand and willed him to wake up. He's a strong lad, she thought, he's had worse and pulled through, but she couldn't help but worry at the sight of him laid in a hospital bed.

'How is he?'

Lena heard Sarah's voice and spun around to see the girl, standing next to Roger. She'd been so absorbed, she hadn't seen or heard them walking through the ward. 'The doctors have said he's going to be fine,' she answered, then added, 'What about you, love, are you all right?'

'Yes, thanks, Lena. I'm a bit on edge at the thought of Godfrey still being out there somewhere, but I'm sure the police will catch up with him soon. I don't know what I would have done without George. He saved my life.'

'That's 'cos I'm Superman in my other job . . .' George quietly groaned.

Lena jumped up from the chair she'd been sitting on. 'George, you're awake,' she exclaimed, and tears began to roll down her cheeks.

'Yeah, but don't look so sad about it.'

'These are tears of happiness, not sadness,' she said, and squeezed his hand tighter.

'Oh, thank God, George. You had us all really worried for a while,' Sarah said.

Lena noticed her voice was still very raspy and the bruising around her neck was visible, though she'd attempted to hide it with a scarf.

'I'm blinkin' starving. Have I been out long?' George asked.

He was putting on a brave face, but Lena could hear his voice was weak and could tell by the way he winced that he was in discomfort. 'It's Sunday afternoon, George. Do you remember what happened yesterday?' she asked gently.

'Mum, he stabbed me in the stomach, not in the brain. Of course I remember. Did any of you bring me any fruit or biscuits?'

Roger laughed. 'Sorry, mate, we've come empty-handed. Trust you to be thinking of food at a time like this.'

'I'll go and fetch a nurse and see if I can't get her to bring you a sandwich or something, but I'm not sure you'll be allowed to eat just yet,' Lena said, then turned to Sarah. 'Keep an eye on him for me, and don't let him try to get up.'

When Lena got back to George's bedside, she noticed a sad look in her son's eyes and wondered if the shock of what had happened was beginning to surface. 'The nurse has gone to fetch the doctor and will be here in a minute. I think you two should go now and let George get his rest. We don't want him overdoing it.'

'All right, but I'll be back tomorrow, mate,' Roger said.

'Keep your chin up. It ain't so bad having all these lovely nurses fussing over you.'

Lena saw Sarah dig Roger in the ribs and thought they looked quite cosy together. Sarah leaned over to kiss George's cheek and said, 'I'll bring Tommy up to see you tomorrow. He's been asking after you.'

'Thanks, you two,' Lena said. 'Don't worry about coming to work for a few days, Sarah. Albert – I mean Mr Bosco – has got cover for both of us.'

'See ya,' George said.

Lena sat beside her son again. Albert had been under-standing about her predicament. Once she had explained what happened, he'd been gravely concerned for Sarah and George's well-being, and insisted that she take all the time off she needed. She promised to have dinner with him once George was on the mend, though at the time of that conversation she hadn't been convinced her son was going to be OK, and was worried sick.

Lena watched George as his eyes followed Sarah and Roger leaving the ward. 'You don't have to put on a brave front now. Tell me how you really feel,' she whispered to him.

'Honest, Mum, I'm all right.'

'You can't pull the wool over my eyes. Are you worried about that man still being on the loose?'

'No, don't be daft. Truth is, I'm wondering what's going on with them two.'

So that was what was bothering her son. He was upset to see Roger getting his feet under Sarah's table. It was bound to happen eventually. After all, Sarah had been harbouring feelings for the man for a long time now. She thought Sarah was a fool, but she was more concerned

244

for George. It wasn't just his stomach in pain. It was his heart too.

Mo looked out of her window when she heard a vehicle pull up outside, and saw Roger's van. 'Your mum's home,' she called over her shoulder to Tommy.

'Yes!' Tommy squealed, and ran across the room and out of the door.

She carried on looking, and saw Roger lean across and kiss Sarah on the lips. Tommy ran from the house, and Sarah climbed from the van, but she never took her eyes off Roger. She's finally got her man, Mo thought, and felt a tinge of sadness. She should be happy for her friend, especially after everything she'd been through lately, but instead had a strange sensation, almost as if she were jealous. She chastised herself and when Sarah walked into the room she said, 'Someone looks a bit happy.'

'Tommy, do you want to go and play with Larry?' Sarah asked.

'Yeah, but what about George? Is he all right?'

'Yes, love, he's going to be fine. I'll take you to see him after school tomorrow.'

Tommy's face lit up. 'Yay! Right, I'm going to see Larry.'

As Tommy ran out, Mo watched as her friend walked across the room, then threw her arms in the air before falling back onto the sofa.

'Oh, Mo . . . he's so . . . so . . . I think I'm in love!'

'Are you dating him now?' Mo asked.

'Yes, he's asked me to be his girlfriend. I know I should be traumatised after what happened yesterday, but I feel like I'm in a dream world,' Sarah said with an exaggerated sigh.

'What a difference a day makes. You was a nervous

245

wreck yesterday, what with the attack and having to give your statement to the police, and today you're like a new woman. It's amazing what an effect a man can have!'

'I know, isn't it! He's only been gone five minutes and I'm missing him already. I can't stop smiling, and I can't stop thinking about him.' Then she added gravely, 'Still, it's better than dwelling on Godfrey.'

'How's George?' Mo asked.

'He's sore but on the mend. Thanks for looking after Tommy for me again.'

'No problem. Sam won't be back for hours yet. He's earning a few extra bob helping one of his mates fix up his motorbike. Do you want something to drink?'

'No, thanks. I've got company tonight so I'm going downstairs to give my room a good clean up, then I'm going to make the most of the taps being fixed and have a soak in the bath before my *boyfriend* visits. He knows I've got Tommy so he said he'll call in with a Muffin the Mule toy for him . . . he's so sweet and thoughtful, don't you think?'

'Seems to be,' Mo said sceptically. 'Just don't go rushing in. He's the first man you've ever dated, and you've got to watch some of these blokes. There's plenty of them out there that are only after one thing.'

'I know,' Sarah said, 'I've seen it often enough with my mum. Roger may be my first proper boyfriend, but I ain't silly when it comes to men.'

Mo wasn't convinced, and a heartbroken blubbering woman was the last thing she wanted to put up with. She could only hope Sarah was as sensible as she sounded.

That evening, Sarah had just applied a slick of pink lipstick when she heard Roger's van outside. Her heart seemed to skip a beat, and though she couldn't wait to see him, she was filled with nervous excitement.

Tommy went to the front door to let him in, and when she saw his masculine physique filling her doorway, all she wanted to do was run into his arms. 'Hello, Roger,' she said meekly.

Roger had a box under his arm which he gave to Tommy. Sarah watched him eagerly opening it and then his voice rose in excitement, 'Muffin! Can I go and show it to Larry?'

'Yes, but I want you back in an hour, young man. You've got school in the morning.'

Once Tommy had gone, Roger approached Sarah and pulled her towards him. She felt a quiver run down her back as he placed his lips on hers and tenderly kissed her.

'It's nice to have you all to myself for a while,' he said, and kissed her again.

This time she could feel his tongue parting her lips and pushing into her mouth. She'd heard about French kissing, but it felt odd, though she tingled with pleasure. He began to run his hands up and down her sides, then reached to the front and softly cupped her breast. She immediately pulled away and turned from him.

'I'm sorry, I couldn't help myself. You're so gorgeous and it's hard for me to keep my hands to myself.'

She spun back around and saw the hungry look in his eyes. She'd seen that look before when some of her mother's punters had eyed her. It was the same look Eddy used to stare at her with too. It made her feel uncomfortable, and she squirmed, but she didn't want Roger to think she didn't like him. 'It's all right,' she said, 'I just need to take things slowly.'

'That's fine,' Roger said and lightly kissed her forehead.

It was a relief to know he wasn't going to try and push her into something she wasn't yet ready for, especially after Mo's warning. She'd enjoyed him kissing her and exploring her mouth though. It had left her quite breathless and wanting more, but she couldn't shake her mother's warning – keep your legs shut.

Chapter 33

In July, after a few complications, George had finally been discharged from hospital. He'd enjoyed his visits from Sarah. He hadn't been so keen on Roger turning up with her on most occasions, but if there was something going on between them, they'd kept it to themselves.

July turned to August and after three weeks of being stuck at home he was ready to return to work on his stall. Sarah hadn't been to see him since he'd left the hospital, and whenever he mentioned her, his mum seemed to steer away from her name.

'Are you looking forward to going back to work today?' his mother asked.

'Yes, can't wait.'

'Just take it easy. Don't go putting a strain on yourself.'

'Mum, stop fussing. You've done a grand job of looking after me and I ain't going to ruin all your hard work by doing myself a mischief on my first day back.'

Lena seemed satisfied with his answer and went upstairs to get dressed, while George drained the last of his glass of milk. Sarah had never said what she'd wanted to talk to him about, but as she hadn't been round it couldn't have been important. She'd probably have forgotten by now. Still, he'd bring it up the next time he saw her and hoped it would be soon.

By the time George arrived at the market, the sun was up and most of the costermongers were set up for the day. He thought it was best to check his stall before unloading his van, and as he walked into the market he heard a whisper go from one stall to another. Then there was a loud cheer, and he heard shouts of 'Welcome back, George' and 'Good to have you back, mate'.

George was taken aback by the display, but pleased to be made to feel so popular. They were a good bunch, and he felt sure that none of them had been the one to have sold Sarah out to Godfrey.

He walked to his stall to the sound of applause, and was moved to see it'd been decorated with bunting and a large sign, hand-drawn in large capitals, which read: GEORGE NEERLY. NEERLY DEAD. NEERLY A HERO.

He turned to his fellow stallholders and did a bow, saying loudly, 'Thanks, it's good to be back.'

Roger was clapping, but George thought his friend looked a bit dubious and was avoiding eye contact with him. 'All right, mate?' he called as the costermongers dispersed back to their stalls.

'Yeah, all good,' Roger answered, then busied himself with some cabbages.

George walked over. 'I thought you might have popped in after work one day to say hello.'

'Sorry, George, I've been so busy. It's great to see you fighting fit again though,' Roger said, patting George's arm.

He was hiding something, George could tell, and it didn't take a genius to work out what. 'You and Sarah . . . are you seeing her now, you know, like a couple?'

Roger slowly nodded his head. 'I hate to tell you, mate, but yes. Look, I'm sorry and all that. I know you like her, but you wasn't getting anywhere with her, and after the attack we got closer. She thinks the world of you as a friend, but, well, she's my bird now. You understand, don't you?'

George felt like he'd been stabbed again, only this time in the back. Roger was his best friend. They'd known each other since they'd been at school together. He wouldn't have treated Roger this way. Where was the man's loyalty? He felt disgusted, but his pride kicked in and there was no way he was going to let Roger see how hurt he felt. 'Sure, I can understand why you'd want to be with her. I get it and hope it works out for you,' George said, adding as he walked away, 'Just make sure don't hurt her, and that's a warning.'

What had started as such a good day had suddenly turned into one of the worst. George knew he'd lost Sarah for good now. With his hopes dashed, he ripped at the bunting, venting his frustration at being let down by his friend and losing the love of his life.

Mo had the hump, and it peeved her even more that Samuel didn't seem to care that she was annoyed with him. 'It's not often we get to have a weekday together, and all you want to do is sit there and paint your stupid pictures,' she complained.

Samuel looked up from his artwork, but continued painting. 'It's no good pouting like a sulky little girl, Mo. You know I've been wanting to get this done for a while now. This will add a bit of colour to this place, and surely you want it to look nice.'

'Yes, I do, but can't you leave it for today? The sun's out, and it's not like you normally get time off work.'

'I know, Mo, but with the hours I work I don't get a lot of chance to paint. I can't stand looking at these dull walls. It's not been the same since your brothers smashed up my paintings. I like it looking bright and colourful in here, it reminds me of home.'

'I don't know why you're bothering. You keep saying we'll be in our own place soon, so does it really matter what this room looks like?'

'We can take the paintings with us, and yes, it does matter to me. I know it's nice weather now, but most of the time this country is so grey and cold. It's so different in Jamaica. I'll take you there one day and then you'll understand how I feel.'

'Yeah, yeah, yeah . . . I've heard it all before, Sam. I'll buy you a house . . . I'll take you to Jamaica . . . I'll buy us a television set, oh, and a motorcar, and there was the record player you promised me. What about the engagement ring? I still haven't seen that! You're full of empty promises and I'm sick of it!' Mo shouted. 'You even made me take back that radio.'

'Not that again, woman. I'm fed up with hearing about it.'

Mo stomped to the window and looked out onto the street. It was a gorgeous day, the sun bright, and surely paintings of some weird poxy flowers could wait.

Samuel placed his paintbrush on his palette and walked over to her. He pulled her close and nibbled gently on her earlobe. 'My promises aren't empty, Mo. I will get you all those things and more, you just have to be patient with me. I'm working hard, for us and for our future family.'

Mo's body flinched at the mention of children. She wasn't prepared to tell him she didn't want any, so strategically changed the subject. 'I know, Sam, I just needed a little rant. I feel better now and I'll leave you in peace to carry on with your paintings, which, by the way, ain't stupid. I'll pop to the shops and fetch us back something delicious for dinner.'

Samuel kissed her goodbye, but she slammed the front door on her way out as the anger that she'd managed to suppress bubbled to the surface again. Stupid, stubborn man, she thought.

As she walked along the road, Mo began to calm down. She'd go to the market and at least she could have a bit of banter with the barrow boys. It felt good to be out in the fresh air and feel the warm sun on her face. She wiggled her hips as she walked and held her chin high. She was aware of heads turning to look at her, and enjoyed the attention, especially from the men. I'm wasted here, she thought, and imagined she was in America, walking down Sunset Boulevard.

Sarah swept the back of her hand over her forehead and wiped away the sweat. It was a scorching afternoon, too hot to be stacking shelves, she thought. During the school holiday, Lena was opening up the shop in the mornings, and Sarah paid Larry's mum a few bob to look after Tommy so she could do an afternoon shift. Mo had offered, saying she was happy to have him without being paid, but she had been so good about how often she'd kept an eye on Tommy that Sarah hadn't wanted to take liberties. Not only that, Tommy liked being with Larry and his mum so it worked out well.

She checked the time. Only another two hours to go. She'd pick up Tommy, sort out his tea and then freshen up before Roger's arrival. Much to her delight, Roger visited her most evenings, and she often prepared him dinner. He'd always bring fresh vegetables from his stall, which sometimes reminded her of Mr Sayers and his allotment.

No sooner had Sarah finished stacking the shelves when the bell above the shop door chimed, and Sarah looked up to see one of her regular customers walk in. They enjoyed a natter while Sarah bagged the woman's shopping, then, when she'd left, she made herself a cold drink. Heaving a sigh, Sarah then took the opportunity to sit down for a while, her mind drifting to the fifty pounds stashed at home. She had big plans for that money, but still hadn't spoken to George. He'd been so ill, and now that he was home again, he was bound to have heard that she was seeing Roger. Unsure of her reception, she hadn't been to see George, but her last thought before she stood up to serve another customer was that she'd have to bite the bullet one of these days. She just prayed it wouldn't be a very awkward and uncomfortable meeting.

The customer came to the counter with a box of biscuits in her hand. It was only then that Sarah noticed the young woman's vivid green eyes. They were the same as her own, the eyes she'd inherited from her father.

'Excuse me,' the woman said, waving the biscuits under Sarah's nose.

Sarah's mind raced, and her heart was pounding. This woman had to be related to her, possibly even her sister. 'Sorry,' Sarah said. 'Half a crown, please.'

The woman fished in her purse for some change, but Sarah couldn't take her eyes off her. She wanted to ask her name, and find out if she was the daughter of Ron Lyons, but she daren't.

The woman handed her the money, then stopped and looked oddly at Sarah.

'Do I know you from somewhere?'

'I – erm – I – I don't think so,' Sarah stuttered. As curious as she was, and as much as she would have liked to know more, she was too afraid of her father to delve.

'You look ever so familiar,' the woman said.

'You've probably seen me in here before,' Sarah answered and quickly looked downwards. She didn't want the woman to notice they shared the same eyes.

'No, I don't think so. I've not been in here before. Oh, well, see ya.'

The woman left the shop, and eventually Sarah began to calm down. She'd just had a close encounter with someone who could be a relative! It would have been so nice to strike up a conversation and get to know the woman, but she knew if Ron Lyons found out, he'd be enraged and that was something she didn't want to risk.

Chapter 34

Later that day, Mo sat on the doorstep and drew long puffs on her cigarette, amusing herself by blowing smoke rings into the air. Smoking was a habit she'd only recently taken up as she thought it made her look more glamorous, like her film-star idols. Samuel didn't like the smell so she usually smoked outside.

She stubbed her cigarette out on the ground and was just rising to her feet when Tommy came flying around the corner.

'Wotcher, Mo,' he said as he ran past her and into the house.

Sarah was behind him and, as she walked towards her, Mo said, 'He's in a hurry.'

'He's a proper live wire. Never walks when he can run. Have you had a nice day with Sam?'

Mo tutted. 'Don't get me started. Make us both a drink of something cold, and I'll tell you all about it.'

'Er . . . I'm a bit pushed for time. Roger will be here soon.'

'Oh, I forgot to tell you, he said he'll be a bit later tonight 'cos he's got to do something for his mum before he can get away. Cor, the atmosphere between him and

George was a bit frosty, so I'm guessing George knows all about you two now.' Mo felt a tinge of pleasure at seeing the smile drop from Sarah's face.

'You've seen them then?' Sarah asked.

'Yes, down the market earlier. Roger was showing off his tanned muscles to all the housewives. He's a bit cheeky, your chap.'

'What do you mean by that?'

'Oh, nothing, forget I said anything,' Mo answered. She wouldn't tell Sarah what had happened, she wasn't that mean, but Roger had flirted with her today and made it quite clear that he fancied her. She knew Sarah wasn't putting out for him, and a good-looking bloke like Roger had his needs. If Sarah wasn't careful, Mo thought, she might find her man's wandering eye would lead him to a woman who *was* willing to please him.

'Well, if Roger's going to be later than usual, you may as well come in,' Sarah said. 'Are you sure he said his mother? I thought she died several years ago.'

'Yep, he said his mum. Forget about the drink, love,' Mo said after glancing at the clock on Sarah's mantel. 'I've just seen the time and Sam will be wanting his dinner. See you soon.'

'Yes, see you,' Sarah said, sounding distracted.

Mo ran upstairs, a roguish grin on her face. That should set the cat amongst the pigeons, she thought, and wondered if she'd hear raised voices from downstairs later.

'How was your first day back?' Lena asked as she dished up smoked kippers for dinner.

'It was all right. Why are we having fish? It ain't Friday.'

'I just fancied some kippers. Is that OK with you?' Lena asked.

'Yes, but they stink the house out,' George said, opening the kitchen window.

They sat at the table to eat, but Lena's appetite had vanished as she felt nervous about broaching the subject of her date with Albert. She noticed George already seemed a bit fed-up, and was pushing his food around on his plate.

'What's the matter? Have you gone off my cooking?' Lena asked.

'No, it's lovely. I'm just not very hungry,' George answered and placed his fork back down on the table.

Something was obviously on his mind, so Lena decided to delay telling him about Albert. 'What's wrong? You've usually got a good appetite.'

'Did you know about Sarah and Roger?'

'What, about them seeing each other?'

'So you did know then. You could have said something, Mum.'

'I thought you'd sussed it when they came to visit you in hospital.'

'Well, I didn't and it wasn't much fun finding out about them on my first day back. I ain't half peed off with him. He's supposed to be my mate.'

'He's nothing but a womaniser, and as for Sarah, I think the girl needs her head testing. I only hope she sees sense before he breaks her heart,' Lena said, pushing her unfinished dinner to one side. 'It can't be easy, having to work next to Roger all day, but try not to let it upset you. I know Sarah is a lovely girl, but she ain't the one for you. There'll be a nice girl out there somewhere, and I'm sure you'll meet her soon.'

'If you say so, Mum.'

'I do, George, so try to stop moping about and cheer up.'

George went through to the front room, and Lena cleared up the kitchen. As she wiped the crockery dry, she wondered if she should try again to talk to George about Albert. She was going to dinner with him tomorrow evening, so she'd have to tell her son soon. George had taken his father's death badly and it had just been the two of them for a lot of years now, and they were close. Lena wasn't sure how her son would take the intrusion of another man into her life.

With the kitchen tidy, she joined her son in the front room. She sat on the sofa, and drawing in a breath, said, 'George, I won't be doing your tea tomorrow. You'll have to fend for yourself, but there's a tin of corned beef in the larder and you can have a bit of salad with it.'

'OK, you off out with Joan and Kath again?'

'Er . . . no . . . I'm going to dinner with Mr Bosco. He's a very nice man, you know, and a widower,' Lena said in a rush as she stared at her son to gauge his reaction. His face didn't show any emotion so she couldn't tell how he'd taken the news. 'George, did you hear me?'

'Yes, I heard you. You're right, he's a nice man, but I don't like the idea of you going out with him. What about my dad, have you forgotten about him?'

'No, of course I haven't and never will, but he's been dead for years now. He'd want me to get on with my life.'

'Maybe, but he wouldn't want you seeing other men!' George said, sounding angry.

'Don't be like that. I loved your father very much, and I always will, but he's gone and I can't bring him back.

It's not like I'm a shrivelled-up old woman. I'm still fairly young and I'd like some companionship. You ain't going to be here forever. Once you've found a good woman, you'll be off and I'll be left here rattling around by myself. Anyway, it's only dinner, not a bloody marriage proposal.'

There was a few moments' silence, then George got up from his armchair and looked in the mirror. 'You're right, Mum. I'm sorry. It's just a bit of a shock to hear you're going to be dating. I never thought you would, but why shouldn't you? You're a smashing-looking woman for your age, and I want you to be happy.'

Lena rose and went to stand next to her son. She looked at her reflection. George was right, she did look good, but she was nervous about going out with a man again. George's father had been the only one she'd ever been with, and they'd been sweethearts since school.

As if George could sense how she was feeling, he took her hand and said, 'You'll be fine. You've got nothing to worry about. If anything, I bet old Bosco's feeling more scared about it than you are.'

'Thanks, love, and I reckon you're probably right. He got himself in a bit of a state when he asked me out. It's not so easy for us oldies, you know, especially second time around.'

George squeezed her hand and Lena smiled up at her son. She was glad he hadn't given her a hard time, and was grateful for his support. Albert Bosco could never compare to her husband, but even so, she was excited about their dinner tomorrow.

Roger turned up just as Tommy was drifting off to sleep. The boy had felt burning hot, probably because he'd been running around with Larry in the heat all afternoon. Sarah had given him a cool bath, but he still felt hot and she was a bit worried that he might have a fever.

When the doorbell rang she went out to stand on the front doorstep, but kept the door half closed. 'I'm sorry, Roger, but Tommy is just going to sleep. He needs his rest and it's getting late now.'

'Come on, Sarah, I've driven over now. Surely you can let me in for half an hour. I'll be quiet, I promise.'

'It's not that. He gets so excited when he sees you and it'll take me ages to settle him again.'

'Come and sit outside then. If he's asleep, he won't notice you're gone,' Roger said.

'Wait here,' Sarah said and after running back to their room to see that Tommy was asleep, she crept out again, gently closing the door behind her. Roger smiled when he saw her, and her heart leaped. She sat on the step and he joined her, placing an arm across her shoulder. Sarah cleared her throat. 'Mo said something a bit odd today. She said you were going to be doing something for your mum.'

'Did I say my mum? I meant my aunt.'

'Mo also said you're cheeky. What do you think she meant by that?'

'Well, I suppose I am really. You have to be, down the market. The women love it, especially the old girls, and they become regular customers. Tell you what, how about I be cheeky now and kiss you . . .'

Sarah had no time to answer and found herself tingling to the feel of Roger's tongue in her mouth. He pulled her closer to him and his kisses became more passionate as his breathing intensified.

'I want you, Sarah,' he said huskily and pushed his hand in between her legs, forcing them slightly apart.

She could feel his hand rubbing on the outside of her knickers, and though it thrilled her, she grabbed his wrist and pulled him away. 'Not here . . . not like this,' she whispered.

'Let's go inside then. Tommy will be out for the count by now.'

Sarah froze. His suggestion brought back terrible memories of pretending to be asleep while her mother had entertained men. The grunts, the groans and the smells, it had been disgusting. She jumped to her feet and straightened her clothes. 'You'd better go now,' she said coldly and dismissively. 'I'll see you tomorrow.'

Roger looked bewildered, but shrugged his shoulders. 'Suit yourself,' he said, then spun on his heel and stomped off towards his van.

'Wait,' Sarah shouted, then ran towards him. She stood on tiptoe and placed her mouth on his. After a long kiss she pulled away and said, 'I'm sorry, I'm just tired. It's been a long day and I think Tommy has got a fever.'

Roger gave her a gentle squeeze. 'I've been waiting weeks for you, and I'll wait longer if I have to, but please tell me you ain't going to hold out on me until our wedding night?'

They'd never discussed sex before or anything related to marriage, so Sarah was staggered at his question. She hadn't really given it much thought, but she loved him and he'd said he loved her too. Regardless of the advice her mother had given her, if they were getting married, what would be the harm? 'Are you going to marry me then?' she said.

'I might,' Roger answered playfully. 'Depends if you're going to be my *proper* girlfriend.'

Sarah understood what he meant and shyly nodded. 'I will be. Goodnight, my *proper* boyfriend.'

She walked with him to the kerb and watched him climb into his van. He waved at her as he drove off, and she waved back, feeling that a milestone had been reached. The milder evening air cooled her flushed cheeks, and feeling elated she looked up to see Mo looking down at her from her upstairs window. She waved again, this time at Mo, but she didn't wave back. Sarah frowned; something didn't feel right. Mo's face was deadpan, then she stepped back and out of sight. It was very strange – maybe Mo hadn't seen her, though she was sure she had.

As she went inside, Sarah thought she heard Tommy moan and dashed to their room, dismissing all thoughts of Mo's peculiar behaviour. She perched on the edge of Tommy's bed and gently stroked his hair, while her mind drifted to thoughts of Roger. His sensual touch had made her quiver with delight, and though they weren't yet married, they were committed and she felt ready to move their relationship on to the next stage.

Chapter 35

The following evening, Lena checked herself one final time in her bedroom mirror. Albert would be here soon, and her nerves were jangling. Her hair was curled to perfection, and she wore a smart brown skirt with a matching jacket, and a white blouse. It wasn't what she'd describe as sexy, and if anything, it made her look a bit like a school headmistress, but she'd deemed the outfit suitable for her date.

Pleased with her appearance, Lena picked up her handbag just as she heard George come home. He was later than usual, but had said he was going to pick up some second-hand stock that he'd been offered for a knockdown price.

'You look . . . nice. Is that what you're wearing for your date with Mr Bosco?' George asked as he came in, a small frown creasing his brow.

'Yes, what's wrong with it?' Lena asked, suddenly having second thoughts about her choice.

'Nothing . . . nothing's wrong with it at all . . . if you were going to meet the bank manager.'

'Oh, George, it's too late for me to change now, he'll be here any minute.'

'Take no notice of me, Mum, you look lovely. You always do. I'm just teasing you.'

There was a knock on the door and when George opened it she could see Mr Bosco, almost hidden behind a large bouquet of flowers. She hurried down the last few stairs. 'Albert, come in,' she invited. 'Are they for me?'

'Yes, I hope you like them.'

'They're beautiful,' Lena said and took the bunch. 'It's been a while since anyone's bought me flowers. George, I've left you a salad and there's some nice crusty bread. Be a love and get a vase out from under the sink. Put these in water for me and I'll see you later.'

'Yeah, will do,' George said as he looked at Albert.

She kissed her son on the cheek and handed him the bouquet, hoping he wouldn't say something embarrassing. Albert looked awkward enough as he stood in the hall so she was keen to get him out of the front door and away from George's scrutiny.

Once outside, Albert held the passenger-side door open and Lena climbed into the car. She was immediately impressed with the red and cream leather interior, and her nose twitched at the smell of polish.

'You look nice,' Albert said as he started the car engine.

'Thank you, so do you,' Lena replied, noting his suit, which looked brand new, and smart shirt. After years of her husband and now her son working with second-hand clothes, Lena had a good eye for quality, and could always tell when something was new.

'I've reserved us a table at Allesandro's. It's a small Italian restaurant in Chelsea. Do you like Italian food?'

Lena had never tasted Italian cuisine, apart from the ice-creams at De Marco's. 'I couldn't say, but I'm sure I will,' she answered and wondered what sort of food it would be. Maybe spaghetti with meatballs? She pictured a scene in her favourite comedy film in which the characters had been given big bowls of the stuff. She couldn't help but chuckle at the memory.

'What's so funny?' Albert asked.

'Oh, nothing really. I'm just remembering an old film with scenes of spaghetti and meatballs,' she answered.

'The Marx Brothers film? *A Night at the Opera*?' Albert asked.

'Yes! It's my favourite,' she said.

'Mine too.'

Lena began to relax and found she was enjoying herself. They didn't only share being widowed, but also the same sense of humour. She'd been hesitant about accepting a night out with a man, but now was glad she had.

'Can I have a jam sandwich?' Tommy asked.

'No, you can't,' Sarah answered firmly.

'But I'm hungry.'

'Then you should have eaten your dinner.'

'But I hate liver.'

'Oh, all right, you can have a jam sandwich, but then it's bed for you, young man.'

'Fanks, Mum. Is Roger coming to see you?'

'Yes, and he should be here soon.'

'Do you think he'll bring me another banana? If he does I'm going to share it with Larry. He said his mum gave him peaches and milk from a tin after his tea yesterday. Can we have peaches and milk from a tin too?'

'We'll see. Now enough questions.'

Sarah sliced the bread, and then looked at the milk.

She'd have to boil it if it was to last. The warm weather was turning the milk quicker, and it didn't help that she had no proper larder. She finished making the sandwich and handed it to Tommy.

He gobbled it down, and she told him to go and clean his teeth. Just then there was a knock on the front door. 'That'll be Roger,' she said.

'Are you going to sit outside with him again?'

'Yes, but you don't have to worry. I'll only be sitting on the doorstep.'

Sarah ran to let Roger in and as she opened the door she thought he looked gorgeous in a buttoned-up cardigan, just like a picture she'd seen of James Dean. 'Hello, Roger. I haven't got Tommy into bed yet, and I doubt I'll be able to for a while now, not once he sees you're here.'

'That's all right. I've got a treat for the lad,' Roger said and lightly kissed Sarah.

Tommy came running from the bathroom. 'Roger, Mum just made me a jam sandwich 'cos I didn't eat my dinner . . . liver . . . erk!'

'Can't say I blame you, but you're a lucky boy. My mum wouldn't have given me anything else if I'd left even a mouthful of food on my plate.'

'See, I'm far too soft with you, Tommy. Now come on, bedtime.'

'Can I stay up for a while? Please, Mum.'

'If you do as your mum tells you, you can have this,' Roger said, and pulled a yo-yo from a pocket of his tweed trousers.

'Cor, thanks, Roger,' Tommy chirped happily as he scrambled into his bed. 'I know how to do the yo-yo 'cos Larry's big sister has got one.'

'Put it under your pillow and you can play with it in the morning,' Sarah told him as she tucked him in. 'Go to sleep now.'

'Night, Tommy,' said Roger.

'Sleep now, I'll only be outside,' Sarah said softly.

Tommy didn't protest, and once on the doorstep, Roger pulled her into his arms. Sarah closed her eyes as she felt his tongue in her mouth and his lips pressing hard on hers. The kiss was a long one, but then he sat down on the step and took her hand, gently pulling her down to sit next to him.

'I've been thinking,' he said, 'it's not ideal sitting out here most nights, and once the winter's here, it's going to be impossible.'

'I know, but what else can we do? I can't leave Tommy by himself.'

'You could move in with me, both of you. There's only me and my dad, and he's down the Labour Club most nights. Tommy would have his own room, and a garden.'

Sarah hadn't been expecting that, and baulked at his suggestion. She couldn't live in sin with him. She could just imagine the gossip. 'I can't do that. What would people say? I mean, we're not married or anything, it wouldn't be right.'

'Mo and Sam live together and they ain't married,' Roger pointed out.

'Yeah, well, it's all right for them, but I've got Tommy to think about. What sort of morals would I be teaching him?'

'It was just a suggestion. We've only been dating a short time and I think it's too soon to think about marriage yet. I thought us living together would be the perfect solution.'

Sarah could tell from the tone of his voice that he wasn't happy she'd declined his offer. Though it had hurt a little that he thought it was too soon to marry, she knew he was right. He'd loosely mentioned marriage before, and one day she hoped for a proposal, along with a nice engagement ring. However, until then, she hoped what she had to say next would placate him. 'I've been really busy lately, but I've been thinking about moving, and you've got a good point about Tommy. He does need his own room.'

'I'm glad to hear that, but in the meantime, are we supposed to sit on this concrete step night after night?' Roger asked.

'Yes, I'm afraid so. I can't ask Lena to babysit – it wouldn't feel right, you know, with George having feelings for me. It'd be like rubbing salt in his wound.'

'You could ask Mo.'

'She's fine about having him during the day, but she only gets one night off a week. It's the only one she gets to spend with Sam, so I can hardly ask her to babysit.'

'Well, I ain't being funny, Sarah, but you're not really his mother. You've made Tommy your responsibility, but he doesn't have to be. You could put him in a children's home. The one round here ain't too bad, and you could visit him at weekends.'

Unable to believe her ears and disgusted with Roger, Sarah jumped to her feet. 'How could you even suggest such a thing? I know I'm not his mother, but I've raised him from the minute he was born and I held him in my arms. I love Tommy and would never, ever, put him in

a home. I'm sorry that you find him such an inconveni-
ence . . . and . . . and I think you should leave now.'

Roger stood up and reached for her hand again. 'Calm
down, woman. Blimey, if I thought you'd react like this,
I would have kept my mouth shut.'

'Yes, well, you should have,' Sarah snapped.

'I'm sorry. Tell you what, I'll help you look for somewhere decent to live. I can run you anywhere in my van
if it helps.'

Sarah felt her mood soften, but Roger's talk of aban-
doning Tommy in a home had hurt her deeply. It seemed
he didn't know her at all, and after the things he'd said
tonight, she questioned how much she really knew him.

Chapter 36

George had been back at work for a month now, but there was still tension between him and Roger. He hadn't seen Sarah in all that time, but heard from his mum that she was doing well, and seemed to be happy with her man. If only she knew what he was really like, thought George, as he saw Roger chatting up the young woman who worked in the café on the market.

'Penny for 'em?' he heard a voice say.

He turned to see an old woman with a stooped back. 'My thoughts ain't worth that much,' George said to her and tried to sound cheerful.

'When you've been around as long as me, young man, you get to know a thing or two. It's a woman, it always is. You love her but she's out of your reach,' the old woman said.

'Yeah, that just about sums it up.'

'Don't give up . . . your time is coming . . .' the old woman said as she hobbled away. 'She'll be yours one day. I can see it, you know. But she'll always yearn for the boy.'

George listened, dumbstruck. He shook his head, thinking she had lost her mind, yet unable to get her words out of his head. Silly old cow, he thought, she didn't have a clue, though he would have liked it to be true.

Another woman, pushing a large pram, stopped at his stall. 'Do you have any new-born stuff?' she asked.

'Yes, a whole box over there,' George replied and went around to the side of his stall where he kept the baby clothes. The woman began to rummage, and George stood waiting, his mind churning over what the old woman had said. He was close to Roger's stall, and when he heard the girl from the café call out, his ears pricked.

'I'll see you tonight then, Roger, and this time you're not shooting off so early.'

George took a moment to digest what he'd heard, and then saw red as his blood boiled. The dirty cheating bastard, he thought. It was bad enough that Roger had pinched Sarah from under his nose, but he felt appalled to think of her being deceived and hurt. She was such a good, honest young woman and deserved more respect than that.

'Excuse me, love,' George ground out to the woman with the pram as he marched over to Roger, fuming.

Roger seemed unaware of his mood and shot him an arrogant smile, which fuelled George further. He raised his arm and pushed hard on Roger's chest. 'How could you? I know your game. What the hell do you think you're playing at?' he screeched.

Roger stumbled back, but his footing was saved as he fell against his stall. 'I don't know what you're talking about. What the hell was that for?' Roger said as he held his hands out in front of him in a calming motion.

'I just heard you – arranging to see that bird from the

café. What about Sarah, eh? I bet she ain't got a fucking clue what you're up to.'

'Leave off. It's got nothing to do with you.'

George was aware that the market had fallen quiet and all eyes were on him, but he couldn't help himself and grabbed Roger's shoulder. He clenched his other fist and punched him, clipping his chin.

Roger's head went back with the force of the blow, but he didn't retaliate. Instead, he rubbed his face and said, 'I'll let you have that one, George, but stay out of mine and Sarah's business.'

'No, I won't! You can't treat her like you've treated all the other women in your life. She's different – special, and I won't let you break her heart.'

'Yeah, all right, she might be special to you, but what you gonna do about it?'

'Either you stop seeing her or I'll tell her what you've been up to,' George said through gritted teeth.

'Tell her what you want, George, she won't believe you. She'll think you're making it up 'cos of sour grapes, and anyhow, I've got her twisted round my little finger . . . How do you like that?'

George puffed out his chest and clenched his fist again, ready to jump on Roger, but suddenly felt strong arms holding him back, and a voice in his ear saying, 'Leave it, George, break it up.'

'Let me go!' George shouted, and glanced sideways at the man restraining him, to see it was Ned the Nose from the ironmonger's stall opposite his.

'I'll kill him, Ned, I'll fucking kill him. Let me at him, will ya?' George shouted as he struggled against Ned's firm grip.

'Calm down, mate, he ain't worth it and the Old Bill are coming down the street.'

George knew it was pointless to fight against Ned. The man was almost twice the size of him and had the strength to match. 'All right, all right,' he said to Ned, then glared at Roger. 'This ain't over.'

Ned released his hold, and George straightened his clothes as he looked around the market. 'What you all staring at?' he shouted.

The costermongers and shoppers looked wary, and quickly resumed their business as George stomped back to his stall. He began packing things away. With what he knew, he couldn't stand there and ignore the situation. Roger might be right, Sarah probably wouldn't believe him, but she trusted his mum. He just hoped his mother could get to Sarah before Roger did.

With Tommy back at school after the school summer holidays, Lena had offered to pick him up every day. It saved Sarah having to pay anyone to look after him, or having to be beholden to the woman who lived above her. Anyway, Lena enjoyed having the lad. These last few days, Tommy's cough had been bad again, so she'd hoped an afternoon spent baking cakes and making pies with him would be a good distraction. Now, the boy and the kitchen were covered in flour. It had been good fun though, and she knew Albert would appreciate her efforts. He'd taken her to dinner on four occasions now, and her cake-making was a small gesture in return to say thank you.

'Can I lick the bowl, please, Lena?' Tommy asked.

'Yes, as the chief cook you've earned that privilege,'

Lena answered. She envied her friends who had grandchildren, and would have loved some of her own, but with George still hankering after Sarah, she doubted it would be any time soon.

As Tommy ate the uncooked cake mixture, Lena began clearing away. She missed George being young, and though the shop had been good for her, she much preferred to stay at home and look after Tommy. It was nice to feel needed again, and she lavished affection on him, which was reciprocated.

Once Tommy finished with the bowl, she lifted him to the kitchen sink. 'Wash your hands, there's a good boy.'

Tommy giggled as water splashed his face. She adored hearing him laugh, and gave him a gentle squeeze, but then, to her surprise, she heard the front door slam. It must be George, but what was he doing home so early? She placed Tommy down and gave him a small towel to dry himself as her son came into the kitchen. His face looked ashen, and she could see there was something wrong.

'I need a word, Mum,' he said, and stalked through to the front room.

Lena quickly removed her apron and gave Tommy a small lump of left-over pastry. 'Here you go, make some animal shapes,' she said, then joined her son.

'It's about Sarah,' George said with a stern face as he paced the floor.

'I thought it probably would be,' Lena answered. He hadn't been the same since the girl had started seeing Roger, and though she wished he'd buck up, her heart went out to him.

'I know for a fact that Roger is doing the dirty on her.'

'Well, that doesn't surprise me. I told you that man was trouble, just like his father. Do you know, his dad tried it on with me once? I slapped his face and he never spoke to me after that, but he'd have got a lot worse if I'd told your dad.'

'Well, the apple ain't fallen far from the tree, but you're missing my point, Mum,' George said, and sat on the armchair. 'Sarah needs to know what he's up to before she gets in any deeper with him, but it's no good coming from me.'

'Why not?'

'Roger will deny it. He'll probably say I'm jealous and trying to cause trouble between them. She'd believe you though, Mum.'

'What, you want me to tell her?'

'Yes, she'll listen to you, you know she will.'

'I don't know, George. I don't think it's a good idea to get mixed up in other people's relationships. I've dropped subtle hints about him, but she's never taken any notice. She's blindly in love with him, and she won't thank either of us for interfering.'

George leaned forward and said earnestly, 'So you think it's best to just let her get on with it, even though I know she's heading for heartbreak?'

'Yes, I do, love. I know that's not what you wanted to hear, but I don't think it's a good idea to get involved. Hopefully, one day soon she'll see Roger for what he is, but until then, stay out of it.'

George leaned back in the chair, 'Mum, you're nearly always right about things, but I don't think you are this time. If you're not prepared to tell her, then I will.'

Lena could see the frustration in his face. His jaw

looked tight and his eyes were narrowed. Although her son's face was heavily scarred, she could read him like a book. If he'd had eyebrows, they'd have been knotted in a deep frown. 'Well, I've said my piece. Just make sure you're telling Sarah for the right reasons,' Lena said, worried that her son's good intentions would be misconstrued.

'What do you mean by that? She's my friend and I'm looking out for her. She deserves to know the truth.'

'I hope for your sake she sees it that way,' Lena said, then went back through to the kitchen to check on Tommy, all the while knowing that trouble was brewing.

Lena looked down at the boy's efforts and smiled warmly. He'd made several little shapes, though she couldn't tell what they were. 'Do you want to come to Joan's with me?' she asked, thinking Sarah would be finishing work soon and it would be best to have Tommy out of the way. George seemed set on telling her the truth about Roger, and she feared all hell was about to break loose.

Sarah was surprised when Roger came into the shop late that afternoon, and listened, shocked, to what he had to say. She now locked up and headed for Lena's to collect Tommy. It was always such a mad dash to get there before George would arrive home, and so far she'd managed to avoid him. This couldn't go on, though, and despite what Roger had told her she still wanted to talk to George about the reward money.

She turned the corner on to Lena's street and immediately noticed George's red van. He was home. Part of her was dreading seeing him, but the other part had missed his friendship. Now, at the prospect of facing him, she couldn't help feeling a little apprehensive. She drew in a deep breath and braced herself, but before she had a chance to knock on the door, George opened it.

'Hello, stranger,' he said, and pulled the door open wider.

'Hi, George. It's nice to see you,' Sarah said as she stepped inside, 'but I didn't expect you to be home yet.'

'It was quiet on the market so I packed up early. Mum's popped over to Joan's with Tommy. She said if you don't want to wait for them, he can stop here the night and I'll run him over to you first thing in the morning if you like?'

Sarah stood in the hallway and hid a smile. It was perfect. It would allow her to have some time alone with Roger. He'd been coming to see her tonight, but lately he'd been showing up later and later, sometimes not showing up at all. He always gave her a good reason, but she was beginning to worry that he was seeing someone else behind her back. Her suspicions had first been aroused when she'd found a long blonde hair on the shoulder of his shirt, but he'd said it must be one of his aunt's. On another occasion, she was sure he smelled of perfume, but she hadn't questioned him as she didn't want to sound paranoid and insecure. Not only that, he'd seemed a bit distant lately, but as she hadn't found anywhere suitable to move yet, maybe it was just because he was fed up with her doorstep. Well, for once they would have her room to themselves and that was sure to make him happy. 'As long as you don't mind, that's great. Thanks, George,' she said, and turned to leave.

'You may as well have a cuppa now you're here,' George said, and closed the front door.

Despite what Roger had said, George seemed fine to her, and anyway, she couldn't really say no, even though she was keen to get home to make things nice for Roger's visit. However, she hadn't seen George in ages and this might be her chance to rekindle their friendship, as well as talk to him about her plans for the reward money. As they walked into the kitchen, Sarah could smell a delicious aroma, and spotted some fresh cakes and pies on a wire rack. 'I can see your mum's been busy cooking with Tommy again. He loves being here with her, she's so good with him.'

'Mum enjoys having him. I reckon she thinks she's his nan. She always wanted a big family with loads of kids, but it never happened for her. When I was younger, she used to babysit all the children on the street. The house was always full and that's how she liked it.'

George poured her a cup of tea from a large brown pot and Sarah sat at the kitchen table. He pulled out a chair opposite her and she was relieved to find that it wasn't as awkward with him as she'd expected. She did notice they both steered away from any mention of Roger. She soon found herself laughing at George's silly jokes, and realised just how much she'd missed his company. 'I'm really glad I've seen you, George, 'cos there's something I've been meaning to talk to you about for a long time now.'

'Funnily enough, there's something I want to talk to you about too,' he answered. 'It's about Roger.'

Sarah braced herself. She didn't want to believe what Roger had told her, thinking that George was better than that, but now feared the worse and hoped to divert him as she said, 'I'm sorry I didn't tell you when I began dating Roger. I was worried it would ruin our friendship.'

'I'll always be your friend, Sarah,' George said softly, 'and it's because we're friends that I have to tell you something. I'm afraid you ain't gonna like it.'

When Roger had come into the shop earlier, he'd said he was worried about George's state of mind. Apparently, George had been spouting off for weeks, saying he would find a way to break up their relationship, and it was getting worse.

'Tell me and we'll see.'

George bit his lower lip for a moment, but then blurted out, 'I'm afraid Roger is doing the dirty on you. He's seeing someone else.'

'I know that isn't true. Roger warned me that you were going to try to break us up, but I didn't want to believe him. To be honest, I expected better from you.'

George reached across the table and grasped her hands, saying earnestly, 'I'm not lying, Sarah, I've seen it with my own eyes. He was chatting up a woman today and they've arranged to see each other later. It ain't the first time either, and it won't be the last.'

George sounded so sincere that Sarah found herself suspicious of Roger again. He'd said he loved her, had talked of marriage, so surely this couldn't be true. They hadn't yet made love, but had come very close to it, and she'd been prepared to give herself to him tonight.

'I'm telling you the truth, Sarah,' George said, unclasping her hands and leaning back in his chair.

She was sure George meant well, in his own way, but even though she had her doubts, he must have got it wrong. 'You must be mistaken, George, 'cos Roger is coming to see me later. He can't be seeing other women.'

'I doubt he'll show up. He's always the same when it comes to women. He's all over his latest conquest for a while, but then his eyes start to stray. I don't want to see him make a mug out of you.'

Sarah didn't want to believe George, but something niggled her, and she got the impression that he was telling the truth. If Roger didn't turn up tonight, there'd be no denying it, and her heart was already beginning to ache.

Mo had been waiting for ages for Sarah to arrive home, and wondered what was keeping her. At last, as she looked out of her window, she saw her friend walking along the street, and noticed Tommy wasn't with her. She ran down the stairs as Sarah was coming through the front door, and said eagerly, 'I'm so glad you're home . . . I've been dying to tell you something.'

Sarah appeared glum, but asked, 'What's up?'

Mo followed Sarah into her room and watched in silence as Sarah kicked off her shoes. There was obviously something bothering her and, as Tommy wasn't with her, Mo asked, 'Is Tommy OK?'

'Yes, he's staying over with Lena tonight. What did you want to tell me?'

'I've got a new job. I'm so happy about it, but I haven't told Samuel yet. I'm not too sure how he'll react.'

'Why, what's the job?'

'I'm going to be a model!' Mo replied, and struck a pose, one hand on her hip and the other held up gracefully.

'That's nice,' Sarah said, 'but why are you worried about telling Sam?'

'He can be a bit funny about that sort of thing. I don't

think he likes other men looking at me. I couldn't turn it down, though, it's too good an opportunity to miss. It all came about last night. I was at work, and when the film had finished, this chap approached me and gave me his card. He said I was just what he'd been looking for and to get in touch. So I did and went to see him today at his studio. He took some headshots and said he'd get me in all the top magazines. I've got to go back to see him tomorrow. Isn't it brilliant?'

Sarah nodded, but looked distracted as she said, 'I'm really pleased for you.'

'Come on, out with it,' Mo demanded. 'You're not yourself, so what's wrong?'

'I'm worried about Roger.'

'Why, has something happened to him?'

'No, he's fine, but I think he may be seeing someone else.'

'What makes you think that? He's here most nights, ain't he?'

'Yes, sort of. He pops over four or five nights a week, but he's started getting here later and later, and sometimes not at all. At first I thought it was because of us sitting outside on the doorstep, but George said something today and now I'm not so sure.'

'You've seen George at last? What did he say?'

'He was at home when I went to collect Tommy. It was funny really, we had a right laugh, until he dropped the bombshell. He told me he'd seen Roger chatting someone up and that they'd arranged to meet tonight. Roger warned me that George would come out with stuff like this to break us up. What do you think, Mo?'

Mo didn't believe for one minute that Roger was the

faithful type. He'd proved that by the way he'd flirted with her, but she didn't want to reveal that to Sarah. 'Maybe George is a bit jealous, or maybe he just got the wrong end of the stick. Is Roger supposed to be coming round tonight?'

'Yes,' Sarah answered.

'Wait and see what happens. If he doesn't show his face, then it could mean George is telling the truth.'

'I'm not so sure, Mo. It can't be much fun for him being stuck on my doorstep. Not long ago he asked me to move in with him.'

'Well then, he'd hardly do that if he's seeing someone else. Are you going to?'

'No, Mo. I just didn't think it was right for me and Tommy. I told him I'd find a new place soon, with a separate bedroom for Tommy, but most that I've seen are riddled with damp. I'll keep looking though, but I don't have much time, not with all the hours I've been doing at work.'

She'd kept that quiet, thought Mo. 'I didn't know you was looking to move out.'

'I've been thinking about it for a while now, but I really like living here with you and Sam. When all that bother was going on with your family, I did look at a couple of places, but the ones I could afford were diabolical. Now I'm earning a few bob more I was hoping to find some-where half decent.'

'If you ask me, it doesn't sound like you really want to move, so are you doing it for you or for Roger?'

'It's for Tommy too. He really should have his own room,' Sarah protested. 'This place is damp and come the winter it'll probably affect his chest again.'

'If you say so, but Tommy seems happy enough here. Just don't let Roger push you into anything you ain't ready for. It's obvious why he wanted you to move in with him, or to get Tommy in a separate bedroom, but take my advice and make sure to get a ring on that finger first.'

Sarah lowered her head, hiding her face. 'We . . . we haven't done . . . done it yet.'

Mo had guessed that Sarah hadn't gone all the way with Roger, and suspected he wasn't going to wait for much longer. She'd met fellas like him before, and regretted giving in to them, only to be left high and dry. It had been different with Samuel. He hadn't tried to persuade her into bed. If anything, she'd seduced him.

There was a sudden loud hammering on the front door that made both women jump. Mo ran to the window first. 'It's George,' she said.

'Oh, no, he can't be here when Roger turns up.'

'Don't worry. You lie low and I'll get rid of him.'

George hammered the door again and Mo hurried to answer it. 'What's going on?' she said. 'Where's the fire?'

'Where's Sarah? I have to speak to Sarah,' George said and pushed past her. He looked frantic and she wondered what was wrong.

'Wait, George,' she called, but he was already running into Sarah's room.

'Sarah, you have to come with me. It's Tommy! Mum's taken him to the hospital. Come on, I'll drive you there.'

'Why? What's wrong with him?' Sarah asked as the colour drained from her face.

'I'm not sure. He's been coughing a lot and Mum said he was burning up. He then seemed to have some sort of fit, so we called for an ambulance.'

'No, oh, no,' Sarah gasped as she frantically pulled on her shoes.

'I'm sure he'll be all right,' said George, 'but get a move on, love.'

Sarah grabbed her keys and hot on the heels of George she dashed out, calling, 'Mo, when Roger turns up, will you tell him what's happened?'

'Yeah, of course,' she called back. What seemed like only moments later, Mo heard the van drive off. She hoped Tommy was going to be all right. She'd seen someone have a fit before and they had bitten off the end of their tongue. Poor Tommy, she thought, hoping that he hadn't done the same thing, and poor Sarah.

Then straight away Mo's selfish side kicked in. She'd been so happy, over the moon at getting a modelling job, but if Tommy didn't make it she'd be expected to be a comfort to Sarah. Instead of celebrating and having a good time, she might well have to attend a bloody funeral.

Chapter 37

On the journey to the hospital, Sarah kept questioning George about Tommy's fit, but as he didn't have any answers she became more and more frantic. They didn't seem to be driving fast enough, and as she tapped her finger and thumb together, she hissed, 'Come on . . . come on . . . get a move on.'

After what seemed like an eternity, they finally pulled up outside the entrance and Sarah grabbed the door handle in a panic to get out of the van. She ran into the hospital, then stopped in her tracks when she realised she didn't know where to go.

George caught up with her. 'This way,' he said.

They turned right and hurried along a corridor where Sarah spotted Lena talking to a man in a white coat. She quickened her pace until she was standing next to them and Lena turned towards her with a solemn face.

'Where is he? Is he OK?' Sarah asked breathlessly.

'I'm . . . I'm . . . Oh, Sarah . . .' Lena groaned.

'What's wrong? Where's Tommy? I want to see him!' Sarah cried, her heart pounding in her chest. Something wasn't right, she could tell by the expressions on their faces.

The doctor placed his hand on Sarah's arm. 'Please, take a seat,' he said, indicating a row of chairs against the wall.

'I don't want to sit down. I want to see Tommy,' Sarah said, and desperately looked from Lena to the doctor for answers.

Lena looked away, dabbing her eyes, as the doctor said, 'Miss Jepson, we did everything we could, but I'm very sorry to tell you that Tommy passed away ten minutes ago. There was nothing we could do for him.'

Sarah saw the doctor's lips moving, heard his words, but they didn't make sense. Her mind refused to accept what she was hearing. This must be some sort of silly mistake and the doctor was talking about another patient. 'Don't be silly. I'm here to see Tommy Jepson and he's had a fit, that's all. Where is he? What ward is he in?'

'Miss Jepson, you don't seem to understand what I am telling you. Your brother has died.'

No . . . he can't be dead, Sarah thought. They've got it wrong. Furiously shaking her head in denial, she began to feel as if the walls were closing in on her. The whole world seemed to stop at that moment, yet she was stuck spinning on the spot. Her legs felt weak, and she crumpled towards the floor, but then George grabbed her around her waist to pull her back up and towards a seat.

'I'm so sorry, Sarah,' sobbed Lena.

Sarah looked up at the woman, but couldn't speak. Lena was crying, but she just felt numb. They said her brother was dead. Tommy, the child she loved like a son. She should be sobbing, hysterical even, yet she felt nothing – nothing but a strange sensation of almost not being there, watching the scene from afar.

'She's in shock,' she heard the doctor say to a nurse.

'I'll fetch her a cup of sweet tea,' the nurse said in a hushed voice, and seemed to vanish as quickly as she appeared.

George was still holding her hand. She could feel the warmth of his palm in hers, and snatched her hand back. If she could feel his body heat, then it was real, and she didn't want any of this to be true. Bile rose in her throat, and she retched. I'm going to be sick, she thought, and covered her mouth with her hand as she heaved.

'Over there,' the doctor said and pointed to a door on the other side of the corridor.

Sarah ran towards the bathroom, but she couldn't hold it any longer, and stopped to lean forward. She placed a hand on the wall to steady herself as she uncontrollably vomited on the corridor floor.

George was by her side and offered her a handkerchief from his pocket. She took it and wiped her mouth. Her own handkerchief was in her handbag. She'd left it behind in her haste to get to the hospital. She wondered why she was having such inane thoughts. What was the matter with her? She had just been told that Tommy was dead.

'Come on, love. Come and sit down again,' George urged.

Sarah couldn't look at him, didn't want to make eye contact, knowing that if she did she would see his sympathy and it might break her. She wanted to stay in this cocoon – this numb bubble of denial and disbelief. She was safe there and wanted to shut out the world around her.

The nurse appeared again. She handed George the cup of tea and then put her arm around Sarah's waist and led her back to the chair. 'Come on, dear,' she said gently. 'Don't worry about the mess. I'll have an orderly clean it up.'

Sarah allowed the nurse to sit her down, and accepted the cup of tea from George as the nurse continued, 'Drink it up, dear, it'll make you feel better.'

How can it make me feel better if I can't feel anything? Sarah thought, but nonetheless she sipped the hot sweet tea.

Lena had stopped crying, but was still sniffing, and as she looked at her, Sarah suddenly felt as though she was being pulled back to reality – a reality she still didn't want to face. This wasn't a nightmare. This was really happening, but her mind cried out against it. She wanted to go back in time, to before Tommy had died, but knew it was impossible. She wanted so much to hold him, to cuddle him for one last time. She asked, 'Please, can I see him?'

'Yes, of course. Nurse, take Miss Jepson to see her brother.'

'This way,' the nurse said, and walked with Sarah towards a set of double doors.

Sarah suddenly realised that George was beside her and she stopped, staring at the doors, not sure that she wanted to go any further. She wasn't sure she could face the horror of what was behind them. Come on, she told herself. You can do this. Tommy is in there and you can't leave him all alone.

'Would you like me to come in with you?' George asked.

Sarah nodded. She still couldn't bring herself to look at him.

The nurse pushed open one of the doors, and Sarah began to take rapid short breaths.

'Are you sure you want to do this?' George asked.

Again Sarah nodded, but looked steadily in front of her. I have to, she thought, desperate to hold Tommy in her arms. She apprehensively stepped forward, feeling that at any moment her knees would give way again, and was grateful for George's arm supporting hers.

The room had no windows, just machines that weren't switched on and a bed. My boy's in that bed, thought Sarah, still holding on to the slim chance that there'd been some terrible mistake, and Tommy would open his eyes to look at her with one of his cheeky grins.

She slowly walked across the room, her eyes fixed on her little brother. He looked so small in the big bed, motionless, with the covers over him up to his neck. He's just sleeping, she thought, and walked around to the side of his bed to peer down at him. She reached out her hand to brush his soft hair off his forehead and frowned. 'Nurse, can you get him more blankets? He feels cold.'

George stepped over and put his arm round her shoulder, saying softly, 'He doesn't need more blankets, love.'

Sarah shrugged off George's arm, and leaned over Tommy. 'Wake up, little man. Mummy's here now to take you home.'

There was no response and tears began to fall from her eyes. 'Please, Tommy, stop playing silly beggers with me. It's time to get up.'

George spoke softly again. 'Sarah, he can't hear you.'

Though she didn't want to accept it, Sarah knew George was right. Tommy couldn't hear her. He would never hear her again. He wasn't going to wake up. The reality finally hit her and she let out an anguished cry as she collapsed onto the bed, clinging to Tommy's lifeless body. 'Tommy . . . my baby! Please, George, do something . . . you have to do something to bring him back.'

'I wish I could, but I can't and you've got to say goodbye now,' George said, as he gently tried to tug her away.

'No . . . I can't leave him alone. He'll be scared if I'm not with him. Tommy . . . Tommy . . . please come back to me,' she begged, then, gasping, she cried, 'I love you.'

Lena sat on one of the seats in the corridor, crying into her handkerchief, but her head shot up when she heard Sarah's screams. It was such an agonising sound, one she'd heard many times during the war. She'd wailed like that when her husband had been killed. Poor Sarah, she thought. No woman should ever have to experience the agony of losing a child, and she was grateful George had been spared when the bomb had dropped.

The doors opened and Sarah emerged with George almost holding her up. She was weeping inconsolably, and, as her legs buckled, Lena rushed over to help.

'We need to get her home, Mum,' George said quietly over the top of Sarah's head.

Lena agreed. She wished she had some words of comfort to offer Sarah, but knew nothing she could say would take away the girl's pain. She'd heard it all herself before, the condolences and phrases such as 'Time heals', but none of it had helped her. She understood how lonely grief could be, and time hadn't healed. She had just learned to live with her heartache.

They managed to get Sarah to George's van, and Lena

was pleased that she didn't protest when they told her she'd be staying with them. The ride home seemed a long one, and was mostly driven in silence, apart from the noise of Sarah crying. She'd stop for a minute or two and seem to pull herself together, but then her face would scrunch and the tears flowed again.

Lena wanted to bawl herself; she loved the boy too and would miss him terribly, but she had to be strong. Her own anguish was nothing compared to Sarah's. The poor girl was bereft, and this was just the beginning of a very long period of mourning.

Chapter 38

Sarah awoke the next morning, and when she opened her puffy eyes, it took her a moment to realise where she was. The sun was streaming through a crack in the curtains in George's room, and she wondered what the time was.

Then she gasped as the shocking memory of Tommy's death hit her again. Unaware of what she was doing, Sarah sat up and an unnatural howl escaped her lips, then she was crying out, 'No . . . no . . . no.'

She was too fraught to hear the tap on her bedroom door, but then George was beside her, sitting on the edge of the bed, 'It's all right, Sarah, let it out,' he said soothingly as he gently rubbed her back.

After a while, her tears subsided, but her voice was a croak as she said, 'I can't believe he's gone, George. For a moment, when I first woke up, I'd forgotten. How could I forget? What sort of mother am I?'

'The best, Sarah, always the best. It's natural for your brain to try and block it out. My mum was the same when my dad died. Do you want to come downstairs for a cuppa or shall I bring you one up?'

George was being so kind that Sarah felt tears welling

again. She took a deep, juddering breath and managed to quell them, her voice shaky as she said, 'Thanks, I'll come down.'

'Mum's gone to open up the shop. She said to tell you not to worry about doing any shifts for a while.'

'Oh, George, I hadn't thought about work. All I can think about is Tommy . . .' Sarah cried as she covered her face with her hands and tears fell again. Her shoulders jerked up and down as her heart broke.

'It's all very raw, love, and you need time to grieve. You stay in bed and I'll bring you up that cuppa.'

George left the room. Sarah blew her nose. Her eyes were sore and she fought to stem her tears. The room looked dim and dreary with the curtains almost closed, so she climbed out of bed to open them. Though it was early, she saw some women sweeping their doorsteps, carrying on their normal everyday activities. Her child had died, and it didn't seem right. How could life continue as normal? She snatched the curtains closed again, and climbed back into bed, preferring the dimness of the room to the bright sunshine outside.

'There you go, love. There was a pot of tea made so I only had to pour it out,' George said as he carried in a cup and placed it on the bedside table.

Sarah thanked him, but couldn't smile. Her world had collapsed around her, and she felt like she would never smile again. She longed to hold Tommy once more, to see his cute face and hear his sweet voice, but he was gone. She looked up and cursed God. 'Why?' she yowled, 'Why would you take such an innocent child? I hate you, do you hear me? I hate you!'

'Oh, Sarah, I wish I could say something to comfort you,' George said, looking close to tears too.

'If He exists, God is supposed to give comfort, but all I can feel is pain. I don't know what to believe any more. If there really is a God, how could he be so cruel? Tommy never did anything wrong, all he brought was goodness to this horrible world.'

'I don't know what to tell you, Sarah. I ain't a believer but there's plenty that are, so I don't know, maybe there is something in it. You've got to see the vicar about Tommy's funeral. Maybe it would help to talk to him?'

'The funeral. Oh, no, I hadn't thought about that. It wasn't long ago that I was burying my mother, but there's no way my Tommy is having a pauper's grave too. No, he's going to have a proper send-off. After all, it's the last thing I can do for him,' Sarah said, trying to hold back more tears.

'You'll do him proud, Sarah, I know you will. This is a bit awkward, especially at a time like this, but I can help you to pay for it.'

Sarah still had the reward money, and though she'd earmarked it for their future, without Tommy her plans held no meaning. At least she would be able to pay for Tommy's funeral. 'Thanks, George,' she said, 'but I can manage.'

'You don't have to make any arrangements just yet, but when the time comes will you at least let me help you?'

'Yes, I'd be grateful if you would. To be honest, I'm struggling to hold myself together and can't think straight. I just keep seeing Tommy's face in my mind, and I can't believe I'll never see him grow up. It's like a part of me is missing and I don't know if I can carry on without him,' Sarah said, and then she broke down again, sobbing.

George pulled her into his arms, and desperate for comfort, Sarah didn't resist.

'Let it all out, Sarah. As I said before, you need to grieve. In time, it will get easier, but in the meantime Mum and me are here to help you through this.'

Sarah could feel George's shirt getting wet as her tears soaked into the material. She'd been strong in the past because she'd had to be for Tommy, but now, without him, she felt lost, as if she had no purpose in life any more.

Mo woke up excited, looking forward to meeting Barry again. She'd enjoyed pouting for his camera, and he'd told her she was a natural. Today he was going to add to her portfolio, and she couldn't wait to be posing for him. He made her feel relaxed in front of the lens, and said she was beautiful. This was the break she'd needed and she believed it wouldn't be long before she was on the front page of *Vogue*, with a career in films sure to follow.

Convinced he would disapprove, Mo hadn't mentioned it to Sam yet. She'd decided to tell him when her picture appeared in a classy magazine, and that way he was sure to be impressed. He would see for himself that she was a proper model, and he'd be proud of her.

Mo went through her wardrobe and tried on several outfits before settling on a simple white blouse and a full swing black and white skirt with a wide waistband. She studied herself in the mirror and thought that with a heavier make-up than usual she looked striking. She wanted a second opinion from Sarah, but hadn't heard her come home last night, and Tommy hadn't pounded on her front door this morning to go to school.

Pleased with her appearance, and convinced it would make a good impression on Barry, she grabbed her handbag and ran downstairs, but when she knocked on Sarah's door there was no answer. Mo frowned. Fits could be nasty, so maybe Tommy had been kept in hospital overnight as a precaution, and, knowing Sarah, she had probably gone out at the crack of dawn to see him.

Oh, well, she thought, she'd have to do without a second opinion. She left the house to head to Queenstown Road where Barry had a small flat and studio above a toyshop. When she arrived, Mo stood outside his door and pulled a small mirror from her bag to check her make-up before knocking.

'Well, I say, look at you,' Barry said, eyeing her with appreciation when he opened the door. 'Come in, everything is set up and ready for you.'

Mo walked past Barry and into the studio. The curtains were drawn but there were bright spotlights angled towards a large bed covered in pink satin. A wooden stepladder was positioned at the end of the bed, and there were large white screens on either side. This wasn't what she'd expected, and it looked a bit sleazy, but she trusted Barry, and was sure he knew what he was doing.

Barry was well spoken and dressed smartly, and his confident manner, along with his knowledge of the modelling industry, had quickly gained her confidence. He looked about twenty years older than her, but Mo thought him rather good-looking, with blonde hair and a golden tan, though he was a bit on the skinny side for her taste.

'What's all this then?' she asked, nodding towards the bed.

'I need you to be relaxed as any tension will show in your jaw, and what better way to relax than on a bed?' Barry answered. 'Now then, before we start I want you to sign this.'

'What is it?' Mo said, worried. She glanced at the paper and saw there were some long words which she knew she'd struggle to read.

'It's nothing for you to worry your pretty little head about. It's just a contract to say that you are happy for me to show your photographs, which I will need to do if we are going to make you a top model.'

'Oh, right, that's fine,' Mo said, taking the pen Barry held out and signing her name where he indicated.

'Right, now that's done, you can put your handbag on that chair, leave your shoes over there too and then climb onto the bed.'

Mo followed his instructions and knelt on the bed. 'How do you want me?'

Barry ascended halfway up the ladder and looked through the lens of his camera. 'Perfect,' he said, and Mo heard the noise of the shutter as he began taking photographs.

'Now, lean back and stretch your legs out,' Barry instructed. 'Good girl, you look beautiful . . . turn to your side, bend one knee up and lift your skirt a little higher. You have fabulous legs, let's show them off.'

Mo wriggled on the satin sheets into poses she thought Barry would like. She found she was really enjoying herself and wasn't the least bit nervous.

'Lovely, now I want you to loosen your blouse, undo a few buttons and show me those ample womanly charms of yours.'

Mo giggled, then undid her top three buttons before pushing her chest forward for maximum effect.

'You are so good at this . . . my goodness, where have you been all my life? Wait . . . hang on . . . it's no good, we'll have to stop,' Barry said, and descended the ladder looking disappointed.

'Have I done something wrong?' Mo asked worriedly.

'No, darling, it's not you, but your skirt is taking all the limelight. You'll have to remove it.'

'But . . . but . . .' Mo said, unsure if she should reveal her underwear for the camera.

'Now come on, don't be coy. If you're going to be a top model you will have to become accustomed to wearing very little. Models pose and show bathing suits on the catwalk, and that's hardly any different to under-wear.'

Mo felt a bit silly and wished she hadn't shown Barry how inexperienced she was. She slipped her skirt off before resuming her position on the bed.

'That's so much better, my dear. Your legs are much prettier than that skirt.'

She soon regained her confidence, and watched with fascination as Barry adjusted the lighting and snapped away.

'Right, undo your blouse and slip it off one shoulder.'

'What, all the way down?'

'Yes, of course,' Barry replied.

As Barry sounded so matter-of-fact about it, Mo assumed this was what models normally did. She didn't want to appear uncooperative or naïve again, so did as she was told, though she wasn't totally happy about it.

'That's fantastic,' Barry said. 'I've got some fabulous pictures and you'll be a star in no time, but now for the money shot. Remove your bra, but keep your back to me and peek over your shoulder. I want you to look deep into the lens and imagine that you're looking at your lover. Be seductive, show him that you want him.'

'I'm not sure about this, Barry. I don't think I should show you my breasts,' Mo protested, thinking how horrified Sam would be if he found out.

'My dear, I'm a photographer, I've seen a thousand pairs of titties in my life, and I can assure you, yours will be no different from any other woman's.'

'But that's not the point. I don't think my boyfriend will like it.'

'Your boyfriend will like it when you become rich and famous. Imagine it, the lovely houses, the cars and the holidays abroad. I doubt he'll complain then, so put him out of your mind and let me see that smiling face again.'

'I'm still not sure I feel comfortable about taking my bra off,' Mo said sullenly.

'If that's your attitude, you're wasting my time. You may as well leave now before I use any more camera film on you. You're a silly girl though, Mo. This is how all the top models and film stars began.'

Mo heaved a breath. 'Really? They've all done this?'

'Yes, how else do you think they got noticed?'

She bit on her bottom lip as she thought about it. Barry was far more knowledgeable than she was on such matters, and she wanted to be a film star more than anything else. Perhaps he was right, and this was the start of something big for her. 'All right, you're the expert,' she said, and slipped off her bra. It wasn't so bad at first with her back to Barry, but then with his continued reassurance, she found herself able to pose full frontal. Then, before Mo knew it, she'd removed her knickers too.

'Right, that's it for today,' Barry said, turning off the spotlights. 'You can get dressed now.'

Mo pulled on her clothes, but then her eyes widened with surprise when Barry held out two pound notes. 'Here, take this,' he said.

'What's that for?' Mo asked as she took it.

'Let's just say you're going to be a hit with my gentlemen clientele. I'll be in touch,' Barry said and opened the front door.

Mo walked down the stairs, her mind racing. His gentlemen clientele. What did that mean? Something wasn't right, she was sure of it. As Mo passed under the railway bridge, the penny dropped and she felt sick. The pictures Barry had taken, the nude poses, were going to be shown to those gentlemen clientele.

She turned and rushed back to bang on Barry's door. Out of breath when he opened it, she panted, 'The photographs you took of me. I want them destroyed.'

'My dear, have you forgotten the contract you signed? It gives me full rights over the prints.'

'But . . . but I don't want men ogling nude pictures of me. If my boyfriend finds out, he'll go mad.'

'Then I suggest you don't tell him,' Barry said offhandedly. 'Now if you don't mind, I'm busy.'

The door closed and Mo slumped. She'd been duped, made a fool of, but worst of all was the fear of Samuel finding out.

Chapter 39

Between them, George and his mother did their best to offer Sarah comfort. George didn't set up his stall that week, and while his mother was at work he held Sarah when she cried, and listened to her when she wanted to talk. He wished he could do more to alleviate her agony.

'Thanks for letting Mo and Roger know about Tommy. I don't think I could have faced telling them. Just saying the words out loud is almost too much to bear.'

'It's not a problem. You know I'd do anything for you, especially during this difficult time. I'm surprised Roger hasn't called round to see you.'

'It doesn't matter. I don't want him to see me like this.'

Sarah was sitting next to him on the sofa, and though it had passed midday she was still wearing a nightdress his mum had given her. Her hair hadn't been brushed, and it worried him to see her so listless. He'd watched his mother sink into a dark depression when his dad had been killed, and he dreaded seeing Sarah go the same way. He felt Sarah rest her head on his shoulder, and said gently, 'I realise you don't want to do it, love, but perhaps now would be a good time to go through the order of service for Tommy's funeral?'

'I can't, George. I haven't got the energy.'

'You can't keep putting it off. I know all of this is harrowing for you, but it's got to be done.'

Sarah sighed. 'I suppose so and I know I've got to face going home soon. I just can't imagine living in that room without Tommy. All his stuff will be there, his clothes, his toys and I – I don't think I can bear it.'

'I could go there before you to sort it all out,' George offered.

'No,' Sarah answered quickly. 'Thanks, but it's something I need to do alone. It's weird . . . I'm dreading it, yet at the same time I feel I want to be near his things. In fact, I think I should go home today, but would you mind taking me to the church first?'

George was relieved to see Sarah responding more positively, but he didn't like to think of her being upset in that room with no one to comfort her. 'Whatever you want, but I don't think you should be by yourself. I could help you to sort things out and then you can come back here.'

'Thanks, but, as I said, I think this is something I need to do alone.'

George nodded, but decided to ask Mo to keep an eye on Sarah. If she couldn't cope he wanted to know about it, and then he'd bring her back here.

Only a couple of hours later, Sarah was sitting beside George as he drove her home. They had been to the church to see the vicar, something she had been dreading, but he'd been so kind that she had managed to make the arrangements without too many tears.

'The vicar was a good bloke,' George said.

'Yes, and I liked his suggestions for the hymns. Tommy used to love "All Things Bright and Beautiful". He learned to sing it in school assemblies. He was right, you know, the vicar, what he said. Tommy was such a bright boy and full of life, so his service should reflect that and not be filled with sombre hymns. I'm not sure I can stand up and do a reading though. I was wondering if you would, or your mum.'

'I could do it, but I reckon my mum would be honoured.'

They pulled up outside Sarah's house and she closed her eyes, taking a deep breath, searching for the courage to step inside.

'We can always come back another day?' George offered softly.

'No . . . I 'm ready,' Sarah said, and climbed out of the van, but when she got to the front door, her hand was shaking. 'George, would you open the door for me, please?'

As soon as they stepped inside, Sarah noticed the familiar musty smell, and cursed herself for not moving Tommy out of the house sooner. Maybe he'd still be alive if she had, though the doctors had told her it wouldn't have made any difference. Tommy had contracted whooping cough, which had led to complications. They'd said whooping cough wasn't caused by the damp or the smog. It was from an infection, but Sarah still believed the mould in their room hadn't helped.

As George was about to open the door to her room, Mo appeared at the top of the stairs.

'Sarah, you're home,' she called and came running down. She threw her arms around her friend. 'I'm so sorry . . . you must be devastated.'

Sarah stiffened at Mo's embrace, fighting to hold back her tears. She appreciated that her friends wanted to show their sympathy, but felt more in control if left alone. 'Thanks, Mo,' she croaked.

'Would you like me to make a pot of tea and bring it down?'

Tea, the answer to everything, but in reality, the answer to nothing, Sarah thought. Still, it was kind of Mo to offer and she didn't want to hurt her feelings. 'Thanks, that would be great,' she said as George slowly pushed the door open.

Sarah stepped in. Everything was just as she'd left it, but it felt empty. Tommy's bed was made, and his school bag was hanging on the end. His short trousers and several shirts were neatly folded on a wooden chair next to his bed, with his tin of toy soldiers on top. The Muffin the Mule game Roger had bought him was poking out from under his bed, as were his sketchpad and paints.

George pushed the door to, and Sarah turned to see Tommy's oversized army jacket hung on the back. It was too much and she gasped, holding her hand to her mouth as silent tears began to flow. She walked up to it and held the material to her face, trying to breathe in the scent of her brother.

'I knew this would be too much for you,' George said, and urged her towards one of the armchairs.

'No . . . I had to come. I want to be here . . . I want to be near his things. I know it sounds daft, but it makes me feel closer to him. I wasn't sure I could do this, but I'm glad I have.'

She sat down, crying quietly, grateful that for once George didn't try to comfort her. Her thoughts were full of Tommy, the room evoking so many memories.

Mo came in carrying a pot of tea and jug of milk. 'Oh, Sarah, I don't know what to say.'

'There isn't anything you can say, Mo,' she said, managing to dry her tears. 'It's so hard. I'm all right for a little while, but then, like waves, it hits me again. Lena says it's normal and this is all part of grieving, but honestly, it hurts so much that at times it's almost more than I can bear.'

'I can't imagine how hard it is for you, but if you need me, I'm just upstairs.'

'Thanks, Mo.'

'When is the funeral?'

'On Monday.'

'Maybe once that's over, you'll begin to feel better.'

Sarah had heard all the platitudes, and though she knew people were trying to be kind, they didn't help. She doubted she'd ever get over losing Tommy, and there were many times that she wished she'd died with him. Nevertheless, she accepted Mo's words of condolence and said, 'Thanks, Mo. I wasn't sure what it would be like coming back here, but actually I think it helps. George and his mum will probably be glad to get rid of me. They must be sick of hearing me crying all the time.'

'Don't be daft,' George protested. 'I'd prefer it if you come home again with me, and I know Mum would too.'

'Don't worry, George, I'll keep an eye on her,' Mo said.

Sarah drank her tea, but as George and Mo chatted she didn't listen to their conversation. Instead she was imagining Tommy sitting on his bed, quietly painting, and she felt her eyes well up again.

George immediately noticed and said, 'Sarah, I'm really not sure about leaving you here.'

'Honestly, George, I'm fine. Anyhow, it's about time you got back to work. You've lost enough business 'cos of me, and I bet everyone is missing you down the market. I know things aren't right with you and Roger, but do you think you two can bury the hatchet and make it up? Life's too short to bear grudges, and I know Roger will be appreciative that you and your mum have looked after me so well.'

Sarah didn't think George looked very happy at the mention of Roger's name, but any animosity between them seemed petty and irrelevant now.

'As long as he treats you right, I haven't got a problem with Roger,' George said tersely.

'Good. Can you let him know I'm home now, please?'

'Yeah, I suppose so,' George answered, with obvious reluctance.

'If you're staying here, Sarah, you'll need some shopping in. Would you like me to pop out and pick you up a few bits?' Mo asked.

'Oh, I hadn't thought of that. Thanks, Mo, but I think I could do with the fresh air. Would you come with me, though, and tell me all about what you've been up to? It might give me something else to think about for a while.'

'Yes, of course, but we'd better get a move on before the shops shut. What are you doing, George? Are you going to wait here 'til we get back?'

'No, I'll leave you to it, if you're sure, Sarah?'

'Yes, and thanks for everything, George,' she said, standing up to hug him. He really had been her rock and good friend, and she didn't know how she would have coped without him.

'All right, ladies, I'll get off now, but I'll be back on

Sunday to pick you up, Sarah. You're coming to ours for dinner, no arguments.'

'I don't know if I'll feel much like eating, but thanks. I'll see you then and it will give me a chance to thank your mum for all she's done,' Sarah said.

Mo listened to the exchange, and couldn't wait to get out of Sarah's room. It felt oppressive, and though she was extremely sorry for Sarah, she hoped she wouldn't keep harping on about Tommy. She had enough to be worrying about without Sarah's troubles too.

'It's a lovely day,' Mo said, appreciating the September sunshine as they walked along the street. Battersea was a stinking dirty area, with the factories billowing out smoke, but she always thought the place looked much cheerier when the sun was shining.

'Yes, it is. Tommy would have loved to be playing out with Larry now. Oh, no, Mo. I haven't told Larry's mum, or the school . . .'

'Don't worry, I've already spoken to Larry's mum and she told the headmaster at Tommy's school. I would have gone and seen your friend Jenny too but I wasn't sure where she lives,' Mo said.

'Thanks, Mo, I don't know what to say.'

'You don't have to say nothing, it was the least I could do.'

'If I talk about Tommy, I'll start crying again, so tell me how the new modelling job is coming along.'

Mo's stomach knotted and her heart raced. She wondered if she should tell Sarah what a big mistake she'd made, but as she felt so embarrassed and ashamed, she decided to keep it to herself. 'Yes, it's great,' she lied.

'Barry's put together my portfolio and is busy getting my pictures in front of the right people. It shouldn't be long before I get my first assignment.'

'Wow, that's fantastic. Have you told Samuel about it yet?'

'No, so don't mention it in front of him. I'm working back at the cinema for now, just until a modelling job comes up. I'll tell him when I've got some work, or my picture in a fashion magazine,' Mo said and her stomach lurched again. The thought of her nude photographs being seen in print had caused her so many sleepless nights and she knew she was looking haggard.

'Well, I'm sure once he sees you looking gorgeous and splashed over all the fashion mags, he'll be ever so proud of you. I've never met any celebrities, but now I'm going to have a famous friend!'

'I wouldn't go that far,' Mo said, trying to play it down.

She swallowed, hoping her lies would never come to light. She knew her photographs were never going to appear in a magazine, at least not the sort Samuel would approve of.

Chapter 40

Sarah had a restless night's sleep, haunted by dreams of Tommy, and awoke in the morning already exhausted. She contemplated staying in bed; after all, she couldn't think of any reason to get up, and her energy was drained. She turned over and pulled the covers around her to try to block out the light. She could hear the voices of excited children on their way to school, another reminder that Tommy was gone.

'Oh, Mr Sayers . . . I hope you're looking after my boy for me up there,' she said out loud, and snuffled into her pillow. She had two brothers in heaven now, both forever young.

Mo popped her head around the door. 'Are you awake?'

Sarah wished she had locked the door now. She wanted to ignore her friend and pretend to be asleep. She wanted to be left alone, to cry when she felt like it, but Mo was already walking over to the bed. Sarah sat up and quickly dashed her tears away with the flannelette sheet. 'Yes, I'm awake,' she said.

'I've brought you down a cuppa,' Mo said.

'Thanks.'

'Oh, look at you. You've been bawling your eyes out

again and you look knackered. Tell you what, I'll go and run you a nice bath with some fancy bubble bath Sam bought me. You have a soak, then get yourself dressed and we'll get you out of the house again. It did you good yesterday . . . Maybe we could go up the Junction and have a look around Arding and Hobbs. You loved it in there the last time we went.'

Sarah knew that Mo meant well, but the last thing she felt like doing was browsing through posh frocks and make-up. 'No, thanks, Mo. I really don't feel up to it.'

'Well, I ain't leaving you here in this state. Bath first, then I'll think of something else. Come on, out of bed and get this tea down you. I'll be back in a minute.'

Mo went off to the bathroom, and Sarah grudgingly swung her legs out of bed and walked over to the window. She pulled open the curtain, but quickly drew it again. The sun was bright, but her mood was too dark to face it. She walked over to the armchair and flopped into it. Everything felt like such an effort, and she couldn't be bothered to fight off her lethargy.

Mo came back into the room. 'Your bath's running. It smells gorgeous in there, and them bombs make your skin feel ever so soft. Keep an eye on it, don't let it over-flow. I'll be back down in an hour and will expect to find you dressed and ready to go.'

Before Sarah could protest, Mo was gone. She liked Mo, but she didn't want to go out. All she wanted to do was hide away for a while and mourn for her boy. She'd slept with his army jacket in her arms, and now walked back to the bed to pick it up. With it draped around her shoulders, she tucked her hands in the pockets, and smiled warmly as she found a half-eaten sticky boiled sweet, covered in fluff. No doubt Tommy had saved it, and even with the fluff he'd still have shoved it in his mouth.

Overcome with emotion, Sarah dropped to her knees. 'Tommy . . . I wish I'd told you more often how much I love you,' she cried. 'I miss you. I miss you so much . . .'

Mo paced back and forth. She could hear Sarah downstairs, crying her eyes out, but couldn't face going to see her. If Sarah had stayed at George's house, it would have been so much easier, but now she felt responsible for her and wasn't happy to be put in that position.

Thankfully the crying at last stopped and she heard the bathroom door close. Sarah was at least having a bath and would hopefully get herself ready. She had to get her out of the house and away from all the memories of Tommy. It had seemed to be a good distraction yesterday, but now Mo decided that the Junction would be too much. Then she had a thought. It was Friday, a good day for a matinee, and Sarah could lose herself in a film for a couple of hours, just as long as the cinema wasn't screening a tear-jerker.

Mo waited a while, then guardedly went back downstairs, hoping to find Sarah had perked up a bit. Of course, she expected her to be upset, but Mo would have preferred her friend to put on a brave face. She realised she was probably a little heartless, but she was much better at offering a joke and a laugh than she was at sympathy. 'How are you feeling now?' Mo asked as she went into Sarah's room.

'Better, thanks,' Sarah said with a sniff, and Mo was

pleased to see her friend was dressed and her hair had been tidied up.

'Good. Do you fancy going to watch a film? It's a bit early yet, so we could go for a coffee and a bun first. I don't think it's healthy for you to sit around in here all day, so what do you think?'

'I really don't want to do anything. Given the choice, I'd much rather stay at home,' Sarah said dolefully.

'Well, I ain't giving you a choice, so come on, we're going out.'

Mo was relieved when Sarah didn't argue. She followed her outside and half an hour later they were sitting in the corner of a small café on the High Street.

'Sarah, I'm not expecting you to be full of the joys of spring, and it's only natural that you're feeling sad and miserable, but I can't leave you to rot in that room. I hope you don't think I'm being a bully or insensitive – I'm just trying to cheer you up a bit.'

Sarah's eyes glistened as she looked at Mo. 'I know, and thank you. Left to my own devices, that's exactly what I would be doing, sitting in my room and crying. To be honest though, Mo, there's no joy for me here, and there won't be in the cinema. It's like nothing matters any more and life seems pointless. It feels like I'm never going to laugh again. The pain inside me is so consuming, and all I can think about is Tommy. It takes over my whole being and I haven't got the strength to fight it off. And . . . I'm not sure if I want to. I feel I should be sad like this forever . . . for Tommy.'

Trust me to open my big gob and start her off again, thought Mo, though she tried to show some empathy in her eyes. 'Sarah, it's early days yet. Give it time, love. I can't pretend to know what you're going through, but I do know that Tommy wouldn't want you feeling like this. Just imagine if it was the other way around, and you had died. If you was a ghost and could see him, would you want to see him upset?'

'No, no, never. I'd want him to be happy and remember me with love.'

'There you go then. Hold on to that.'

'Mo, can we just leave it for now? I don't believe in ghosts. Tommy is dead, he can't see me, and I can't help feeling bloody miserable. Look, thanks for dragging me out, but I want to go home now,' Sarah said. She shoved back her chair and almost ran out of the café.

Mo quickly found some coins in her handbag and threw them on the table. She was cursing herself for saying the wrong thing, and ran to catch up with Sarah. 'Wait . . . I'm sorry,' she called along the street.

Sarah stopped and turned, her shoulders slumped. 'No, Mo, don't be sorry. It's me who should be apologising. You go off and watch the film, and I'll head home. If it's all the same with you, I'd rather be by myself for a while.'

'If that's what you want,' she said, inwardly pleased. It suited her that way. When Sarah was happy, she was good company and fun to be around, but Mo was finding her grief difficult to deal with. 'I'll pop in to see you later, make sure you're OK.'

Sarah nodded, and Mo watched as she trudged off. Selfishly she hoped that Sarah would find it too hard to live in that room now, the memories too hard to bear. If Sarah moved out, she wouldn't have to put up with her crying all the time, something that she now realised could go on for weeks, months or even years.

Sarah knew Mo had good intentions, and though she had tried, she couldn't force a smile or drive the devastating thoughts of Tommy from her head. As she walked along, she decided to take the long way home. She wanted to go through Battersea Park, a place that held so many precious memories of Tommy and Mr Sayers. They were both gone now, but she would hold their memories in her heart forever.

She wandered around the park, gazing at the trees Tommy had climbed and recalling his squeals of delight. The hills he'd run up and tumbled down, and the pond where they'd fed the geese. Mr Sayers' allotment had long gone, but now she strolled the paths they'd once walked together, and though her pain was deep, her memories were fond and she never wanted to let go of them. She'd been meandering for a long time when she found herself at the Guinness Clock, one of Tommy's favourite places. It began to chime five, and the intriguing mechanisms sprang into action. She looked to her side, as if Tommy was next to her, and recalled him trying to guess the sequence of the clock's movements. First the windmill would spin, then the soldier would pop up . . . no, it was the other way around. He never did guess it correctly . . . and, with a sob, Sarah knew that now he never would.

Chapter 41

George had set up his stall, but had spent the rest of the day fretting about Sarah. At least Mo was with her, but he still didn't like leaving. Roger had stayed out of his way, but as they began to pack away their wares, George knew he had to pass on the message from Sarah. He strolled over to Roger's stall and picked up an orange, which he threw in the air and caught.

'Are you going to buy that orange, or are you training for a new circus act?' Roger asked sarcastically.

At the man's tone, George felt his temper flare. He remembered what Sarah had said, and fought to calm himself. She wanted them to be friends, but he knew that could never be. Roger had seduced Sarah the moment his back had been turned, but that wouldn't have been so bad if he'd given her the respect she deserved. He thought about throwing the orange in Roger's face, but that would probably turn into a fight and the man wasn't worth the bother. Instead he said calmly, 'Sarah asked me to tell you that she's back home now.'

'Oh, right, thanks for letting me know.'

He didn't sound interested, and George frowned. 'Will you be going to see her?'

'Er . . . yeah, I suppose so.'

Alarm bells went off in George's head. Something didn't seem right and Roger hadn't even asked how Sarah was. 'You suppose so! You've made no attempt to see her since Tommy died, and now you *suppose* you'll go and see her?'

'Yeah, well, you and your mum have been looking out for her, but if she's back home now, I'll go to see her.'

'Are you sure about that?' George asked.

'Leave off, will ya, George? I'll call in on my way home, not that it's got fuck all to do with you.'

George had placed the orange back in the crate, but now his fists clenched. He wanted to launch at Roger and smash his smug face in, but he knew that any more friction between them would only add to Sarah's grief. Instead he began to walk away, but said, 'Be good to her. Sarah's fragile, and it's Tommy's funeral on Monday.'

He didn't wait for Roger to respond, and went back to his stall to pack up. He loved Sarah, and always would. He wished he was going to see her tonight instead of Roger.

Sarah arrived home exhausted from ambling around the park for most of the day, and lay down on Tommy's bed to rest her aching legs. She felt different, pleased to be home, and, though still heartbroken, she'd taken some pleasure in spending the day reminiscing. The scent of Tommy filled her nostrils and tears flowed again until, exhausted, she fell asleep.

A knock on her door woke her, and when it opened, Roger walked in. 'Mo let me in the front door,' he said.

Sarah was surprised to see him and scrambled from

the bed, noticing that he had a bunch of flowers in his hands.

'How are you?' he asked, handing them to her.

'Just about coping.'

'I'm sorry for your loss.'

There was no warmth in his voice and Sarah thought it a strange thing for him to say. Roger was talking to her as if he was a casual acquaintance, not her boyfriend. 'Thank you for the flowers,' she said. 'They're lovely. I'll put them in some water.'

Roger followed her to the sink, and when she turned around to look at him, she wanted him to take her in his arms and hold her until all her pain went away. 'I've missed you,' she whispered.

'Come here,' Roger said, and held out his arms.

Sarah immediately fell into them, her body once again wracked with grief.

'It's all right. You have a good cry, my girl,' Roger said, and stroked the top of her head with one hand while holding her close with the other.

Sarah fought to stifle her tears. Roger would look after her now, and though he couldn't take away her suffering, she felt some comfort.

He pulled away slightly and cupped her face in his large hands. 'Look at you, all worked up and blotchy-eyed,' he said, and kissed her gently on the lips.

Sarah kissed him back, but her nose was blocked and she could hardly breathe. She felt Roger's tongue in her mouth and all at once she felt the exciting, tingling feelings he always made her experience. He kissed her harder, and her body responded with fevered passion. It felt so good to be loved, and she relished the comfort of being able to forget her grief for a while. When Roger undid her skirt and it dropped to the floor, she didn't protest. He pressed his body up against hers, and she stumbled backwards until she was leaning against the sink. Roger slipped her top off over her head and lifted her bra to kiss and caress her breasts. He then picked her up in his strong arms and sat her on the edge of the sink. Her legs seemed to naturally part, and Roger stood in between them as he pushed his hard manhood against her. She could feel him fumbling between her legs, and as he kissed her fervently, she felt him pull her knickers to one side. There was a pain as his penis entered her and she fought against him as his hips began to thrust back and forward.

'Roger . . . it hurts . . .' she said, squirming.

'It's all right,' Roger said, and pushed harder and faster into her.

'No . . . Roger . . . please stop, you're hurting me . . .' Sarah said and could feel her body clenching as she tried to pull away from him.

He was pounding into her now, and she recoiled as he grunted and dug his fingers into her shoulders. That noise, the one she'd heard so many times when her mother had entertained men. She hated it and again pleaded with him to stop, but he threw his head back and shouted in triumph as he reached his climax.

Sarah couldn't bring herself to look at him as Roger pulled himself away from her. There was something wet in her knickers and she quickly closed her legs. She jumped down from the sink, feeling sick inside.

'I know it wasn't much fun for you, Sarah. It was your first time and it always hurts, but it'll be better for you the next time,' Roger said as he buttoned up his trouser fly.

Sarah hated what had happened. She'd wanted him at first, his touch had brought her comfort, but then she had come to her senses and begged him to stop. 'You really hurt me,' she cried.

'Oh, come on, it wasn't that bad. You can't get a bloke going like that and then expect him to stop. Sorry if I got a bit carried away, but that's the effect you have on me.'

Sarah sniffed. Her mother had warned her to keep her legs shut, and after the pain she'd just experienced, she could understand why.

Roger smiled softly and pulled her into his arms. 'Forgive me?'

Sarah nodded. Maybe he was right, she should have stopped him before it went that far.

'I can't stay. I've got an early start in the morning, but how about we go for a drive on Sunday?' Roger said.

'I can't. I'm having dinner with George and Lena.'

'All right, but do you want me to come to Tommy's funeral with you on Monday? It means I'd have to shut up my stall for the day and lose a good day's business, but if you want me with you . . .'

Sarah got the impression that he didn't really want to accompany her, and she was deeply hurt. She hid her feelings and said shortly, 'No, don't bother. I'll be fine.'

'Look, I'm sorry about earlier, but I'll make it up to you next time. How about I call in on Tuesday?'

'If you want,' Sarah answered, but she was feeling hugely disappointed.

As Roger left and the door closed, Sarah collapsed onto

her bed and screamed into her pillow. It wasn't supposed to be like this! Tommy shouldn't be dead, and Roger shouldn't have been so callous. He'd acted as if he didn't care, about her or about Tommy.

Worse, Roger wasn't going to the funeral. He didn't seem to realise how much she would need his comfort and support, and now she began to question whether he really loved her. She'd let him brutally take her virginity when all she'd wanted was love and tenderness. 'What have I done?' Sarah moaned, and once again cried her heart out as she longed to see her brother just one more time.

Chapter 42

'It's a bad state of affairs, Albert. The poor girl is bereft,' Lena said as she straightened her black hat in her mantel mirror.

'Has George gone to pick her up?'

'Yes, we thought it would be better to leave from here. I don't like the thought of her being on her own after the funeral, so I'm going to suggest that she sleeps here tonight too.'

'You're a good woman, Lena. Are you sure I should be coming with you in the car? I'm not family.'

'Albert, neither are we. The girl hasn't got any relatives, so we're the closest thing she has to a family, and yes, I'm sure. Just don't mention anything about our engagement. I haven't told George yet, not with all this going on,' Lena said, and took her ring from her handbag to gaze at the diamond. 'I can't wait to wear this, but it's happened so quickly. I think we should give George some time to get used to us being together.'

'How do you think he will react?' Albert asked.

'He's a good boy, he'll be fine once he gets over the shock. Blimey, come to that, I think I'm still in shock myself,' Lena said and laughed.

'I've known for a long time that I wanted you to be my wife, and as it was your birthday yesterday, it seemed like the appropriate time to ask. I'm just glad you said yes as I didn't have another birthday present to give you if you had said no to the ring.'

Lena looked lovingly at the man sitting on her sofa. He was so different from her deceased husband. She'd never thought she'd be able to love again after losing him, but Albert had shown her it was possible to fall in love more than once in a lifetime, and though she felt a small sense of guilt, she was looking forward to becoming Mrs Bosco. She heard a door slam. 'That sounds like George's van,' she said, and went to look through the front room window. 'They're here. Oh, dear, look at Sarah, my heart goes out to her.'

George came in with Sarah behind him, and Albert stood and doffed his hat.

'Sit down, Sarah,' urged Lena. 'We've got a little time before the cars arrive. George, pour her a good size brandy, it'll help to steady her nerves.'

Sarah sat on the sofa in silence. She looked dazed, and her swollen eyes gave away the many tears she'd shed. 'Oh, God, I'm not sure I can do this,' she said, her voice breaking.

'Yes, you can, and you will. This is your chance to say a proper goodbye to Tommy and we'll all be there to support you.'

'Here, drink this,' said George as he handed Sarah the brandy.

Sarah downed it, then pulled a face that showed how horrid it tasted to her.

'Good girl,' Lena said. 'It'll help you to get through the day. George, pour her another one.'

Sarah didn't argue and quickly drank the second glass as Lena said, 'I know it doesn't seem the right thing to say, but the weather is good. The day I buried your father, George, do you remember? It was chucking it down, bloody awful it was. Tommy was a little ray of sunshine, so it's appropriate that the sun is out to see him off today.'

'Well said,' Albert commented.

'Thanks, George. I think the brandy has helped to dull the pain,' Sarah croaked.

'That's good. I'm glad.'

'Sarah, love,' said Lena. 'I know you're hurting, and you will for some time yet, but this time next year, things will seem a little better.'

'I've been trying to stay positive for Tommy but it's so difficult. I keep thinking of all the bereaved mothers who come in the shop. They buried their sons and husbands during the war, but the way they've got on with their lives is an inspiration to me, and so are you, Lena.'

'That's the spirit, love, every time it hurts, let it hurt. Let it hurt 'til you can't cry no more. That pain will never go away, but in time you'll find yourself going for longer and longer periods of just living and doing day-to-day stuff.'

'Yes, I've been told that time heals, but it doesn't feel like it at the moment,' Sarah said sadly.

'One day you'll find you can put a sticky plaster over the wound, but there are times when it will still weep. When the plaster falls off, you'll feel the pain again, but yes, with time it will become easier,' Lena said. She saw George discreetly wipe a tear from his eye, and Albert bowed his head. As for Sarah, Lena was impressed at how brave the girl was being. She knew it wouldn't last though.

When the hearse arrived and she saw the coffin, she was bound to break down. Lena remembered how difficult it had been for her to walk out of the house when the hearse was waiting outside with her husband in it. She was sure that's when it would hit Sarah, and when it did, they'd all just have to be there for her and hold her up if she threatened to fall.

The hearse pulled up outside. George had struggled to get Sarah out of the door, but she'd eventually relented. One look at the small white coffin though, and her legs went from under her. It was agonising to see, but they managed to get her into the car, where they followed Tommy on his final journey. As though her emotions were frozen, Sarah sat woodenly, staring ahead, while Lena quietly dabbed her eyes.

When they pulled up to the church, George was surprised to see how many people were waiting to pay their final respects. As he'd expected, there was no sign of Roger. He was disgusted that the man wasn't there to support Sarah.

As George led Sarah towards the chapel, Mo and Samuel stepped forward, but Sarah hardly seemed to notice that they were there. She wasn't crying, but she looked so lost, so bereft, her face as white as a sheet.

'How's she been?' Mo whispered.

'Not good,' George answered.

'It's a lovely turnout, Sarah,' Mo said. 'Lots of mums from Tommy's school are here, and so is his teacher. I've met your friend Jenny too, she's really nice.'

Sarah didn't respond. She was locked in a world of grief, and moved stiffly. The vicar stood by the entrance to the church, and took Sarah's hand, but she remained silent.

George led her inside to a front pew, and after a few minutes the organ began to play. George glanced behind to see that everyone was seated, and then the vicar walked down the aisle in front of the bearers carrying Tommy's tiny coffin. It was placed on a plinth, while Sarah stared ahead, and he wondered how much longer she could hold it together.

The service began; they sang hymns, said prayers and Lena did well with the reading. George could tell she was nervous, but the things she said about Tommy were very moving, and he could hear quiet snuffles echoing through the church. Still, Sarah remained silent. She had opted to have Tommy cremated, saying that she couldn't stand the thought of him being buried underground, all alone in the dark.

To the sound of the final hymn, a curtain was drawn across the plinth, hiding the coffin, and George felt a surge of sorrow. He swallowed the lump in his throat, fighting tears, and in his head said a final goodbye to the bright, bonny boy he had become so fond of. He reached for Sarah's hand and found it cold. She still sat stiffly beside him.

The service over, people filed out and George gently urged Sarah to her feet. Outside, condolences were offered, and then he led Sarah to where the flowers and wreaths had been placed. She barely looked at them, but George saw his mother collecting the cards. In time, maybe Sarah would want to read them, he thought. For now, she was tapping her finger and thumb together, something he'd noticed she did whenever she was upset or worried.

'I am so sorry, love,' a young woman said.

At last Sarah spoke, but only to say curtly, 'Thanks, Jenny.'

'Sarah, I wanted to let you know that I've got another job. I'll still be an apprentice seamstress, but the pay is much better and it's in a fashion house on the other side of London. My mum's sister lives in the area, so rather than forking out the fare to travel back and forth each day, I'm moving in with her.'

Sarah just nodded, and George wasn't sure that she took any of this in. He was worried about her state of mind and said, 'Come on, Sarah, let's get you home.'

'Bye, Sarah,' said Jenny.

There was no response again, and with unshed tears in her eyes Jenny walked away. George called out to his mother and Albert and all of them returned to the car. It was a silent journey home, his mother as quiet as Sarah. There wasn't going to be a wake; Sarah hadn't wanted one, saying that she couldn't bear to prolong the day. He knew his mother didn't approve. She felt that everyone who came to the church should be asked back to the house, and at least offered a sandwich or something. However, she hadn't interfered, but instead had done all she could to support Sarah, and George knew she'd continue to do so for as long as Sarah needed her.

When they arrived home, George drew his mother to one side and said, 'Mum, I'm worried. Sarah's behaviour doesn't seem normal.'

'I know, love. There was hardly a dry eye in the church, but Sarah hasn't shed a tear. Maybe it's some kind of coping mechanism, but if she doesn't snap out of it, we may have to call the doctor. You go and sit with her while

I make a pot of tea. I don't know about you, but I'm parched.'

Albert stayed in the kitchen, while George went to sit beside Sarah in the front room. In an attempt to break through her wall of silence, he reached out to take her hand and said, 'It was a lovely turnout for Tommy,' but once again she didn't respond, her hand limp in his.

'Sarah – are you all right, love? Can I get you anything?'

At last some movement, a small shake of her head.

George gripped her hand tighter, and said earnestly, 'Sarah, please say something. I'm worried about you.'

At last she turned to look at him, panic in her eyes. 'No . . . no . . . I don't want to talk. I'm scared, George . . . scared that if I let myself feel . . . if I let myself cry . . . I'll never be able to stop.'

'You can't keep it all bottled up, love,' he said and gently pulled her into his arms. 'Come on, let it all out.'

Just as he heard one, small, sob, his mother walked into the room carrying a tray. George shook his head at her and she quickly walked out again, while he gently began to stroke Sarah's hair. She broke then, tears at last flowing, her body shuddering while George continued to hold her – listening to her heart shattering and wishing he could take away her pain, but knowing that he couldn't.

Chapter 43

Two weeks had passed since Tommy's funeral, and Sarah was back at work in the shop. Lena had thought it was too soon, but the girl had insisted she needed to keep her mind occupied.

'I'm proud of you, you know,' Lena said as she helped Sarah stock the refrigerators.

'Oh, why's that?' Sarah asked.

'Look at you, back at work and getting on with things. It took me a long time to get over my husband's death. In fact, I'm sure George has told you, I didn't cope very well and took to my bed for quite some time. You should give yourself a pat on the back, young lady.'

'I'm back at work, but I'm only just about functioning. To be honest, Lena, I'm having to force myself to get up every morning, and I'm finding it difficult to smile at our customers,' Sarah said, and Lena could see her eyes were filling with tears.

'Even so, you're doing great so don't beat yourself up. Make us both a drink, love. I think we deserve a break after filling up all the lard and butter shelves.'

A few minutes later, Sarah came back onto the shop floor and the two of them sat behind the counter with their cups of Camp coffee. Lena took a sip and grimaced. 'I'm still not keen on this stuff.'

'Sorry, I should have made tea.'

'No, it's all right. It makes a change and I suppose I'll get used to it. Sarah, there is something I've been meaning to tell both you and George, only I haven't found the right time,' Lena said, and tapped her ring finger on the side of her cup, hoping Sarah would notice the diamond.

'Oh, what is it?' Sarah asked.

'It's about me and Albert . . .' Lena said and looked directly at the ring on her finger.

'Oh, my goodness, Lena, you're engaged!' Sarah exclaimed, and jumped up from her stool. 'Let me have a closer look at that ring,' she said, taking Lena's hand.

'Yes, he proposed on my birthday, and well, I know we haven't been dating for very long, but we've known each other for years.'

'I'm so happy for you. When are you going to tell George?'

'Tonight, I suppose, but I'm worried he might fly off the handle for a bit. What do you think?'

'He doesn't have a problem with you dating Albert and he always talks very highly of him. I'm pretty sure he'll be pleased for you.'

'I hope you're right,' Lena said. George had accepted that she was dating Albert, but marriage might be another matter. 'When I lost my husband, I never expected to be happy again, but I am, and in time you will be too.'

The women drained their cups, and an hour later Lena finished her shift. 'I'll see you tomorrow, love. I'll let you know how George reacts to my engagement.'

'Good luck,' Sarah called.

Lena hoped the shop would be busy for the rest of the afternoon. It would give Sarah less time to think. Since Tommy's death she had lost her zest for life and her smiles were forced. It saddened Lena, but for now she had other things on her mind. She was keen to cook George's favourite dinner, and when he was sitting happy and replete, she'd tell him about her forthcoming marriage.

Sarah locked up the shop, and as always, dreaded going home to her empty room.

Roger had been round last night and said he'd be round again that evening. It was only the thought of being all alone in her room that had made her agree, but Sarah now found that she wasn't looking forward to seeing him. He wouldn't let her mention Tommy's name, saying it would only upset her, and only seemed interested in pestering her for sex again. After her first traumatic experience with him, she'd manage to hold him off, but she could see he was becoming increasingly frustrated with her. He didn't seem to understand that she wasn't ready for fun, and though he tried hard to make her laugh, it didn't work. She didn't want to enjoy herself, not yet, it was too soon. How could she laugh? She thought she'd feel guilty if she did. Couldn't he see it was impossible for her to enjoy herself when her heart was still in pieces?

Mo was coming down the stairs as Sarah arrived home. 'Off to work?' Sarah asked.

'Yep, they've asked us all to come in early. Gawd knows why, but I've gotta dash. I'll see you tomorrow,' Mo said hurriedly and was gone.

Sarah reluctantly went into her room. She ached for Tommy, missed him so much, and couldn't bring herself to remove any of his things. Roger had told her it was unhealthy and she was creating a shrine to him. Lena told her to take no notice of what he said and to do things in her own time. She had never voiced an opinion about him, but Sarah sensed that Lena didn't like Roger.

She made herself a cheese sandwich, then quickly freshened herself up. It wasn't long after when she heard Roger's van pull up outside, but she didn't get butterflies in her stomach like she used to. In fact, she felt her mood drop at the thought of having to fight him off.

'Hello, gorgeous,' Roger said when she opened the door.

'Hi,' Sarah replied, but didn't feel like saying much else.

'You're not still moping about, are you? Come on, Sarah, you've got to buck your ideas up,' Roger said as he followed her into her room.

'I'm just tired, that's all,' she answered.

'Come here, sexy, I'll liven you up,' Roger said as he pulled her towards him, his hands creeping up to her breasts.

'Roger . . . please . . . I'm not in the mood.'

With that he abruptly let go of her. 'You're never in the bloody mood, Sarah, and I'm not in the mood to put up with it. Your brother is dead – get over it, before it ruins the rest of your life. I'm going, but think about what I've said.'

With that, Roger walked out, slamming the door behind him. Shortly after, Sarah heard his van drive off. It felt like she was losing him, and maybe she should have chased after him, but she couldn't find the energy or the inclination to win him back, and his words had left her seething.

Mo walked the aisles of the cinema, ushering people to their seats, and then hung a tray around her neck that carried sweets and cigarettes. It wasn't the most challenging of jobs, but she liked the attention she'd invariably get from men.

'Hey, miss, over here,' Mo heard a man call. He was sitting with two other smartly dressed men near the aisle seats. They'd been a bit rowdy during the first half of the film and she'd politely requested they kept the noise down, but during the interval they'd become raucous again.

'What cigarettes do you have there?' the man asked.

The lights were up during the interval and Mo could see the men more clearly. They were older than she'd originally assumed, so she expected better behaviour from them.

'Don't I know you from somewhere?' the man asked, studying her face intently.

'I don't think so, sir,' Mo replied. She was used to men hitting on her and though she enjoyed flirting, there was something about this man that unnerved her.

'Yeah, I do . . . I've definitely seen you somewhere before . . .'

Mo went on to list the cigarette brands she was carrying, but the man suddenly cut in.

'I've got it – you're the lady in the postcards . . . you saucy little minx. I tell you what, lads, she's got a great pair under that uniform.'

The penny dropped and Mo was mortified. The man must have seen her naked photographs. Postcards, she thought in horror as she realised that the pictures must be in circulation. 'You must be mistaken,' she said hastily, and ran from the auditorium.

In the staff room, Mo quickly removed her tray, grabbed her coat and hurried out onto the street. Once there, she sucked in the fresh air and tried to steady herself. She'd probably be sacked for running out like that, but didn't care. It was too risky to go back in there again. If that man had recognised her, then surely others would too. Oh, God, would men who had seen the postcards recognise her in the streets too?

Mo kept her head down as she made her way home. Samuel would question why she was back early, but she'd pretend to be unwell. All the times she'd hidden from her violent family she'd felt her room was a prison cell, yet now it felt like her sanctuary, and she couldn't wait to be back in it.

Chapter 44

Sarah had struggled, but managed to get through another week at work. Despite walking out on her, Roger had been round to see her a couple of times. She managed to brush off his advances by telling him she was on her monthlies and now, as the sun rose on Sunday morning, Sarah found she wasn't looking forward to going out with him later that day.

She loved him and wanted to feel the way she had before Tommy died, but at the moment being with Roger was such hard work and she was beginning to resent that he behaved as if Tommy had never existed. She would've spoken to Mo about the situation, asked her advice, but she hadn't seen her all week. Samuel said Mo was ill in bed with flu and she hoped her friend would recover soon.

Sarah sighed heavily as she poured some cereal for her breakfast. She really didn't want to go out with Roger today, but couldn't face his annoyance if she broke their date to his face. It was cowardly, but she decided to avoid him, and pop round to see George instead. Lena had said she and Albert were going out for the day, so George might welcome her company. She hadn't seen him all week, but Lena had told her he'd taken the news of her engagement well, better than she'd expected. She had laughed, saying that her son seemed more worried about who was going to look after the house and cook his dinner once she was married and had moved in with Albert. Typical man, thought Sarah, but she knew that Lena had spoiled him and that living on his own was going to be a rude awakening.

A couple of hours later, Sarah knocked on George's door, to be greeted with surprise, but a warm welcome.

'Wait 'til you see this, Sarah,' he said animatedly, and showed her through to the front room.

Sarah's eyes widened. 'Wow, George, you've got a television.'

'Yep. Well, I reckoned if my mum's going to be moving out I'll need the company. It takes a bit of adjusting with the aerial, but once I've got it right, it's a really good picture.'

George showed Sarah how the television worked, and she watched with fascination. 'Tommy would have loved this,' she said, glad she could talk freely about him with George.

'Funny you should say that 'cos I thought exactly the same thing,' George said, and smiled warmly at her. 'Anyway, what brings you here today?'

'I'm supposed to be going out with Roger, but I've done a runner. Don't get me wrong, George, I do love him, but he's not very caring about my feelings. I can't mention Tommy in front of him, and it's hard not to 'cos he's always in my thoughts.'

'You know what I think about the man so I won't harp

on about it, but I've known Roger a long time and he's always had a selfish streak. He doesn't take life seriously, and if it ain't fun, it bores him,' George said.

'Yes, I got that impression too. You don't mind me hiding out here with you, do you?'

'You know you're always welcome here. Mum left me some lunch so do you fancy a bite to eat?'

Sarah was peckish and happy to share George's lunch. They talked about Albert and Lena's forthcoming wedding, though no date had been set yet, the weather, the latest music, but mostly they talked about Tommy. 'Thanks, George,' Sarah said afterwards. 'It's been good to share so many lovely memories.'

'I miss the little man, and it's nice to talk about him, especially his day at the funfair.'

Sarah helped George to wash up, and then went back to the front room to sit on the sofa. She felt so much better. She'd enjoyed sharing memories, laughing at Tommy's antics, and crying a few times. It was just what she needed and now she felt ready to face the week ahead with renewed vigour.

Mo had convinced Samuel to go to work, saying that she felt much better. He got extra in his pay packet for working on Sundays, and she knew he hated turning the overtime down. In truth, there was nothing wrong with her, but it gave her a good excuse to hide away from the outside world and anyone who might have seen her photos.

It was about half past two when Mo heard a knock on the front door. She climbed out of bed to look out of the window and saw Roger's van. She'd heard Sarah go out earlier and knew she hadn't returned, so, puzzled, she threw on her dressing gown. She quickly checked her reflection in the mirror, and though she was only wearing a touch of mascara, she was happy with her natural appearance, and ran downstairs.

Roger was just walking off back towards his van.

'Hey, are you looking for Sarah?' Mo called.

Roger spun around and once again she was struck by his ice-blue eyes.

'Yes, I thought she knew I was coming over to take her out today but she doesn't appear to be home.'

'I heard her go out this morning, but I've no idea where.'

'That's odd,' Roger said, though Mo didn't think he seemed bothered.

'In that case, she's bound to be back soon. Do you want to come up to my place and wait for her? I'm bored stiff and could do with a bit of company,' Mo said, well aware that her red satin dressing gown had fallen open to reveal her low-cut matching nightdress with lace that stretched across her large chest.

'Yeah, all right,' Roger agreed.

As he followed her upstairs, Mo wiggled her hips, sure that his eyes would be on them, and as they walked into her room, she gestured towards the sofa. 'Take a seat, love. Sam's at work, doing a spot of overtime, some political VIPs or something, so, as you can see, I'm on my own.'

'You're having a lazy day then?' Roger asked as he took a seat, eyeing her nightclothes.

'You could say that,' Mo replied, 'but I've been pretending to be ill all week.'

'Have you? Why have you been swinging the lead?'

Mo was desperate to share her sordid secret, and thought that unlike Samuel, Roger was broad-minded enough to understand. 'I've made a right balls-up . . . a really big mistake and now I don't know what to do about it.'

Roger rolled his eyes, 'Come on, Mo, it can't be that bad. What have you done?'

'Promise you won't say anything if I tell you?'

'Scouts' honour.'

'No, I mean it, Roger. You can't tell a soul.'

'I know how to keep my mouth shut, Mo.'

'Yeah, well, I've been really stupid. I should have known better, but I let this bloke talk me into taking my clothes off to pose for photographs. I thought he was genuine and was going to make me a top model. Instead, I've been humiliated and now I think my nude shots are being brandished about all over Battersea. I'm so ashamed and can't face going outside.'

'Blimey, Mo, I thought it was going to be something really bad. That's nothing to worry about, not nowadays. I've seen plenty of pictures of nude women, and don't think anything of it. If anything, you'll probably be someone's pin-up now and you've every right to be proud of that, especially with a gorgeous body like yours.'

'Do you really think so?'

'Yes, I know so. Cor, I wish I had one of your photos . . . I'd keep it next to my bed and admire it every night.'

Mo wasn't normally one to blush, but she could feel her cheeks burning. 'That's nice of you to say so, but what about my Sam? I know him and he'll be furious if he finds out.'

'He may not, so stop wasting time worrying about something that may never happen. If it does ever come out, deal with it then.'

'Yeah, you're right. Thanks, Roger. I feel a bit better about it now,' Mo said, and sashayed over to the sofa to sit next to him.

''Ere, Mo, have you got any of your photos? I'd love to have a look at them.'

'No, cheeky, I ain't,' Mo replied with a naughty grin, and didn't push Roger's hand away when she felt it sliding up her thigh.

'How about you give me a private viewing then, pose for me like you did for the photographer?' Roger asked lustily.

'Oh . . . I don't know about that . . .'

'Go on, it'll be our secret. I'm getting really turned on thinking about your beautiful body.'

Mo saw Roger's face inching closer to hers, and their lips met. She returned his kiss and groaned in pleasure as his hand slid between her legs. It was seductive, irresistible, and she responded to his touch.

'Please, Mo . . . pose for me,' Roger asked as he pushed her nightdress off her shoulders to flick her erect nipples with his tongue.

Mo gently pushed him away to remove her dressing gown, then slipped her nightdress off. It fell to the floor, leaving her naked, and she relished the look of desire in Roger's eyes. Then she slowly walked across the room and lay on the bed to pose, just as she had for Barry, and asked huskily, 'Do I look good?'

Roger groaned, rubbing his bulging crotch. 'Oh, yes, Mo, you're stunning,' he said, then walked over to stand by the bed.

Mo reached out and undid his trousers, freeing his erect manhood. She smiled, and said, 'Well, look at that. I think you want me.'

'Oh, yes, I do, but like this,' Roger growled and climbing on the bed he roughly flipped her over, then pulled her up at the waist until she was on her knees.

Mo moaned with delight as Roger took her from behind. She loved it that he was so commanding as he held her hips and thrust furiously in and out of her.

'Yes, yes,' Roger panted.

Mo's pleasure mounted, and she was about to reach an explosive orgasm when the door flew open and she saw Samuel's horrified face.

'What the fuck are you doing with my woman?' Sam screeched as he ran towards Roger.

Roger scrambled from the bed and desperately tried to pull up his trousers, while Mo jumped in between them. 'Please, Sam, it's not what you think!'

Samuel roughly pushed her aside. 'I know what I saw . . . you filthy tart . . . and as for you!' He flew at Roger.

'No, Sam,' Mo cried out, but Samuel was beyond listening.

With clenched fists he pounded Roger's face, over and over, Roger crying out in pain as blood spurted.

Mo jumped on Samuel's back, screaming, 'Get off him, you're going to kill him!'

He shook her off, and continued to pound Roger until the man fell to the floor unconscious. With blood dripping off his fists, Samuel stood over him, while Mo cried, 'Oh, Sam, what have you done? Is he dead?'

'I hope so,' Samuel spat, but then Roger groaned.

'You black bastard,' he said as he regained consciousness. 'I'll have you for this. You won't get away with it. I'll get the police on you.'

Mo panicked. She knew the police would come down hard on Samuel, and he'd no doubt go to jail. 'Quick, Sam, you've got to get out of here.'

Blood was running from Roger's nose, and dashing it away with the back of his hand he winced and said, 'You can run, but you won't get far. I'll have you nicked for this!'

Mo grabbed pound notes from the biscuit tin and shoved them at Samuel. 'Go! Go before he calls the police!'

Samuel looked at Roger and then blinked, his wild eyes clearing as he seemed to come to his senses. He took the money and headed for the door as Roger tried to stagger to his feet.

Mo grabbed her dressing gown from the floor and wrapped it around herself, then tried to help Roger, but he shrugged her off. 'I'm sorry, Roger, I wasn't expecting him home so early.'

Roger just glared at her, but then he managed to get to the small sink where he splashed water onto his face.

Mo realised she was shaking, and sat on the edge of the bed, just as the door flew open again. Her heart sank when she saw a confused-looking Sarah standing there.

'What the hell is going on? I've just bumped into Samuel in the street. Please tell me it isn't true,' Sarah cried, but as she judged the scene before her, she already knew it was.

'I'm so sorry, Sarah – we didn't plan on this happening. It just sort of did. One of those crazy heat-of-the-moment things,' Mo answered.

Sarah saw that Mo could barely look her in the eyes.

'How could you? You're supposed to be my friend!' she snapped, then turned her attention to Roger. 'As for you, George was right all along. You said you loved me, yet you jump into bed with my so-called best friend.'

Roger spun around from the sink, and Sarah didn't know if she was more shocked to be looking straight at his naked body or his battered face.

'Don't come that one with me, Sarah. What did you expect? I've tried to be patient, but if you ask me, you're bloody frigid!'

Sarah gazed open-mouthed at Roger. 'I've just lost my brother, but all you care about is getting me into bed. You disgust me, the pair of you,' she said, turning to glare at Mo before fleeing the room. Her mind was in turmoil, and she still couldn't quite believe what she'd seen. She couldn't face going into her room, knowing they were both upstairs and possibly laughing at her. She was devastated by Mo and Roger's betrayal and headed for the man who now felt like her only true friend.

George was surprised to see Sarah on his doorstep. She'd only left about a half hour ago, but one look at her tear-streaked face told him something was terribly wrong. 'What's happened?' he asked.

Sarah fell into his arms and sobbed, 'Oh, George . . . you won't believe what I walked into.'

George held her close and could feel her shaking as she cried into his chest. 'Come on, let's get you inside,' he said, and led her through to the front room. 'Sit down,' he offered, then fetched her a damp flannel to wipe her face.

'I've been such a fool,' Sarah said. 'I was nearly home

and saw Samuel running up the street. He was in a bit of a state and told me he'd just beaten Roger up. He said he'd found him in bed with Mo. Well, I thought he must have got it wrong – you know he can be a bit paranoid sometimes – but when I walked in, it was true. Roger was stark naked and Mo . . . she said sorry.'

Sarah began to cry again, so George put his arm around her shoulder. How could Roger have done this to her? The girl had been through so much already, and Roger must have seen her vulnerability. 'I could bloody kill him. This is typical of Roger, but I'm surprised at Mo.'

'I can't believe it. She's supposed to be my friend and I trusted her. As for him, I've always had my doubts but he's such a good liar!'

'I don't know what to say, except the bloody pair of them deserve each other and I hope they both rot,' George said.

'I loved Roger, but when Tommy died I found that he wasn't the man I thought he was. He seemed so insensitive and it hurt that he didn't come to his funeral.'

'You didn't say anything.'

'I know how you feel about him and I didn't want to add fuel to the fire. Oh, George, how can I go home now? I don't want to live in the same house as Mo. Samuel's never coming back – he said Roger's getting the law onto him. How can I rest in my room knowing what's going on above my head with the love of my life and my best friend?'

George flinched. She'd described Roger as the love of her life. The words had cut him, but he hid his feelings well. 'You can stay here until you get something else sorted. Tell you what, write me a list of what you need and I'll go and pick it up.'

Sarah's tears had dried, but now she looked pensive. 'Thanks, I'd appreciate that, but I want to come with you. I don't care if I never see Roger or Mo again for as long as I live, but as I'm never going back there, I want to take everything, including Tommy's things.'

'I understand and don't worry. I'll make sure they keep out of your way. They'd have to get past me to get to you and that ain't gonna happen.'

Chapter 45

It was half past six on Monday morning. George and Sarah were sitting at the table as Lena fried some sausages, but both looked half asleep. Lena had heard Sarah crying in the night. The poor girl was devastated by Mo and Roger's betrayal, and following so soon after Tommy's death, no wonder it had knocked her for six. Lena had suggested that she take the day off work, but Sarah refused, saying that she'd rather be at work than sitting at home brooding.

Lena dished up breakfast, which both George and Sarah ate in silence. She was itching to share her news, though worried that her timing was inappropriate. Still, it might give Sarah something else to think about. 'It's been an absolutely terrible past few weeks, especially for you, Sarah, so I think we could all do with something to look forward to.'

'You ain't wrong, Mum. Have you got anything in mind?' George asked, perking up a bit.

'As it happens, I have,' Lena answered with a teasing grin.

'Well, spill the beans then,' George said as he mopped up the last of his egg with a slice of bread.

'Albert and I have set a date for the wedding,' Lena said, and though she'd tried to sound calm, the excitement in her voice was obvious and she couldn't suppress a whoop of delight.

George got up from the table and walked around to his mum, placed his hands on her shoulders and leaned over to kiss her on the cheek. 'That's lovely news, Mum. Congratulations. So, when is the special day?'

'In November. I know it sounds a bit sudden, but we don't want to wait any longer. It's only going to be a small affair, but it'll be a special day and boy do we all need one!'

'Congratulations, Lena, that's wonderful news,' Sarah said, but Lena could see the smile on Sarah's face was just a front, masking her pain.

'After the wedding, I'll be moving into Albert's house. That means you'll be able to have my room, George, and if Sarah would like to live here permanently, she can have yours. It'll save you looking for somewhere else to rent, Sarah, and it's ideal here for you, just up the road from the shop. What do you think?'

'Hang on, Mum. That might cause a bit of gossip.'

'You know you'll be in separate rooms so your conscience will be clear, and the only people who will gossip are those with dirty minds. Now then, what do you think, Sarah?'

'Yes, that sounds perfect, thanks, but how do you feel about me living here, George?'

Before George could answer, Lena said, 'He'll be more than happy about it, and glad of the company, won't you, George?'

'Suits me,' George said, and gave a thumbs-up sign.

'Good, that's settled then. Albert wants me to stop working, so Sarah, we are going to promote you. You'll be the manageress and you can take on an assistant. I've every confidence in you. Do you think you're up to it, love?'

'Lena, yes, definitely. I don't know what to say,' Sarah answered, sounding surprised.

'Thanks will do, and of course your wages will be increased to reflect your new position.'

'Well then, thanks, Lena. I won't let you down,' Sarah said, looking brighter.

Lena had seen how Sarah worked and trusted her. She felt the added responsibility would do the girl good and help to take her mind off the tragedies that had surrounded her lately. 'I was also hoping you'd help me with the planning and arrangements for the wedding too. Like I said, it's only going to be a small do, but there are still lots of arrangements to make.'

'I'd love to help,' Sarah said.

Lena felt pleased with herself. Sarah looked happier. With a smile she said to her son, 'George, would you like to give me away?'

'With pleasure, Mum, but will I have to pay Albert to take you off my hands?'

'You cheeky sod,' Lena said and smiled.

It would take time for Sarah to feel anything other than sadness, but Lena felt sure her upcoming wedding day was a good way to start getting the girl back on track.

Sarah went upstairs to dress for work. This would soon be her own room, and she liked the idea. She'd always felt at home in Lena's house and found it luxurious compared to her damp room.

Unbidden, the images of Mo and Roger returned and she tried to push them away. She had cried herself to sleep last night, and now despised the woman she'd once considered a close friend. Thankfully, when George had run her back to the house yesterday, Mo had kept out of the way, and Roger's van wasn't outside.

As for Roger, she wished she'd listened to George in the first place. Her own instincts had told her too, but she'd dismissed them, and now regretted it. It was a lesson learned, and now she'd never forgive him for being unfaithful to her at a time when she needed him the most.

Her eyes began to well up again, but she clenched her jaw tightly. She refused to cry over either of them any more. Once dressed, she applied a touch of lipstick and was reminded of the reward money she had tucked away in an old handbag. She'd had big plans for this money, but since Tommy's death she hadn't seen the point in anything any more. Now, though, she'd been given a promising opportunity in Albert's shop, and with her increased salary and affordable rent at George's, she wasn't sure what to do with the money. For now, it would remain tucked in the handbag, something to think about in the future. Drawing a deep breath, Sarah went downstairs to face another day.

George was over the moon for his mum. He liked Albert and could see how happy he made her. As he set off for work, the only blight on his landscape was the thought of having to stand next to Roger all day and not punch his face in. Sarah hated violence, and he'd promised her he wouldn't touch the man, but it went against the grain.

It wouldn't be easy to rein in his temper, but he would do his best to ignore the man whom he had once considered a friend.

Thankfully, when George arrived at the market, Roger was nowhere to be seen. According to Sarah he'd taken a beating, so he was probably too embarrassed to show his face, thought George. He hoped he'd stay away for a long time. Having to work in such close proximity with the bastard who'd hurt Sarah would be a struggle, but at least today he'd have a reprieve.

The morning wore on uneventfully, and George was getting fed up with answering questions about Roger's whereabouts. At least a dozen housewives had enquired, and he saw a familiar face approaching him. It was the girl from the café, the one he'd heard making arrangements with Roger.

'Hello, do you know where Roger is today?' she asked.

George could see why Roger had been interested in her. She was striking, with olive eyes and mahogany hair, but she was younger than George had first thought. 'No, love, and to be honest, I couldn't give two hoots. I'll give you a bit of advice – if you've got any sense, you'll stay well clear of him.'

'I've heard you and Roger have had your differences in the past, so why should I take any notice of anything you say?' the girl asked, then marched off haughtily before George could answer.

'I'll tell you why,' he shouted, ''cos his girlfriend caught him in bed last night with someone else's woman!'

The girl spun round and looked at George with disbelief. 'You're just bloody jealous of him 'cos he's got the looks and you've got – well . . . look at you, you're hideous,' she spat, then walked off again.

George reeled. He felt as though he'd been smacked across his face, but the girl was right, he *was* hideous, and it was no wonder that Sarah wasn't interested in him. He'd learned to live with his scars, and sometimes forgot he had them, until he caught sight of his reflection and was reminded again.

'Take no notice,' a woman said who'd been within earshot of the unfriendly exchange. 'She's just a silly little girl who doesn't know what you've suffered. As for Roger, we all know what he's like and she'll find out for herself the hard way.'

The woman was just a few years younger than his mum and had been friends with her for many years. 'Thanks, Kath, but she's right. I am hideous, and I've got no chance of anyone taking me on when I look like this.'

'You just need someone who can look past your scars, George. Keep your chin up, lad. I have a feeling that there is just the girl for you out there. Leave it to me, lad, I might have a nice surprise for you.'

The daft bat, thought George fondly, wondering what Kath was on about, but before he gave it any thought, a customer required attention and he found himself busy for the rest of the day.

Chapter 46

The following two weeks passed in a bit of a whirl for Sarah. She'd employed a nice young girl, Violet, to work in the shop with her. She'd been pleased that Lena approved her choice. She'd been busy during the day training Violet up, and her evenings had been filled with discussing what type of outfit Lena would wear. The woman refused to entertain a wedding dress, saying she hadn't worn one for her first marriage, so didn't need one this time. Anyhow, she was too old to be a blushing bride.

George had taken Sarah to a concert at Battersea Town Hall on Saturday night, and they had been for a long walk in the park on Sunday. Now it was Monday morning again and she was back behind the counter at work.

'Violet, I'm going to make us a drink. Would you like tea or coffee?'

'Neither, thanks. I'm not keen on them.'

'What about some orange squash?'

'Yes, please.'

Sarah went into the back room, but a few minutes later she heard the bell over the door ring, and went back into the shop. It was Violet's second week, so she didn't want to leave her alone. 'Good morning,' she chirped, but was horribly surprised to see two policemen standing in the shop with their backs to her as they spoke to Violet.

Her heart began to race as she feared her father might be paying her a visit, and if he was, it wouldn't be a friendly one. When the policemen turned around she blurted, 'Oh, I thought one of you was Sergeant Lyons. Ron Lyons.'

'Sergeant Lyons retired, miss, and moved down to Cornwall.'

'Oh, I see,' Sarah said, puzzled.

'Are you Sarah Jepson?' one of the constables asked.

'Yes,' Sarah answered, her heart still racing.

'We're investigating an alleged assault that took place in a house that you live in.'

'Yes,' Sarah muttered.

'Roger Brooke sustained substantial injuries during an attack which we believe was carried out by Samuel Edwards. We haven't been able to locate Mr Edwards since the assault, but we believe you were the last person to see him. Did he tell you where he was going?'

'No,' Sarah said, thinking that even if she knew she wouldn't tell the police. As far as she was concerned, Roger deserved what he got, and she hoped that Sam got clean away.

'So you have no idea where he can be contacted?'

'No,' Sarah said brusquely.

'Thank you, Miss Jepson, sorry to have bothered you, but if you do happen to hear from Mr Edwards, please let us know immediately.'

Sarah nodded, but she knew it was unlikely that she'd ever see or hear from Samuel again. As the policemen left, she walked out to the back room again, her thoughts on Ron Lyons. Surely he was too young for retirement? It crossed her mind that maybe he'd run away from her to protect himself and his wife against his past mistakes.

Good, Sarah thought. She had been frightened of him and his threats, but now it was another chapter of her life she could lay to rest.

George's heart had sunk when he'd seen Roger turn up on his stall, but he'd had a couple of weeks to calm down, and was now only simmering. Sarah seemed to be recovering from the heartache Roger and Mo had caused her, though he knew it would be a long time yet before she would get over losing Tommy, if ever. They'd talked for hours, and getting things off her chest seemed to do Sarah good, but she still refused to allow George to lamp Roger one.

He looked over at the man, pleased to see the remnants of the beating that Samuel had given him.

'So it's to be in November, George. Are you getting excited?'

George tore his eyes away from Roger to see Kath standing in front of him, carrying her usual woven cane shopping basket. 'Hello, Kath. November? Oh, yeah – my mum's wedding. To be honest I'll be glad when it's done and dusted. All I hear at home nowadays is her and Sarah talking about dresses, cakes, hairdos and all the other stuff. It's driving me bonkers.'

'Well, you can't blame your mum for pushing the boat out a bit.'

'Don't get me wrong, I'm really happy for her, but what she said was going to be a small do is suddenly turning into a full-blown affair. Mark my words, she'll be booking Westminster Cathedral next.'

Kath laughed. 'You do exaggerate, George. Anyway, me and Joan are going to organise a bit of a ladies' get-together before your mum's big day. You'll have to tell Sarah to join us.'

'I will. It'd probably do her good. Oh, and by the way, Kath – what were you going on about the other week? You know, all that stuff about you having a surprise for me?'

'You'll see soon enough,' Kath said, then winked mysteriously again at George as she walked off to do her shopping.

Blinking women, thought George with an affectionate smile. He'd never understand them.

Mo woke up and looked at the clock. It was gone lunchtime, but it wasn't unusual for her to sleep for most of the day. She didn't have much reason to get up. Since Samuel had beaten Roger up she hadn't seen either of them, or Sarah, and now spent her days and nights alone.

She'd sent several letters to Samuel, hoping they would get through to him via his brother's address, but hadn't heard back. She didn't know where he was, and missed him so much that her heart ached. As she climbed out of bed, Mo stepped over an empty brandy bottle. The room looked like a tip, but she didn't care. The biscuit tin was now empty, all the savings gone. She'd given the lot to Sam, but now rent was due and she had no means to pay it. She doubted she even had a job to go back to, not after being absent for so long without word. Things were pretty dire for her, and were made worse when she picked up the milk, sniffed it and found that it had soured.

Mo heard a knock on the front door, and covertly looked through the window. Her heart hammered when she saw it was Mr Terence doing his rent collection. There was nothing she could do – she couldn't pay him, and if he found out she was alone and jobless, he'd throw her out.

Mo climbed back into the bed and buried her head under the pillow, hoping Mr Terence would go away. Finally, the knocking stopped and she heard his car drive off. She'd managed to avoid him, but she wouldn't be able to hide forever. It would only be a matter of time.

Throwing back the bed covers again, Mo walked to the mirror and looked at her reflection. She was a mess, and so was her life. She had no man, no friends, no family, and it wouldn't be long before she had no home. She had one thing going for her, though – her looks. She could tidy herself up and visit Barry. He'd never make her a top model, but he would pay her to pose for pornographic photos. She'd done it before, and on reflection, it hadn't been so bad, and now, without Samuel's feelings to consider, she'd be prepared to do whatever Barry wanted, just as long as he paid the right price.

Chapter 47

There were only three weeks to go until Lena's wedding, and on a Thursday evening Sarah was at Joan's house with Kath and George's Aunty Min. She thought they were a lively bunch of women and liked being with them.

Lena suddenly yelped, and Joan said, 'Sorry, love, I didn't mean to stick you with a pin, but this dress needs to be taken in a bit more.'

'With all the running around I've been doing it's no wonder I've lost a bit of weight,' Lena tutted.

The long dress was in ivory, with a matching bolero. Sarah said, 'You look beautiful.'

'Thanks, love,' Lena responded, smiling warmly.

'Right, that's you done for now, Lena. Come on, you're next,' Joan said, ushering Sarah to her.

She stood on a small footstall as Joan pinched in the material on the waistband of the bridesmaid dress Sarah was wearing.

'You've lost a bit of weight too,' Joan commented.

'I hope you ain't working too hard in that shop and you're eating the sandwiches I pack you,' Lena said sternly.

Aunty Min stood up and beckoned Lena to the corner of the room. 'Leave the girl alone,' she said quietly. 'Don't

357

you remember how the weight fell off you when your Les was killed?'

'Yes, you're right, it did. I don't think I ate much for several months after he died. Poor Sarah, she puts on ever such a brave face though. Credit to her, she's coped much better than I did,' Lena answered.

'She's a good girl,' said Aunty Min, her voice hushed. 'I've only met her a handful of times but I'm ever so fond of her.'

'Me too. If I'd had been blessed with a daughter, she's just what I would have wanted,' Lena said sincerely.

They didn't think Sarah could hear them, but she'd heard every word. She found herself blushing. She wasn't used to having women fussing over her, or giving her compliments and showing affection

'I didn't tell you, Lena, but I've lined up a date for your George,' Kath said.

Sarah's ears pricked up. George was going on a date, and she found that she didn't like the idea. But why? He was her friend and she should be pleased for him, yet instead she found herself thinking that if he was seeing someone else, she would miss his company.

'He didn't say anything to me,' Lena said.

'That's 'cos I ain't told him yet. But you know my niece Julie, well, she said she'd love to go out with him.'

'Julie . . . ain't she a bit young for him?' Joan mumbled through the pins she was holding in her mouth.

'She's eighteen,' Kath replied.

'Blimey, time flies. She was just a nipper the last time I saw her.'

'Yeah, well, you should see her now. All grown up and very pretty too,' Kath said proudly.

'Have you told her about George's scars?' Lena asked.

'Yes, and I also said what a smashing man he is. She's training to be a nurse and things like that don't bother my Julie. She's one of them who only looks for the good in people,' Kath said. 'I've always said she's an old soul, and she's got a heart of gold.'

'Ah, she sounds lovely, Kath. When's George supposed to be taking her out then?' Lena asked.

'Saturday night. There's a big dance thing on over in Carshalton where she lives. She said she'd like George to take her.'

'Oooo, I say. Fancy that, your George taking a young lady out! It's about time, he's a lovely chap and he deserves to have a nice girlfriend,' Aunty Min said.

'He's got to ask her out first. I told her that George might not have the nerve, so she's going to come with me to the market tomorrow and make it obvious that she likes him,' Kath said with a wink.

Lena heaved a sigh. 'I hope this girl is right for him. After all, he's been barking up the wrong tree with you, Sarah.'

'We're friends, close friends, and I'm really fond of George, but just not in that way,' Sarah said, her cheeks flushing again.

'Right,' said Joan, 'I've finished pinning your dress so you can take it off now. Just make sure you don't lose any more weight.'

'I'll try not to.'

'Albert seems to be a lovely man,' Aunty Min said.

'Yes, he is, and a wonderful cook too. He's always spoiling me with fancy lunches,' Lena said, and patted her tummy.

'Cor, a man that can cook! I can see why you're marrying him now,' Kath said.

'There's more to Albert than just his cooking. It's the little things he does for me, like when he knows I'm coming over, he always has my favourite biscuits in, even though he ain't got a sweet tooth. He's a proper gent, holds doors open, puts Vera Lynn records on when I know he can't stand her, and yesterday he told me I can redecorate his house to my taste. He wants me to feel like it's my home.'

Sarah liked Albert but, hearing Lena talk about him, she realised Roger had never been thoughtful like that with her.

'You've got yourself a good one there, Lena. My Bob was like that. Nothing was ever too much trouble for him. He used to go out of his way to make sure I was happy. I remember this one time, when I was pregnant with Emily. I had a craving for mashed potatoes, of all things, but I was out of spuds. It was late in the evening and all the shops were closed, but my Bob walked for seven miles in the rain, jumped over the fences at Hampton's fields and dug me up a whole bleedin' sack full of potatoes. He got home after midnight, drenched through to the skin and with a bad back after lugging them spuds all the way home. As if that weren't enough, he peeled and boiled them too,' Joan said.

'I remember that,' Kath said, ''cos I asked him why he just didn't go down the allotments to pinch some.'

'Yeah, the silly bugger said he never thought of that. Still, we ended up with enough potatoes to last us a month,' Joan said and laughed.

The more Sarah listened to the women exchange fond

memories of their late husbands, the more she realised Roger had never loved her. The only thoughtful thing he'd ever done for her was bring her a bunch of flowers and a toy for Tommy, but that was probably only to impress her so he could charm her into bed. She cringed at the memory of him brutally taking her virginity. No love had been shown, and she regretted letting it happen. It had been so soon after Tommy's death and she'd been all over the place mentally, craving comfort when there had been none.

A couple of hours later, after the women had enjoyed several glasses of sherry, their laughter was interrupted by George knocking on the door.

'Tell Mum and Sarah I'll be in the van outside when they're ready,' George said to Joan when she answered the door. 'But tell them not to rush. It sounds like you ladies are having fun in there.'

'Come in, George,' she invited, and opened the door wider just as howls of laughter bellowed from the living room.

'Nah, I'll wait out here. That sounds like a blinking witches' coven in there,' George said, grinning.

Joan walked back to her large lounge and said to Lena, 'It's George. He's come to pick you and Sarah up, but he said to take your time.'

'He's another one who'd make someone a good husband,' Kath said, 'and you never know, if him and Julie hit it off, we might be having another wedding.'

Sarah's stomach lurched. It was one thing to feel strange about George going on a date, but she'd never imagined him married.

George hadn't been sitting in his van for long when Joan's front door opened and the group of women emerged. He was winding down his window when Kath came over.

'Hello, George. I'm glad you're here. I'll be popping up to see you tomorrow at the market with that surprise I was on about,' she said.

'Oh, Kath. I hate surprises. Tell me what's going on . . . please,' George asked.

'Well, just in case you don't bite, I'll give you the heads-up. It's my niece Julie. You've got to ask her out. She wants you to take her to a dance on Saturday, so make sure you've got your shoes polished and a comb in your inside pocket. She's ever so keen to meet you. You'll like her, George, she's pretty and clever too. See, I told you to leave it to me, didn't I?' Kath said and winked at him again.

'Yes, you did, but I wasn't expecting a date. I'm not sure, Kath. I mean, I'm sure your niece is a lovely girl, but—'

Kath interrupted, 'George, you're going on the date so shut up. You can't let Julie down. She's been looking forward to this dance for ages, and anyhow, when was the last time you went out?'

'OK, OK,' George said, but glanced at Sarah. He'd much rather be taking her out, but she would always be out of his reach and he'd resigned himself to the fact they would never be anything more than friends.

'Good, see you tomorrow then,' Kath said firmly.

George reluctantly nodded and got out of the van to open the other door for his mum to get in.

'See, my Albert ain't the only bloke with good manners,' Lena said as she climbed in. 'See you soon, ladies, and thanks for a good laugh tonight.'

George opened the back doors for Sarah. 'Sorry, it ain't

very comfortable for a lady in the back of my van but I have made you a wooden bench to sit on.'

'It's fine, George, thanks. Tommy used to love riding in the back, and I'm sure I will too. It beats walking home at this time of night.'

They set off. Lena relayed funny bits of the evening's conversation, but George noticed that Sarah seemed very subdued. He hoped she hadn't been overwhelmed by the women. After all, they could be quite boisterous when they all got together. 'Are you OK in the cheap seats at the back there?' he asked.

'Yes, I'm just tired,' Sarah answered.

He could see she wasn't tired and knew something was bothering her, but he'd have to get to the bottom of it when his mother wasn't around.

On Friday morning George found Sarah quiet over break-fast. His mum was acting a bit odd too, smiling and winking at him as he left for work.

He was now busy on his stall, but his heart was hammering in his chest as he kept an eye out for Kath. Thankfully, the first part of the morning whizzed by. Then, when he was showing a customer a dress that had caught her eye, he heard a voice say, 'Hello, George.'

George turned to see Kath, and beside her a diminutive, pretty young woman. 'Hello, Kath. None the worse for wear this morning then?'

'Cheeky. I only had a couple glasses of booze. George, this is my niece Julie. She's training to be a nurse.'

'Hello, Julie, pleasure to meet you,' George said nervously. She was much better-looking than he'd been expecting.

363

'Nice to meet you too,' she replied, looking straight up at his face with none of the usual horror or shock that George was used to.

Suddenly finding himself stuck for anything to say, he stammered, 'So . . . so you're training to be a nurse?'

'Yes, and I love it. I'm on a children's ward at the moment,' she said, seeming to study his face again. 'One young lad was in a house fire, and will have facial scarring like you.'

'Poor kid,' George murmured.

'You seem to have learned to live with your disfigurement, and plastic surgery has come a long way.'

'When you've got a mug like mine, you ain't got a lot of choice,' George said, though he kept his voice cheery.

'Oh, it's not so bad,' Julie said, smiling coquettishly up at him.

Her smile looked flirtatious, but as that was highly unlikely, George decided he was misreading her expression and said, 'Nice of you to say that, but I know I ain't pretty.'

'You'll do,' Julie said softly.

'It sounds like my niece is smitten with you, George. There's a dance at the Town Hall next week. You should ask her if she'd like to go with you,' Kath said bluntly, with one of her familiar winks.

'Aunty Kath!' said Julie, her face flushing.

'There's no need to be coy. You'd go, wouldn't you?'

'Well, yes, if George would like to take me,' Julie answered, and looked shyly at George.

'Go on then, George, ask her,' Kath demanded.

George couldn't believe this was happening – that this lovely young woman would want to go out with him. 'Er, well . . . would you—'

'Yes, I'd love to,' Julie interrupted.

'Right then, that's sorted,' Kath said. 'I'll leave you two to make the arrangements while I go to that stall over there to buy myself a new wooden spoon. It might come in handy for any more stirring I have to do,' she laughed.

George still felt a bit bemused, almost bamboozled into asking Julie for a date, but when she smiled at him again, he was glad that he was taking her out, pushed into it or not.

Chapter 48

November drew in. One day, at closing time, Sarah was about to lock up the shop when the bell over the door chimed. She felt a little irritated, but plastered a smile on her face, one that dropped as soon as she saw that the customer was Mo, looking sheepish. 'Get out,' she snapped. 'I've got nothing to say to you.'

'Sarah, please, hear me out. I'm so sorry for what I did. I'll never forgive myself for being such a terrible friend.'

'I'll never forgive you either, and you was *never* my friend. Real friends don't do what you did. Just bugger off. I want nothing to do with you.'

'Please, Sarah, I wouldn't have come but I'm desperate,' Mo pleaded, looking on the verge of tears.

Sarah walked behind the counter, feeling better about putting a barrier between her and Mo. She wasn't scared of the woman, but seeing her had reopened her wounds, and Mo's pleading was rubbing salt into them. 'What you did is unforgivable. Tommy had just died, and you saw the state I was in, but it didn't stop you from sleeping with Roger. Now you've got the audacity to come here and stand in front of me, say you're sorry and expect me to say, oh, that's OK. Well, it's not. You're a bitch, I hate you and I wish I'd never met you,' Sarah spat.

'I know, and I know all that,' Mo said as she sniffed through her sobs, 'but I don't have anyone else to turn to. What I did was the lowest of the low, and I've regretted it every day since. If I could go back and do things differently, I would, but I can't and now . . . now . . . I'm pregnant.'

Sarah sat down on the stool behind the counter as the shock of Mo's words sunk in, but it didn't change how she felt about the woman. 'What do you expect me to do about it?' she said. 'Go back to your family, they'll take you in now you're not with Sam.'

'I can't . . . I don't know who the father is. If the baby comes out with dark skin, they'll disown me. It could be Roger's child, but he won't have anything to do with me, and I can't find Sam. I've been modelling to earn some money, but I can't do that for much longer, not with my belly starting to swell. I'll have no money, Sarah, and if I can't pay the rent, I won't have a home.'

Sarah didn't like to see anyone in this sort of state, and she knew how it felt to be all alone in the world with a child, but her heart was hard towards Mo. 'You brought this on yourself. You cheated on a good man who loved you, and that worked out well for you, didn't it?' Sarah said sarcastically. 'If you think I'm going to help you, then think again. You're not worth the dirt on the bottom of my shoe. Now get out.'

Mo's persona suddenly changed. She stopped crying and glared at Sarah with a look of pure hatred. 'I made a mistake, Sarah. I've put my hands up to it, guilty as charged, but it was one mistake, that's all, and boy, I'm paying the price for it. I'm going to lose everything because I've got this . . . this . . . this thing growing in my stomach. Look at you though. You've got it made now with this cushy job and the Neerlys have taken you in as one of their own, yet you stand there looking down on me, and you think you're so much better. Just remember, I know where you came from. Your mother was a tart and you once slept rough, scavenging on the Thames for stuff to sell. You had help when you needed it most, so I thought you of all people would understand.'

'Don't put this at my door, Mo. When Tommy died, and I needed you the most, you was too busy sleeping with my boyfriend to give me a second thought. You had it all, but it was never enough for you. You wanted more, and well, now you've got it, only a baby wasn't what you had in mind, was it? An unmarried mother, goodness, what will people say? Go and look for sympathy elsewhere 'cos you won't be getting any from me.' Sarah strode from behind the counter, past Mo, and swung the door open. 'Get out,' she said calmly.

Mo walked past Sarah and spat in her face. 'All right, I'm going, but I'll leave you something to think about. If you'd been more of a girlfriend to Roger and not a cold fish, he wouldn't have been in my bed,' Mo snapped, then left.

Sarah rushed to lock the door and leaned against it, then took a hanky from her pocket and wiped the spit from her face. She was relieved that Mo had gone. She just hoped she would never came back. Mo seemed to think she had it made, but the truth was that she still grieved for Tommy. He was still her first thought when she woke up every day, and her last before she fell asleep at night. She put on a front, a mask to hide her pain, but sometimes it slipped, especially when George took Julie out. She wanted him to be happy and hated her selfishness, but if they became serious, she worried about her future. If they eventually married, not only would she lose her home, she would lose her best friend too.

'Hello, anyone home?' George called an hour later as he walked through the door.

'In here,' Sarah shouted back from the kitchen.

'Hello, love, where's Mum?' George asked.

'She's having a last fitting and won't be home for an hour or two. You'll have to put up with my culinary skills tonight. Mushroom omelette?'

'That'll do. I hope you've had a better day than me. I bloody hate working next to your ex-boyfriend all day, the smug git. You'd think after getting a good hiding from Samuel that he would have changed his ways, but no, not him. He's playing the girl from the café and another from the library.'

'If they're anything like I was, they'll fall for his lies. Talking of Roger, you'll never guess who showed up in the shop today.'

'Go on,' George said.

'Mo, asking me to forgive her before telling me she's pregnant.'

George nearly spat his mouthful of hot tea out across the table, but gulped it down. 'Blimey, she's got some nerve. Are you all right?'

'Yeah,' Sarah said with a sigh. 'Mo doesn't know whether the baby is Sam's or Roger's. She has no idea where Sam is, and Roger doesn't want anything to do with her.'

'So what was she after? Money?'

'I think so.'

'I hope you didn't give her any. I know how bloody soft-hearted you can be,' George said.

'No, I didn't. I stood my ground and told her to get out.'

'Well done. It can't have been easy for you and let's hope that's the last you see of her. I wish I could say the same about Roger, but unfortunately, unless another pitch comes up on the market, I'll have to look at his lying mug every day.'

It was just as bad for her. She wasn't forced to look at Roger every day, but there wasn't a day that passed when she didn't think about him.

Chapter 49

'You look nice, love,' Lena said to George as he walked into the front room the following evening. 'Does this mean you're seeing Julie again?'

'Yes, we're going to the pictures.'

'Have a nice time,' Sarah said, trying to sound upbeat but thinking she had failed.

George had only just left when Lena said, 'Sarah, I need to talk to you, but it's not good news, I'm afraid.'

'It's all right, Lena, whatever it is. Me and bad news are well acquainted,' Sarah said. After losing Tommy and the deceit of her best friend and boyfriend, Sarah felt as if nothing could touch her emotionally any more.

'The thing is, love, Albert and me,' Lena said, coming to sit on the edge of her armchair, 'we've been talking about a honeymoon. He wants to take me travelling. I've only ever been as far as Brighton, so I'm a tad nervous about it, but Albert wants me to see Europe and meet his family in Italy.'

'That's wonderful, Lena. I didn't know Albert had Italian relatives.'

'His parents moved here before he was born, and his

real name is Alberto. He hasn't seen his extended family in years and now wants to visit them.'

'So, what's the bad news?' Sarah asked.

'Well, as we'll be travelling around Europe too, the only way we can really afford it is by selling the shop. Albert thinks he'll get a good price for it, and he's already had a couple of interested parties so I don't think it'll be on the market for long.'

'I see,' Sarah said.

'I know this isn't good for you, but there's always the possibility that the new owners would keep you on. If not, with a glowing reference from Albert I don't think you'd have a problem finding another job.'

Sarah's mind raced. With the reward money that she still had squirrelled away, and her good salary from Bosco's, she'd managed to save a decent amount. Maybe this was just the push she needed to set her original plan into action.

'I really am sorry, love,' Lena said.

'Don't be silly. Your honeymoon sounds like it's going to be wonderful and there's no need to worry about me. I have plans of my own.'

'Really? What plans?' Lena asked.

'I haven't told you, or George, but a while ago I came into a bit of money. I had planned to do something with it, but then Tommy died and my life sort of got put on hold. Now, though, I think I'm ready to do something with it.'

'I'm intrigued,' said Lena. 'Tell me more.'

'Well, when I first started working in the shop, do you remember telling me that I was a natural?'

'Yes, you picked everything up so quickly.'

'Do you think that George loves working on the stall?'

After a moment's thought, Lena answered, 'I wouldn't say he loves it. I don't think he minds it in the summer, but he hates the winters. And he's made it more than clear that he can't stand working next to Roger. I don't think there's a night that's gone past that he ain't come home and moaned about it.'

'Right then,' Sarah said with a rare smile. 'I'm thinking of renting some premises and setting up a second-hand shop. I'd like it to be in partnership with George. He'd do all the stock acquisition, and I'd run the shop. We know there's no shortage of demand for good quality second-hand gear around here, so what do you think?'

'That's a smashing idea! If anyone can make a shop run well and turn a good profit, it's you. With George doing the buying, well, we know he's got a good eye for that sort of thing. Funnily enough, he's always wanted to expand into stuff other than clothing, but he's never had room on the stall.'

'Lena, don't say anything to George yet. I want to make sure I can find affordable premises first and, if I can, I'd like to put it to him myself.'

'Mum's the word, but thinking about it, there could be a problem. You said you want a partnership with George, but I don't think he's got much in the way of savings.'

'Some of the cash I have rightfully belongs to him,' Sarah said.

'How come?'

Sarah told Lena about the jewellery. 'So you see, I want to repay him for the money he spent on it.'

'Well then, it sounds like you've got it all worked out.'

'I hope so. If George agrees to a partnership, I'll start looking for premises straight away.'

'I can't see him turning such a good opportunity down. I think this calls for a bit of a celebration! Get the sherry glasses out and there's a box of posh chocs in the top cupboard that Albert bought me,' Lena said.

Sarah hoped that Lena was right and felt a surge of excitement. She'd had her own doubts and didn't really believe she'd be capable of pulling it off. After all, she'd had little schooling, and had never run her own business before. But she trusted Lena; the woman was wise, and her belief in Sarah gave her the confidence boost she needed.

It would be wonderful to be her own boss, to have her future in her own hands, and at last some of the deep sorrow that plagued her lifted a little.

The next morning, George was sitting in the kitchen and, when Sarah joined him, he noticed that she looked different, brighter somehow. He knew mornings were difficult for her. It was the waking up followed by the realisation that Tommy wasn't there, and he'd heard her crying many times as the sun rose. But this morning he could see there had been no tears.

Sarah poured herself a cup of tea from the pot, then sat opposite him at the table just as his mum walked into the room with a silly grin on her face. When she exchanged looks with Sarah and winked, George knew they were up to something.

'Did you enjoy your date with Julie?' his mother asked.

'Yes, it was fine,' George answered, his voice flat.

'Is it getting serious between the two of you?'

'Serious? No, it's a bit early for that.'

Sarah abruptly stood up and said, 'I'm just going to the bathroom.'

No sooner had she left the room than his mother said, 'How do you feel about this girl, George? Do you like her?'

'Yes, she's all right, Mum . . . but she ain't Sarah,' George replied honestly.

'I thought as much. Give it time though, Julie may grow on you.'

'What, like fungus?' George asked and chuckled. In all fairness, he liked Julie. She wasn't bothered about his scars, and they got on well. He'd had the impression that she'd been expecting a good-night kiss when he'd dropped her home, but he couldn't bring himself to make the move. It didn't seem right, not when the only woman he really wanted was Sarah.

Sarah came back into the kitchen and sat down at the table. George thought she looked quite sexy with her just-got-out-of-bed hair, and tried not to make it obvious that he was eyeing her lustfully.

'Albert's coming to pick me up later and we'll be moving some of my things over to his house. Are you going to be around today, George? We could do with some strong muscles,' Lena asked.

'Yes, no problem. We can take my van as well if you want. Let's face it, Mum, the amount of shoes and bags you've got ain't going to fit into Albert's boot.'

'Very funny, but you're probably right. I'd better start packing. I need to chuck a lot of stuff out.'

'Hang on,' George said. 'Don't you dare throw anything away! Hello – your son has a second-hand clothes stall!'

'Oh, yes, of course, sorry, George. You can go through it before I chuck it out,' Lena said, and, winking at Sarah again, she added, 'and of course, you'll want to sort through it too.'

George couldn't imagine that Sarah would want anything of his mother's, but the atmosphere in the kitchen was cheery. It was nice, almost like before tragedy had struck, and he was pleased to see a glimmer of the old Sarah shining through.

Chapter 50

Lena's wedding day finally arrived, and her house was a hive of activity with Aunty Min, Joan and Kath all buzzing around. George had been sent to Albert's for the night, and instructed to ensure the groom remained calm today. He also had to make sure that he got him to the church on time.

'Sarah, sit down. I'll do your hair next,' Kath ordered.

She did as she was told. Kath was a dab hand with hair, and Joan was busy finishing off the final details on Lena's dress. Aunty Min flapped around looking busy but actually doing very little.

'For Christ's sake, Min, you're making me nervous. Find something useful to do, like making us all a cup of tea,' Lena barked at her sister.

'Someone's a bit tetchy this morning,' Kath said with a laugh. 'Relax, love. It's a beautiful autumnal day, and everything is going to be a perfect.'

'Sorry, ladies, and sorry, Min. I didn't mean to snap. I don't know why I'm so bloody nervous, it's not like I ain't done this before!'

'You ain't having second thoughts, are you?' Joan asked.

'Don't be daft. I'm looking forward to being Mrs Bosco,

it's just all the faffing about with hair, my dress, the flowers and cake . . . I ain't used to so much fuss.'

'Well, get used to it, woman, because today is your day, and we're going to make sure you have the best day of your life,' Joan said, then Kath added, 'And you're going to look absolutely stunning.'

'I know, but you don't think I'm too old for all this dressing-up malarkey, do you?' Lena asked as she studied her reflection in the mantel mirror. Her hair was in rollers and she was wearing a face pack made of raw eggs and honey that Kath had smothered on her earlier.

'Lena, you're going to look beautiful, and no, you ain't going to look like mutton dressed as lamb if that's what you're worried about. It isn't often a woman gets a second chance at happiness, so just grab it with both hands,' said Kath as she brushed Sarah's hair.

'Yeah, I agree,' Joan said. 'We've had rotten austere times since the war, what with all the men who didn't come home, the rationing, the London smog and the slum housing round here. It's about time something nice happened, and thanks to Albert telling you to arrange a street party, all your friends and neighbours are going to have a day they'll never forget. You're lucky to have a man like him, and you should be bloody proud of yourself. If I'm honest, I'm a little bit jealous,' Joan said.

The room fell silent, then Aunty Min snuffled. 'Blimey, Joan, that was a speech and a half. Someone get me a hankie, please.'

'Bugger that tea,' Lena said, 'open up whatever bottle you can find in my cabinet.'

The women laughed, and Sarah found herself able to

join in. At last she was rebuilding her life, and what Joan had said made her feel more determined than ever.

George waited outside the church for his mum to arrive. Guests had arrived and filled the church. He'd been surprised at how calm Albert appeared, and had left the man standing in the front by the altar, waiting for his bride. He knew that when his mum had married his dad, it had been in a register office, but this time Albert had insisted on a church wedding. He was pleased Lena had chosen this church to marry in. He'd been christened here years earlier, and it was a different church from the one where Tommy's funeral had been held.

The highly polished grey Austin car pulled up, and George watched as his mother climbed out. He had never seen her looking so glamorous and regal, her smile warm as he walked to her side. Sarah followed his mother. The sight of them looking so glamorous almost took his breath away. He wished it was Sarah in the bridal gown and he was the groom, but he knew his dreams were unattainable.

'I'm so proud of you, Mum. You look beautiful and Albert's a very lucky man.'

'Stop it, you'll have me in tears and I don't want to smudge my make-up,' Lena said with a nervous giggle.

'Right, let's do this,' George said, and indicated to one of the ushers to open the church doors. The organ began to play the 'Bridal March', and George proudly walked down the aisle with his mum on his arm, and Sarah behind.

The service went well, with Lena and Albert repeating their vows flawlessly. George looked around and spotted a few tears of joy, then his eyes set on Sarah. She must have felt someone staring at her and turned to look at him, offering the sweetest smile. His heart leaped. He was dating Julie now, but he didn't think he'd ever stop loving Sarah.

Everything had passed without a hitch, and now, as the car turned into her street, Lena was bowled over by the sight of the long tables and chairs, the bunting and the pretty decorations that lined the road. All her neighbours were ready to greet her, and as she climbed from the car, a loud cheer went up.

'I present to you Mr and Mrs Bosco,' a booming voice shouted.

'Thank you, each and every one of you,' Albert said. 'This has made our day perfect. Now, let's eat, drink and be merry!'

Lena thought it was out of character for Albert to be so loud and extroverted, but maybe, like her, he'd had a couple of drinks to calm his nerves. He'd been so generous with the street party, ordering barrels of beer, with sherry for the ladies, and many of the neighbours had chipped in with home-made cakes, sausage rolls and sandwiches.

As the hours passed, Lena sat back and watched her friends dance to the sound of a man with an accordion and another with a guitar. Everyone was enjoying themselves, except George. He looked sad, and hadn't taken his eyes off Sarah. She worried about him. He said he was seeing Julie, she knew his heart wasn't in it.

Sarah was twirling around with some of the children. She must miss Tommy so much, especially on days like this, Lena thought, but once again she admired the girl's strong spirit.

'Are you all right, Mrs Bosco? You look very deep in thought there,' Albert asked.

'Yes, my love, I couldn't be happier. It's so nice to see everyone having a good time.'

'You and your friends have done an amazing job organising all of this,' Albert said, 'but I'm finding myself rather weary. Would you mind if we go home now? I'm looking forward to getting my new wife to myself.'

'We didn't organise it all. You sorted out the booze for us. Anyway, I'd very much like to go home now,' Lena answered. 'Let's see if we can just slip away without anyone noticing.'

Home, Lena thought. Today she was leaving behind the house she'd shared with George since her first husband had been killed. It felt strange, and though she was sad to be leaving, she was also excited about starting her new life with Albert. As soon as the shop was sold they'd be off on their travels, and she was so looking forward to their future together.

Chapter 51

It had been a month since Lena's wedding, but many of the customers who came into the shop still talked about it. It had certainly been a day to remember, though Sarah wished Tommy had been there to share it with her. The shop was now under offer, and Lena had told Sarah that Albert had accepted a very fair price. She'd felt awful about having to let Violet go, but had heard the girl had a new job, which eased her conscience somewhat.

Sarah had seen a few empty shops, but hadn't yet found one in a decent location. She was due to see another one shortly, and was hoping the premises would be more promising than the others she'd viewed. Lena had told her about this one, saying that Albert had put a word in for her, and had offered to come with her. The shop was ideally situated on a busy stretch between York Road and Battersea Park Road. It wasn't far from where she worked now, but was on a main street instead of up a back one.

Lena walked into the shop now and said, 'Hello, love, are you ready?'

'Yep, fingers crossed this is better than the others,' Sarah said, and went through to the back to collect her bag. She turned the sign on the front door to 'closed', then locked up. 'It was good of Albert to have a word with Mr Burrows about it.'

'Well, it's been a shoe shop for as far back as I can remember, and from what Albert told me, Mr Burrows is desperate to rent it out so he can retire. The shop became too much and he's been losing money hand over fist.'

'What about his family? Aren't any of them keen to take it on?' Sarah asked.

'You haven't heard the gossip then? His eldest son was working with him but he's in prison now for theft. He went down last month for quite a stretch. They reckon the judge made an example of him and he got a longer sentence then he deserved. His other son went off to live in Australia a year ago and his daughter is married with four kids.'

'Why hasn't Mr Burrows put the shop up for sale?'

'He did, but when he didn't find a buyer, he decided to rent it.'

'At least it'll give him a regular income,' Sarah mused as they walked to the shop, and soon they were standing outside the dark-green frontage. Sarah liked the double-aspect large windows and could already picture herself displaying their goods.

The agent arrived, and shook their hands. 'This is a prime location,' he said, unlocking the door.

'So far, so good,' Sarah said, feeling a tinge of excitement. She had a feeling this was going to be the one and couldn't wait to get inside.

The windows let in lots of natural light, and the floor space was good. The shelves were dusty, but as the premises had been empty for at least a month, that wasn't surprising.

'Just through this door, you have a back yard with rear entrance vehicle access,' the agent said.

Sarah stepped into the yard and looked around, feeling elated as she went back inside. The interior of the shop needed a lick of paint, but that was something easily tackled. 'What do you think, Lena?' she said.

'I think it's perfect. If George can pick up second-hand furniture, he can do restoration work out there, or it could be used for storage. I don't think you're going to find anything more suitable, and it's a fair price too.'

Sarah turned to the agent. 'I'll take it,' she said, hoping she hadn't jumped the gun.

The agent looked pleased, and said, 'I'll tell Mr Burrows, and draw up a rental agreement. If you come to my office on Monday you can sign it, and as long as you pay the first month's rent, I will give you the keys.'

Sarah was chewing on her bottom lip as they left the premises and said to Lena, 'Maybe I should talk to George before I sign the rental agreement. He might not want to go into business with me.'

'Of course he will. He'll be over the moon. Just make sure I'm there when you tell him.'

'All right,' Sarah agreed. 'When everything is done and dusted we'll bring him here and tell him together.'

Once she'd struggled to get out of bed and see any future for herself or any light at the end of a very dark tunnel. Now she was about to embark on a new venture as a business owner. Sarah smiled to herself. Things were looking up.

George was packing up his stall when he spotted the little bent old woman who had spoken to him in riddles. He'd met her once before, only briefly, and remembered he thought she was a bit odd. She was making a beeline for him again, and he braced himself.

'Young man,' she croaked. 'You're not with the woman you're destined to be with!'

George shook his head, thinking the daft old bat made no sense, but then she scuttled off. Yet the more he thought about it, the more he knew she was right. He liked Julie, but she wasn't the one for him. He didn't know if he was destined to be with Sarah, but if he couldn't have her, he didn't want anyone.

George finished packing up his stall and went home. His journey passed quickly as his mind turned, mulling over the Julie problem. It was early evening when he arrived home. Sarah appeared to be in an extremely good mood, though his own didn't match hers. He was supposed to be taking Julie out again next week, but wasn't looking forward to it. He knew he had to tell her that he wasn't going to be seeing her again, but worried that it would upset her.

'What's bothering you, George?' Sarah asked later that evening as they sat together in front of the black and white images on the television.

'Nothing,' George answered.

'Don't give me that. You only rub your chin like that when you've got stuff on your mind.'

George smiled. Sarah knew him too well. 'All right. It's Julie,' George said.

'What's the matter, has she given you the elbow?'

'No, it's the other way round. I'm gonna tell her I don't want to see her any more. She's nice, but she ain't the one for me. I just don't know how to tell her. I don't want to hurt the girl. Any suggestions?'

'You could say it's you who has the problem.'

'How do you mean?' George asked.

'Say something along the lines of "I really like you, Julie, you're a lovely girl" and all that sort of stuff, but then tell her you prefer blokes,' Sarah said with a wicked grin.

'Sarah! I couldn't say something like that. Apart from anything else, it's against the law. Is that the best you can come up with?'

He liked it when Sarah laughed at his mock horror. It was nice to see her mucking about again.

'I don't know then, just tell her the truth. Women ain't stupid, you know, we can normally see through a bloke's lies . . . and before you say anything, I did say *normally*. Obviously, there are the few exceptions, Roger being a good example, but if you're honest with her, she'll appreciate it more.'

'What, tell her I don't love her?' George asked.

'Maybe not quite as bluntly as that. Start by saying you can't help who you fall in love with, and you can't force it to happen. Tell her how wonderful she is, and how much you hoped you would have fallen for her, but it just didn't happen. Yes, she may be upset at first, but she'll get over it, and she won't be left with a bitter taste in her mouth 'cos you haven't deceived her.'

'All right, I'll take your advice,' George said, but knew that he couldn't be totally honest with Julie. He could hardly tell her that he was in love with someone else, someone who would never see him as more than a friend.

George switched the television off, and Sarah warmed some milk. He could imagine it was the same at Albert's house, and once again he wished Sarah was his wife.

Chapter 52

The weekend passed quickly and on Monday Sarah went to see the agent to sign the agreement for the new shop. It took surprisingly little time, and now she was holding the keys in her hand. It was official, she was the proud new owner of the old shoe shop on the main road, and she couldn't wait to get started with the renovations, but the first thing she wanted to do was arrange the shop signage. Once that was done, she planned on introducing George to his new business.

That evening, George went to see Julie, and Sarah was sitting up, waiting for him to come home. She heard his van pull up outside, and her heart skipped a beat. She thought it was strange that she felt so pleased to see him arrive home early, and even more happy that he'd given his girlfriend the heave-ho. She had no right to feel jealous of George being with Julie, but she had been, and was now glad she had him back to herself again.

'How did it go?' she asked as soon as George came through the door.

'Nothing like you said it would,' George said with a chortle.

'Oh, what happened then?' Sarah asked.

'We were sat in my van, and I said everything like you suggested, but she suddenly turned into a crazy woman. First, she slapped me around the face, then she accused me of all sorts and called me every name under the sun. I was shocked, to say the least. I thought she was such a sweet little thing, but she turned the air blue with her language. Honestly, Sarah, I've never even heard a navvy swear like that. Once she'd said her piece, she got out of the van and slammed the door. Thank Gawd for that, I thought to myself, thinking that was the end of it, but then she started whacking my van with her handbag. I was trying to turn the keys in the ignition, and in all my fumbling, I dropped them. By the time I managed to get started and drive off, she'd knocked off my wing mirror!'

'Blimey, George, sounds like you had a lucky escape and did the right thing by dumping her. Cor, can you imagine what it would have been like if you'd been married and had upset her in any way? Has she done much other damage to your van?' Sarah asked, trying to hold in a fit of giggles. She shouldn't laugh, she thought, it had obviously been quite traumatic for George.

'Thankfully not a lot, just a couple of dents on the bonnet. She's as nutty as a blinking fruitcake, but who'd have thought it, eh? Wait 'til I see that Kath, I shall be having words with her about her mental niece!'

Sarah began to chuckle and George asked indignantly, 'What's so funny? I've just had an encounter with the devil woman, and you find it amusing?'

Sarah's chuckle turned to a giggle, and tears began to roll down her face. 'Oh, George,' she managed to splutter but couldn't stop laughing. 'I can just imagine the look on your face when she hit you. I wish I'd been a fly on the wall.'

'She frightened the bloomin' life out of me.'

Her giggling must have been infectious, as George started laughing too. 'That's the last blinking time I take any advice from you about women,' he said. 'I don't know why we're laughing, I was scared for my life.'

Sarah laughed harder. 'George, Julie is tiny compared to you. I can't believe you were scared of her.'

'You're horrible to me, you are. I don't know why I love you,' George said.

Sarah suddenly stopped laughing. George had declared his love again, but this time it felt different. She no longer saw his scars, and realised she could only see the wonderful man who was her best friend, one who had never let her down. It was then that Sarah realised that her feelings had changed and she began to wonder if she loved him too. Confused, she jumped to her feet and ran from the room to dash up to her bedroom, wanting time alone to sort out her muddled mind.

Could she have fallen in love with George without noticing? That would explain the jealousy she'd experienced towards Julie. Suddenly, her stomach flipped, and she felt the familiar butterflies she'd had when she'd met Roger.

She heard George call to her, 'Sarah, what's wrong?'

She couldn't answer him, and closed the bedroom door before throwing herself onto her bed. Was it possible? Had she really fallen in love with George Neerly?

The following day, George was still kicking himself. Fancy telling Sarah again that he loved her! He hadn't meant to say it – it had just slipped out. He hadn't seen her that morning, and when he arrived home from work there was no sign of her. She was keeping out of his way, but she wouldn't be able to avoid him forever.

When he heard the front door open, he fixed a smile on his face, determined to somehow lighten the atmosphere, but it was his mother who walked into the room.

'What are you doing here?' he asked.

'Well, that's a fine way to greet your mother.'

'Sorry, Mum. It's nice to see you and now that the shop's been sold I expect you've come to tell me that you're off on your travels?'

'No, that's not it. I want you to meet me tomorrow at the back of the shoe shop on the main road, the one that shut down.'

'What for?'

'I've got a surprise for you.'

'What sort of surprise?'

'I can't tell you. I've been sworn to secrecy. Do you know how to get around the back?'

'Yes,' George replied with a furrowed brow.

'OK, then just make sure you're there first thing in the morning. I'm so excited so I'm going to shoot off now before I let the cat out of the bag.'

George was left with his mind whirling. It seemed like a very strange request.

He sat in his armchair and racked his brains, but he couldn't think of a single reason why his mother would want to meet him by the shoe shop. He heaved a sigh, but then the door opened again and Sarah walked in. He tensed, but she smiled at him, saying pleasantly, 'Hello, George.'

'Hello, Sarah. I've just had the strangest visit from my mother.'

'Have you now,' Sarah replied, but something in the way she said it made George think she already knew.

'She wants me to meet her tomorrow morning behind the shoe shop on the main road but she won't tell me why, only that it's a surprise. Do you know anything about it?'

'No, I haven't a clue,' Sarah answered.

She wasn't a convincing liar and George got the impression that both she and his mother were up to something. 'You do know, Sarah. I can tell when you're fibbing so please spill the beans.'

'Nope, I'm not saying a word. And I'm warning you, if you keep on at me about it I'll chuck a bucket of cold water over you.'

'Please tell me, Sarah,' George begged.

'I'm going to get the bucket. I mean it! Blimey, you've only got to wait 'til tomorrow to find out. I bet you was one of those kids who got up at silly o'clock on Christmas morning to see what Santa had left you.'

'Yep, and I still am. OK, I'll shut up about it 'cos I know how bloody stubborn you can be. I'll be wasting my breath trying to get it out of you.'

Sarah smiled as she looked at him, but it was a strange smile, almost one of fondness. George was relieved. At least his declaration of love hadn't ruined their friendship, and though he'd prefer her love, friendship was better than nothing.

'Is everything ready?' Lena asked as she walked into the old shoe shop the next morning to find Sarah flapping around like a woman possessed.

'Yes, I think so. Oh, Lena, I'm worried sick. What if George doesn't want to do this?'

'Sarah, take a few deep breaths and calm down, love. We both know George is going to be thrilled to bits, so stop panicking and relax,' Lena said. 'He's going to be here in twenty minutes, and he'll wonder what's wrong if he sees you in this state.' The girl looked like a nervous wreck, but Lena knew her son was just about to get the surprise of his life, and she couldn't wait to see the delight in his eyes.

'OK, I'm calm . . . sort of. Let's wait for him outside. You know him, he's so eager to find out what's going on, he's bound to show up early.'

Just as the women stepped into the yard, they saw George's van pull up.

'Blimey, here we go,' Sarah said excitedly to Lena.

She was tapping her finger and thumb together, but Lena couldn't understand what Sarah was so worried about. This was a wonderful opportunity for George and he wasn't daft enough to turn it down.

'I knew you two were in cahoots,' George said as he walked towards the women. 'Now, is someone going to tell me what this is all about?'

Lena looked at Sarah. 'Go on, love, put him out of his misery.'

'Well, I know you hate working down the market in the winter, and I also know you'd like to have more stock to sell but haven't got the room,' Sarah said.

'Yes, but what has that got to do with meeting you here?'

'Welcome to your new premises!' Sarah exclaimed.

'What premises?'

'These,' said Sarah, flinging open the door. 'Come on, come inside, George. I've rented this shop, and . . . and

I want you to come into business with me. We can sell second-hand clothes, and furniture too.'

'Are you serious?' he asked.

'Yes, very. As you can see the shop needs a bit of work, but between us we can soon sort that out.'

'Bloody hell, this is a lot to take in.'

'George, just put Sarah out of her misery, will you? She's been fretting that you won't want to be her partner,' Lena said, rolling her eyes.

'I'd love it, but I don't see how we can afford to take on a shop. There's the rent to pay, and stock to buy.'

'Don't worry about that for now. I'll explain everything later, but trust me, we can afford it.'

'Right then, Sarah, you're on,' George said. 'Let's shake on it.'

Lena was so pleased to see her son beaming from ear to ear. It had been a while since she'd seen him this excited about anything. 'Oh, George, I'm so happy for you. I know that you and Sarah will make the shop a big success,' she said, chuffed for him. She and Albert would soon be off on their travels, and she could leave knowing that her son's future looked bright.

Sarah shook George's hand, but her heart was hammering in her chest and her mouth was dry. This was it. This was going to be the big reveal.

'I've got to say, Sarah, you couldn't have picked a better position. These windows are great too. Blimey, for someone who doesn't like surprises, this is the best one I've ever had. Gawd knows how you two managed to keep this quiet from me, but well done,' George said, and Sarah was pleased to see he was beaming from ear to ear.

'George, it won't be the finished article, but I've done a mock-up of our shop sign. Come out the front and I'll show it to you,' she said nervously.

George and Lena followed her outside and she watched his face as he read the sign. His jaw dropped, then he looked at her, and back to the sign again.

'Oh, Sarah,' Lena said, her eyes flooding with tears.

Sarah held her breath as she waited for George's reaction.

As he read the sign out loud, it slowly seemed to dawn on him. 'I can't believe this. "Mr and Mrs Neerly New Shop." Is . . . is that you and me?' he asked, sounding unconvinced.

'Yes, George, if you'll still have me.'

'But . . . but I don't get it.'

'When you told me again that you loved me, I realised that I love you too. So, George Neerly, will you marry me?'

George threw his arms around her and she felt herself being lifted off the ground as he swung her around and kissed her hard on the lips. 'Of course I will, you amazing woman! You've just made me the happiest man on this planet,' he said as he lowered her back to her feet. 'Did you hear that, Mum? Have you seen that sign? I'm getting married!'

Lena nodded, hardly able to speak through her tears. 'I'm so happy for you both, but as this means Albert and I will have to put off our travels until you tie the knot, don't leave it for too long.'

'We won't,' Sarah said, and seeing the love for her in George's eyes, she knew she'd made the right decision. Since Tommy's death, she hadn't expected to feel happy again, but she felt a surge of happiness now. Though the pain of her loss would never leave her, she now knew there was room in her heart for joy too. 'I love you, George Neerly,' she said, 'and I can't wait to be your wife.'

The hardest choice she'll ever make . . .

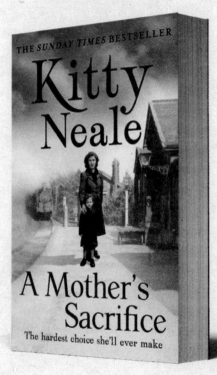

A heart-rending drama perfect for fans of Katie Flynn and Nadine Dorries.

You can never leave a bad man behind . . .

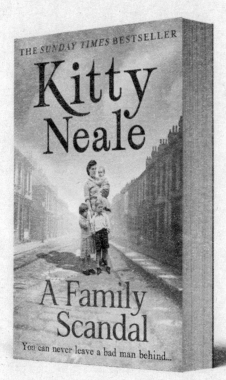

A gritty and emotional family drama
from the *Sunday Times* bestseller.

A Family Scandal is your next must-read!

How far would you go to find happiness?

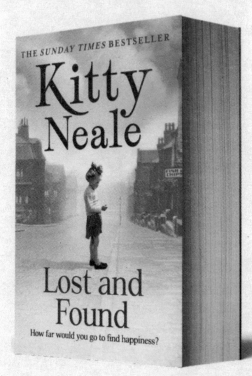

Bullied by everyone around her for years, has Mavis Jackson finally found happiness?

Or has she jumped straight from the frying pan into the fire?

A mother must fight for
all she holds dear . . .

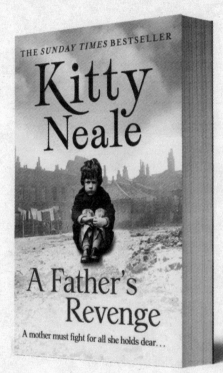

**In this tale of revenge and family feuds,
a mother must put her life on hold
in order to save her son from
her abusive ex-husband.**

Abandoned and alone, you'll do anything to survive . . .

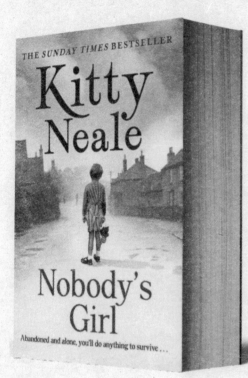

Left on the cold stone steps of an orphanage,
only a few hours old and clutching
the object which was to give her name,
Pearl Button had a hard start to life.

But will adulthood be any better . . .?

The past *always* comes back to haunt you . . .

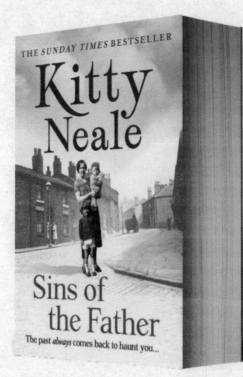

Desperate. Degraded. In danger . . .

Emma Chambers has a way out of the poverty-stricken life she lives – but it might just destroy her to take it . . .

The only person she can rely on is herself . . .

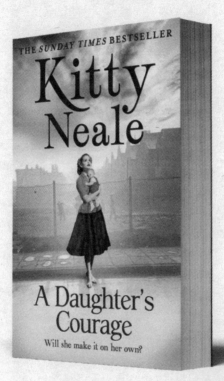

Does Dorothy have the courage to make it on her own? Or is someone waiting in the wings to save her?